INITIATION RITES

Soon the van pulled off on a deserted narrow pathway, and Fat Phil said, "Everybody out."

They piled out of the van, most of them with beers in their hands. Klaus and Snake and Mongo and Phil stood by the van. Harry Wolfe and Rax got a couple of steps before they realized no one was going with them, and they were standing alone. They turned toward the others.

Fat Phil reached into his pocket and drew his gleaming hammerless revolver. He aimed it, from the hip, at Wolfe. The others also drew their guns. Snake and Mongo had .45 automatics. In Klaus's hand was a huge, ugly .44 Magnum revolver.

All the guns were leveled at Wolfe.

They've found me out, he thought. And they're going to kill me.

CODE ZERO

ZERO

DEATHRIDE

D. A. HODGMAN

A GOLD EAGLE BOOK FROM

WORLDWIDE®

TORONTO • NEW YORK • LONDON
AMSTERDAM • PARIS • SYDNEY • HAMBURG
STOCKHOLM • ATHENS • TOKYO • MILAN
MADRID • WARSAW • BUDAPEST • AUCKLAND

First edition July 1992

ISBN 0-373-63405-6

Special thanks and acknowledgment to
D. A. Hodgman for his contribution to this work.

DEATHRIDE

Copyright © 1992 by Worldwide Library.
Philippine copyright 1992. Australian copyright 1992.

1

When the tan figure swung out from behind the concrete blockhouse and faced him, Harry Wolfe moved quickly. His gun hand flashed down under his windbreaker and closed on the textured polymer grip of his Glock 17 pistol. In an instant his hands met, the gun hand pushing and the support hand pulling in the isometric Weaver lock. As the three green dots of his gun sights lined up in the center of his opponent, he pulled the trigger twice.

He saw the figure spin back away behind the blockhouse. He broke and sprinted to the side, his finger extended rigidly away from the trigger of his black automatic pistol. There were two more of the tan shapes standing behind a woman in gray whose face was contorted in a silent scream. He shot each enemy carefully in the face, two shots each.

The hostage was safe now, and Wolfe was up and running again, hurdling a fifty-five-gallon drum that lay on its side, the pistol coming up into his line of sight as he jumped into a stop position behind a heavy wood barricade.

The Peppers were there, as he knew they would be. Four of them, gray and ugly and threatening. It would finish now.

The first was only ten paces away. He lined up on the body's center of mass and fired twice, hearing the impact of the bullets hitting home. He saw his enemy quiver and knew he was going down, and with the confidence born of training he swung his gun toward the others.

The remaining opponents shuddered as Harry's bullets slammed into them: one slug for the one on the left, and two for the one on the right, who was going down as the one on the left shook groggily from the single bullet that had hit slightly low. Wolfe's next shot smashed him onto his back.

The last surviving opponent was twenty-five yards away, the width of a city street. Wolfe took an extra fraction of a second to line up the triple dots of his gun sights before he stroked the trigger rhythmically.

One. The bullet hit the last of the Peppers belly high, barely moving him. *Two.* The 9 mm slug struck higher, center chest, and the gray assailant jerked another couple of inches backward. *Three.* Recoil was tracking the Glock pistol upward now, and the last bullet struck Pepper in the face. Even though his mind knew his last enemy was falling now, his finger was already pressing the eight-pound trigger of his pistol. *Four.* The last bullet hit the chest as Pepper landed flat on his back, bounced once and lay still.

Behind Wolfe a shrill whistle pierced the wind. "Unload," came a booming voice behind him. "Show clear. Scorers, prepare to move forward and reset."

Wolfe pressed the small square button below and behind the trigger of his pistol, and the magazine with the few rounds left came free in his hand. He slipped it into his pocket and worked the slide. The last DEA-issue Winchester Subsonic 9 mm cartridge popped free through the ejection port and fell safely to the ground.

When the range officer glanced at the gun and nodded approvingly, Wolfe thrust it back into his Summer Special holster that rode inside the waistband behind the right hip. He pulled a handkerchief from his back pocket and stuffed it into the butt of the gun to keep the blowing sand out of the mechanism, then raised his hands to show clear.

He moved forward with the range officers to score his targets. The three khaki-colored cardboard silhouettes who'd drawn his fire had each been hit twice. When the range officer pulled the first one back out from behind the concrete barricade on its swinging frame, Wolfe saw that the two holes in the center of its chest were about four inches apart.

The other two still were motionless behind the life-size black-and-white picture of the screaming woman. The head of one showed small holes like snake eyes. In the second, centered where the nose would be, was a keyhole shape where two of the copper-jacketed bullets had gone through in almost the same place.

"Dammit, Wolfe," the range master said, "you're the only guy who gets away with shooting a minor caliber up here. How do you get every bullet into the exact center?"

Wolfe flashed him a relaxed smile. "See, I've got a smart gun. It knows you guys give bonus points for major caliber when we shoot .45s, and only minor caliber points for a little 9 mm. It knows it has to get the shots dead center 'cause that's the only place a 9 mm gets the full five-point value."

The bearded range officer just grunted as he turned with his pen and clipboard. "A hundred percent for the Pepper Poppers," he said as his assistants ran forward. Wolfe watched as they reset the heavy, gray steel humanoids. "I don't know why you use that damn 9 mm. You *know* these things are set so a .45 can take 'em down with one hit, and you gotta hit 'em at least twice with that mousegun of yours. Christ, it looked like you hit that last one three times."

"Four," said Wolfe absentmindedly. He was looking at the stopwatch the assistant linesman was holding up in front of the range master. It read, "O8.74."

The range officer was shaking his head. "Eight and three-quarter seconds. You beat the guys with the .45s *and* the guys with the three-thousand-dollar .38 Super compensator guns. And you did it with that plastic piece of shit, and all the extra bullets you had to fire. If you had to reload, like with a .45, you couldn't have made it."

"That," said Wolfe, "is why I carry a gun I don't have to reload as often as you do."

The range master snorted. "What's that thing hold, seventeen or eighteen bullets?"

"Twenty," said Wolfe. "I use the Plus-Two extenders on the magazines."

Exasperated, the man with the beard said, "Harry, I've been watching you shoot for a few weeks now. I know your boss makes you carry a 9 mm. But, Christ, did you ever stop to think that if you got a .38 Super or even a .45, you could have a damn good crack at being state champion, maybe even national champ? Especially if you got rid of that hideout holster and got a real competition rig, like an Ernie Hill?''

Wolfe laughed. ''I haven't really thought about it, Bob. But I don't want to win a trophy. All I want to do is save my ass when the time comes. That's why I shoot with what I carry. It isn't a game with me like it is for you guys.''

The range master rolled his eyes. Suddenly there was a sharp beeping sound.

Wolfe's hand went automatically to his beeper, shutting it off. ''I've got to make a phone call. You got a pay phone around here?''

''You kidding?'' The range master spread his hands broadly. On the windswept high desert of the Wes Thompson shooting range, an hour north of Los Angeles, there were no phones to be had.

Wolfe grimaced, turned and sprinted toward the parking lot. Even though his eyes were shielded from the wind-whipped sand by his Gargoyle shooting glasses, he squinted against the flying grit.

It took him a minute to get down to the parking area. He popped open the door of his G-car, a government-issue white Ford sedan, and reached for the cellular phone on the dashboard. He punched in the number.

''Wolfe,'' he said when the connection was made.

A woman's voice on the other end said, ''Straight from the director. Call your special number right away. Code Zero. You're needed immediately.''

High on the wind-whipped hill that was known on the Thompson range as Eagle's Nest, Bob the range master looked at the parking lot far below and saw Harry Wolfe's white Ford back out of the lot, turn and head rapidly toward the gate. ''Son of a bitch,'' he said. ''If I'd just won the match, I'd sure as hell stick around to get the first-place trophy!''

WOLFE RELOADED his Glock in the car one-handed as he sped the fifteen miles toward the nearest truck stop with a pay phone. Strapped to his left ankle was a Strahan Custom revolver in a Ken Null leg holster. It had been loaded with six .357 Magnum cartridges the whole time, in spite of the Thompson range rule that no guns be loaded on the property. Wolfe considered it a forgivable civil disobedience. He detested being without a loaded gun in reach. Too many people had tried to kill him.

The wind that tore through the valley of Saugus, California, was blunted by the building's corner where the pay phones were located. Wolfe noted that he was the only one standing there. He punched in the secure number, and at the tone from Pacific Bell, hit the memorized number of his untraceable phone card. The people at the range thought he was a bodyguard for a Los Angeles executive, and thus one of the rare Southern Californians authorized to carry a loaded and concealed weapon. They had no need to know that his job was something else entirely, and that the authority that armed him came from a higher plane than the California statutes.

When the phone was answered, he said simply, "Wolfe."

The man on the other end got to the point quickly. "Harry, we've got a bad one. Fatal shooting, in the director's office. About forty minutes ago. The director wants you here for this one. He said to tell you, Code Zero."

Something other than the wind sent a cold shiver down Wolfe's spine. How ironic that Code Zero should be literally his occupational category, yet he'd shudder whenever he heard the term at the beginning of an operation.

"What can you tell me now?"

"Just that there's a United nonstop to Dulles Airport leaving LAX in about two hours, and your reservation's already confirmed."

"I'll be there," said Wolfe.

2

The director slumped back in his luxurious leather swivel chair, his eyes closed. He did not need the video players in the corner to relive the nightmare. Death had come padding to him softly, right here to his mahogany-paneled office. He could not shake the image.

He forced his eyes open. Goddammit! He didn't deserve this. His people didn't deserve this!

He shot to his feet, his two hundred pounds jarring the floor. His dark and powerful hands clenched and unclenched. This shit had not been in the job description.

He couldn't help looking past his glass-topped desk. The bloodstains in the thick, light green pile carpet were turning dark brown already. Some thoughtful office person had removed the leather-upholstered chair that Brian Voit had been sitting in when it had happened. But the bloodstains weren't going to come out, he knew.

Not out of the carpet, and not out of his soul.

The director turned away, toward the window with the green drapes. Beyond lay a panorama of a Washington street scene, the kind that tourists pay the guides to show them. But the director didn't see that. He saw his reflection in the glass instead.

The face was strong and chocolate-colored. The face of the first black man to hold a position this high in the war on drugs. The President himself had appointed him, within hours of the death of the former director. When his predecessor had died with his young family in the flaming wreckage of their car that had been time-bombed to explode in front of their church, the war on drugs had gone to a new level like a video game going to the next-toughest plateau. Only this time the deaths weren't just on liquid crystal display.

The man whose reflection stared back at the director from the glass was head of Centac, whose name was a contraction of the Drug Enforcement Administration's central tactical group. Originally they had been to the drug war what Eliot Ness and his Untouchables had been to the war against organized crime in Chicago so many decades before: a team of lawyers and accountants and a handful of people who were more spies than agents. They had tied together the giant narcotics conglomerates with cohesive investigations that had ended in mass arrests and the sweeping destruction of major dope cartels.

But law enforcement, like anything else governmental, is run by people. People love glory, and Centac had stepped on the toes of too many inside and outside the DEA who had wanted the glory of the arrests for themselves.

Its founder had retired from the DEA to take an undersheriff's position in Florida, and his replacement had tried to up the stakes. The Colombian drug lords had dealt with him: they had set the bomb that incinerated him and his family in front of their church.

But the Medellín Cartel had not realized what a Pandora's box they had opened. The death of the director had triggered a backlash, a reaction that had morally empowered the President of the United States to do what had never been done before in the battle against the poisoners of America.

Centac had acquired new powers. Though supposedly under the auspices of the Drug Enforcement Administration, it was actually an elite and separate group that carried credentials of both Centac and DEA. The new director, the man looking at his reflection in the glass at this moment, had been placed in charge—and he reported directly to the President of the United States.

Only some fifty agents were directly assigned to Centac. Exactly seven of them were authorized for Code Zero. Those seven people, the director and the President were among the very few who knew what Code Zero stood for.

Code One used to be as high as it went. It meant unlimited budget, unlimited manpower authorized for an operation considered so important that it *had* to succeed. After the assassination of the previous director, the President himself had authorized Code Zero.

The director remembered his awe as he'd sat alone in the Oval Office with the President of the United States, and he remembered the President's words....

"AS YOU WELL KNOW," the President began, "I had some background in Intelligence before I entered politics. I knew better than most politicians what a crippling blow it was to this country when our covert services were stripped of the power to sanction an enemy with 'extreme prejudice.' Nonetheless, I accepted it, then and now—those were the laws of the land, the laws I swore an oath to administer. Assassination would now be used legitimately only against operatives of enemy entities when a state of war had been declared."

The President looked the director in the eye and smiled wryly. "Well, war has been declared. What happened in front of that church was no less a declaration of war than Pearl Harbor. You've heard my predecessors talk about declaring war on drugs. You heard me reaffirm my commitment to win that war in my address to the nation today at your predecessor's funeral.

"The war is declared," the President announced. "The sanctions no longer apply, morally and legally speaking. Actually the 'legally' is arguable, and that is why what is being said today does not leave this room. That is why my office recorders have been shut off, and why you have been screened for recording devices before entering the Oval Office."

The President's mirthless smile seemed to intensify. "When I was associated with this nation's Intelligence branch, I had to tell men frankly that I could not publicly stand behind them. Actually, when they were caught or killed, we only disavowed them officially. Their families were always taken care of. We had separate, untraceable funds for that. The kind of funds I'm going to make available to you."

The smile was gone now as the President spun in his swivel chair to face the director intently. "Before, you had Code One. There were funds made available to you to pursue truly major drug investigations, funds that were not allocated to you on any official annual budgets. Now, however, you have something more.

"I call it Code Zero. I am authorizing you, right now, to terminate with extreme prejudice the people responsible for the murder of the director of Centac.

"That authorization will not end when those men are dead, but will continue to be available to you. When the central command of this country's war on drugs—which I believe is the most important war of our time—is violated by dopers who kill, you now have the power to exterminate them.

"You'll need to put together a very select cadre. I don't want to know who they are. I only know that I don't want them to exceed a dozen personnel, and I want them to be people you have a hold on that goes beyond the civil service, and I want none of them to ever know more than half of the others' identities.

"There are some people who cannot be controlled while alive," the President continued, "and you will know who they are. You will not abuse this power I give you today, because if you do, you will wake up dead one morning. Only when they kill your own kind—or, for that matter, if they kill *me*—will you employ Code Zero. I expect to be reelected, but if I am not, I will leave the money and the power in place for you in such a way that you can always access it."

The Chief Executive of the United States paused and took a breath before he said, "If I'm wrong about you, you'll leave this room now and go back to being a senior administrator in the Drug Enforcement Administration. At least, for so long as you'll be comfortable there. Of course, this conversation will not have taken place.

"But if I'm right about you, you're going to walk out of here as the newly appointed director of Centac. And within ninety days you will sit here with me again and satisfy me

that the men who did this blasphemy in front of the church
are burning in hell, and that you are responsible."

The President stopped talking. The pause was long and
pregnant. Then the tall black man allowed himself his own
small smile when he said softly, "It sounds like a plan to
me...."

IT SEEMED AGES LATER as the director looked at his ghostly
reflection in the window of his own executive office. He saw
short curly hair more iron gray than it was before, and a face
more lined than it had been that day in the Oval Office. It
was the face of a man who had selected a team—no, what
had the President called it, a cadre—that had gone beyond
even the President's expectations.

He had not stood in front of the President to report suc-
cess in ninety days. It had taken only forty-one before the
Colombian plotters had been brought to justice by steel and
by flame. It had sealed the director's position as a member
of the President's innermost circle.

There had been five Code Zero operatives to start, all with
a dark secret somewhere that gave the director his power
over them. Soon there had been a sixth.

Then had come the seventh, a woman of Centac who had
undergone an unbelievable nightmare when kidnapped by
what the director called drug demons. She'd been rescued by
one of his Code Zero men, and had herself avenged what the
kidnappers had done. She was, he reflected, the first of his
cadre who was truly clean, who had never done anything
that he, the director, could not send the agent to prison for
if they turned on each other. But she'd been made Code
Zero only after that bloodbath was over, and was as yet un-
proven in his mind.

But they had never faced a situation such as this one.

The director turned away from the window and looked
again at the carpet. The bloodstain was still there. He wondered if it would ever go away, at least in his mind, even after they tore this rug up and laid down the new one to
replace it.

There was a buzz on his intercom. "Sir, Agent Wolfe is here."

"Send him in," said the director in a voice that sounded flat and dead.

He walked to his desk and, as the President had done for him that day in the Oval Office, flipped the hidden toggle switches that killed the automatic audio tape recorder and locked out the hidden VCR Minicam.

Several steps away, across the deep pile carpet, the heavy teak door opened. Harry Wolfe, the Code Zero operative he had summoned, walked in.

The director waited for the massive door to shut fully and sound-seal itself before he told Wolfe, "Lock it behind you. I've already told my receptionist we're not to be disturbed."

3

"One of our agents is dead," the director told Wolfe. "Brian Voit, age twenty-nine. In this office. In that chair. Quarter to five last night."

Wolfe followed as the director walked toward the TV/VCR complex at the end of one of the oak-paneled counters in the office. The director picked up two videocassettes. "One of these was taken here. The other was left on my desk by Agent Voit. That's the one I'll show you first. It looks as if he set it up alone in a motel room and did it himself."

The director inserted the cassette and pressed Play. Static swirled on the screen for a moment, and then Wolfe saw the bare pastel walls of a motel room, with a nightstand in the background and a rumpled bed on the left of the screen.

A man walked into view of the camera, obviously having set it up. He was stripped to the waist. He wore grungy jeans, and there was elastic bandaging around his ribs. The butt of a small-frame Smith & Wesson revolver protruded from his right hip pocket.

The man sat on the bed, turned and looked at the camera. "My name is Brian Voit," he said in a flat voice. "Centac, Phoenix office."

Wolfe was stunned. This man was supposed to be twenty-nine years old. He looked between forty and fifty. The eyes were hollow and dark. The fairly long, dark hair was matted and filthy. He wore a dark beard, two or three inches long, obviously well trimmed but also looking dirty and greasy.

The eyes were pale blue and bloodshot. The eyes of a haunted man, Wolfe thought.

"Four days ago I was taken out for my initiation into the Princes of Hell. I do not believe they burned my cover.

There were four of them, all made members of the Princes. Rax, Mongo, Fat Phil and one I hadn't seen before. Huge guy, six-five, close to two-seventy-five, mostly muscle. White male, of course, blue and blond. Clean shaven, medium hair. Didn't have 'the look.' Standard club colors.

"They took me outside my parents' house—3625 Dundee Road, Tempe, Arizona. I don't know how they found me there. We'd been working the op out of the L.A.-San Diego axis. I know nobody followed me. They just somehow knew I'd be there...."

The man on the screen was starting to choke. He turned away from the camera, put his hand over his face, then walked out of view toward the right. The image went dark for a moment.

When it came back on, the view was the same, but now there was a 12-pack of Budweiser on the bed, its top torn open. Brian Voit walked from the camera to the bed again, then sat down. He had an open can in his hand.

He took a deep breath, then looked at the camera and said, "Sorry about that. I'm gonna try like hell to hold together long enough to get this right.

"Anyway, I'd called home for messages and found out that my mom was real sick. She's had two heart attacks, and here she was, down with severe bronchitis. My dad begged me to come home and see her. Said she'd been calling for me.

"So I let my supervisor know where I was going to be, and told Fat Phil I had to take care of some personal shit, I'd be out of L.A. for a while. He didn't ask me anything, just said it was cool. I took my Harley to Arizona. Didn't take long. I made Phoenix in four and a half hours."

The man on the screen paused and took a long drink of beer. "I got to the house a little after four in the afternoon," he went on, his voice beginning to tremble slightly. "My younger brother Tom was there, and his wife and their two little girls. Mom was in pretty bad shape. She had an oxygen bottle by the bed and everything. My dad was holding up okay—he's sixty but in good shape for his age. Anyway, my mom was kind of in and out of it, crying a lot, talking about what to do after she was dead. We were all trying to cheer her up.

"About six I thought it'd be a good idea to go out, get a big bucket of chicken or something for the family to eat. Took the keys to my dad's station wagon. I got halfway into the driveway, and two cars pulled in. Gray Ford van I'd never seen before—stripped down, didn't look like a biker van—and a blue Chevy sedan that could have been a rental.

"Four people got out of each. They were dressed like bikers, half of them wearing Princes of Hell colors. Except for one, I knew all the Princes. It was pretty dark and I couldn't really see the four that got out of the Chevy, the ones I didn't recognize.

"Fat Phil come up to me and said, 'Don't look at them, kid, look at me. I'm the one you're running with tonight.' He grabbed me by the face like this—'' Voit paused on-screen to show his own hand coming under his chin, squeezing hard and forcing his lips into an obscene pucker "—and Phil said 'it's intro night, boy.'''

The man on the screen looked away from the camera. "I tried to tell them, hey, what the fuck you doin', this is my old folks' place an' my mom's sick... But the four I didn't know were already in the door and Fat Phil was saying, 'Don't sweat it for them, sonny. Don't you know we're the only family you got now?' And he said, 'You be cool, they be fine.'

"Rax and Mongo grabbed me from behind. Phil patted me down and took my gun. Colt .45 automatic. Then somebody pulled a hood down over my head and shoved something up under it.

"I recognized the smell from drug-awareness training at the academy. Ether. I tried to hold my breath. Didn't do any good."

The man on the screen paused to swill down another gulp of beer. Wolfe took the opportunity to glance over at the director. The big black man was staring, riveted, at the TV screen. Wolfe could see that his hands were opening and closing, making the muscles and veins stand out angrily.

"When I woke up, we were in the desert," the man on the screen said after a moment. "They dragged me out of the van. Even though I had a headache from the ether, my eyes were pretty much adjusted to the dark.

"There was a campfire and a pickup truck, an old Ford, Arizona plates. Oh, I remember, the one at the house that looked like a rental had Arizona plates, too, but there were California plates on the van. I don't remember any of the numbers except the pickup by the fire. Arizona HE 6546, that's Helen Edward six-five-four-six.

"There were two more Princes by the fire, and what looked like a woman curled up in a sleeping bag. I could smell marijuana. The Princes were the two we've got on file, Snake and Thumper. Thumper said, 'Yo, bros! You got our in-duc-tee!' "

The man on the camera still looked at the lens, but he seemed to be staring into space. He did not speak for a while, and then he said, "And Phil told me, 'Initiation night, boy. Real easy one for ya, too. Don't hafta steal nothing off nobody. All's ya gotta do is pork yerself some fine teen pussy.' He gestured at the girl who was huddled in the sleeping bag. I could see her shoulders shudder when he said it.

"Phil said, 'Thumper, m'man, unpeel that fine surprise we got for our wannabe here.' Thumper reached down and ripped the sleeping bag open.

"I could see the girl. She was naked and looked very slight, with a real small backside. Could have been a little boy with his clothes off, the way she was all curled up. She was shivering. She had dark skin and dark hair.

"Fat Phil said, 'Turn the little bitch over.' Thumper reached down and grabbed her by the hair and jerked her onto her back.

"She screamed. She covered her face. I could see she had little buds for breasts. She tried to cross her legs, and I could see she just had a little wisp of pubic hair.

"I looked at Phil and said, 'For crissakes, man, she's a *baby*, she can't be fourteen, fifteen!' Phil grins at me an' he says, 'Old enough to bleat, old enough to shear.'

"I said, 'Fuck you, man, I ain't no baby-fucker.' That's when the new one, the big clean-cut guy, just out of the blue hit me in the ribs. I think it was his fist, but he must've had knucks on, I could feel the ribs break. I kind of lost my wind and went down to my knees. I heard Phil's voice. 'I give you an easy initiation, an' you chicken out on me? Well, no freakin' way. You're gonna do it now!'"

Brian Voit's words choked off into a sob. He lurched forward, off the bed, his hand coming up as if reaching for the camera. Sure enough, the screen went black.

It came on almost immediately, but Wolfe could tell that there had been a long pause before Voit had started his Minicam again. There were several empty Bud cans in sight now, and the beer case was turned over on its side on the bed. Only a few full cans were visible inside.

Voit walked back into the picture. He took the revolver out of his hip pocket and set it on the nightstand. It was indeed a Smith & Wesson, Harry saw, a short-barreled stainless-steel one. Probably the 5-shot Model 60. The little .38 was a popular backup gun among the agents.

This time Voit did not look at the camera. He stared at the floor, a can of beer between his hands. There was more tremor in his voice now, and he was noticeably slurring his words.

"I looked at her. Her eyes were white all the way around. Her face was all bruised from being slapped. She tried to say something in Spanish, and that bastard Thumper smacked her in the face with his open hand.

"They pulled my jeans off and threw me on top of her. I couldn't . . . I couldn't get hard. I don't know if I could've got turned on to the finest-looking woman in the world under those circumstances, but not a young girl, man, no way.

"One of them kicked me in the ribs. I almost passed out. The girl was screaming. I couldn't breathe. The ribs were already busted on one side. Then she was talking in Spanish, saying something like, 'If you don't, they'll kill us both.'

"I pretended to hump her."

Fear had given way to anger now. Wolfe could see Voit's teeth grinding, the masseter muscles of his jaws standing out in his cheeks. Voit didn't seem to know that he was crushing the half-full beer can as he spoke.

"After a while they dragged me off her. Rax said something about me being a phony motherfucker because I didn't have a hard-on, and I said something about I came already, and he hit me. Phil said, 'Look down there an' see if there's any come,' and Thumper started laughing and said, 'Hey, man, you took so long gettin' here an' we didn't have nothin' to do... so we had ourselves some fun with the little spic... there's lots of donations down there already.''

"I swore at him and said, 'Look at that poor kid. She didn't ask for nothin'. It ain't like fuckin' a sheep!'

"And Mongo comes up and says, 'That your only problem, man? I'll make her a fuckin' sheep.' He pulls out this Buck knife, and I see Rax grin real big and hold her leg down. Mongo starts to cut her leg.

"That's when the stranger, the clean-cut one, comes up and hits me another uppercut in the ribs, on the other side this time. I can feel bone break and I can't breathe at all and I'm down on both knees. And I see Mongo cut the Princes of Hell brand into her thigh. While she's *screaming!*''

The man on the screen extended his index finger and slashed letters in the air in front of him. It looked like a cattle brand, with the capital *H* extending from the stem of the *P*.

"They pulled the hood over my head. I heard Fat Phil say, quiet like he didn't want me to hear him, 'Get him outa here now. You guys clean up. Let's bring his candy ass back where we found it.'

"With the hood over my head, and trying to breathe, I couldn't keep track of time. It was half to three quarters of an hour before the van stopped. On the way Fat Phil was telling me how nice my sister-in-law looked, even if she was a little long in the tooth. My sister-in-law is twenty-four. He told me if I turned rat my whole family was going to die screaming.

"As soon as the van came to a stop, they pulled the hood off my head. I could see the other ones running out of the house, my parents' house. Two of them jumped in the back of the Chevy, and the other two come running up to Fat Phil. One of them says, 'Trouble, man. Ol' lady got all hyped about us bein' in there. She starts havin' a conniption fit an' goes into seizure, man! Then everybody else goes hysterical! We hadda slap 'em around, tie 'em up. Couldn't do nothin' for the ol' lady without callin' 911, right? She bit the big one. Wasn't nothin' I could do, Phil, honest to Christ.'"

Voit put his hands to his face, trying to compose himself. Wolfe could tell he was gritting his teeth to keep from crying. At length Voit lowered his hands, and tears were streaming down his face as he said through his clenched teeth, "Phil must have known he couldn't kill everybody right there in a suburban neighborhood. He said to me, 'This is your fault, you fuckin' candy ass. You wanted to be a Prince of Hell? You can't even take care of yer own family. Look, it wasn't our fault your ol' lady bit the big one. You lied to us, told us you didn't have no family!' Then he hit me in the face with his open hand.

"'We're outa here,' he said. 'Get in the house an' take care of shit. You even think about ratting on us, just remember—we know where yer fucking family is! You rat us out, yer mom's gonna be the lucky one!'

"I felt a boot on my ass. They shoved me out of the van onto the lawn. The pain in my ribs was unbelievable. I was trying to get my breath. I couldn't do anything. I heard the van and the rental car pull out and take off.

"I managed to get up and I went in the house. I didn't hear anything inside at first. I started yelling 'Mom! Mom!' I ran into her bedroom...."

Suddenly sobs convulsed the man on-screen. He threw his half-full beer can at the camera, and the room seemed to tilt crazily, then turn on its side. The camera was pointed now at the inside of the motel room door. In the background was the sound of a man sobbing violently. After a while the scene whirled kaleidoscopically again. Wolfe and the director watched as the camera was roughly shoved back into position, aimed at the bed. They saw Brian Voit stagger back toward the bed, stumble and catch himself, then drop into a sitting position, exhausted. He was still crying.

"My mother was dead," Voit went on, the words painfully wrenched out of him. "Her eyes were open. Her face was all bluish gray. She was lying there staring at the ceiling. Her pupils were all wide and black, and her eyes were halfway rolled up in her head.

"My father was on the floor. They'd tied him up with towels and sheets. There was a facecloth from the bathroom in his mouth. I pulled it out.

"My father looked me in the eye for a minute, and then he said, 'Damn you. God damn you! You did this! *You!*'

"I heard thumping, like stomping, in the next room. It had been my room when I lived there. I ran out of my parents' room and into my old room. My brother was there, and his wife. They were both tied up with sheets, too. The kids were over in the corner, the two-year-old and the three-year-old, crying their heads off. They'd gagged the grownups but they hadn't gagged the kids.

"My sister-in-law was naked from the waist down. When I came into the room, she turned her face away from me. My brother just looked at me. I never saw hate like that in my life!"

The haggard man on the screen looked at the camera, his own eyes red with hatred.

"You fucking *failed* me, Director," a red-faced Brian Voit screamed into the camera. "I hung my ass out for five years for DEA and Centac! They told me in the DEA Academy we'd always have the best training, the best Intelligence!

"But it was a lie! I was working the 'Customs Connection' on the Mexican border when I got the chance to get close to the Princes of Hell! My field supervisor said he talked to you, Director, and you thought it was a good idea to try to get accepted into the club. Going to be Centac's first big op on the outlaw bike gangs that run the methamphetamine factories. Code One op, the whole bit!"

Voit was sobbing now.

"But you didn't give me shit for information! You told me an outlaw bike gang would wait six, twelve months to initiate a wannabe. You said they'd never be able to find out my real identity, find out where my family was!

"You know what you made me do? You know what you did to my family? You going to show me some way I can ever look my dad or my brother or my sister-in-law in the eye again?" Voit was shouting at the top of his lungs.

"I felt like going into the club headquarters. Or the headquarters bar. I was going to smoke Fat Phil and Rax and Mongo and all those other bastards right *there!* Hold back the trigger on my subgun and blast 'em to shit!

"But I wouldn't get them all, and they'd get me before I did, and if I even got one of them, they'd know where my family was. They'd *finish* with my sister-in-law. And her kids. And my brother. *And* my father.

"So I only have one way out. I'm going to be dead, and they'll know I'm dead and can't testify against them. You couldn't even use this fucking tape, could you? Even if I was sworn. You want me to be sworn?

"Okay. I solemnly swear that everything on this fucking tape is the truth, the whole truth, and nothing but the truth, so help me God! See, my right hand is up and everything! But you won't send them to jail with that, and you can't keep them from getting at my family. My family, which *you* compromised by making me do this thing half-assed!

"Once I'm dead, they'll know they're safe, and they'll know there's no point screwing with my family anymore. I'm sending a copy of this tape to Fat Phil. When I kill myself, he'll know it wasn't a fake. And so will you.

"Oh, believe me, you fat old office bastard, so will you!"

Suddenly Brian Voit launched himself from his seated position, swinging his right fist at the camera. The room spun crazily, and the camera's mike recorded the crashing sound as the whole apparatus toppled to the floor. Wolfe could see a booted foot swing toward the camera lens, coming crazily in from the side, and then the screen went black.

The director moved forward. Without bothering to rewind, he punched Stop and then Eject on the VHS player, withdrew very gently the cassette and put it aside as if he didn't want to harm it. He picked up the next cassette and looked at Wolfe.

"Harry, you probably won't be surprised to know that this office is bugged. The lens is behind the mirror by the wet bar.

"He had called for an appointment, and said it was urgent and personal as well as agency involved, and that he couldn't trust his supervisor. Harry, you know I've tried to be open with you guys. I also knew it was out of the ordinary. We'd had no idea of what had happened in Tempe.

"I had flicked on the machine just before he walked in. What you see is what you get. This is yesterday, starting at about 5:40 p.m."

The director pressed Play.

This time there was no static. The image came up instantly on the screen. The director could be seen behind his huge desk on the left, and on the right was Brian Voit. He was clean shaven now and wearing a suit. He appeared younger, closer to his own age, except for the still gray and hollow look about the eyes.

"Thank you for taking the time to see me, Director," said Voit, the voice strangely calm compared to what Harry had just seen.

"My door is always open, Brian, you know that. Now, what is it that you needed to tell me that you couldn't share with your supervisor?"

"This," said Voit, placing a small manila-wrapped package on the big desk. It was obviously the videotape. "There's a lot in here that I didn't really think I could tell you in person, at least, not without you calling some guys with a straitjacket to take me away in."

Wolfe saw the director say soothingly, as if to a child, "Now, Brian, it can't be all that bad." Beside him, Wolfe felt the director wince as he heard his own platitude.

On the screen the director leaned forward across his desk, his hands folded, waiting expectantly for an answer. Brian Voit imitated his action, leaning forward, too, until their faces were only inches apart. Wolfe could hear the tremor from the other tape creeping into Voit's voice.

"You told us we were the elite," Voit said. "You said we'd face the deadliest danger, but that you'd make us the best-prepared agents in the world *to* face it. Well, you lied, you bastard. I've paid the price. Now you're going to pay it."

Almost imperceptibly the director's hand began to edge toward the top drawer of his desk. "Don't move," barked Voit. His hand flashed under his jacket, and suddenly a silver snub-nosed revolver was leveled at the director's face. It was the Smith & Wesson Voit had possessed on the previous videotape. Wolfe saw the director freeze in midmotion.

"What are you going to do?" asked Voit on-screen, his lips coming back from his teeth. "Call the boys to haul me away? Go for a gun in your own desk? You old bastard, don't you even want to hear me? Don't you even want to hear what you've done to me?"

There was a beeping sound, and on the video screen both men's heads turned involuntarily toward the intercom on the desk.

They heard the director say calmly, "Son, if I don't answer it, they'll send people in here."

Voit answered, "No problem. Just reach over carefully and press the button. Want to bet your secretary's got some TV newspeople in the hall?"

The director's hand slowly and carefully reached for the intercom, pressed the button. "Yes?"

A woman's cultured voice was heard. "Director? There are two news teams here. They said they were told to be here at exactly this hour for an important announcement."

The director looked at Voit, watched a nervous grin spread across his face.

"Just in time," Voit said. He cocked the hammer of the little silver-colored revolver that was pointed at the director's head. The implacable black face showed no trace of fear.

Voit sighed, long and deep.

"Avenge me," he said.

Then Brian Voit turned the gun in his hand, shoved the muzzle into his own mouth and pulled the trigger.

4

The director's hand flashed to the machine, slapping rather than pressing the Stop button. The screen went to static.

The immaculately dressed man turned away. "Harry," he said, "I'm sorry. I didn't think it would affect me that way. I see now why Brian knocked over the video machine when he did. You just . . . go ahead and finish the tape."

Wolfe pressed Rewind for an instant, then Play. The tape started where it had left off.

Wolfe watched the gun enter the mouth of the young agent. Voit closed his eyes hard, squinting them shut, and yanked the revolver's trigger back with a hard, fast pull.

The blast of the shot was muffled. It was, of course, inside his head.

Wolfe had seen other men shot on camera. In the age of the evening-news Minicam, it was common now for the media to get to the danger scene before the shooting was complete. Many of these real-life "snuff films" had been made into law-enforcement training, and Harry had seen more than his share.

Mostly, though, the camera would jerk violently when the shot was fired. It was usually hand held. It was a reflection of the fact that Man was at least partly civilized, so that the camera person would flinch when the death bullet was unleashed, making the camera jump at just that moment.

But the director's security camera had been locked in place in a bracket mount. It had no nerves. It was still as the shot was fired.

Brian Voit's eyes went wide open. The body convulsed once, jerking upright in the chair, then collapsed instantly like a bag of laundry. The silvery revolver, its front half now dark with blood, tumbled between his feet and bounced once on the carpet.

The head lolled across the back of the chair in front of the director's desk. Blood was everywhere. A thin, persistent trickle of it appeared instantly at Voit's left ear, draining down into his dark suit.

But the blood poured from the nose and mouth as if from a spigot. The DEA-issue cartridge for a .38 Special revolver like the one Voit had put in his mouth was a Remington 158-grain hollowpoint, loaded to Plus-P velocity, which meant more powder, more pressure and more power. The giant blood vessels that fed Voit's brain had been torn apart.

The dark red fluid gushed like a carmine waterfall from the nostrils and the mouth, the mouth that hung slack and open. It poured across the front of the young man's suit. The body did not twitch at all.

Over the intercom a voice could be heard screaming, "Director! Director!"

The director's face changed quickly. First the mouth was agape in horror as Voit did what he did. Then the jaw immediately tightened into resolve. The director's hand flashed under the desktop, and for an instant Wolfe expected the video to plunge into blackness. But instead, the director had hit the emergency button that locked the massive door to his office. Wolfe saw the big black man lurch to his feet, reach for his intercom and bark, "Condition Red! I have a man who has shot himself in here! Get me paramedics *now!*"

Then, on-screen, the director's hand went under the table again. The door released, and it was like opening a floodgate. The camera's lens angle wasn't wide enough to take in the doorway, but Wolfe saw the tableau bathed in intense white light from behind as the newspeople's lights and cameras came through the doorway.

In the background was a chorus of gasps and exclamations. "Jesus Christ! Oh . . . my . . . God!"

A blond woman, holding a microphone covered with audio foam, rushed into camera range. She stopped short as she found herself next to the dead man in the chair. Blood was still rushing freely from the mouth and nostrils of Brian Voit.

Wolfe watched as she stared into the face of the dead man, and he saw Brian Voit's eyes move. They seemed to look around for an instant, and then to fix on the blond woman with the microphone.

Wolfe saw her mouth open in a silent scream. Then her own eyes rolled up in her head, her knees buckled and she swooned and fell to the floor.

On the left of the screen, the director's hand flickered at his desk. This time the video *did* go black.

Wolfe reached forward and pressed Stop. He turned. The director's back was to him.

The broad shoulders inside the expensive suit were slumped, and the man's head hung dejectedly forward. The chief of Centac asked, "Did you see his eyes?"

"Yes," answered Wolfe. "So, it seems, did the news lady."

"He couldn't have been still alive, could he?"

"Impossible, sir. At that angle the bullet had to go right through his medulla. It would have been instant. The thing with the eyes was just a post-mortem response."

The director shook his head. "I'm going to see those eyes as long as I live, Wolfe. I'm going to hear Brian Voit's words. 'Avenge me.' That's what he said. Avenge me!"

Wolfe stepped forward and placed a hand on the director's shoulder. The man was trembling. Harry couldn't tell if it was tears or tension or a mix of both.

The director's voice was soft. "I will, you know. I *will* avenge him. You, too. If you're up for it."

Wolfe turned toward the mirror where he knew now the camera had been. The director caught the gesture. How he saw it with his back turned, Harry would never know.

"We're not recording, Harry," the director said with a small sigh. He turned and faced the agent, extending his own arms out to the side. Wolfe knew what he meant.

Harry slowly extended his own arms out sideways. The director's hands ran over him, collar to toes. They did not pause as they passed the holstered Glock, the knife in the right front pants pocket, or the custom snub-nosed .357 Magnum in the holster strapped to Wolfe's left ankle. The expert hands were looking only for a microphone, what agents call a wire.

The director stepped back, extending his own arms. Wolfe fulfilled the ritual and patted down his commander. The only thing he felt out of the ordinary was a small revolver butt-forward in front of the left hip. Under his hands, however, his chief's body was not only hard, but seemed to be vibrating with the stress.

Wolfe stood back. "Sir," he began, and the director instantly cut him off.

"Give me a minute, Harry," he said. "I've been through my share of shit. I created Centac out of the ashes of what it was. I avenged the man who used to sit at this desk when he and his family were murdered. Correction—*we* avenged him.

"And we're going to avenge this, too."

"Understood, sir," said Wolfe. "But, my God, the press was here—"

The director cut him off with a raised hand. "It's all over the country. You must have seen today's papers. CNN had it on the air as early as last night.

"The kid gave us a fucked-up hand to play with. He knew that there's no safehouse arrangement, no reestablished identity program for the family of a compromised drug agent. We've got the system in place through the Marshal's Service to do that for scumbags that rat on their own kind, but no, nothing like that for our own people when the other side makes them targets."

The lips were drawn back bitterly from the white teeth of the senior narcotics commander. "Everyone from the Tempe Police Department on up has been notified, and the Voit family is being watched as closely as the President's family right now. The Princes of Hell are going to be especially leery of any possible infiltration, not just now, but in the foreseeable future."

Wolfe asked, "Who knows about the first videotape?"

"No one. In the CBS station's footage, where you can see everything from when the door to this office burst open a second after Brian shot himself, the manila envelope is plainly visible on my desk. But it's hiding in plain sight. It never occurred to anyone to examine it.''

Wolfe said one word. "Investigators?"

A grim smile curled the director's lips. "D.C. homicide, naturally, felt a need to be here. So did FBI and a few lawyers from Justice Department. By then, of course, the TV cameras were gone and the envelope was *in* my desk. No one ever had the bad taste to ask. Hell, they never even saw the second videotape, Harry. Very little has gone to the public—just the footage from the CBS affiliate coming through the door, along with Brian's file photo. All anyone knows is that he was a DEA agent and that he shot himself in my office. I've been holding off my FBI interviews until tomorrow. I've already hashed it out with the President."

"And?"

"And," the director answered, "the story is that a young agent who was assigned to the investigation of methamphetamine labs operated by outlaw bikers walked into my office and shot himself. 'The investigation,' as the news hounds like to say, 'continues.' What I'm saying is, we've got a little time."

"I was told it was Code Zero," said Wolfe.

The director nodded. "It most certainly is. You know why we created the Code Zero concept. I never thought we'd use it for an agent-involved suicide. But Harry, those bastards killed that boy as surely as if they'd blown his brains out in the Arizona desert. I don't think we'll be able to hide from the press what went down with his family. The world is going to know pretty damn quick just what happened to young Voit, and why. If the outlaws think they can get away with that, then everything Code Zero was developed to stand for is meaningless."

"It'll be the biggest Code Zero since the first one," Wolfe told the director.

"I know that," the director said softly. "Voit said there were ten people along on what they did to him and to his family. There were only half that many initial targets when your team made things right with the people who murdered my predecessor."

"It was more than that by the time we were finished," Wolfe observed.

"Yes. They got in the way and they paid the price, and they were all dope-sucking scumbags that deserved what they got. If some more Princes of Hell get in the way, let 'em fall. They belong with the rest.

"Your designated targets of priority are the six involved in kidnapping our agent and making him rape, or try to rape, that young girl. And the four who held his family hostage, raped his sister-in-law and scared his mother literally to death. And, within those eight, particularly the ones who did the young girl."

Wolfe asked, "Do you think we can find her?"

The director looked at him with eyes that seemed dark and dead. "We've found her. Take a look on my desk. Far left corner. Came in today."

Wolfe stepped to the desk and picked up a fax of a teletype. The federal headquarters of the various U.S. law-enforcement agencies didn't get all the teletypes from every state, but this one apparently had been faxed from a Centac or DEA regional office. Wolfe felt himself grow cold as he read it. It began with the current date.

Maricopa County, Arizona. Corpse discovered in desert 2 Mi. off I-10, Hispanic female, age approx. 14-15, height 4′ 11″, wt. 94 lb. long black hair, brown eyes.

Wolfe could barely make himself read the clinical descriptions of the different modes of rape. He gazed down at the floor for a minute to try to contain his rage, then finished reading the fax.

Cause of death, suffocation. Multiple bruises, lacerations on head, face. Initials carved into left thigh with edged instrument, appear to be stylized letter "P"—Paul—directly over letter "H"—Henry—in caps. Unidentified this time. Contact Detective Lt. John Casey, Maricopa County Sheriff's Office.

Wolfe set the communiqué back on the director's desk. "Jesus."

"You see why I called it Code Zero, Harry?"

Wolfe nodded grimly. "Who do you want on the team?"

"You're in charge," said the director. "It's going to have to be up close and personal. I doubt that we can infiltrate with more than one man ... and one woman."

Wolfe's head snapped up. "You want Carmelita Morales?"

The director met Wolfe's gaze. "She's the only Code Zero person we've got, of the seven, that's female. She's the only one who hasn't been blooded yet."

"I would have thought," Wolfe said dryly, "that killing one perpetrator and sending the other to living hell would have pretty well qualified as being blooded."

The director shook his head. "She didn't really do that as Code Zero, did she, Harry? She did it straight line-of-duty, self-defense or in the defense of another agent. You're not going to tell me you don't know the difference."

Wolfe nodded. "*She* knows the difference. And she's ready for Code Zero. I'm just not sure yet that it's an infiltration job."

"That's the way I want it, Harry. It can't be SAND— search and destroy—which worked for the first Code Zero. It won't work for this one. These bastards need to be taken from the inside out. We're working entirely inside our own country now. If you and Carmelita don't see it that way after your briefing, see me and we'll talk about changing it."

Wolfe nodded. "Accepted. Is Carmelita still at the academy in Quantico?"

"Yes. I'd like you to go down there to pick her up for this. I'll give you the documentation you'll need to get her out of her teaching duty."

"You mentioned a briefing," Harry said.

The director lowered his head. "I can still hear Brian Voit saying, 'You didn't give me shit for information!' I'm not going to have that on my head again. I know you're a lot more experienced than Brian was, and I know you're familiar with the way the outlaw bike gangs work, but I'm not going through that again.

"Brian already had all the info DEA could give him on the outlaws, at the academy at least. By the time he'd fallen into his chance to hook up with Princes of Hell, it was too late for us to pull him back out and give him a briefing on the details of that particular outfit.

"The two Federal agencies that seem to have the most experience with outlaw motorcyclists in general and the Princes of Hell in particular are the U.S. Marshal's Service and the Bureau of Alcohol, Tobacco, and Firearms. Apparently the Princes' gunrunning has been a whole lot more observable than their drug running. In any case, a top expert from each agency will be here at noon to give you and Morales the best possible briefing available to us."

Wolfe nodded. "What about Voit's family? Have they gone to the press?"

The director shook his head. "All they know is that Brian was trying to infiltrate a drug gang on his own and it got too big for him. As far as they know, their son was DEA, not Centac, and DEA has already said—truthfully—that they don't have any investigation going on the Princes of Hell, and whatever Brian was doing must have been strictly on his own. They're as bitter as Brian, Harry. They may decide to talk to the press soon, and there's nothing I can do about it if they do. That's one reason why things are going to have to be done quickly."

"I understand, sir," said Wolfe.

The big man in the expensive suit sat down at last in his expensive swivel chair. "You'll understand when one of your own kills himself in front of you, Harry. For now I'm just glad you've accepted the assignment."

5

Fat Phil Newell, President of the Princes of Hell Motorcycle Club, Inc., settled his 326 pounds back in his BarcaLounger. "It's good to be alive," he said aloud.

He meant it sincerely. Phil's BarcaLounger sat in the middle of a extrawide mobile home on a desolate hillside in Little Tujunga, California, that overlooked what was called locally the Canyon District. The club's corporation, PHI, was registered with the state and owned eighty acres. Next to the mobile home was a huge corrugated-metal Quonset hut that housed a full motorcycle repair shop, an eighteen-wheel tractor trailer, several vans and countless motorcycles. A few of the latter were near-antique Indians, and the rest were a panoply of the Harley-Davidson line. Most had been heavily customized, and more than half were "choppers," with long forks and souped-up engines.

The inside of the mobile home was cleaner than the dwellings of most of the members. One wall was lined with trophies. Backed mostly in denim but sometimes in leather, these were elaborate patches and embroidered rocker panels that other men had once worn to designate their affiliations.

From left to right, they read Hell's Angels MC, San Berdoo; Hell's Angels MC, L.A.; Pagans MC; Satan's Slaves; Iron Horsemen.

Next to them was a series of police patches. There were more than twenty. Above them hung a black police baton with a handle almost six inches down from one end, and a crossed pair of regular police nightsticks, one in blond hardwood and one dark with a rubber grommet—which looked like part of a crutch tip—a third of the way up. The patches represented Los Angeles Sheriff's Office, LAPD, the California Highway Patrol and several other agencies.

All the patches and rockers, both from police departments and motorcycle clubs, were mounted upside down.

The room was redolent of marijuana. Beer cans, mostly Budweiser but a few Coors, were strewn everywhere. Against every door leaned a weapon of some kind: a Remington pump shotgun with a short barrel, an M-16 or a dainty .30-caliber M-1 carbine.

A dozen or more people lounged about the room. Eight of them were male and, like Phil, wore unkempt shoulder-length hair and long, grizzled beards. The majority wore T-shirts with various emblems of the Harley-Davidson motorcycle company. About half wore sleeveless denim jackets festooned with patches, buttons and medals. On the back of these—right-side up, and proud—was a huge embroidered patch depicting a red-faced horned devil with vertically-irised eyes like a cat's and a forked tongue protruding obscenely from his mouth. Above the head was a rocker that said Princes Of Hell, and below the demonic figure were the letters, MC/L.A.

There were four or five women. Most of them wore jeans or denim cutoffs that were skintight, obviously with nothing under them, and they wore nothing under their T-shirts, either. Some were men's T-shirts, some French-cut ones that left less to the imagination. All their armpits were shaven. Several had tattoos visible on shoulders or thighs.

One woman knelt lovingly next to Fat Phil Newell, her arms folded across his right thigh, where she rested her head. She was careful not to touch the revolver in Fat Phil's right front pocket. Fat Phil hated it when people went near his gun. She kept her distance from it as she nuzzled his leg through the soiled, worn denim of his jeans. In reward, Phil stroked her long, dirty brown hair like a kitten.

"It's good to be alive," he said again.

In front of them was the screen of a giant television. It was tuned to CNN "Headlines News." The impeccably coiffed woman on the screen was saying, "Federal law enforcement was shaken today when a narcotics agent shot himself to death in the office of the Director of Centac, the Drug Enforcement Administration's central tactical group."

The camera cut to the director's office, zooming in on the chair with its back to the camera, in which sprawled the body of the young agent. The small red crater of the .38 slug's exit wound was evident through Voit's dark hair. The camera, as if in shame, switched to the desk in front of the body, behind which the director was yelling toward the cameras, "Get clear! We need paramedics in here!"

The TV screen was now filled with a close-up of the stainless-steel Model 60 revolver, stainless no longer, covered instead with blood as it lay in the darkening pool between the sprawled feet of the young man in the chair.

The CNN voice-over continued, "The Drug Enforcement Administration at this hour has said only that the young narcotics officer who committed suicide in the director's office had been assigned to the Los Angeles area, and had not previously shown dangerous signs of burnout."

A picture of Brian Voit, the official bureau photo that looked like a yearbook picture, came on the screen. The woman's voice-over intoned, "The Drug Enforcement Administration says tonight that the investigation continues into the circumstances that led Agent Brian Voit, twenty-nine, to take his own life so dramatically today in Washington."

The image cut to a studio in Georgia, where an impossibly handsome man with a razor cut said solemnly, "More proof, Susan, that police work is a terribly dangerous job. We cut now to a live CNN update in Birmingham, Alabama, where a SWAT team has surrounded an escaped gunman who snatched a police officer's revolver and shot him to death, and then took hostages inside this day-care center—"

Fat Phil pressed a button, and the image died. "Hon-ey," said the woman at his knees, "I was watchin' that!"

As though he were casually swatting a fly, Fat Phil back-handed her across the face. She sprawled on her back on the cheap carpet of the clubhouse trailer. Her hand flew to her face, and she started to speak, but then she turned away. She rolled up on her right elbow, her left hand going to her mouth. It came away covered with blood.

Two big men were standing behind Fat Phil's reclining chair. The tallest, six-five, glowered under the blond hair that fell over his forehead and said, "That's him, all right. I *told* you we shoulda killed him!"

The other man, only slightly shorter and wearing the club colors, said, "Henry's right, Phil. I said from the beginnin', the little cocksucker was the heat."

Fat Phil's left hand flicked out from the easy chair in a back-fist movement, and caught the speaker between the legs. The big bearded man grunted, clutched his groin and went to his knees, making a mewling sound.

Phil didn't even turn around to look at him. He just roared from his chair, "Knew it from the beginning, huh? Then why the fuck didn't ya tell me before we took him out to break him in? Why didn't ya tell me that before we left him to go back to his head pig?"

The man on his knees didn't say anything except utter another strangled sound of pain. The larger man who'd been standing next to him said, "Phil. Give Rax a break. He don't trust nobody ain't already wearing the colors. If any of us knew the little guy was heat, it never woulda got as far as it did."

The obese man in the BarcaLounger grunted. "Fuck it. It's done, it's done. Still a waste of a good initiation. What it tells me is we're getting soft. Ain't had a fuckup like this in so long, we weren't ready for it. And that old hag dropping dead on us, shit, we weren't ready for that, neither. We been getting pretty goddamn sloppy, is what it is, and that's what pisses me off."

Fat Phil burped loudly, and then went on. "Ain't had a fuckup during an initiation in so damn long, we just blanked out and walked away. We probably shoulda done them all. Turns out okay, though. Put the fear of God in those yuppie fuckers at his house. I don't see them coming back for any more of us, do you?"

Klaus Richter, a huge blond man sitting next to Phil's chair, laughed out loud. "No way in hell, my friend. They want no more of the Princes at all."

The words comforted Fat Phil. ''Yah. Yer friggin' right. Still, we gotta tighten up on the initiations. Matter of fact, let's put a moratorium on new members. Them DEA bastards are gonna come after us for blood, if they got any more balls than that last little prick they put on our ass. Remember that, bros—next motherfucker wants to join up with us, ain't no more mister nice guy.''

The woman at his side on the floor was still dabbing at the blood on her mouth. Fat Phil reached out with his right hand, grabbed her by the hair and pulled her head into his groin.

''C'mere and gimme some skull,'' he said. ''I wanna celebrate. Ain't every fucking night we get on CNN!''

6

Wolfe parked the gray G-car he'd taken from the DEA motor pool near the building where the physical training was housed. The morning was still young. He had left D.C. early, going against the bulk of the traffic, and the trip to the Marine base that housed the FBI and DEA training centers was an unusually clean shot as far as northern Virginia traffic went.

At the security entrance he was given an identification card to clip on to the lapel of his suit. It was the same suit he'd worn the day before: to make the airport in Los Angeles to race back to Washington, he'd had to fall back on the small suitcase he kept in the trunk of his issue vehicle. The shirt and underwear, at least, were fresh, and if he needed more, he'd have to buy them here.

Walking down the pristine hall to the gym, he was struck by the quiet. With a defensive-tactics course in session, you could usually hear cries, grunts and hollow thumping.

He swung the door open silently, but the instructor still caught his movement instantly. The stunning brunette turned toward him and smiled and waved without breaking a word in her sentence as she faced her class again.

"The reason the old-fashioned police arm-bar doesn't work against a bigger person for most of you," she was saying in her strong but still feminine voice, "is that it was developed at a time when the average police officer was a male, selected for size and strength. A petite female or small-statured male simply can't apply that technique to a stronger man. That's why I think you're better off with the variation we'll work on today. Even if you're six-two and two hundred pounds, there's someone out there who's bigger than you by as much as you are bigger than me."

A hand went up among the twenty or so gym-suited agents. It belonged to a strapping red-haired man about twenty-five. "Excuse me, ma'am," he said sarcastically, "but are you saying you've got an arm-bar that would let you put me down?"

Carmelita Morales sighed demurely. "Why don't you step up here and we'll see," she said softly and evenly.

He did. The recruit was well over six feet. He dwarfed Carmelita, looming more than half a foot over her. "Sir," she said, "I'd like you to come with me, please." One of her small, light brown hands closed over his wrist, and the other lightly cupped his elbow.

Wolfe grinned. He knew what was going to happen.

The big red-haired kid flexed his biceps, resisting violently as he cocked his left fist to smash Carmelita in the face. Then there was a sudden flash of movement as the 125-pound woman threw her right hip back in a hard pivot, her long black hair swirling in a halo. As the big recruit was jerked off balance, Wolfe could see the soles of both his gym shoes. He landed on the padded floor with a heavy thud that shook the gym.

"Sir," said Carmelita firmly, "please stop resisting!"

Instead, the young man scrambled with his legs, trying to get his feet under him. Carmelita demurely looked skyward, shook her head and dropped her hips.

"Yaaaaahhh!" The red-haired man's half roar, half scream of pain tore through the gym. The palm of his free hand slapped a fast tattoo on the floor of the gym, the universal signal of submission.

Carmelita let go of his arm. It fell heavily to the floor. The recruit rolled onto his side, grimacing and pulling his hurting arm in against his belly.

The rest of the students burst into appreciative laughter. One of the other men said, "Can you show us that on him again?"

"No," said Carmelita with a soft smile, "but I'll show it on you."

A moment later this one, too, was facedown on the floor, his face contorted in agony and his palm slapping the floor as fast as a beaver's tail. "The secret," Carmelita explained, "is to pivot back with your outside hip at the first sign of resistance. This jerks your opponent off balance, and it also hyperextends his arm, like *sensei* holding the board for you to break. Remember, a flexed elbow is a body weapon, but a hyperextended one is a fragile thing waiting to be broken. I didn't break these fellows' elbows, even though they're carrying on as though I did, but it wouldn't have been hard. Would it, guys?"

The last one, rubbing his elbow, shook his head sheepishly. The red-haired recruit, just getting up, merely glared at her.

She clapped her hands. "Okay," she said, "you're due for a break. Take ten, and don't work on that technique until we start up again."

The students began to drift away, and she turned and strode toward Harry, her face breaking into a wide and perfect smile.

They met with a handshake, not a hug. "Carmelita, you look terrific."

She cast her eyes down modestly and brushed a hand at her long hair. "You're looking good, too," she said softly. Wolfe could see that she was parting her hair on the side now, brushing it over to cover the ugly scar high on her forehead, the scar from the bullet that had almost killed her a year ago.

"Got someone who can cover you on DT? The director wants you on something high priority."

"Immediately?"

"Yesterday," Wolfe said.

7

When Wolfe and Morales entered the conference room, three people were already seated at the far side of the long table, opposite the director, whose ebony face looked more haggard than either of the agents had ever seen it. They sat down on either side of him.

"Right on time," the director said. "Gentlemen, meet Carmelita Morales and Harry Wolfe, two of our best agents. Carmelita, Harry, we've got quite a team to brief us today." He pointed at the gray-haired man on the left who looked about sixty. "This is Duane Boche, from MAGLO-CLEN. He'll give you a briefing on what the Princes of Hell seem to be up to lately."

The director turned to the man in the middle, a thirtyish man with brown hair and a mustache, wearing khaki trousers and a blue blazer. "Bob Halloran, U.S. Marshal's Service. He's spent a lot of time with the only informant anyone seems to have been able to get out of the gang. He'll tell you what he knows about the operation."

The director turned to a disheveled man of average height, who sat at the right of the group. He wore torn, faded jeans and a sleeveless, dark-stained denim vest over a plain black T-shirt. His straight black hair flowed to his shoulders and melted into an untrimmed but carefully combed beard that reached to his upper chest. "Don McAllister, BATF. His people have done the most in the investigation of the Princes. He'll give you a rundown on the suspects identified so far."

After everyone shook hands, the older man, Boche, stood up. "Good morning," he began. "I'm here from MAG-LOCLEN, the Mid-Atlantic/Great Lakes Organized Crime Law Enforcement Network. We cover eight states for the Regional Information Sharing System under the National

Institute of Justice. We serve American law enforcement the way INTERPOL serves American and European police, as an information-gathering center and data bank on criminal suspects and gangs. Because of the short notice, my counterpart for the Southwest couldn't be here today, but he's furnished me with a pretty good background package for you.

"The Princes of Hell Motorcycle Club, Inc., was actually founded as a California corporation four years ago, listing one Phillip Newell as chairman of the board. I suspect you'll be hearing more about Mr. Newell from the other gentlemen present. The group was chartered as a nonprofit corporation whose purpose was 'to promote safe recreational motorcycling and contribute to charity.' Please try to keep a straight face. Routine tax returns are in order, indicating typical expenses and dues income from a fraternal organization with slightly under one hundred listed members.

"In fact, a hundred members sounds about right from what we've been able to determine. However, even though they make a big deal about donating to toy collections for poor children at Christmas and things of that kind, charity does not seem to be their major goal in life.

"Phillip Newell, a.k.a. Fat Phil, is a former member of the Hell's Angels. He's probably the only Hell's Angel in history to be kicked out of that club for being too disgusting even for the other outlaw bikers. It seems his taste in female companionship ran toward the very young. However, the man has a genius IQ, knew the inner workings of the Angels and set out to create a club that would beat Hell's Angels at its own game.

"Contrary to popular belief, Hell's Angels don't go around terrorizing small towns, or at least, they haven't since about 1949, when they sacked the little town of Hollister, California. At that time the motorcycle club consisted of a bunch of misfit World War II vets who called themselves POBOB, which stood for 'Pissed Off Bastards of Burbank.' After the Hollister incident, which inspired the

Marlon Brando movie *The Wild One,* the club changed its name to Hell's Angels.

"The Justice Department estimates that there are currently some 856 outlaw motorcycle gangs on the North American continent, many of them in Canada. We believe that just about half of them are affiliated, openly or subrosa, with one of the so-called Big Four—Hell's Angels, Pagans, Bandidos and Outlaws.

"The brighter clubs have worked hard to become heavy hitters in the world of organized crime. On both coasts they often hire out as enforcers and hit men for Mafia families. There is a subgroup within the outlaw biker culture that runs through all the gangs, which calls itself the 'Filthy Few.' These are men who have committed murder for money and are available to do it again. They usually work for organized crime, occasionally but very rarely hiring out as independent hit men.

"The gangs are feared even by the Mafia. When a *capo* in Philadelphia, Philip 'Chicken Man' Testa, got crossways of the Pagans, they blew up his Cadillac with him in it. There was no retaliation for the murder. The feeling among the traditional crime families is that the outlaw bikers are insane fanatics, who will wipe out your family to the last person if you screw with them. There is reason to believe that this assessment is absolutely correct.

"The gangs have proven extremely difficult to infiltrate. The initiation ritual for full-fledged membership, after six to twelve months' probation as a wannabe, is to commit a serious felony before the eyes of made members of the group. It was incorrectly stated at a Senate subcommittee hearing a few years ago that one had to commit murder to join. That is not true, except for the Filthy Few.

"In the past it was possible to infiltrate by taking some motorcycles from the property room, screwing with the VINs—Vehicle Identification Numbers—and leaving them out somewhere. You could set it up to look as if you were stealing motorcycles, which is always a major outlaw bike gang activity.

"That, I'm afraid, has changed. Starting with Hell's Angels, the trend among the outlaw gangs has been counterintelligence. They infiltrate law enforcement. Chicago police at one time had identified four made members of the Outlaws on their patrol force.

"However, throughout the bike gangs, the bikers use their women like chattel. In addition to treating them as lower life forms personally, they force them to work in everyday jobs to support them. They place emphasis on putting their women to work in positions of advantage, say clerical staff with Social Security, a state's department of unemployment compensation, or a welfare department, where they can assist in processing fraudulent claims. They also seed their women as secretaries and clerks in police department records bureaus. This gives them direct access to Intelligence files, allows them to confirm the criminal backgrounds of wannabe members, and allows them access to the NCIC—National Crime Information Center—computers. This is why the old ploy of faking the theft of a motorcycle no longer works. NCIC also allows the tracing of guns by serial numbers. More than one undercover agent has come to grief when his gun was taken by gang members and its serial number was run through NCIC, and the gang learned that the gun had been purchased by a law-enforcement agency even though it was not a typical service revolver.

"Let's get back to Hell's Angels, and why Fat Phil wants to one-up them. In addition to his humiliation at being kicked out of the club, he knows how financially successful they've been.

"It is estimated that if Hell's Angels went public, they'd be a Fortune 500 company. The best profit opportunities seem to be in meth and ice labs. The methamphetamines are the drugs of choice for the outlaw bike world, and the rage today is ice. Why take meth when you can have supermeth? Mexican brown heroin is also a hot item, although its use is forbidden by some gangs.

"Gunrunning as a major moneymaking venture seems to have tapered off among the big outfits, and this is where the

Princes of Hell come into the picture. Newell is trying to make his gang the kings of the gunrunners. We believe they have a good-sized machine shop near Los Angeles, which produces fully automatic submachine guns and converts semiautomatic weapons to full automatic. They also have at least one good-sized meth factory going somewhere around San Diego. While other gangs have been engaging in money-laundering operations, there's no indication that the Princes of Hell have done anything similar. It is believed that Mr. Newell maintains a series of safe-deposit boxes in Los Angeles area banks with some very large stores of folding money.

"The group is considered *extremely* dangerous. Their preferred initiation rite seems to be sex with underage girls, sometimes forced sex. The feeling is that no undercover cop will volunteer to do that, and it gives them another layer against infiltration. It's something the outlaw bikers picked up from the Satanists."

Duane Boche lowered his notes. "Any questions?"

Wolfe shook his head. Carmelita said, "Mr. Boche, you mentioned that their initiation rites were derived from Satanist practices. Does that, and a name like 'Princes of Hell,' imply any actual ties with devil worshipers?"

"No," replied the man from MAGLOCLEN. "The devilish names some of these clubs adopt seem to exist just for their counterculture impact. Throughout the outlaw bike culture, there seems to be a predilection for any kind of behavior that would shock an ordinary citizen. They call it 'showing class.' You'll see the male members tongue-kissing in public to shock people, but there is no homosexual undercurrent in the gangs. If anything, they're homophobic. Similarly there's no actual Satan worship involved. They had simply observed that sexual initiation rituals with children had kept the Satanist cults virtually impervious to infiltration by police, and adopted the procedure themselves, using primarily young teenage girls."

There were no more questions. Boche sat down and the bearded man stood up. "Don McAllister," he said, reintroducing himself in a gruff voice. "I'm with BATF. Be-

cause of the heavy traffic in illicit weapons among the
outlaw bikers, the Bureau of Alcohol, Tobacco, and Firearms has probably dealt with them more than any of the
other federal law-enforcement agencies. Because it's one of
my areas of specialization, I've also been able to gather a lot
of Intelligence from state, county and municipal police in
areas where the bikers are strong, and where biker activity
concentrates. That includes the areas of the three major
outlaw 'runs' every year, all of which key around major
championships in conventional motorcycle racing. Sturgis,
South Dakota, Daytona, Florida, and Laconia, New
Hampshire.

"Mr. Boche here was right on with what he told you
about the outlaw biker life-style. Let me fill you in a little
more.

"First, they're all racists. Without exception. Remember, I'm not talking about the ordinary motorcycle enthu-
siast. Police tend to say 'biker' when they mean 'outlaw
biker.' The outlaws call themselves 'one-percenters.' It
comes from a statement made years and years ago from the
American Motorcycle Association, which said that outlaws
comprised only one percent of motorcycle users. Actually
it's probably a tiny fraction of one percent. But the outlaws
were perversely proud of it. You'll often see patches or tattoos on them that say 1%.

"Let me fill you in on the patches while we're talking
about them. Mr. Boche told you about 'colors.' This will be
the club's symbol, which is very jealously guarded. It's like
a trademark except that if the outlaws find you using their
trademark, instead of suing they kick the shit out of you.
Hell's Angels, for example, has a death's head with wings
on the side. Princes of Hell have a well-hung devil in a red
swimsuit with a blood-dripping pitchfork. The original
patch had been a naked devil with a huge penis, but they had
to stop using it because local cops were using the obscenity
codes as an excuse to bust the members.

"Over the club emblem you'll have a big rocker with the
name of the club on it, always ending in 'MC' for 'motorcycle club.' Under the emblem, there'll be a rocker that has

the name of the jurisdiction you're affiliated with. Hell's Angels, for example, has chapters all over the world. Princes of Hell, to the best of our knowledge, only have two chapters, L.A. and San Diego.

"Mr. Boche mentioned that they treat their women like chattel," McAllister continued, looking pointedly at Carmelita. "If you're bringing in a female undercover, you can't overemphasize that too heavily. There are two categories of women to the outlaw bikers. One is 'sheep.' They're women who literally belong to the club. They'll probably have a tattoo on their buttocks or thigh or breast that'll say something like Property of Princes Of Hell. They're in effect resident whores. Any club member in full standing can have sex with them on demand. Any probationary member has the same privilege if there's a made member around who says it's okay. The Princes of Hell went a little beyond tattoos. They supposedly had a branding iron made up with their own brand, a letter *P* with a long stem and an *H* growing sideways out of the bottom."

McAllister didn't notice the Centac people exchanging glances. He had just described the brand cut into the leg of the young rape victim.

The bearded BATF agent continued, "The second category of woman for the outlaw bikers is 'old lady.' They use the same term for their mothers as for their wives and lovers. If you're a biker's old lady and another biker touches you without the first biker's permission, it's a capital offense. The biker who 'owns' the woman can shoot the guy and the club will cover it up. However, it's a gesture of hospitality for a biker to share his old lady with another outlaw who's visiting him.

"One thing you'll have to remember in particular," he said, looking pointedly again at Carmelita and Harry, "is that while a *made* member's woman has 'old lady' status, a probationary member's wife or girlfriend is on thin ice. On a run or at a club meeting or beer blast or something, a wannabe's girlfriend or wife will generally be accorded the same hands-off status as a regular member's woman. But when things get rough, it's not unknown for the wannabe's woman to get gang-banged. They call it 'pulling a train.' If it happens, the most the prez—the club president—will do is order a slap on the wrist for the regular members who did it.

"You've got to understand. The outlaw bike gang culture is made up of misfits. People who never could have made it in ordinary life. Bright guys are rare exceptions. Phil Newell? He's bright, but he's a demented sociopath.

"Your typical outlaw bike gang member is a loser who's found his last haven. Some of the clubs require new members to sell everything they own and give it to the club, like a monk signing himself into a monastery with an oath of poverty. The club becomes everything. Before your parents, before your religion, before your children, there is the club.

"Get in a brawl with a made member, unless you're a made member of the same club, and every club member in the place'll be all over you. When made members fight each other, everyone stands back.

"They fight to kill. They train in what the police have come to call 'outlaw karate.' It's really just stylized street fighting. They wear motorcycle boots and engineer boots, heavy and steel capped. They'll kick for the knees and the testicles, and when they get you down, they'll stomp in your head and your rib cage. The eyes and the throat are standard targets in any kind of a street fight.

"You can also expect weapons to be used. They're big on belts. Until California passed a law against it, the favorite belt for bike outlaws there was a length of driven chain. Now, what they like is a regular Garrison belt with a heavy buckle on it. They'll knead the leather with neat's-foot oil until it's real soft and supple. They like to whip their belts off and swing them around like flails. Or they will use belt-buckle knives. See what I'm wearing?"

The people around the conference table looked at McAllister. His well-worn brown belt had a rectangular bronze-colored buckle. It looked massive and heavy, but showed no indication of a blade.

Harry Wolfe said, "The belt-buckle knives I've seen are easy to spot. They've got a regular buckle with a stud for the hole in the belt where they fasten it. I don't see that there."

McAllister grinned, and his hand flashed to the belt. In an instant, three inches of shiny double-edged dagger extended from his hand. "You're right," he said, "that's the typical form. This one is called 'the Monk.' You can't spot it like the others. Also, notice my belt is still fastened. With the other belt-buckle knives, when you pull the knife you lose the buckle and your pants could fall down. That's a problem for many outlaws, because they tend to have big beer guts except for the ones that pump iron. General rule is that the skinny ones will use the belts for fighting or use the belt-buckle knives, and the fat ones will have something like mine, or they carry a knife separate."

Carmelita looked intently at the Monk knife. "I want one of those," she said.

McAllister grinned and replied, "I'll get that arranged before I leave."

McAllister turned his attention back to the rest of the group. "You remember I told you about the patches, or started to. In addition to the colors, which are generally worn on the back of a sleeveless leather or denim vest, their vests will be nothing less than festooned with patches. Here's a few things to watch for.

"First, they're not just patches. They're usually only sewn on three sides and left open on the top. That means every patch you see is actually a little pocket, a little stash pouch for contraband. Sometimes they keep their spare cash there. Sometimes pot. These guys smoke marijuana as casually as they drink beer.

"But the patches will also contain stuff like handcuff keys, razor blades, small folding knives and little guns. The outlaw bikers are more into trick weapons than James Bond. They like 2-shot derringers, and the little minirevolvers, 5-shot .22s and .22 Magnums.

"Most of these guys have heavy criminal records, and they know that a charge of felon in possession of a firearm will land them back in the slammer. Whenever they go out at night, they expect to get into trouble. For that reason, they don't usually carry guns unless they're intending to use them.

"That doesn't mean they don't have them around. They use their women as mules. The women carry their dope for the most part, and the women carry their guns. You have to understand what kind of woman becomes a biker woman. She's usually got no self-esteem at all. Most of them are battered. They live in an environment where a man who doesn't slap his woman around a little is considered something of a pussy. These women desperately want the approval of their men. They'll carry guns and drugs for them to get that approval. In my experience, at least half of these women would kill for their man without hesitation. Any time you're getting in trouble with these people, watch their women. They're the ones you can expect to be passing them guns, or maybe shooting you in the back.

"The outlaw biker's taste in guns follows his taste in motorcycles," McAllister went on. "Big, powerful, American made and usually customized. These guys fancy themselves super-right-wing patriots. They buy strictly American. That's the main reason for the emphasis on the Harley-Davidson motorcycle. It's like an icon to the bikers.

"For guns, expect Colt .45 automatics, or something like a 9 mm. Smith & Wesson or a Ruger, American made. Revolvers tend to be Colt, Smith, Ruger, Dan Wesson, and usually some kind of a Magnum, .44 or .357.

"When shit gets serious, they haul out the big stuff. What they generally do is take the regular semiautomatic version, the AR-15, and convert it to an M-16 machine gun by installing an auto-sear. That's home-workshop stuff as far as they're concerned. For close-range assassination," McAllister continued, "they like sawed-off shotguns. Their assassination method, club to club, is fairly standard. Either they place the muzzle of the shotgun to the forehead or the back of the head of the victim, or they make him or her suck the muzzle of the gun before they pull the trigger. It seems to give a certain kind of person a psychosexual kick to kill like that. Either way, the head is shattered, the brains literally blown out.

"Knives are a big part of their culture, and not just the belt-buckle knives we talked about earlier. A folding hunting knife, almost invariably the Buck brand, is standard wear among the outlaws. It's as common as a Harley-Davidson T-shirt. They don't have a lot of finesse in their knife-fighting techniques. They go for raw cutting power. About half of their techniques will start with the blade to the rear, instead of pointed to the front the way most Americans fight with knives."

Carmelita interrupted. "Is there any particular form or style they'll use in knife fighting?"

"I've got a book I want you both to read. It's called *Bloody Iron,* and it was written by a couple of guys from the Iron Cross Motorcycle Club named Jenks and Brown. It's pretty much a bible of how you can expect these guys to fight with knives."

Wolfe raised a hand, and McAllister nodded to him. Harry asked, "Is the same true with guns? Do they tend to be good shots? Any particular style to their shooting?"

McAllister cocked an eyebrow in appreciation. "You know," he said, "you're the first lawman I ever briefed who asked me that. It's something I generally save for the end of the talk. Yeah, they know how to shoot. They even have their own damn shooting matches, made up to be a damn good approximation of one of our advanced assault courses. They shoot with two hands on the pistol whenever possible, sometimes the Weaver stance with both elbows bent and dynamic tension exerted on the gun with the shooting hand pushing and the support hand pulling, sometimes the isosceles stance with both arms just locked straight out.

"Also, they'll usually have multiple spare magazines available. If the woman drifting close to the outlaw you're worried about has a gun in her purse, she's probably got a couple of spare clips or a couple of spare speedloaders.

"You will need," said McAllister after pausing a moment for breath, "to know your way around motorcycles. The machine to know is the Harley-Davidson. It's the only American-made motorcycle still produced. Your two primary Harleys in use by the outlaws are the 74, a raw power machine, and the Sportster, which is probably the lightest, most nimble bike Harley ever manufactured.

"Naturally it's the kiss of death with those people to ride a Japanese motorcycle. They call them 'rice-burners.' Your typical outlaw is likely to ride a 'chopped' Harley, called either a 'chopper' or a 'hog.' They refer to motorcycles generically as their 'ride' or their 'sled,' and you'll see them sometimes modified into tricycle form. Your typical trike rider is someone like Fat Phil, who is so huge or so obese that he overbalances a regular two-wheeled machine."

McAllister took another breath, consulted his notes and added, "You'll find that the vehicles themselves are equipped with weapons. The gas tank cap between the driver's legs is often modified with a push dagger brazed to the cap. The guy reaches forward to open his gas tank for a fillup, and wham—he slaps his palm at you and you've got four inches of steel embedded in your chest. You've seen the long rods coming up from behind the driver, called 'sissy bars' by regular bikers. The outlaws modify them a little. They're removable, and sharpened to spear points.

"A few of the outlaw bikers have gone even further. A motorcycle handlebar is replaced by a length of PVC pipe about the diameter of a 12-gauge shotgun shell. The end of a nail is inserted at the bottom to make a crude, fixed firing pin. The tube that replaces the handlebar is now threaded and screwed down so the shotgun shell inside has its cap, its primer, very lightly touching that nail. They'll slip a rubber sleeve over the whole thing.

"When they want to fire it, they just twist, and the screw threading drives the primer down on the nail and fires the shell. You get a blast of double-ought buckshot, full power, coming out of the end of the handlebar. To a bystander, the firing motion would look like the twist of the wrist you'd apply to the handlebar controls if you were going to change gears on a normal motorcycle."

McAllister paced around the room briefly to stretch his legs and refresh himself, then he continued where he'd left off. Transportation options such as tractor trailers, pickup trucks and personalized vans were discussed, then he launched into a rundown on "wings," detailing the oral sexual exploits that are perceived as points of manly pride by bikers.

McAllister paused and let it all sink in on his audience before he said, "One final, particular sign to watch for. You remember I told you about the Filthy Few, the outlaws who have killed for money and are ready to again. Their sign is the double lighting bolts of the Nazi SS. Remember, these guys tend to be total white racists. Any street cop who works anywhere near Laconia, Sturgis or Daytona can tell you that when you've got a roadblock up to stop an outlaw bike run, you never have a black man or a Hispanic officer—or a female officer of *any* color—on the team. These guys are total sexists and racists and won't submit to an order from a woman, or a black man, or what they consider a 'spic.' There are Hispanic bike gangs, but they're all Hispanic. There are black bike gangs, but they're all black. There flat ain't no such thing as an integrated outlaw motorcycle gang, not on this continent and not anywhere else I know of."

Don McAllister took a long pause. "Any questions?"

"I have one," said Carmelita. "Let's say a Hispanic female is introduced to a gang like this as the girlfriend of a white guy who might be a wannabe or a member of another club. What problems do you see there?"

"Okay," said McAllister. "When I was undercover with the outlaw bikers, I never saw anybody bring in a black woman. Hispanic women? Once or twice. It's all going to depend on whether he's respected or not. Either way, she could probably expect to take some shit from the other biker women. If the guy's respected, she'll take a little shit and that'll be that. If he's not, she's history. It's that simple, Agent Morales."

Carmelita nodded. McAllister looked at Wolfe, who shook his head. No questions.

McAllister sat down. The man in the middle, the one wearing the blazer, stood up. "Bob Halloran, United States Marshal's Service," he said from under his bushy brown mustache. "Don was right. His outfit does more with the outlaw bikers than anyone. However, we seem to be the ones who get stuck keeping track of their activities and giving most of the lectures. Don't ask me why." He grinned, and McAllister grinned back.

"The Marshal's Service," Halloran continued, "is who gets custody of the bad guys who turn on the other bad guys. We're in charge of the Witness Relocation Program. We get the scumbags who rat out the other scumbags, and after they're locked in to courtroom testimony, we're in charge of keeping them alive.

"Everything you've heard from these other two guys about outlaw bikers is true. In spades, it's true. Rat out these guys, and you can expect them to come and murder you and your whole family in your beds, rape your women and kill your dogs and your cats.

"Anyway, we got one of the few CIs—Confidential Informants—that ever came out of the Princes of Hell. The *only* one, to my personal knowledge. The Princes got a fifty-K price on his head. You show them proof you cooled Johnny Bob Hopkins, they'll give you fifty grand, cash on the barrel head.

"I got Johnny Bob himself on tape, talking from one of our safehouses. I'll be showing you a few sequences that will shed some light on the functioning of the Princes." Halloran looked at the director, who held up his hand.

"Let's take a break," he said. "It will help things to sink in, and we can all use a cup of coffee. Harry and Carmelita, this can be a good opportunity for you to discuss your gut feelings. I don't want you to feel pressured."

He stood and walked toward the door. "See you all in twenty minutes."

8

When they were all back in the conference room, still nursing cups of coffee, Halloran took a VHS cassette from an attaché case in front of him and walked over to the bank of video machines. He inserted the cassette and pressed Play.

There was static, then for a moment, a blue field, upon which golden yellow letters suddenly appeared. "Our video people do good work," Halloran said appreciatively. The letters read Case 019046. U.S. Marshal's Service. Princes of Hell MC, Inc.

The camera cut to a nervous-looking man of average size. His hair was dark, coming over his forehead in a widow's peak, and had obviously been cropped to about two inches in length recently. The face was darkly tanned, and light tan lines showed near the hairline, where hair had obviously been longer before, shielding the face from the sun's rays. Similarly the lower part of the face and the area where a mustache would be were the same white color. He was obviously a long-haired, bearded man who'd recently undergone a close shave and a haircut.

The face no longer hidden by the beard showed a receding chin and an overbite, and nervous eyes that darted back and forth. The man wore a dirty white T-shirt. Filmed from the waist up, he showed no other clothing.

An off-camera voice, male with an African-American accent, asked, "Johnny Bob, tell us why you're running from the Princes of Hell."

"The pigs got some shit on me, an' I found out right quick Fat Phil wasn't gonna cover me."

"What did the cops have on you, Johnny?" the voice prompted.

"I was charged with having a roll in the hay... with my sister's girl."

"How old was she, Johnny? Your niece?"

The man on the screen dropped his eyes. "Sixteen, sumpin' like that."

"Come on," said the voice beyond the screen, taking on a hard edge for the first time. "How old was your niece, John?"

"Okay, okay," whined the man on camera. "She's like, in *actual* years, she's like ten or something, okay? But in *real* years, she's about nineteen going on fuckin' thirty, all right?"

He shrugged, then started to look angry. "When I called Fat Phil from the substation after the San Diego cops dragged me in, he starts yellin' and' screamin' and havin' a conniption fit, callin' me twenty-seven kinds of names like baby-rapist.... A case of the pot callin' the kettle black—then he starts really screamin' about how I was never a member of his club when I tole him that. Fat Phil an' the Princes was gonna sell *me* out, so I sold them out first."

The man on the screen was obviously becoming agitated.

Halloran, having introduced the CI, fast forwarded to another segment. "You'll find this quite relevant," he said as he again pressed Play. The picture went black, then came back on. Now Johnny Bob was wearing an orange Harley-Davidson T-shirt. It was obviously a second sitting before a video camera that the Marshal's Service had edited. There was also a different voice asking the questions. The accent sounded white Southern.

"Johnny Bob, tell us about your gut feeling so far as these boys in the Princes. Fat Phil, Rax and the others."

Johnny Bob, who seemed reinvigorated this time around, answered eagerly on-screen, "You mean, gut feelin's about busting 'em? Tell ya right now, Fat Phil's gonna go down shootin'. He ain't never outa reach of a gun. Rax? He's a fuckin' power-lifter, man. About six-three, he's gotta be two-fifty if he's an ounce. Ain't got muscles ripplin' all over him like Schwarzenegger, but he goes for raw strength. He looks fat, but Rax ain't got an ounce of fat on him, man. He'll rip ya apart as soon as look at ya."

The new off-camera voice said, "What's Rax's position in the club? And why do they call him Rax?"

Johnny Bob grinned nervously for the camera. "Rax is the sergeant-at-arms for the club. The enforcer. At least, till Klaus came along. But he's still plenty bad. They call him Rax 'cause when ya fuck with him or the prez, he racks ya up. Big-time."

The off-camera voice said softly, "Who's Klaus? And why do they call him that?"

Before he answered, Johnny Bob furtively looked around. He was in a safely guarded Marshal's Service training studio, surrounded by heavily armed guards, but still he looked over both shoulders before he leaned forward conspiratorially and answered, "Klaus is a bad, bad, bad fucker! Filthy Few and beyond, man! Don't swear, don't drink, don't even screw, at least not in front of nobody. Don't do ice or meth or take a toke or nothin'. They call him Klaus cause it's his name!

"But he's a stone killer, man! Way I understand it, Fat Phil hired him in off the Pagans to do a hit for him, an' Phil got him to stay on somehow. Tell ya the truth, I think Klaus is gonna be the next road captain or somethin'."

The off-camera voice said, "Road captain. Explain that, Johnny Bob."

The man on-screen answered nervously, "Shit, everybody knows what a road captain is. When you go on a run, the road captain's up front, leadin' the whole gang. The prez is to the side an' back, out of the line of fire. If the pigs stop the run and just gotta arrest the guy who looks like the leader, the road captain takes the fall an' the prez is still free in the middle of the gang to keep everything up and runnin'. It's stronger than vice-prez, really."

"Who," said the soft voice off camera, "is road captain now for the Princes of Hell?"

"That's Thumper. He's so big he could be Fat Phil's twin brother. I think they call him Thumper 'cause he likes to hit ya with shit—with one of them black police flashlights, a two-by-four, or whip on ya with a drive chain off a Harley 74."

The screen flickered again. The background was different this time—the dark blue curtains of a motel room—as Johnny Bob came back on-screen wearing a dark blue sweater. Except for the white marks where his beard and long hair used to be, he looked like a burned-out executive dressed for a casual weekend. However, the illusion disappeared as soon as he opened his mouth.

"Whaddya want?" Johnny Bob was asking on this new segment of video, leaning back casually in his chair against the indigo curtains. "Bitches are bitches. At least Princes know how to keep 'em in their place."

"Tell us about that, Johnny. Tell us about keeping them in their place."

The new off-screen voice was familiar to the Centac team. They'd heard it before any of this video had come up on-screen. It was the voice of Bob Halloran, the man from the Marshal's Service. They looked at him as the video played. Halloran looked back at them, shrugged and turned his head toward the screen just as Johnny Bob began talking again.

"Bitches? Shit, man, that's the neat thing about runnin' with guys like the Princes. You wanna piece of ass? You *got* a piece of ass. You want some head? Snap your fingers an' you got it, man!"

The face of Johnny Bob tightened into a glower. "Only thing I didn't like about bein' with the Princes, was that ol' lady of Phil's. That Doreen. Goddamn, what a superbitch. She's damn near six foot tall, gotta be two hundred pounds if she's a fuckin' ounce...good head on her, pretty woman an' all that, got this long dark hair an' big tits that stand up hard without a bra...but man, she's a *mean* fuckin' bitch."

Like a straight man Agent Halloran came on the tape with his disembodied voice and asked, "How mean is she, Johnny Bob?"

"I'm here to tell you, man," Johnny Bob answered on the screen. "She once got jumped by three assholes that was gonna rob her an' rape her, I guess. Now, all I know about this shit is two things. One, there's this news clipping on the wall of the club—I swear to God, I think it's out of the *L.A.*

Times—an' it says, 'Three men found dead on suburban street. Two shot to death, one with a gunshot wound and massive skull fractures. Record check shows all three have sexual assault records.' After her 5-shot revolver was emptied, she just kicked their heads in . . . you gotta remember, she's a big broad.

"The other thing I know is when we were all shit-faced at the clubhouse one time, Fat Phil was braggin' how Doreen done it, an' Doreen didn't wanna talk about it. An' Phil said, 'Show the gun you made me get for ya.'

"An' Doreen pulls out this nickel-plated Colt Detective Special .38 revolver. Phil says, 'Break open the cylinder, show 'em why you made me get you that,' an' she did, an' she's got these bullets in the cylinder. When you count 'em, it's got six bullets in it, not five like she had in that Smith & Wesson that time. In front of all of us, she says, 'Next time you send me out there with a gun with only five bullets in it, sweetheart, it's grounds for divorce.' Everybody laughed their ass off when she said that. I'll never forget that fuckin' gun. It had this long-stemmed rose engraved on the side of it, on the right side like sneaking around from behind the cylinder part an' goin' under it.

"Man, I don't never wanna fuck with that bitch. That Doreen is one cold cooze. She'd kill your ass as soon as squeeze it. You see, that's the kind of person Fat Phil has around him. If somebody like Doreen is his main squeeze, what do you figure his bodyguards are like?"

Bob Halloran moved forward and touched the Stop button on the videocassette player. Harry and Carmelita both noticed that he didn't hit Rewind, and realized instantly that there was something left to see.

Halloran stood up. "If you two are looking at infiltrating these clowns, you want to think about it a lot before you do it. The Princes are really layered. There's a bunch of wannabes that get to go on runs. There's ten or fifteen made members that work the submachine-gun factory Phil set up in the basement of a house in Long Beach. Another ten or twenty work the ice lab in the foothills of Capistrano. Then there's the real inside clique, Rax and Thumper and all the rest, and apparently now this guy Klaus. You'll have to have passed the initiation before you ever get in close to the guys you want for a Centac bust.

"Listen real careful, now. This is the part where he talks about the initiation ritual." Halloran reached down and touched the Play button.

It was still Halloran doing the off-camera questioning, and they heard him ask, "Johnny Bob, what's the story on the initiation ritual?"

The man on the screen curled his lip. "They're gonna come an' get ya when ya least expect it. Most gangs—clubs—it's six months or a year before ya get initiated. Phil says they are nuts to do it that way. Says that gives a narc or a punk who's gonna turn fink all that time to get shit on ya. He likes to grab ya for yer initiation as soon as the guys in the inner circle figure yer club material.

"Before they ever think about takin' ya out for initiation, you're gonna hafta do some dope with 'em. You're gonna hafta do some meth."

Off camera, Halloran asked, "Crystal?"

"Nah," said Johnny Bob, "ain't no bikers gonna stick needles in themselves. Fat Phil got that much from the Angels. Anybody uses a needle, they figure he's a junkie piece of shit. No, they do pills."

"Tell us," said Halloran's voice, "about the initiation itself."

"Phil says it's gotta be like 'Candid Camera.' You know. 'Suddenly when you least expect it.' Like that.

"Fat Phil's always along. So's the inner circle, or most of it. Rax, Thumper, Big Henry, them guys. They're gonna scoop ya when yer with somebody ya care about. Usually yer woman, maybe yer kid, yer family. Whatever.

"Anyway, next thing ya know, yer gonna be on top of some young stuff. Phil an' his guys are all witnesses. Like, they can testify against ya for statutory rape or something they can hold over ya. I dunno how Fat Phil figures he can ever testify when he set it up an' he's standin' right there the whole time. I just know that's the way he does it.

"How often," asked the marshal, "do they rape the person they're holding hostage while they're waiting for the guy they're initiating to be brought back?"

Johnny Bob shrugged. "I dunno. Half the time. They did my ol' lady, but I don't think it was rape. She was a slut anyway. I guess they figured she was just biker hospitality, ya know?"

That was the end of the film.

Halloran walked to the VCR and shut it off.

"Like I said, I don't know how the hell you're going to infiltrate, but I wish you two all the luck in the world. You're going to need it.

"Any questions?"

Wolfe and Morales both shook their heads. The director stood up. "Gentlemen," he said, "I'd like to thank all of you. I don't know about these two, but I've learned a lot this afternoon." As everyone stood, he added, "Don, will you still be in this afternoon?"

"Affirmative," said the shaggy BATF agent. "Headquarters, I'm on the third floor. Have the receptionist buzz me when you get off the elevator." He left with the others.

When the door had closed, the director said, "I've asked him to help you to pick out the hardware you'll need. Now that they're gone, do either of you have any questions?"

Carmelita spoke first. "How much time do we have for preparation?"

"I'm hoping a couple of weeks will do it," the director answered, "but there's no rush. I don't want you going into this half-assed. Two weeks is what's budgeted now, but if you think you need more time, call me."

Then Harry said, "Halloran made a good point about needing good luck. Is there any reason this couldn't be done as an outside cleanup, the way we did the first one? Or last year's?"

The director shook his head. "Last year's situation had to be a SAND. The two of them were running too fast to be pinned down, let alone infiltrated. They were highly publicized mad-dog killers, lone wolves, and the sentiment of the entire country was against them. Anyone who read the newspapers expected them to be killed in a shoot-out with law enforcement. It was only a matter of time.

"The first one, Harry, was done primarily outside the United States. Here we're talking about eight or ten American citizens, however unsavory they might be. It's going to have to appear to have happened from the inside."

Wolfe cocked a skeptical eyebrow. "I won't argue. I'm not sure about the two weeks, though. I've been working out of the office lately. It'd take me a year to grow hair and a beard that would fit in like Don's."

"That will be gotten around," the director answered confidently.

"One other thing," said Wolfe. "One obvious thing is that this is an outlaw motorcycle culture. I hate to tell you this, sir, but I haven't been on a motorcycle since I was in college. And that was a little Honda."

The director smiled. "I'm sure you'll pick it back up. Don will see to that. I've made arrangements with his supervisors to take him on special assignment to help groom the two of you, if you think it'll help."

"It'll help," said Wolfe, and Morales nodded.

"If you want it," the director said, "it's there. You will be fully prepared for this, in every way."

"Sir," said Wolfe, "have you given any thought to how we're supposed to infiltrate? Raping teeny-boppers isn't my style."

The director snorted. "I didn't think it was. It's going to take some doing to get you a quick acceptance. I do have one idea I'm going to work on this afternoon. Thanks for bringing it up. If it doesn't fly, I'll leave it up to you. Right now I think you two ought to grab some lunch. Then get on over to BATF and see how you like the goodies McAllister's going to have for you. I suspect you'll feel like James Bond seeing the armorer."

"Care to join us for lunch?" Wolfe spoke more softly than he had before.

The director shook his head and dropped wearily into his leather-upholstered chair. "The thought of food makes me puke. Don't say it—I know you warned me. Since the night

Brian shot himself, I've been going back again and again to that talk you and I had last year. A post-shooting-trauma program for the agents. When this is over, I'm going to sit down with you personally and work out the nuts and bolts, see what I'll need for a budget to implement it. In fact, I'm thinking seriously of putting you in charge of it."

The director shook his head wearily before he continued. "You know, Harry, when you first came to me with that proposal, I thought it was bullshit. Post-shooting trauma? Hell, I was in a shooting when I wasn't two years on the job. The son of a bitch killed my partner and shot me in the arm. The backup agents had to pull me off his body. My gun was empty and I was still pistol-whipping the prick. But feel bad about it? I wish he was still alive so I could shoot him again.

"I told you that then, and you asked how I felt about my partner being killed. I wanted to hit you for that. You said that was the sort of aftermath feeling you were talking about, not any guilt for shooting the scumbag who killed my partner. I was too angry to see what you were saying then. That's why your proposal has been in my file ever since.

"And since Brian shot himself... Harry, the things I'm feeling are like a playback of those training videotapes you gave me. The nightmares. The flashbacks. The feeling that everyone's looking at me different. And, at the moment, the appetite disruption."

The director shook his head sharply, as if to throw off something unpleasant. "Go on, you two. Have lunch, drop over to BATF and see Don McAllister, and call me in the morning."

The two agents looked at each other, shrugged and walked to the door. When it closed behind them, the director touched his intercom and told his chief secretary, "Get me the San Diego office."

9

It was nearly 3:00 p.m. that day when Harry Wolfe turned the G-car into the underground parking garage that served the Justice Department building in downtown Washington, D.C., which also housed the Bureau of Alcohol, Tobacco, and Firearms. U.S. Capitol Police, the uniformed guardians of the central government buildings, checked their ID cards and waved them through.

Harry found a slot, and he and Carmelita Morales slid out of the car. Neither had been to this building before. They weren't familiar with the security measures, particularly the ones for people who told the armed personnel at the central reception area that they were headed for the third floor.

Fifteen minutes later Don McAllister was waiting for them as they emerged from the elevator. He led them down a series of locked corridors. Several gates later they were inside one of BATF's many armories.

"You're going to need to look right with whatever you're carrying," McAllister was saying, "and if my feeling for what you're going to get involved in is right, you're damn well going to need to be *good* with whatever you're carrying. What are the two of you doing for weapons right now? And not just guns."

Harry turned toward Carmelita, with an unspoken gesture that said, You first.

She told the agent, "Agency-issue service pistol, Smith & Wesson 6904, 9 mm. I used to carry a *bali-song,* but lately I've been carrying a Spyderco Clipit that Harry gave me."

"No good," said McAllister. "Anything agency issue, they can trace. You know they've got access to police data banks. Look, I assume your cover is going to be as his girlfriend," McAllister said, nodding toward Harry. When Carmelita responded affirmatively, Don continued, "You'll be carrying his guns, and I think it'd be a good idea to have at least one for yourself. Something small, with some power, would be good, maybe a .380 automatic or a little .38 revolver. You have any preference?"

Carmelita shook her head. "Not really. I qualified with the revolver when I went through the academy. I can go with what you've got. If it makes a difference, I'd rather have fewer shots with plenty of power than a lot of shots with a small caliber."

McAllister nodded. "Okay. Now, I don't know what the director told you, but we only have a limited number of clean, untraceable guns here. You know how the system works to retrieve serial numbers. Guns are on file from when they're made to when they're stolen to when they're recovered and it's been that way since 1968.

"We recover a lot of stolen guns. Most of them go back to the owners, or to the insurance companies that paid for the losses if the thefts were insured. We do have a deal with one particular underwriter, giving us the use of certain recovered weapons for which they've reimbursed the owners. If the guns disappear, we just pay them the dollar value, and that's that. Still, given the fact that fewer than one out of a hundred stolen guns are recovered, that doesn't give us a whole lot to play with. If you want something small, with some power, I've got a mint-condition Smith & Wesson Bodyguard .38 Special snubnose. Built-in hammer shroud so there's nothing to snag when you pull it out of a pocket or a purse.

"Now, for the knives. The outlaw bikers are as much a knife culture as they are a motorcycle culture or a drug culture. They think *bali-songs* belong with Japanese motorcycles—they figure butterfly knives and rice-burners go together, you know? That would be out. The Spyderco? They see that as a police knife. It would burn you the second they saw it. I'll give you some steel that'll fit you right in. Trust me, okay?"

He turned to Wolfe. "What about you?"

Harry said, "Primary weapon is a Glock 17, 9 mm. Government issue. My backup is a Smith & Wesson .357 Magnum. A gunsmith in Georgia named Trevor Strachan chopped and channeled it down for me. It's the size of a Chief Special .38, two-inch barrel.''

McAllister whistled softly. "I've heard of those, but I've never seen one. Got it on?''

Harry leaned against the wall and drew his left foot up to his right thigh. He slid the gun from the Ken Null ankle holster, opened the cylinder and dumped half a dozen .357 Silvertip hollowpoints into his palm. He handed the gun and the rounds to McAllister. The agent took the gun and left the ammo in Harry's hand.

"Okay if I try the action?''

"Sure.''

The gun clicked a few times. "Ooh,'' sighed McAllister ecstatically. "Beautiful! Traceable to you, no doubt?''

Harry nodded yes. McAllister sighed and handed back the gun. "No good, then. I'm telling you, they'll find an excuse to examine your weapon and trace it. Remember, this is an armed culture we're talking about. You and Fat Phil ever do get together, you can bet your ass he'll ask to see your piece, and he'll be suspicious as hell if you don't let him look at it. He'll be handing you his at the same time. Like dogs sniffing other dogs, you know? Only thing is, he'll have a couple of his guys backing him up with their own guns. Now, even if you had an untraceable Glock, it would never fly with the outlaws.

"The Glock is made in Austria. It's got a polymer frame, so everybody calls it a plastic gun. Remember, the biker's gun is almost as much a reflection of his own ego as his motorcycle. He wants it big, he wants it steel and he wants it American made. They also know a lot of cops use Glocks. You wear one around those guys, it'd be like taking a motor scooter on a run to Sturgis. They'd kind of pick up that you weren't one of them, you know?''

"Understood,'' said Harry. "What do you recommend, then?''

"Colt .45 automatic is pretty much the standard gun with that crowd. You familiar with it?''

"Yes. The only difficulty I ever had with them was not always feeding hollowpoints."

"No problem," said McAllister. "These guys figure that anything but GI-type hardball, the round-nose full-metal-jacket bullet, is subversive anyway. You almost never see them with hollowpoints in their .45s. In any case, the gun I've got set aside for you is a nice Series 80 Colt Government Model, stainless steel. The feed ramp was throated out at the factory so it feeds hollowpoints. Totally reliable. Excellent condition, too. Came out of the same batch as the .38 I'll give your partner. Now, you carry a knife like she does? She said you gave her the one she uses now."

Wolfe nodded. "Spyderco Clipit, police model, with the plastic Endura handle and the serrated edge, three-and-three-quarter-inch blade."

"Same deal," said McAllister. "Great weapon, wrong place. These guys carry hideout blades with James Bond gimmick stuff, or they carry a good old Buck. Those, we've got plenty of. You guys like the Spyderco design, the quick one-hand opening, no problem. There's a company in Canada makes a bolt-on attachment called the One-Armed Bandit. It goes on a Buck folding hunting knife, makes it open about as fast as your Clipit. Heavier, not as fancy, but you'll blend right in and it'll get the job done."

"Belt carry or pocket?" Wolfe asked.

McAllister grinned. "Pocket or pocketbook for her, belt for you. They wear theirs on the right hip, where you carry your pistol, in a leather sheath. I've got one here, a special one that was made by Tom Bleeker, leathersmith out in California. Check it out."

He picked up what looked like an ordinary open-top sheath for a folding knife. The Buck in his other hand was well-worn but in good shape. The stoning marks on the edge told Harry it would be razor sharp without his having to touch it.

McAllister closed the blade halfway, then twisted the knife into the sheath. It looked like a closed knife in a leather scabbard. Harry could have sworn he'd seen a flash of steel from the side of the sheath.

"Et voilà," said McAllister. In an instant he grabbed the handle of the knife and pulled. There was another flicker of polished steel, and the extended blade was in his hand, locked open. "See how it works? The sheath actually holds the knife inside, just short of closed, with the edge resting on a rubber roller. As you pull on the handle, the knife will open. It's as fast as drawing a fixed-blade hunting knife from a sheath, but the difference is that it's legal to wear. That's why all these guys wear folding knives on the belt. They're legal, at least in some places. Real fighting knives aren't legal anywhere. Most places, even people with pistol permits can't carry a good double-edge fighting dagger."

He handed Wolfe the Buck knife in the trick Blocker sheath. "That one's yours. And these, Agent Morales, are for you." McAllister reached into a cardboard box. He withdrew an identical Buck knife, without a sheath but with a stud on the rear of the blade near the handle. He flicked it with the thumb of his right hand, and the blade was extended, gleaming wickedly. This knife, too, was well-worn and had recently been resharpened. Carmelita took it appreciatively.

The hand disappeared into the box once more. It came out with two worn brown belts, each featuring a tarnished rectangular brass buckle. "Size 34 for you, Wolfe, and a twenty-five-inch belt for you, Agent Morales. I hope I guessed right."

"Bingo."

"Right on."

"Practice with them," said McAllister. "The belts are the ones I showed you this morning. The Monk. Pull forward on the buckle, and the dagger comes out in your hand, and your pants don't fall down. Best belt-buckle knife on the market. Now, come on down the hall and I'll issue you that .38 revolver and the .45 automatic."

"What about holsters?" asked Wolfe.

McAllister made the sign of the cross with his index fingers. "You kidding? These guys all got felony records, man. They know a holster is presumptive evidence that they've been carrying a gun, and their parole gets revoked or they go down for felony in possession of a weapon. This little lady's going to have to carry it for you—which is why she wants to shoot it as much as you do to get used to it, 'cause she's probably going to be more able to get at it when the shit hits the fan than you are. When you carry it, just stuff it in your pants, Mexican style. That's the way all the bikers carry when they pack a concealed pistol.''

The BATF agent paused. "Uh, Agent Wolfe? If you can go on down the hall there, last door on the left, you can start getting the feel of that .45 stainless. It's right on my desk. I have a question for Agent Morales. I'll have her back with you in a second."

Wolfe's eyes met Morales's. No threat, the secret glances said. Without a word Wolfe turned and headed down the hall.

When they were alone, McAllister said, "Agent Morales, I don't want you to think I'm being forward, but I just wanted to say I couldn't keep my eyes off you this morning. I'm sorry. I noticed you don't have a ring on your left hand, and I was wondering if you might be free tonight...."

Even with her dark skin, Carmelita's blush was evident. She lowered her eyes demurely, then looked up at McAllister from under her long, dark lashes. Her teeth showed white in a gentle smile as she said softly, "I'm really flattered that you ask. You're a very attractive man. I guess you know that. But I never date law-enforcement agents. I'm sure you understand."

McAllister looked crestfallen. Carmelita reached over and took his wrist, squeezing it warmly and gently as she said, softly and urgently, "Why can't you quit BATF and be an insurance man or something? God, I'd love to go out with you! But you understand why I can't."

As they walked toward his office together, McAllister was thinking, You've still got it, man! If she ever quits this job, she's yours!

And Carmelita Morales was thinking, Mother was right. Always let them think you would if you could. Let them down gently. Their egos are so fragile!

10

United States Deputy Marshal Rick Garland stood at the window of the town house in Denver when he heard the phone ring. The inside of the glass reflected the face of a handsome black man about thirty-five, wearing white shirt and tie, and no jacket to conceal the black SIG-Sauer 9 mm automatic holstered at his right hip.

"I'll get it," said a voice behind him. It was his partner, Deputy Marshal Vern Quigley, a lanky young redhead who still had freckles on his face. Garland turned and watched Quigley press the button of the inexpensive tape recorder that was hooked on to the phone, then pick up the receiver and say, "Yes?"

There was a pause, and Garland saw the partner snap the recorder back off as he said, "Sure, Bob, he's right here. Hang on."

The redheaded agent turned and yelled, "Yo, Johnny Bob! Halloran for you."

Marshal Garland turned the opposite way to watch Johnny Bob Hopkins rise from the couch he'd been sprawled on, peel off his Sony Walkman and saunter to the phone. Since it was another marshal calling, they didn't bother to monitor the conversation.

As the former outlaw biker took the phone, the lanky man walked toward his partner at the window. "Bob Halloran," he said softly and unnecessarily.

Garland grimaced. "Those two are soul brothers. I don't know which'd be worse, baby-sitting this damn baby-raper or baby-sitting Halloran."

Quigley smiled. "I know what you mean. Halloran's sort of like a stereotype on a cop show. But even if he's an asshole, he's our asshole. At least he's honest. And he'd kick the crap out of Johnny Bob as soon as we would, if he had an excuse."

On the phone the informant was saying, in a soft, conspiratorial tone, "Fat Phil don't spend that much time at the biker bars, Bob. He likes to kick back where he feels safe. The clubhouse, mostly. Its lower-level members hang out at the bars. Fat Phil only goes in there about every Saturday night, kinda like a Mafia don showin' up to let guys pay tribute an' ask for favors an' shit.

"Where? Depends where he is. Up in L.A. there's the Red Wing. Fat Phil kinda made it the unofficial club bar 'cause it's the nearest one to the clubhouse up in the Canyon. That way, he gets into a bar fight, he's got a fast, straight shot back to the club to ditch his guns an' cover his ass before the cops even think to look for him. It's right off the exit you take for the Comfort Inn. Go by the hotel and it's second right.

"Same deal in San Diego. Good hour outa the city, when you get up to the edge of San Juan Capistrano, there's a joint called the All Done Inn. It's a regular hangout for bike clubs, not just the Princes. He's only there when he's checkin' on things in San Diego, the meth lab, ya know?"

"Yeah, sure. Anytime, Bob. Me? Doin' fine, just jumpy as hell is all." Johnny Bob dropped his voice to a small whisper. "I still think it sucked puttin' a nigger marshal in on me like that. You oughta see the way the fucker looks at me...yeah, well, that's cool. Stay in touch, huh, bro?" He hung up the phone as if he hated to let go of it.

Turning, he saw the two U.S. marshals staring at him.

"Bobby just needed some info," Johnny Bob said importantly.

Garland sneered at him. "We didn't ask what he wanted."

"We don't give a damn what he wanted," Quigley added.

Johnny Bob's eyes narrowed. "You don't give a fuck about me, do you?" It was the voice of a petulant child.

"We're not here to care about you," the red-haired marshal answered. "We're here to keep you from getting your ass shot off. If you wanted us to care about you personally, you wouldn't go whispering 'nigger this' and 'nigger that'."

Johnny Bob sneered.

"That's yer fuckin' attitude, I fuckin' told ya, just gimme my own guns an' some credit cards. I'll find my own place, so's you won't be stuck with me an' I won't be stuck with you. Call me to testify, I'll be there."

It was the black marshal's turn to curl his lip derisively. "That all you want, Johnny Bob? Gun and a credit card and a little girl's school to bide your time in, maybe? Our job is to keep your ass intact, like Vern said. It isn't to have you insulting our intelligence. Nobody's going to be happier when they've got a case against your club and you're done testifying and you're off someplace we won't have to see your face, with some name we're never going to hear. Until then, we're stuck with each other. Only difference is, they won't let us wear Walkmans to drown your bullshit out."

Johnny Bob's eyes narrowed. "I don't have to take this shit. I don't have to eat any more microwave junk, either. It's half-past noon. Let's go eat a real lunch someplace. You guys got the credit card. I wasn't here, you'd fuckin' have to feed yourselves. We all go out to lunch, man, it's like I'd be takin' you out. Let Uncle Sugar pay for it all!"

The black marshal grunted. "Take a black dude to lunch, right? God, Johnny Bob, the next thing I hear, you will be turning yourself in to the NAACP."

"Actually," said Quigley softly, trying not to let things turn into a shouting match, "getting out of here for lunch doesn't sound like a half-bad idea. Putting three of us who can't cook in the same safehouse was not the smartest idea Washington ever came up with."

11

Richard "Rax" Higgins, twenty-eight, sat behind the wheel of the rented blue Pontiac sedan parked a block down the street from the Denver town house where the two U.S. marshals were keeping tabs on his former biker brother. His fingers drummed on the dashboard. He was not comfortable in clean jeans, an oversize polo shirt and a blue nylon shell jacket. Six foot three and two hundred fifty pounds of power-lifting muscle, he looked like a professional wrestler. The dark beard that came to the top edge of his pectoral muscles only enhanced the image. His long hair had been braided, and the braid wound up under his blue baseball cap. The logo on the cap read, innocuously, Coors.

In the passenger seat next to him was an even larger man. Klaus Richter was precisely six feet, five inches tall. The width of his shoulders filled his half of the front seat, actually pressing against the passenger window. He weighed two hundred and seventy pounds, all of it sculptured muscle. Hatless, his medium-length blond hair was now combed straight back from his forehead.

He, too, wore clean, but stone-washed, blue jeans and a yellow T-shirt with the logo Gold's Gym. His nylon shell jacket was like Rax's, but dark green.

Beneath it, tucked into his waistband and invisible, was a blue-steel Smith & Wesson .44 Magnum revolver with a four-inch barrel. He carried it behind his right hip, butt forward. That way he could place his fists behind his hips with the elbows out, and anyone looking from the front would see only a big guy taking an intimidating stance, not a man whose hand was already on his gun in a drawing position.

Behind the wheel Rax was twitching. He liked guns, but he wasn't used to carrying one. Either Cindy, his old lady, or whatever sheep he was with usually carried his .45 in her handbag. Now the Colt Lightweight Commander was inside the jeans just back of his right hip, butt pointed to the rear for a straight, right-hand draw. With no holster to keep it in place, it shifted of its own weight. It dug into his side.

"Pain in the ass," he grunted. "This what the fuckin' pigs go through, when they're doin' surveillance on us?"

"Probably," said Richter.

"They oughta pay 'em more, then," groused Rax as he reached down and moved the pistol to a more comfortable position.

Klaus looked at him coldly. "Really? What *do* they pay them?"

"How the hell should I know? You know what I meant!"

Klaus Richter looked at Rax and smiled condescendingly. "No," he said coldly and flatly, "I don't know what you meant. I do know that your group was infiltrated and that you told Phil that you knew the guy was no good, and Phil says he doesn't remember you saying that before. You were there during the initiation. You really should have said something."

The bearded man twisted in his seat to glower at the huge man who had just spoken. "*You* was fuckin' there, Klaus! And you didn't say nothin', and you didn't do nothin'!"

Klaus Richter smiled coldly. "I didn't have the knowledge you said you had. I didn't *fuckin'* say anything or *fuckin'* do anything because it was not my concern. It was yours." Richter's emphasis on the four-letter words was contemptuously sarcastic.

Rax stared at him, his face darkening. "Think yer mister big shit, don't ya? Always talk perfect, don't swear, don't drink, don't even drop a pill. Think bein' Filthy Few means yer shit don't stink?

"Fuck you, Klaus! I ain't scared of you!"

Klaus chuckled. "Sure you are, Rax. You're scared of me. The only question is, are you as scared of Phil? Or maybe even more scared of Phil?"

"You mean the other night? Forget it, man, he just tapped me. We're brothers, man, we do that stuff to each other all the time. Don't mean nobody's scared of nobody!''

"Really," said Klaus coolly. "When was the last time you smacked Phil in the balls?"

Rax was fighting to maintain control. "Phil is the prez, man, and I'm the sergeant-at-arms! My job is to make sure nobody lays a fuckin' hand on the prez! You think I'm gonna smack 'im myself?"

The big blond man chuckled. "Oh, excuse me," he said. "You were just telling me it was something you did to each other. I assumed it went both ways."

The driver's eyes narrowed. "Pushin' me, ain't ya, Klaus? You don't know why I don't hit the prez of my own club? Man, you supposed to be a bro an' you don't *know* that? I suppose Pagans, where you're supposed to come from, lets guys slap their prez around? You come in here, lookin' like the athletic director from the Yuppie Club or somethin', an' everybody takes you at face value. Big shit, 'cause you been to Berea!"

"My friend," said Klaus cryptically, "I teach at Berea. And I can tell you right now, you wouldn't qualify for the recruit class."

Rax was seething with hate. "Think yer hot shit, Filthy Few? Well, remember somethin', man! After today, we're both Filthy Few! Unnerstand?"

Klaus Richter's smile was mocking. "It takes more than killing a man to make Filthy Few, Rax. It takes more than killing for money. Otherwise, every wino who killed another wino would be Filthy Few. But don't sign the loan until you've got the collateral, my friend. So far, all you've done about it is talk. And saying 'fuck' doesn't make you a member of Filthy Few. Nor," he said contemptuously, "does killing some stupid little girl in a desert."

Rax was about to blurt an answer when Klaus snapped, "Look!"

Rax turned. Three men were leaving the town house, walking toward a powder blue Chevy sedan parked across the street. They were all wearing jackets and ties. Rax recognized Johnny Bob instantly, even without the beard. On his left was a gangly white guy with red hair; Rax figured him to come apart instantly with one punch. On the right was a black guy, built a little stronger. Rax figured him for two or three punches.

"Drive," Richter ordered. Rax turned the ignition and snapped the Pontiac into gear, easing it forward. They came to the cross street just as the Chevy sedan pulled away from the curb. Rax smoothly came away from the stop sign in a right turn and drove straight at a steady pace. The car with the protected informant was now eight or ten carlengths behind.

"Give them a few blocks, then take a right. Real casual. Don't look in the rearview mirror. They'll see the reflection, and the eye contact will put them on alert," Klaus said.

"I fuckin' know what I'm doin'," Rax growled back. "Listen, mister Filthy Few, it was *our* guy, Squirrel, found out where this rat fink was, remember? Pagans an' Filthy Few didn't have nobody inside the phone company could bug his ol' lady's phone, get a number trace when he called, did they? But the Princes did, an' we got him now, an' we can do him all by ourselves!"

"You should have told Fat Phil that," said Klaus. "If he thought you were competent to do this yourselves, he wouldn't be paying me to go along to supervise."

"Supervise," sputtered Rax. "Man, he sent you so I could watch you an' see if you really had the balls to off some dude in cold fuckin' blood!"

Klaus chuckled again, softly. "We'll know soon who's doing what, won't we? And whether Princes of Hell are strong enough and smart enough to be represented at Berea. For now, it's time for you to take the next right. Let the cops and the fink keep going. We'll go down a few blocks, then double back. When they get back to their little safehouse, we'll have a nice little welcoming committee waiting for them."

12

When Klaus used the copper pennies to short out the alarm system in the town house just before they broke in, Rax couldn't keep himself from blurting, "How'd you do that?"

Klaus answered, "If you ever make it to Berea, you'll find out." Rax cursed himself for asking.

It had been a blessing when Klaus said, "I'm going to wait around the corner of the kitchen alcove in case they come in the back door. You get on the other side of that stereo entertainment center by the front door. Whichever way they come in, they'll have to go by one of us." That meant that they wouldn't have to talk to each other.

For the hour and a half they waited, the silence was golden. Rax knew he couldn't have taken any more from Klaus. But when they came back, Rax knew he'd show them who was who. Drop the marshals, but leave them alive, Fat Phil had said, and Rax would perform it to perfection. He'd even stomach Klaus on the plane ride back, even if he had to get a seat on a different part of the plane. He'd even take a different plane if he felt like it. They'd be ditching the stolen guns after this job anyway, so he didn't have to worry anymore about being responsible for that suitcase with the undeclared pistols.

Waiting off the kitchen, Klaus Richter cracked his knuckles and smiled.

This thing with the Princes of Hell was having its ups and downs, but all things considered, more of the former than the latter. It had been more than a year since Fat Phil Newell had petitioned the Pagans to affiliate his chicken-shit little motorcycle club with their organization. Pagans made some inquiries, and the word came back that Fat Phil was known for preferring very young stuff.

That would normally have resulted in an automatic rejection. But the Pagans were fully aware from their Intelligence sources that Fat Phil Newell had put his brains to work, had rounded up some misfits like himself and was making money hand over fist with his meth lab and his submachine gun factory.

They also understood Phil's motivation. Acceptance and approval was what the fat man needed. He wanted his top lieutenants to go to the outlaw biker encampment in Berea, Kentucky. Staffed by ex–Special Forces men and ex-cops who'd gone to the side of the outlaw bikers, it was considered as deadly a fighting school as anything outside the KGB. Having men who were graduates was the ultimate mark of honor for a prez of an outlaw bike club. It was comparable to a police chief whose captains had graduated from the FBI Academy.

The Pagans wanted to take over the Princes of Hell. But they wanted to do it quietly and smoothly, without a shooting war that would bring the police down on them from California to Philadelphia, and possibly even affect Berea, Kentucky, where the training camp open to the made members of the Big Four gangs was ensconced. Berea was sacrosanct to the outlaws. It was their Switzerland, their neutral zone in a constantly shifting field of battle. However the Pagans, Outlaws, Bandidos and Hell's Angels felt about one another at any given time, Berea was off-limits. It was holy ground to the true outlaws.

And Klaus Richter was a senior instructor in the cadre of the outlaw biker academy in Berea. Now thirty, he'd been an outlaw biker since joining a now-disbanded club affiliated with the Pagans when he was an eighteen-year-old black belt in *goju shorei* karate. Diagnosed as a psychopath by the school psychologists, kicked out of his house for beating his brother almost to death in an argument over who would watch TV that night, Klaus had been an atom in search of a molecule to join. He'd found it with the outlaws. His imposing size, his fighting skill and, later, the body he'd sculpted with the countless long hours in the gym had all combined to make him someone to be feared.

The one thing he'd missed about school was learning. He had continued his reading and, self-taught, considered himself a master of arts or equivalent. He didn't drink or smoke. He'd done drugs only when he'd had to during club rituals like initiations. On a run he'd open a beer and sip at it for a couple of hours, and finally stopped even that charade once he had been accepted.

Klaus Richter had killed his first man at the age of twenty-four, and within a year he was an inducted member of the Filthy Few. Since then, it had been uphill all the way.

Because he often had to travel by plane to get to his deadly assignations, the heavy hitters in the outlaw biker culture gave him special permission to dress his own way. Polo shirts, suits, clean shaven, haircut like a movie actor. Each of the heavy clubs had its own cadre of members who looked like straights, the better to work in the outside world to be their emissaries when necessary. To Klaus, looking the way he did was the mark of the executive. The shaggy-haired, long-bearded bike rider who looked as if he had stepped off the cover of *Easyriders* magazine was to be sneered down upon, like someone showing up at a board meeting wearing a leisure suit.

Now he was going to kill Johnny Bob Hopkins, the fink who had ratted out the Princes of Hell and was now under guard in this safehouse. Safehouse? Klaus laughed to himself. They hadn't even left an armed man inside the place when the two marshals had taken their charge out for lunch!

A search had shown them that there was only one heavy weapon in the whole place. It was a witness-protection gun, a sawed-off shotgun expressly made for this particular function by the Marshal's Service. The Remington pump shotgun had been sawed off at each end, leaving just a sloping pistol grip for the gun hand, and the pump handle at the front for the other. The muzzle of the gun terminated just ahead of the pump handle. The barrel was only a bit over thirteen inches long. The gun held four 12-gauge shotgun shells in the magazine and a fifth in the firing chamber. Klaus had examined the weapon. The shells were red plastic with high, brass bases—Winchester double-ought buckshot.

He figured two such guns with two agents involved. One of them must be carrying the other in addition to his pistol. None, Klaus believed, was wearing body armor: the closet had displayed three identical Second Chance bulletproof vests, hung neatly on heavy-duty hangers.

The vests still hung there. The agents, Klaus knew, hadn't worn them because they were complacent. Well, he didn't need them, either. He had the upper hand. No one was going to shoot him.

Besides, he thought, flexing the muscles of his massive body, the vests were too small to fit him anyway.

There was the sound of a car pulling up out front, a motor shutting off. Klaus heard Rax whisper excitedly, "They're here! They're comin' up the front walk!"

"Be ready," Klaus said coldly. The big blond man moved quickly, silently, through the rooms until he was diagonally opposite the front door of the town house, behind the wall that opened onto the dining room. The .44 was still in tight behind his hip. The marshals' own shotgun was steady in his hand.

There was the sound of a key in the lock, and the door swung open. Vern Quigley entered first, his hand under his coat and tight on the butt of his holstered Smith & Wesson 9 mm automatic. He moved to the right, toward where Rax was hiding.

Behind him through the door came Johnny Bob Hopkins, shoulder to shoulder with the black marshal, Rick Garland. The marshal had one hand under his coat. He glanced left and right and didn't see Klaus in the shadows behind the wall. He moved straight ahead toward the kitchen, his back toward Klaus.

Rax was the first to move. As the gangly redhead came almost abreast of him, the biker swung his .45 automatic down hard on the marshal's wrist.

"Aah!" Quigley cried out as the hard metal of the blue automatic crushed his radial nerve against the bone behind his wrist. Quigley's fingers went numb. The pistol fell from his hand. He was turning toward the threat when Rax swung his meaty left fist with all his weight behind it. The blow broke Quigley's lower jaw out of its socket and spun him halfway around. Rax swung his fist back, hammering it into the nape of the marshal's neck, and Quigley grunted as he dropped to his knees. Rax put every ounce of strength into the third punch. It smashed into the base of Quigley's skull, and the marshal slumped to the floor, unconscious.

Gettin' old, thought Rax. Figured this one for only one punch. An' that fuckin' Klaus had to see it.

Where *was* Klaus? Rax pivoted, and frowned when he saw that the situation was in hand.

When Rax had moved, the thud of his Colt Commander on Marshal Quigley's wrist had made Marshal Garland turn reflexively, his hand coming out from under his coat with the sawed-off Remington shotgun. It was then that Klaus had uttered two short, sharp syllables.

"Uh-uh!"

Garland froze. He looked up and saw the blond giant leveling the gaping maw of the Remington shotgun at him, and recognized it instantly as Quigley's weapon, the one they'd left behind in the town house. He could see the finger tight on the trigger. If he went for the rest of the movement to bring his own witness-protection gun to bear, he knew he'd be killed before he completed the swing.

"Shit," muttered Garland.

"Let go of it," Klaus whispered, his voice taut with excitement. Garland sighed and let go of the shotgun. It swung back under his jacket, hanging from a harness on his left shoulder.

Two feet away Johnny Bob Hopkins was frozen in fear. "Oh, Jesus," he moaned, his voice trembling. "Oh, God."

"Shut up," snapped Klaus. "You sound like an idiot child with a filthy mouth."

"Klaus, man," Johnny Bob said in the quavering voice, "Jesus, man, don't do it!"

"Why not?" sneered Klaus. "Will these big bad Feds hurt me if I kill you?"

Rax came into the room. "Rax," bleated Johnny Bob. "Rax, man, be cool, okay?"

"I'm cool, you fink," Rax growled. "You're gonna be cool, too, in a fuckin' minute!"

Johnny Bob's face crumpled. As he began sobbing, a dark stain emerged on the crotch of his pants, spreading downward. "Oh, Jesus, oh, Jesus..."

"You want your Jesus?" Klaus's voice was hard and mocking. "I didn't know you loved Jesus. You probably didn't call Him until now. But I'll tell you what. You can tell Him yourself.

"Now!"

Inside the small town house, the blast of the short-barrel 12-gauge was as deafening as a grenade.

Flame bloomed from the muzzle of the shotgun, and eight feet away a red hole the diameter of a man's circled thumb and forefinger appeared in the chest of Johnny Bob Hopkins. He had been cringing back away from the gun muzzle when the shot went off, and his body jerked backward four feet, the soles of his shoes coming up off the carpet. He landed heavily on the soft pile. Blood gouted thickly from his chest, pouring onto the carpet beneath him.

As Klaus pumped the action of the shotgun, he yelled at Garland, "Don't move!" The black marshal stood frozen. He knew that his one chance now was to stay cool. In the Marshal's Service Academy, they'd said that the guards would be shot down in the opening moment of the killing of the witness if the guards were in fact expendable. If that wasn't the case, his instructors had said—if the killers didn't want to bring down the predictable extra heat of shooting down a federal lawman—a marshal caught with his pants down would probably be disarmed but left alive.

Marshal Garland froze, staring into the black hole of death that the huge blond man was aiming at him. He heard the man behind the shotgun say, "Finish the rat fink."

A man almost as big as this one, but darker and bearded, stepped forward. There was a blue automatic in his hand. Garland recognized it as a short-barrel Colt Commander, probably a .45 caliber. He couldn't help but wince as the burly bearded man put the muzzle to Johnny Bob's head and pulled the trigger.

The .45 wasn't as loud as the shotgun, but it was still explosive. The body on the floor convulsed once and was still. Brain matter and blood oozed from the crater in the center of Johnny Bob's forehead, and Garland knew beyond doubt now that he had failed.

"Get his cuffs and cuff him," Rax told Klaus hoarsely.

"Don't tell me what to do," Klaus said abstractedly. "Did I ever tell you what the difference was between me and the cops?"

Rax blinked at him. "What?"

"The difference is, only cops handcuff the people they kill."

Rick Garland knew what was going to happen. The shotgun was hanging under his left arm, too far away for a quick draw. Instead, he felt his hand going for the 9 mm pistol on his hip.

He didn't make it.

Just as his hand closed on the sharply checkered plastic grip, Rick Garland saw the orange flame blossom from the muzzle of the gun in front of him, and it was as if a giant hand had clutched his chest from the inside and jerked him backward. There was no pain, but he couldn't breathe and he seemed to be floating in space. He tried to pull the SIG from its holster, but his arm seemed to have lost all its strength. And then, almost in slow motion, he saw the blond man pump the action of the shotgun again, back and forward, and another fireball erupted at the muzzle. Everything went black.

Klaus Richter reflexively pumped the shotgun again as the black man's body thudded to the floor a couple of feet away from the corpse of Johnny Bob Hopkins. The first blast had caught the marshal squarely in the center of the chest, the second, dead in the face. All nine of the .33-caliber buckshot pellets had struck en masse, and it was as if the facial features had been pulled inside the black hole where the shotgun charge had entered the head before pulping the

brain. It looked as if a rubber mask had been crushed together, leaving no real face at all.

"You weren't supposed to kill the cop," screamed Rax.
"Fat Phil told us not to kill the cops!"

Klaus looked at him and smiled. "Then we'll let the other
one live. He's still out, isn't he?" They both looked. The
red-haired marshal was still sprawled unconscious in the
next room.

Klaus turned slowly and looked Rax in the eye. There was
a long moment and then, even though Rax still held a
loaded, cocked .45 in his hand, Klaus could see that he was
in charge.

"What it is," Klaus explained softly, "is that we came to
kill the fink, and we did. We split fifty grand for that.

"But," said Klaus, a smile beginning to spread on his
handsome face, "I do niggers for free."

13

They came off the highway on the panhead Harley-Davidson chopper, sweeping past the Spanish hacienda-styled Comfort Inn, banging a right at the next corner into Sylmar. In a few minutes they were there.

Red neon lights, shaped like Air Force wings, glowed over the roadhouse. Redundantly the neon below said in cursive script, Red Wing. As Wolfe shut off the Harley, he reflected idly on what red wings meant to outlaw bikers. A symbol of having performed oral sex on a menstruating woman. He wondered how many of the thousands of motorists who drove by each day had any idea what the bar was named after.

As soon as Wolfe killed the engine, he felt Carmelita Morales slip off the pillion seat behind him. Her presence was comforting. Not just because she was hard and trained and proven...not just because she had two guns in her purse, and he was carrying none...he just felt comfort from her sheer presence, he realized.

He felt cold, naked. His newly shaven head was only part of it. Even in the summer, it was cooler in the Canyon than it was below, in the city of Los Angeles. And riding a motorcycle was like establishing a wind-chill factor. He missed his Second Chance Deep Cover bulletproof vest. The thing was a great windbreaker. It would fit his cover, if he needed it, except for two things. The Second Chance brand was only sold to cops, and outlaw bikers only wore them on heavy-duty runs. In either case, it would have been a giveaway.

That was why Wolfe wore only a black T-shirt with the inscription, Friends Don't Let Friends Ride Rice-Burners. Like his jeans, the shirt was permanently darkened with the grease from working on his bike with Don McAllister. He wiggled his toes inside his Nasty Feet, long, heavy engineer boots that he'd only become accustomed to wearing in the past few days.

He turned toward Carmelita. Her black hair was long, loose and free. Her breasts were free, too, under a black Harley-Davidson T-shirt over which a long-stemmed red rose had been embroidered. The cold wind she must have felt on the back of the bike had done its work: her nipples were starkly erect beneath the cotton fabric. Or maybe it was the excitement.

"Tell you what," he said. "Let's do something we haven't had a chance to do for a while, and follow the plan. You go on in, right into the ladies' room, and I'll fuck with this bike for a minute and go in myself. We'll catch up inside. If it looks like we should get together, we will."

Carmelita smiled, winked and sauntered toward the door. Wolfe's eyes scanned the parking lot. No outside bodyguards—Fat Phil must feel pretty damn safe here. But, hell, not seeing bodyguards didn't mean anything. Wolfe didn't see DEA agents, either, and they were the ones who had sent him the message that Fat Phil and some of his inner circle were here. That confirmed what Johnny Bob had said to Halloran. When they got the word that their informant and one marshal were dead, with the other still in a coma, the director had decided to accelerate the operation.

Harry Wolfe felt strangely calm as he walked up to the door of the Red Wing. His T-shirt was untucked and hanging over his belt. He reached back one more time to check that the Buck knife was in its Block speed sheath, and then he walked inside.

A Johnny Paycheck song was playing softly in the background. The interior stank of cigarette smoke, but Wolfe could detect no aroma of marijuana. That was no surprise. One For All, All For One was the biker's code: you take care of us, we take care of you. Pot smoking on premises would give the liquor license authorities grounds to shut down the bar. It was understood that inside the Red Wing, beer was the abusable substance of choice, and Jack Daniel's was the maximum substance allowed.

Wolfe looked around. The place was a square box. On the back wall was the bar, flanked on either side by the ladies' and men's rooms. There were no booths. Round tables with chairs were scattered throughout the rest of the place, and it was full.

It was an outlaw night. Wolfe had walked in wondering how many of the denizens would be outlaws. He realized to his horror that almost all of them fit the profile. The place looked like *Easyriders* magazine come to life.

In the far right corner, near the sign that said Fire Exit, sat the man he recognized as Fat Phil.

The man's pictures hadn't done him justice. He was, Harry could see, grotesquely obese. His gut spilled over on his lap halfway to his knees. Harry understood now why Phil carried his gun in his side pants pocket. He couldn't possibly reach anything near his waist.

At Fat Phil's right sat a big man with yellow hair and yellow beard, both long and unkempt. On his left was a tall woman with long brown hair.

Jesus, Harry thought, she's beautiful.

The woman's hair was long and brown and clean. It hung straight past her shoulders and down her back. She was about Harry's height, perhaps a little taller, perhaps a little shorter. She looked smaller surrounded by huge men. Her breasts were full and heavy and firm, protruding against a light blue shell blouse. She wore no makeup. She needed none.

Doreen, Wolfe thought, remembering the briefing. They didn't fully describe her.

Wolfe walked casually to the bar. The bartender glanced at him as if to say, What are *you* doing here? When their eyes met, Wolfe just smiled and pointed at the draught tap labeled Budweiser.

The barkeep filled a schooner for him with a look of contempt on his face. He slapped it down on the bar in front of Harry, staring him in the eye. "Two bucks."

Harry asked, with an intentionally innocent voice, "Can I run a tab?"

"No," the barkeep growled through his grizzly gray beard, "but you can pay for yer fuckin' beer."

Wolfe reached into his hip pocket, took out a roll of bills and carefully peeled off three singles. "Brew, and a buck for a tip," he said.

The man behind the bar reached over and carefully separated two of the three dollar bills, letting the third fall onto the bar. "Keep yer tip," he snarled. "I own the place. Doncha know it's a fuckin' insult to tip the guy that owns the joint?"

Wolfe left the crumpled dollar on the bar. "Hey, no, I didn't know that. Sorry, bro."

The bartender took the two dollar bills in his hand and walked away, muttering.

The door slammed open behind him, and Wolfe stopped himself from turning around, instead glancing into the mirror over the bar. The image he saw there told him instantly who had just entered. Thumper. There couldn't be two heavy, bearded bikers with buckteeth. Wolfe watched as Thumper swaggered to the table where Fat Phil, Doreen and the yellow-haired man sat waiting.

"Yo, prez! First lady! Henry! How's it goin'?"

Harry sipped his beer as Thumper sat down with the Princes.

The bar mirror showed two or three men for every woman. Most of the men were long-haired and bearded, but three or four had shaven heads or closely crew-cut hair. Several wore earrings. The typical dress, almost a uniform, was the bike logo on the T-shirt and torn, greasy jeans. Knife pouches were as standard as holsters in a police squad room, and worn in the same place on the strong-side hip.

In the bar mirror he could see eyes on him. The regulars were assessing the new guy. No one appeared to be wearing colors.

It was a little past midnight, Saturday night blending into Sunday morning. Harry had timed his late arrival deliberately. He knew that the night would not pass without his being in a bar fight with at least some of these people. He knew some people hated to fight drunks because of the blows they could absorb and keep coming; it wasn't called "feeling no pain" for nothing.

But Harry's study had taught him outlaw bikers would take punishment and keep coming anyway. Most of them would rather die than show fear or cowardice. Besides, once they got back to the clubhouse, there were enough drugs and booze to erase any pain.

No, Harry had decided, it would be best to let them get as drunk as his good fortune allowed. Slow their reflexes, mute their awareness, reduce their balance. He knew that sudden turning movements in particular would destabilize someone who'd had too much alcohol. That was something he could use to his advantage in a fight, more than any perception of how many blows a man could take.

Carmelita was still in the ladies' room. He saw Doreen get up and saunter in, too. Without seeming to, he kept his focus in that direction. He didn't want anything to happen out here without a backup. Carmelita had the guns. If anything went down in the women's rest room, he'd have to be alert to help her. He knew she could take care of herself against any woman alive. He also knew that if they thought the prez's lady was in trouble, the male bikers in the bar would tear the rest-room door off its hinges to come to her aid.

He sipped his beer and bided his time.

HER BAG over her shoulder, Doreen Newell strode into the ladies' room. The Latino woman at the sink, with a shoulder bag over her black T-shirt, was brushing her long dark hair. Their eyes met in the mirror. Doreen smiled. The woman in the mirror smiled back.

Doreen joined her, setting her own bag down. She reached in carefully so neither her revolver nor Phil's would be visible, and extracted her own small hairbrush.

Doreen asked casually, "First time here? I haven't seen you before."

"Yeah," answered Carmelita. "We were just drivin' by, ya know, saw the bikes, looked like our kind of place."

"Who you with?"

"My guy's out at the bar."

"I didn't see him. What's he look like?"

"Harley T-shirt," said Carmelita.

"Honey, that's everybody in here!" They both burst out laughing.

"I'm sorry," said Carmelita. "About the middle of the bar? T-shirt says Harley on the back, and Friends Don't Let Friends Ride Rice-Burners on the front?"

"Okay, I saw him," said Doreen. "Skinhead? He's cute." Carmelita shrugged.

"I'm Doreen Newell," the taller woman said, extending her hand.

Carmelita reciprocated. "Elita Suarez."

"Nice to meet you. It took guts for you to come in here."

"Why's that?"

"Well, in case you didn't notice, this place is whiter than white. Nothing personal. Just watch yourself. Some of these guys think any woman who's not as Anglo as the queen of England is a target of opportunity, if you catch my drift."

Carmelita analyzed the big woman carefully. There was no threat in her voice or her look. She was giving her a sincere warning.

"Hey, thanks. I appreciate your telling me. But I can take care of myself."

Doreen looked at her skeptically. "I hope your guy can, too." The voice was still free of menace.

"I don't worry about it," Carmelita said. "Nice meeting you."

She turned toward the door.

WOLFE SIPPED his beer, trying to loosen up. His muscles were so tight they were almost locked, even though he'd pulled over to the roadside before coming to the Red Wing and done his stretching exercises in anticipation of the fight. He knew the feeling. It had been the same way when he was young, fighting in the karate tournaments.

In a way, it felt good. The depression had grown heavy the past couple of years. He had joined the DEA to help good people, and to put criminals behind bars. He wasn't afraid to fight them. But since Centac and Code Zero, he'd found himself on an express train rushing toward the dark side of his soul. He would wake up in the middle of the night with the faces of men long dead, fresh again before his eyes. He had wanted to be the village constable, he realized, not the village executioner.

This was different. The place was full of weapons, but he didn't expect anyone to die tonight. The fighting would be fierce, though, beyond that of his full-contact days in the dojo. There would be no referees. He would be hellishly outnumbered. If they got him on the ground, they'd stomp him until he was crippled for life. He knew a policeman retired on disability who was wheelchair-bound after a stomping by a biker gang.

Timing would be everything. Wolfe turned on his bar stool, in time to see a black-and-white police cruiser roll past outside. He heard someone at Fat Phil's table snarl, "Fuckin' heat on out there tonight, or what?"

He heard Newell answer with a nervous giggle that didn't seem to go with his huge body, "Saturday night at the biker bar. You're a deer hunter, you hunt where there's deer. You're a county mountie, you hang out near the Red Wing. Don't sweat it, man. Just don't have nothing on ya if they start pulling us over when we leave."

Carmelita drifted out of the rest-room area, toward the bar. Her eyes met Harry's. When he smiled, she went to him and perched on the stool to his left.

She bent to his ear and whispered, "I talked with Doreen Newell in the ladies'. She actually seemed nice. Told me the place was full of scumbags who'd treat a Latin woman like shit."

Wolfe grinned. "Let's hope so," he said softly, and gestured at the bartender for a draft beer for Carmelita.

COREY LANE, twenty-two, sat at a table in the far corner of the Red Wing, diagonally across from Fat Phil and his group. A helmeted death's-head adorned his T-shirt. He stood five-eight and weighed about a hundred sixty pounds, but the wispiness of his beard made him look thinner.

Corey called himself "Spider," but almost no one else did. He bused tables at a cheap restaurant in Pasadena and lived with his parents. All his money went to support his customized Harley Sportster. He would have sold his soul to be invited to join the Princes of Hell. Now, he saw an opening to "show some class."

He gestured to the man he was drinking with, a pimply-faced hanger-on named George Doolittle. "See that spic bitch at the bar, with the skinhead?" When George nodded, Corey asked, "Think I could take the dude?"

George swigged at his beer, burped and said, "Maybe, if you caught him by surprise."

Corey grinned. Here was his chance to impress Fat Phil. He stood up and swaggered toward the bar where Carmelita and Harry were sitting.

"Hey, Conchita," he said loudly, "how's tricks?"

Harry didn't even turn. He just watched in the mirror and grinned. Carmelita turned slowly on her bar stool and said, "Fuck off, creep."

The bar had grown suddenly, ominously silent.

"Hey, now," sneered Corey. "That any way to talk? I bet you don't talk that trash to your white bosses when you're cleanin' their house an' shit, right?"

Carmelita's dark eyes narrowed. "Helluva choice for a bar, honey," she said loudly to Harry. "When it's geek night, they ought to put up a sign to warn people."

Corey flushed bright red. "I don't take that shit from no bitch," he snapped. "I think you oughta have yer mouth full, keep you from sayin' that shit."

Harry burst out laughing.

Corey turned on him. "You think that's funny, asshole? What'd you do if I just grabbed this little spic and walked out with her?"

Harry ostentatiously sipped his beer before he answered, "I'd watch her kick your ass all by herself."

"Yeah?" Corey's left hand lashed out and grabbed Carmelita's right wrist. "C'mon, Conchita! We're out—"

He didn't get to finish the sentence.

Her left hand came down on Corey's, trapping it where it was on her wrist. He instinctively tightened his hold, and Carmelita swung her two hands down, then up and over. Corey's arm was jerked out straight, his palm up toward the ceiling as she peeled it off her wrist.

"What—"

Carmelita pivoted smoothly off the bar stool and threw her hips back. The movement swung him away from her, and he lost his footing. She let go, and Corey sprawled to his hands and knees on the floor. Carmelita quickly slid the shoulder bag off, dropped it in Harry's lap and stood lightly balanced on the balls of her feet, her hands loose in front of her.

Corey Lane scrambled to his feet. He screamed, "You fuckin' bitch!" and dived at her.

She ducked under his wild right-hand haymaker, stepped in and drove a knee in deep just below his belt buckle. The air whooshed out of him as he slammed into the bar. Carmelita followed with a hard right elbow to the back of the head. Blood spattered on the dark wood of the bar as Corey's face was slammed into the hard surface.

With her left hand Carmelita grabbed his long, greasy hair and jerked his head back. Then, pivoting her hips to drive her whole 125 pounds into the blow, she hammered a right-hand reverse punch just over his left ear.

Corey Lane slumped to the floor, unconscious.

George Doolittle had started moving forward to back Corey's play. He was six feet away from Carmelita and Harry when Corey went down, out cold. George froze.

Carmelita spun on him, eyes flashing. "You want some, too? What is this, a geek tag team?"

"H-hey," George stammered, "this is bullshit! I don't fight no broads!" He turned on Harry, trying desperately to save face. "You can't keep yer broad in line, you shouldn't bring her places!"

He realized how stupid it was as soon as he said it. Titters of laughter came from the corners of the otherwise silent barroom. Exasperated, George stuck his left index finger out at Harry and said, "I mean it, man!"

Calmly, casually, Harry brought up his right hand and trapped George's extended finger. He brought his four fingers up behind George's first knuckle, his thumb trapping the finger in place, and then Harry swung his hand down toward his own belt.

Even through the alcoholic haze, the pain was excruciating. George Doolittle went down to his knees.

"Aah! You fuck!" His right hand went to the knife pouch on his belt.

Harry exploded out of his chair and drove his right knee into George's face. He felt the cartilage give way as George's nose caved in. Wolfe brought up the knee again. And again. The last knee-lift caught George Doolittle under the chin, breaking his jaw with a sharp crack and snapping his head back as he passed out. He had never cleared the knife from the leather.

Wolfe was still holding the limp, extended finger. He paused for a moment, then tightened his grasp and whipped his hand downward. There was an audible snap as the finger broke at the base joint.

Wolfe threw the limp hand back in the unconscious man's face. He turned expectantly toward the table where Fat Phil and the others had been sitting, to face the attack.

But nothing was happening.

Phil and Thumper and Henry and the rest sat motionless. They were watching, but their faces were expressionless. Only Doreen, sitting next to Fat Phil, seemed animated. She was leaning forward in her seat, watching Harry and Carmelita with frank, admiring fascination.

It took Harry a minute to realize what was happening. Then it came to him. These two weren't Princes! Gang members would fight like commandos for one of their own but couldn't care less for some wannabe that got his ass kicked.

The bartender came storming up. "What the fuck you think you're doin'? You can't come in here and—"

Then the bartender caught Fat Phil's eye. Fat Phil was frowning and slowly shaking his head no.

The bartender's words caught in his throat. He turned away from Harry and yelled into the back room, "Bobby! Karl! Drag these two assholes out of here!"

Harry and Carmelita glanced at each other. Soon background chatter from the tables began to fill the Red Wing again, and a Johnny Cash album came on the jukebox. They sat back down on the bar stools.

She looked at him expectantly, raising an eyebrow. He shrugged. There was nothing left to do but see what happened.

Wolfe turned to his beer for a moment, paused and then said loudly, "Hey, bartender, got a towel? There's blood all over the bar here. And a couple more Buds. I think somebody bounced a tooth into mine."

FAT PHIL made a come-here gesture with his index fingers. The people at his table closed in around him, and others started moving in from around the barroom. Rax walked through the door with a sleazy-looking biker woman on his arm, and Fat Phil beckoned him over, too.

"Here's the deal," said Fat Phil. "I dunno if this dipshit just walked in or what. Ain't wearin' no colors. I let that shit go by 'cause if a couple wannabes decide they're gonna be assholes, it ain't no skin off our nose if they can't take care of themselves."

Doreen said softly, "I talked to the woman when I was in the john. Her name is Elita. She said they were just driving by, saw the bikes—it looked like their kinda place."

"Okay," said Fat Phil. "Maybe the guy's just a lone wolf."

Henry asked, "How come you didn't let the bartender kick 'em the fuck out?"

Fat Phil frowned. "This is our bar, man, leastwise when we're sitting in it. That fucker don't decide what goes on in here, just 'cause he owns it. We're here, we own it. We decide who gets kicked out."

Thumper looked around. "We got like ten made members here, Phil, an' about twenty, thirty other people. Think it makes us look bad, for this guy an' his broad to slap them punks around without our say-so?"

"Yeah," said Fat Phil. "That's a problem. Tell ya what. Rax, give it a minute or two, and if the two of 'em don't beat it, go see what they're made out of. They *do* get the fuck out, we'll all follow 'em into the parking lot. If there ain't no pigs around, we'll see what they're made of out there."

Ten minutes later the Red Wing was humming again. Rax was wandering around, a Marlboro in one hand and a long-neck Bud in the other. On his arm was Cindy, the woman he'd walked in with. She was twenty-eight, divorced, and a mother of three who had abandoned her kids almost a year before to ride with the Princes. Beneath her tight-fitting shorts was a tattoo that read Property Of The Princes Of Hell.

The clock read 12:24.

Rax felt confident as he looked at the back of the guy sitting with the Hispanic chick. His eyes ran up and down Wolfe's body. Buck knife in a pouch on the right hip. No surprise. Biker wallet in the left hip pocket, with a chain hooked to a well-worn black Garrison belt. No big deal there, either. No bulges at the boots or anywhere else. That meant probably no guns, at least, none on him. The Latino chick had the shoulder bag, and that told him one thing—handgun. That's where biker women carried their men's guns. That's where Cindy was carrying his new little Colt Officer's .45 automatic. It didn't feel as comfortable in his hand as his old Lightweight Commander, but he'd had to ditch that in Denver after it had fired the bullet through Johnny Bob's head. It was one of Fat Phil's inviolable rules: do somebody with a piece, the piece is history. Rax had told him that all it needed was a new barrel—he'd picked up the spent shell casing, so they couldn't trace the extractor or breechface marks—but you couldn't argue with the Fat Man.

Rax took a swig out of his beer. He and Cindy were pretending to be wandering around the room saying hi to their buddies. Casually he leaned down and whispered in Cindy's ear, "Go ahead. Do like I told ya a minute ago. I'll be right behind."

IN THE BARROOM MIRROR, Wolfe saw Rax and the ugly biker woman coming toward them. Rax was not meeting his glance in the mirror. Wolfe felt his nerves tingle. Not meeting your eyes meant they were going to pounce. It was going to happen after all. Harry felt the tension singing in his veins, like vibrations on a taut wire. It felt good.

Rax, he knew, was a power-lifter. He was giving away more than fifty pounds to the biker. He knew he'd have to avoid the fists. The heavy bull neck meant muscles too strong to allow the head to spin from a blow, so Rax would be almost immune to the classic knockout punch to the jaw, the target that had put his last opponent down. Throat, eyes, groin, locked joints—Harry knew he would have to attack the soft targets and keep his distance.

Rax and Cindy were almost on top of them. Rax nudged Cindy, and she said, "Hey."

Carmelita and Harry turned slowly. Cindy said, "Hey, good-lookin'."

Harry looked at Carmelita and grinned. "She talkin' to you or me?"

Cindy's fake smile disappeared. "I'm talkin' to you, man! What do I look like, a dyke or sumpin'?"

Harry turned slowly on his stool and grinned at her, keeping Rax in his peripheral vision. "You really want me to answer that?"

Cindy curled her lip and shook her bottle-blond hair. "Hey, I just figured, you let a woman do half your fightin' for ya, ya must dig babes that like to fight. That your bag, honey? Ya like rough sex?"

The bar was totally silent now.

Wolfe looked past Cindy and stared Rax straight in the eyes. "Honey," he said loud and clear, "if I want rough sex, I'll force your boyfriend."

It took a moment for the words to penetrate. Then Rax's face darkened with fury, and he stepped in toward Harry, swinging his huge right fist.

Wolfe pivoted gracefully off the bar stool, feeling the power of the huge fist as it brushed past his left ear. Rax had driven his massive weight behind the blow, expecting it to connect, and the miss carried him forward, off balance.

Wolfe swung his right elbow, full power, into Rax's throat.

He saw the big man's eyes widen with the shock of the impact. Harry's body had turned to the left with the force of the blow, cocking him for a left hook, and he smashed his left fist full strength into the center of Rax's face. He felt the big guy's nose flatten under his fist. Blood sprayed.

Rax drove himself toward Wolfe, trying to get hold of him, bring him down under his bulk. Wolfe slid smoothly to his right, found himself on the big man's left, and drove his right foot forward in a piston kick that buckled Rax's left knee. Rax toppled away, taking two bar stools with him as he sprawled to the floor.

As Rax went down over the bar stools, Cindy pivoted away. She'd been in the middle of bar fights before, but never with another woman involved. Men wouldn't hit her in public. But this brown broad had just taken down a guy a few minutes before, and she felt threatened.

Carmelita was moving away from the bar now. She turned her back toward Harry, watching for threats. She found herself staring Cindy in the face.

"Get away from me, you spic bitch," Cindy screamed. She reached inside the purse to get her hands on Rax's gun to make sure the Mexican broad wouldn't tangle with her.

Carmelita recognized the movement. She lashed out with her right leg, kicking Cindy on the side of her left thigh, crushing the common peroneal nerve against the femur underneath. Cindy shrieked and went down, still grabbing at the insides of her bag. Carmelita cursed silently, let her right foot come down to be the pivot point and threw her left foot forward in a roundhouse kick.

The blow caught Cindy on the jaw. Her head snapped around from the impact, spinning her brain inside the cerebrospinal fluid until the arteries that connected the brain to the rest of the system could stretch no more. The impact shut off the supply of blood to her brain for a moment. Cindy fell back on the floor unconscious, the victim of the classic knockout blow. Her hand flopped back out of her purse. Empty.

Rax was facedown on the floor, trying to get up. His arms instinctively went into a pushup position. At the moment when the elbows locked, Wolfe knew he had his chance.

Leaning to the right, his weight on his right leg, he drew up his left knee to chamber the kick and then drove his heel straight down. The side-kick caught Rax on the point of his locked left elbow, and it shattered the joint with a crunching sound like a board breaking.

Rax cried out and pitched forward, his bulk no longer supported by the ruined arm.

The bar went up for grabs.

Harry was facing the door. On his left Fat Phil, Henry and Thumper loomed up from the bikers' head table, moving forward. Doreen sat where she was, her hand snaking inside her shoulder bag.

To his right there was more movement. Half a dozen outlaws were up from their tables and moving in fast. They halted when a surprisingly high-pitched voice yelled, "Stay back! He's ours!"

It was the voice of Fat Phil.

The room stood still.

Wolfe faced him. The big man was in the center, Henry at his right shoulder, the bulky Thumper at his left. He moved slowly toward Harry, the other two keeping pace.

"You picked the wrong bar, my friend," said Fat Phil. His eyes were bright with nervous tension.

"See that guy on the floor you just fucked up? He's a Prince of Hell, and so are we."

Wolfe hawked in the back of his throat and spit contemptuously on the floor. "Princes of Hell? What are you, vampires? Shit, man, if you're a vampire, I'm a werewolf."

"Ooh, man," chuckled Fat Phil softly. "What you are, is a *dead* son of a gun." The trio moved slowly forward.

"What's the matter? Ain't got the balls to fight me one on one?" Wolfe's voice echoed coldly through the bar. But it worked. The three men stopped.

"Thumper," said Fat Phil, "he is yours!"

Thumper's mouth opened in a bucktoothed leer. He reached inside his leather jacket and withdrew a long black flashlight.

Wolfe asked, "What's the flashlight for, punk?"

"To see inna dark, asshole," said Thumper, coming forward.

Wolfe grinned. "Then you're going to need it."

Thumper pounced, cocking the flashlight over his right shoulder, intending to bring it down on the top of Wolfe's skull.

But Wolfe was quicker. He lunged forward, into the blow, his right hand coming up in a palm-heel strike to Thumper's elbow. The blow drove Thumper's arm and shoulder back, rocking his whole body backward and off balance. With the other hand Wolfe reached quickly under the big biker's arm and grabbed the clubbing end of the flashlight, pulling it down under Thumper's arm toward himself as he continued pushing Thumper's arm up and over.

Thumper screamed. There was a sound like canvas ripping as Wolfe executed the final aikido movement that tore apart the rotator cuff inside Thumper's shoulder.

The big biker fell heavily on his back, gritting his teeth against the unbelievable pain. Wolfe had literally torn his arm out of the socket.

Henry and Fat Phil lunged forward.

But Wolfe had the five-cell flashlight in his hands now, and he remembered the staff techniques his *sensei* had drilled him on so intensively those many years ago. He pivoted, driving the butt end of the flashlight into Fat Phil's huge belly. It seemed to sink halfway in. A rush of breath exploded through Fat Phil's matted beard. He sank to his knees, clutching his distended abdomen.

Now Big Henry was on him, clutching Harry's left arm with one huge fist as he cocked the other to hammer Wolfe in the face. Harry released the flashlight from his left hand

and grabbed Henry by the forearm. He pivoted back as the big man swung, and Henry's fist went harmlessly by his head.

Harry's right hand still held the heavy flashlight just above its globe, upside down. He swung it now, pulling hard with his left hand to straighten Henry's left arm out in front of him, so it would be there as though a *sensei* were holding a board for him to break.

The muscles of Henry's big arm did not muffle the crunching sound of his elbow breaking as Harry smashed the flashlight down on it with all his strength.

Henry went to his knees. Harry looked around him like a trapped animal. Others were moving toward him, but they were still a distance away. Fat Phil was struggling to his feet. Henry was trying to get up.

Big Henry was the closest, and therefore, the most dangerous.

Again Wolfe swung the flashlight down, and the blow caught Henry just above the left eye. It fractured his skull and shattered his orbital socket with a sickening crunch. Henry dropped to the floor, unconscious. His eye was bulging from the socket and turning dark with blood from inside.

Fat Phil had regained his feet and was turning toward Harry. "Motherfucker," Phil wheezed, "you need that flashlight to fight me?"

Everything stood still for an instant in a deadly tableau. then Wolfe yelled, "I can take you with my hands, fat boy!"

He threw the flashlight. Fat Phil ducked instinctively, but Wolfe had intentionally aimed it over his head. It struck the window of the bar with an explosive crash and disappeared into the darkness of the parking lot in a shower of crystalline glass.

As if on a signal, the others lunged at him. Fat Phil was the nearest, and Wolfe knew this would be his last chance. He threw himself at the gang leader, and with his hip back to start, pivoted his entire body into a punch that sank his fist forearm-deep in Fat Phil's body.

SERGEANT BOB TESTA of the L.A. County Sheriff's Department had been cruising the area at about twenty past twelve when he got a call on the car-to-car channel from one of his eleven patrol units.

"Things might be warming up at the Red Wing," the field car told him. "The bartender just helped a couple of guys out into the parking lot. They didn't look like they wanted to go. One of them was covered with blood. We decided to do a field interview. We stopped them a block away and did the FI. They told us nothing was wrong, they just fell down. Think we might have a good bar beef ready to blow up?"

"Good bet," said Testa over his radio. "Stay on top of it. I'll be there in ten. If things start popping before that, use your own judgment. And remember, that's a Princes of Hell hangout."

Testa put the mike back in its tongue-in-groove rack and told his rookie driver, "Bang a turn on the next off-ramp. We're heading to the Red Wing. Looks like whoever tipped us that the Red Wing was gonna get hot tonight was right."

HARRY HAD BEEN in the middle of the fighting, and Carmelita standing alone, when Fat Phil yelled "Stay back! He's ours!"

Everyone had frozen, thank God. Even Carmelita.

Almost.

Watching all those men get up from their chairs, watching their lips peel back from their teeth, she knew things were getting serious. Only a couple of them even looked at her. They were focused on Harry and Fat Phil.

It gave her time to slip her right hand into her shoulder bag.

Like Harry, she had won her share of karate tournaments. She also knew her limitations. She had two weapons to choose from, the little 5-shot .38 revolver and the big 8-shot Colt .45 automatic.

It was an easy choice. Her small, strong hand closed over the checkered walnut stocks of the Colt .45. She let her index finger slide inside the trigger guard and put the tip of her thumb on top of the safety catch, ready to drive it down into the Fire position if she had to. She held the gun inside the shoulder bag. No one was within ten feet of her yet. Even the barflies at the bar had backed off. That was stupid. It was a tactical failure she was fully prepared to take advantage of. The obese bartender was down at the far end of the bar, on her right. His hands were clearly visible. That was fine. She didn't trust him.

She didn't turn when she heard the sounds of the fight. Discipline kept her watching what a police trainer would call her "area of responsibility." She realized she didn't need to look.

The faces of the bikers she watched were mirror enough. There would be a thud and the crunching sound of a bone breaking, and their jaws would drop agape. If Harry had been hurt, she knew, they would have broken out in wolfish grins. Instead, they wore the shocked expressions of people watching underdogs kick the crap out of bullies.

But then there was a shattering of glass, and the final thudding sound of Wolfe's fist sinking into Fat Phil's belly, and someone cried, "Save the prez!"

Everyone lunged forward. Two of them got past her and two were coming in on her when she cleared the .45 automatic from her bag, thumbed off the safety, pointed the pistol at the floor a few feet ahead of her and fired.

The blast of the big automatic was like a grenade going off. A splinter-edged hole appeared in the hardwood floor inches ahead of the feet of the nearest of the two outlaws coming at her.

The world seemed to go into silent, frozen motion.

There were smacking sounds behind her on the left, where Harry was. There was no time to look. She could only hope that he was all right. She had enough to worry about.

Her left hand came up to support her right hand on the big, shiny automatic, her shoulder bag swinging free under her arm, still holding the .38. Her gut instinct told her to yell "Police, don't move!" She choked off that reflex born of training, and instead, shouted as loud as she could, "Back off, jerks!"

Behind her there were impacts, grunts, a crunching sound. She heard a collective gasp as if several people had seen something horrible, and then there was a loud thud on the floor.

From outside she could hear sirens. Suddenly, blue-and-red reflections flickered against the windows of the bar.

Someone shouted, "It's the fuckin' pigs!"

DOREEN NEWELL SAT, enraptured, as the fight unfolded. The guy with Elita wasn't big by any outlaw standard, but he could sure as hell fight. The thing that impressed her most was watching him sit back with a smile while Elita beat up that little jerk who grabbed her by the arm.

In her world, women were to be slapped around or fought over. If she ever slapped a guy in front of Phil, he would have been humiliated. When they got home—if he waited until then—he would have beaten her, yelling, "Think I can't take care of my own woman? You gotta make everybody around me think I'm a pussy whose wife has to fight for herself while I'm right there to protect her?"

Instead, this new guy had enough confidence in his female partner to let her fight by herself, and when someone else tried to gang up on her, then he had smoothly and efficiently beaten the shit out of him.

Doreen liked what she had seen.

When Phil moved forward with the others to beat the crap out of the new guy, she felt sad. This Latino woman was a soul sister, and it wasn't right that her man got beaten up just for being where the Princes hung out. There were too damn few men who had respect for their women. Phil wasn't one of them. He feared her, in a way, but he damn sure didn't respect her.

She felt a pang of remorse when she realized that in her heart she was siding with the new guy when Phil and Henry and Thumper faced him. Elita's boyfriend appeared hardly bigger than Doreen herself—probably a little smaller, to tell the truth. She remembered the night the three scumbags had tried to drag her into the dark and rape her. As big as she was, she could never have fought them the way this man did.

Thank God she'd had the gun. She enjoyed watching this guy fight without one, as much as she'd enjoyed watching the Latin sister punch out the guy who'd grabbed her. She felt a vague irritation with her man: if Fat Phil was supposed to be the lord of the bar, why had he let a man touch a woman that way at all?

And then Elita's guy had ripped Thumper's arm out of the socket—she shivered when she heard the sound of the cartilage ripping, but it was a strangely excited shiver—and she heard the skull crunch when he smashed the flashlight down into Henry's head. Well, Henry. She'd been at the clubhouse enough when Henry would grab some poor girl's head, call her a sheep and force himself down her throat. She remembered Phil doing it to her, and having to clench her eyelids tight and try to fight the gag reflex. The sound of Henry's skull crunching had been music to her ears.

And when the man sank his fist into Phil's guts, God help her, she'd felt no protective instinct toward Phil at all. Instead, she had a flashback to the last time Phil had punched her in the stomach, driven her to her knees and pulled her head under the sickening overhang of his belly.

Someone yelled, "Save the prez!" Doreen knew what would happen now. They'd descend like a wave on Elita and her boyfriend, and crush their ribs and their skulls and their genitals, under the weight of their heavy boots. Doreen felt a wave of anger, of rebellion, when she heard the cry.

Then there came the deafening blast of the shot, drowning out the crash of the flashlight turning the window to flying shards, and now everyone was yelling and screaming and moving.

Doreen found herself on her feet. Her right hand had gone inside her shoulder bag without her thinking about it and closed on the black rubber handle of her snub-nosed .38 revolver.

She knew what she had to do.

SERGEANT TESTA'S CRUISER was just pulling into the lot of the Red Wing when the flashlight came flying out the window in a shower of glass. Testa saw that the first on-scene cruiser had just pulled in at the northwest corner of the building. He knew he should tell the rookie at the wheel to swing around and cover the southeast corner, so police eyes would now be watching all four walls of the building and prevent anyone's escape.

But he also knew that a fight was on inside. The old cop rule was, "Let the barfighters burn themselves out, call an ambulance for the losers and arrest the winners." Still, he was a thirty-two-year-old man whose decade of police experience hadn't quite yet burned him out. He didn't know how many innocent people were trapped in the melee inside. He only knew that if there was even one, he had to bring his team in to shut off the harm where it was born.

His cruiser was on the west side of the building, facing south. Testa barked into his radio mike, "We need backup at this location! Advise the first unit to block the southeast corner!"

He was up and running, the PR-24 baton in his hand.

Then he heard the shot.

Testa hit the ground rolling, coming up behind a pickup truck near the door. Without his brain telling them to, his hands went into action. They thrust the baton into its belt ring and the right hand cleared the Beretta 9 mm automatic from its Safariland SS-III holster while the left hand reflexively scooped the portable radio from its belt-mounted carrier. His thumb keyed the mike as he barked, "Unit 12, shots fired, Red Wing. Repeat, shots fired. Requesting backup. Condition Red."

WOLFE TURNED IN TIME to see two grungy-looking outlaws he couldn't identify rush past Carmelita. He was on automatic pilot by now, and his body went back to the dojo.

Wolfe pivoted in a spinning back-kick, his torso gaining momentum as it spun before his right leg came up off the floor and pistoned straight out into the chest of the first onrushing attacker. The sound of the ribs breaking inside the man's muscular chest was like the sound of a hornet's nest being crushed, but accompanied by the thud of heavy impact. The man gave a strangled cry and dropped to the floor, clutching at his solar plexus.

The second man kept coming. He feinted with a right cross, and Wolfe moved to his own right to escape it, only to see the left fist sweeping toward his chin in an uppercut.

There was no time to stop the fist itself. Wolfe just continued moving to his right and threw his own right hand out in a hard slap to the man's shoulder.

The fist missed Wolfe by more than eight inches. The man had committed his whole body weight forward into the blow, and it carried him in that direction, off balance after Harry's hard slap hit his shoulder. Harry found himself facing the attacker from the left side.

Wolfe didn't think about the movement. He just watched his body follow its training and do it. Wolfe's right elbow smashed into the man's left temple with a hollow, cracking thud. Wolfe could tell that the thin skull wall over the occipital had given way.

But his attacker was still up, staggering for balance. Wolfe's elbow had just struck the man above the ear and skidded over his head. Harry took it as he found it.

He let his right hand finish the motion, looping down behind the man's neck as Harry drove his left palm hard into the man's face, pushing it back into the noose of Harry's arm.

The man was now bent backward, his head face-up under Harry's right arm that encircled his neck. Harry drove his right hand toward himself, tightening the flesh and bone noose into what judo masters called *hakimi-waza*, the deadly neck-breaking technique taught only to black belts.

Harry Wolfe finished tightening the hold . . . and executed it.

He felt, and heard, the sound of the man's neck breaking, and felt the man go limp. He let the man go. The body fell to the floor like a corpse.

From somewhere very far away, Wolfe heard someone scream, "It's the fuckin' pigs!" He had never heard the sound of Carmelita's .45 automatic discharging at more than one hundred forty decibels.

All he heard was the thrumming sound of the blood rushing in his veins and pounding in his ears. Wolfe widened his stance into what his *sensei* had called *kaizin-dache,* and coiled himself forward to fight, his hands turning into the claws of the creature he was named after and his lips coming back from the teeth like his namesake's.

THE RED WING had turned into bedlam. The red-and-blue lights of the police cars outside cast an eerie light. Some employee who had been through raids before found the light switch and flipped it down. The interior of the Red Wing plunged into darkness.

Carmelita instinctively moved to her right, the .45 still in a two-hand hold but pulled in toward her belly now, the muzzle of the shiny pistol still pointed in front of her. Her back touched the bar.

A hand grabbed her left arm. Carmelita turned, her finger on the trigger, and in the dim light she saw the face of Doreen Newell.

There were two Carmelitas now. The intellectual one said, "She's got a gun! Shoot!"

But the Carmelita that lived in her guts said, "Wait. *Wait!*"

Carmelita took her finger off the trigger and thumbed the safety catch up into the Safe position.

"Let's go," gasped Doreen insistently. "Let's *go!*"

Carmelita couldn't go. Harry was fighting for her life. She turned toward him. He was standing alone, with three men down at his feet, his fists clenched. The blue-and-red lights flickered, shadowed as men came running toward the door of the bar. The cavalry was here.

"Let's go," Doreen said again, almost pleadingly this time. Carmelita knew that Harry would be okay now that the cops were here. She also knew that the plan was for her to be out of there before the cops arrived. She was carrying the guns. They could square a gun arrest away later, but it could be the straw that breaks the camel's back. And they couldn't replace the untraceable guns they'd need later.

The cops were almost through the door. With the lights out and the police strobes outside flashing through the windows, the inside of the Red Wing was an insane kaleidoscope of red-and-blue light.

"Where?" Carmelita asked insistently.

"Follow me," said Doreen.

The big woman moved, and Carmelita crouched and ran in her wake. Men cursed as they bumped into them. One grabbed at Doreen's arm, bringing her up short with the power of his locked hand. Carmelita reached over Doreen's arm and shoved her .45 in the man's face. "Out of the way, scumbag," she hissed.

The man fell back and melted into the darkness. Doreen was moving forward again, and so was Carmelita. Then they were through the back door and into the parking lot.

A quarter moon lit the area. They were still surrounded by flickers of red and blue, but they were from the front of the building. Carmelita could see that Doreen had a nickle-plated revolver in her hand. She tightened her fist around the butt of her own Colt .45.

Doreen gasped, "You okay?"

Carmelita nodded. She was watching the nickle .38 revolver in Doreen's hands.

"Let's ditch the guns out of sight," said Doreen, following Carmelita's glance. She tucked her Detective Special into her own purse and nodded urgently to Carmelita as if to tell her to do the same. She did.

Doreen asked, "You got wheels?"

Carmelita shook her head. "Came on the back of my guy's bike."

"Shit. Me, too," said Doreen. "Look, we can't save either one right now. But you're carrying your guy's gun, and I'm carrying mine, and they know we've gotta get outa here, and *now*. Right?"

"You got it, sister," Carmelita answered. There were sirens in the distance and shouts inside the bar.

"Let's move," said Doreen. "We're two blocks from a little tavern I know. I'll call somebody to pick us up, and we'll have a drink and get home in time to bail out these assholes we hang out with. Cool with you?"

"Cool with me," said Carmelita tensely.

Doreen turned and began to sprint with surprising grace for a woman her size. Carmelita followed her at the same speed. Behind them the red-and-blue lights were growing more intense.

SERGEANT TESTA WAS the first one through the door of the Red Wing, his Beretta 9 mm automatic ready and held ahead of him in a two-hand hold. In seconds other officers were behind him, their own 9 mm automatics and .38 revolvers held level.

The scene before him was devastation. "Police," he barked. "Don't move!"

No one did.

"Who's got the gun?" Testa yelled.

No one answered.

The darkness was lanced by the twenty thousand candlepower beams of high-intensity flashlights until the bar looked like a grotesque light show. There was a man on the floor clutching a broken arm. Testa could see a bone shard sticking out between his fingers. Another man, hugely fat, was on his knees, clutching a belly covered by a long beard. Testa recognized the bent-over fat man as Phil Newell, President of the Princes of Hell. A third man was rolling around in agony, holding on to his shoulder, and a fourth was not moving at all, his head lolling at an odd angle. One more was rocking on his heels, nursing his chest and making strangled gasping sounds.

A dazed, bleached-blond woman loomed into the flashlight beams. A heavy shoulder bag swung from her arm. Blood dripped from her swollen mouth.

"Him," she screamed, pointing at Harry. "Him an' his spic bitch!"

"Check that bag," barked Testa, and a female officer moved forward, holstering her own Beretta and plucking the bag from Cindy's shoulder. The officer reached inside for only an instant before she said, "Gun, Sarge. We've got a gun in *this* bag!"

By now Testa had followed Cindy's pointing finger toward Harry Wolfe, and the flashlights of the other officers moved to frame the man. Wolfe's face looked hideously skeletal in the glare of the flashlights.

"We're taking them in, all of them," Sergeant Testa barked. "Take the blond for illegal possession of a firearm. Take everybody else for disturbance of the peace. And, until we've got something else, take this one for mayhem, aggravated assault, and what the hell, possible conspiracy to commit murder." He was looking at Harry.

Choking as he got his breath back, Fat Phil Newell grinned. The sergeant saw him show his teeth.

"And Fat Phil, too. Phil, what do you know about this?"

Fat Phil wheezed, "My name's Phil Newell. I don't know a fucking thing about it."

"And *him*," snapped the sergeant. "Mayhem, aggravated assault, disturbing the peace and everything you've got on the ugly one there."

In the flickering light-lanced darkness, Harry felt the hands of the police officers close on him.

He did not resist.

In the background Wolfe heard the sergeant say, "Some people got out of here. Tell the responding units to close a net. And what the hell's the ETA on the ambulances?"

14

It was thirteen minutes to one when Carmelita Morales, a.k.a. Elita Suarez, and Doreen Newell found themselves at the door of the Felicitous Fern. As Doreen opened it, a slender young man in skintight white pants and a matching vest said petulantly, "I'm terribly sorry, but we're closing."

"No problem," said Doreen, slightly out of breath, as she pushed herself the rest of the way through the door. Carmelita followed and closed the door behind her.

The slender man stamped his foot. "Miss," he said insistently, "I said that we're—"

He stopped talking when Doreen Newell's large, strong hand closed over his throat. She leaned forward, into his face, and he could smell the mixture of perspiration and Chanel.

"Closed," Doreen said for him. "I heard you already. You're closed. But California law allows you to stay open for private parties who rent the establishment. What do you charge per hour for private parties like that?"

The young man had no idea what this Amazon was talking about, but what she said sounded suddenly and amazingly logical. "Uh, two hundred dollars an hour?"

Doreen released her hold on his throat. He gasped and rubbed his neck as she turned her purse so he couldn't see what was in it, reached inside and drew out a handful of hundred-dollar bills. "Here you go. This hold you for an hour or two?"

The young man nodded.

"Fine. Lock it behind us. We came here to get away from bars where they let in assholes."

The young man obeyed, and Doreen and Carmelita sat down in a candlelit corner.

"Our own bar," said Carmelita nervously. "I kind of like it."

"Me, too," sighed Doreen. "Kid, I'll have a Ward Eight. Elita, you don't have to drink beer with your guy anymore tonight. What do you really feel like drinking?"

Carmelita smiled, still nervous. "Before I decide, what the hell is a Ward Eight?"

"I was going to ask that myself," the young man said querulously, still holding his throat.

Doreen sighed. "God, it's hell living on an uncivilized frontier. A Ward Eight is a shot of good whiskey—we'll go with Canadian Club—a shot of grenadine, and mix it with equal parts of grapefruit juice and lemon juice, over shaved ice."

"Sounds good," said Carmelita. "Make that two."

The young man shuddered. "Heavens! No wonder you have to pay hundreds of dollars to get people to make this for you!"

Doreen stood up. She towered over the waiter. "I'm kidding," he shrieked. "I'm kidding!" He scuttled toward the back room.

Doreen looked down. "Hey, stop laughing," she said.

"I'm sorry," Carmelita giggled. "It's just that you did that so beautifully."

Doreen smiled and sat down. "So," she asked Carmelita, "this the first time you've had to leave a bar at a high rate of speed?"

Carmelita cast her a conspiratorial grin. "It was the first time it turned into a zoo like *this*. When assholes try to hit on me, Johnny lets me handle it myself. He gets a kick out of it. I was going to take the second one, but I guess he thought the guy was sneaking up behind me or something, and he dropped him. I figured it was over then. And then, a few minutes later the big guy and the bimbo came up on us like they'd been planning it."

Doreen nodded. "They were. It pissed them off that you could walk into their bar and show some strength. They had to show you who was in charge."

"Hey," said Carmelita, "we didn't go in there to start anything!"

"Hey, I know that." Doreen smiled. "But look, I see you wearing that T-shirt with a Harley-Davidson emblem over the long-stemmed rose. If they made that thing with a long-stemmed rose, and the Harley logo under it, then dammit, even I might wear it. But that's the whole biker thing—guys and their bikes on top, women somewhere down below. It just pisses me off, that's all. The problem with you and your guy was, it was their bar, so they had to be in charge, you know?"

The young man came out with their drinks and set them ostentatiously on the table. "My supervisor," he said, "would like to know just how long we can expect to stay open for this special party of yours."

Doreen looked at him coldly. "Tell him we'll be here until our money runs out, or until we decide to get the fuck out."

The young man sighed. "I was afraid of that," he said as he retreated again.

Carmelita tasted her drink. "Hey, that's good!"

Doreen sipped hers and grimaced. "I'm glad *you* like it. God, you can't get a decent Ward Eight west of Boston."

"So," said Carmelita, "you were going to tell me about how it was in the bar tonight."

"What's to tell," said Doreen casually. "But I've got a couple of things to ask you. First, where did you learn to fight like that?"

Carmelita grinned and decided to tell the truth. "I grew up in the *barrio* in East L.A. It wasn't a safe place to be a young girl. I was lucky enough to have some big brothers. One of them got into karate. He brought me to the dojo. It kind of went from there."

Doreen nodded. "Yeah, but one thing the bikers always ask kinda comes home. I hear 'em talking about all the fights they been in, and the one thing that comes up is, 'Did you ever get your ass kicked?'

"Well? Did you?"

Carmelita's grin turned rueful. She decided to stay with the truth. She brushed her hair back, revealing the ugly scar at the edge of her hairline. "Does that answer your question?"

Doreen leaned forward reflexively. She looked Carmelita in the eye. "What happened to the guy who did that?"

Carmelita told the truth one more time. "I think that he's sorry now."

"Were you the one who made him sorry?"

Carmelita nodded in the affirmative.

There is a lie detector, some say, that exists only in women and only understood between women. What Carmelita had said was the truth. And Doreen knew it was.

The big woman sat back and sipped her Ward Eight. "I believe you."

"I know," said Carmelita. Both were speaking the truth. Then Carmelita said, "And I have a feeling you've been there, too."

Doreen raised an eyelid over her Ward Eight. "A few times, Elita. I've been there a few times."

She sighed and continued, "My father took a walk before I was born. I guess you could say that was the first in a long string of men who fucked me over. When I was four, my mom married a guy that kicked the shit out of her. She stayed with him till he started kicking the shit out of me, too, and she left him when I was six. When I was eight, she married number three, and he tried to screw me. I told Mom. She didn't believe me. I went through hell for a year until she walked in and saw him doing it, and then she believed me.

"She said it was my fault. She said I seduced him. She sent me to live with her sister.

"One of my teachers did it to me when I was fourteen. I loved him, honest to God. I trusted him, but he only wanted one thing from me. I got out from under him—literally—when I was fifteen.

"When I was not quite sixteen, I met Phil. He had the Harley, the apartment, a life. Christ, Elita, he had a life, and he offered me a part of it. Does anybody wonder why I went off with him and married him?

"I was a big person by then, Elita. When you're taller than the boys, you intimidate them. When you're stronger than some of the boys, you really intimidate them. Do you know what it's like to feel like a cow? To be told you look like a cow? If enough little weak people tell you that, you start to believe it.

"So I went with Phil. The one thing about him, he made me look petite. So does everybody around him. Ever since I've been Phil's old lady, anybody in his inner circle has to be bigger than me. Six feet plus, since I'm six feet one. Over two hundred pounds, since I was a hundred seventy the last time I got on the scales.

"Funny thing with that. Fat Phil thinks having a big woman makes him a big man... he likes to have me with him, to show me off. But you know something? He only wants really small, really young ones these days. That's all that turns him on. I reach for him, and he says if he wants to have sex with something big an' fat, he'll just masturbate. Figure it out, huh?"

Doreen took a long swallow of her drink.

Carmelita said, "Wow. Sounds like you've been through the wringer. But at least he wasn't as abusive as the men before in your life, right?"

The tall woman burst out laughing. "I'm sorry, I don't mean to laugh. You just don't know the story. Phil's definition of a woman is no different from the guys around him. They think a woman is a life-support system for a vagina. And for a mouth. It's the same to them. A woman's mouth isn't something for them to listen to, Elita. A woman's mouth is something for them to stick their dick in." Doreen took another mouthful of her drink and swirled it over her tongue, as if to cleanse her mouth.

"So," said Carmelita, "why do you stay with him?"

Doreen was still smiling. "Honey," she said, "I don't have anywhere else to go right now. But he doesn't hit me anymore, and he doesn't want to have sex with me anymore, so there's no pressure. I carry his guns for him, just like you carried your gun for your man tonight, and I stay along, and I'll see how things come out."

There was a silence and then Carmelita asked, "What made him stop hurting you?"

Doreen leaned back in her chair and grinned. She looked away from Carmelita, and it seemed that she was sorting out the words, trying to tell the truth without being incriminating. "It's a long story," she began, "and it's enough to say that one night people like Phil tried to make me do things I didn't want to do, and I didn't let them. Let's just say that what they tried to do wound up hurting them a lot more than it hurt me.

"I came back to Phil after that, and it was kind of funny. A part of him was proud that I had overpowered men who were like him. A part of him, though, was scared. It's like he identified with them.

"Our sex life had been tapering off, anyway. It was dead after that happened. Phil would tell everybody about what happened and how strong he thought I was, but he was afraid of it inside. In the meantime, Phil seemed to be turning more and more antifemale. He had this thing about hurting a woman—made him feel more of a man somehow. When he realized he couldn't do it with me anymore, he stopped trying to hurt me, and it was like we had worked out an unspoken truce. I'd be there for him, I'd run bail for him, I'd be with him to show everybody how he was man enough to take care of a big woman even though he never touched me anymore, and I'd even carry his gun for him. And I would get to go where I wanted so long as none of his asshole biker friends would ever see me there. And that, I guess, brings us up to date."

Doreen Newell heaved a sigh and drank the rest of her Ward Eight. She snapped her fingers, and the young man in the background moved quickly toward the bar to get her a refill.

"So," Doreen said to Carmelita, "it's your turn."

Carmelita smiled. "Well, I pretty much told you. I learned to fight when I was young. I took control of my life. I guess I haven't been hurt as much as you, so I haven't got as much to talk about." She didn't catch her hand before it unconsciously went to the scar on the side of her forehead, and she saw Doreen smile.

"So, tell me about your guy," said Doreen. "I told you about mine."

"He's nice," Carmelita said simply, deciding quickly to stay with the truth once more. "I met him down around Miami. He got me out of a thing that wasn't good for me, with a couple of guys, and we've been off-again, on-again, together ever since. He's got no racist in him, and he's got no sexist in him. I think when he looks at me, he doesn't see 'female' and he doesn't see 'Latin.' He just sees, 'Is she strong enough to back me up, can we talk to each other, can we care about each other.' You know?"

As the young man came forward with the drinks, Doreen said with a bitter laugh, "No, I don't know. I don't know what it's like for a man you respect to see you as an equal. That's never happened to me. I'm not sure I really even know what making love is supposed to be like. I've screwed enough, God knows, but I'm not sure if I've ever even made love with a man. I'm not sure what the words mean anymore." Doreen took a long drink from her fresh glass.

Carmelita didn't know what to say to that. Her mind was racing for a response when Doreen said, "How's your guy? What's his name? How is he that way, you know?"

Carmelita almost choked on her Ward Eight. "John? Well, he's . . . he's great, you know?"

Doreen leaned forward. "Come on," she said. "Really. Tell me what it's like to sleep with him."

Carmelita had never been to bed with Harry. But she knew the man, and quick answers are the resource of any DEA or Centac agent. She gave herself a second and began smoothly, "Great, Doreen. I mean, you saw what happened tonight. He lets me take care of myself, right? Well, that's the way it is with him sexually, I guess. He lets you do what you want, and he does what you want. Gentle, caring, good for all night. What can I say?" Carmelita had run out of words, and she tilted her drink to her mouth to cover herself.

"Good," murmured Doreen. "Can I have him?"

"What?"

Doreen looked offended by Carmelita's response. "I said, can I have him? I mean, you say he's good for all night, so that means he's a renewable resource, right? It's not like I was taking something away from you or anything. And honey, I did get your ass out of there alive and away from the cops tonight, right?"

It was too much for Carmelita. She burst out laughing. "Okay, okay, give me just a minute here, Doreen. You got me out of there, and you're absolutely right, you done me a favor."

"A big favor," said Doreen. "You had just fired a gun in public. You are still carrying a loaded goddamn gun. I've just aided and abetted your little fugitive ass, is what I've done."

Carmelita was still smiling. "Why?"

"Because—" Doreen smiled back "—you remind me of me. Only with more of a chance, all right?"

Carmelita instinctively reached her hand across the table. Doreen took it. The grasp was warm and mutual.

"You have strong hands," Doreen said, sort of surprised.

"So do you," said Carmelita with a modest smile. "So, you still want to sleep with my boyfriend?"

"I'm not sure yet," said Doreen. "Is he really good in bed?"

"The best," said Carmelita warmly. "He's kind and good and gentle and he only does what you want to do."

"Does he make you come?"

"He'll make you come, Doreen," said Carmelita. "He'll make you come and come and come. I guarantee it."

Doreen made a soft animal sound. Carmelita could swear that the tall, beautiful woman was purring like a kitten.

"I'm going to hold you to that," Doreen said dreamily. "And now, I think it's time to find us a phone and call someone who'll get us someplace safe for tonight. Unless, of course, you have somewhere else you want to go."

Carmelita shrugged. "John and I are running free. We were going to find a place to crash after we'd had a beer at the goddamn Red Wing."

"Then come along with me," said Doreen. "Judging by the number of police lights I saw there, nobody got out. If they didn't get out, they'll be in the county jail until at least morning, which is as soon as they start the bail hearings on a weekend. I've got to get some cash to get Phil out, and to get your guy out, too. Unless you've got, oh, five grand."

Carmelita forced herself to gulp. "Five grand? For a bar fight?"

Doreen smiled ruefully. "I've spent my time hanging around these guys, honey. That last guy your boyfriend dropped didn't look like he was going to get up for about six months. All the witnesses are going to say he's a karate man, and that's like saying he had a gun and used it. I'm betting the D.A.'s office is going to charge aggravated assault on your guy. That's fifty thousand dollars bail, standard, and that means five grand cash up front to pay the bondsman if you want your superstud out of jail before Monday."

"Wow," said Carmelita softly.

"So," Doreen continued, "you want me to bond your guy out?"

"Hey, I'd really appreciate it," said Carmelita. "I don't have five grand."

"No problem," said Doreen, beginning to rise. "Time to get out of here. Hey, I'm not trying to do to you what Phil did to me—I mean, put pressure on you to do anything you don't want to do. When I said I wanted to go to bed with your guy, I didn't mean that was necessary for me to help you, you know?"

Carmelita looked up at the six-foot-tall woman. Even in the dim light of the after-hours bar, Doreen Newell was stunningly beautiful. A Playboy Playmate, just a few years older and a third or a fourth larger in dimension.

"I'm doing him a favor more than I'm doing you one," said Carmelita softly. "Christ, Doreen, you're a knockout. You're the last woman in the world who'd have to pay for it."

Doreen smiled skeptically. "I have to wonder, when you say that, why you're so confident that you can give him to me, just like that."

It was Carmelita's turn to smile. No more miz nice girl. "Look," she said, "I've got my time into this bike shit, too. You let your guy Phil do what he wants with women who want to be with him, for whatever reason. Well, I can do that with my guy, too.

"Why does your Phil come back to you? You've got something that is important to him, that he doesn't get anywhere else. And you know that, don't you?

"Well," Carmelita continued, "it's the same with me and my guy. Since we met in Miami, we've got something between us, something special. And it doesn't have anything to do with sex.

"You want him, Doreen? You got him. You'll have to set up the time and the place. Christ, we walk in the Red Wing, and they're gonna kill us just for being there? Johnny and I ain't the ones to pick the place, are we?

"But if you want him, you got him. I know I can speak for that, because I care about him very much, and I think he cares about me very much. And I know he loves to make love to beautiful women, and you are definitely that. So it's a guarantee, Doreen."

"Fair enough."

The tall woman smiled. "Fair enough," she said again, tossing her long brown hair. "But I'll believe it when I see it."

It was Carmelita's turn to shake her head. "You won't just see it. You'll feel it. You saved my ass tonight. If you want my guy, you got him. It ain't taking away. It's sharing, because I want to do something good for you, that you need, like you did when you took care of me tonight, all right?"

Doreen Newell took a long breath before she said, "Christ, if only women could run these things, huh, Elita?"

15

The sheriff's office was ruthlessly efficient. As the battered bar fighters from the Red Wing emerged from the official green-and-yellow van inside the sally port—the secured entrance through which it had to pass—they were surrounded by uniformed deputies, some still holding the PR-24 batons that looked like chunks of black angle iron. Sergeant Testa—medium height, stocky with muscle instead of fat and darkly mustached—barked, "Standard process for the ones that didn't go to the hospital. Except these two." He pointed to Fat Phil and Harry.

"These are our two prime movers, gentlemen. I don't know who started what, but I don't want either of them mingling with the others. Put them separate."

"It's been a busy Saturday, Sarge," said a tall black deputy. "No isolation cells left unless you want to run them all the way over to the county farm. If you want them separate from the rest, there's only one partly filled tank we can use."

"Do it," barked Testa gruffly.

The next thing Wolfe knew, he was in a room that looked like a high school gym locker. Uniformed men with PR-24s stood around as another deputy ordered Wolfe to strip for a search. He obeyed wordlessly when he was told to bend forward and pull the cheeks of his buttocks apart. A plastic-gloved finger probed roughly for contraband.

"He's clean," the examining deputy said.

Another deputy threw Wolfe a shapeless orange jumpsuit stenciled on both sides with the word Prisoner. Wolfe sneered, "Don't I get the louse spray like before?"

A deputy glared back at him impassively and answered, "Only if you're here more than twenty-four hours. Don't worry. We'll delouse your jail suit after you're gone." Then he wrapped a chain around Wolfe's belly and clapped his wrists into the handcuffs that were hooked in front.

A clerk at the booking desk enumerated his clothes, wallet with his new ID and other personal property. They had to hold the clipboard down for him so he could sign the property manifest with his cuffed hands.

Then the guards walked him through steel door after steel door until they came to a cell the size of an average bedroom. They opened the door before uncuffing him. He walked in before they could shove him in, and the door closed behind him. The deputies' footfalls echoed away. Wolfe didn't speak until the last steel door had clanged behind them.

Three big, ominous-looking black men surrounded him. One, dark as coal, was his own height but twice as wide, muscles bulging heavily through his tanker shirt. The man was clean shaven.

The second was six-four, bearded, well over two hundred pounds. When he grinned at Wolfe, a gold tooth was visible ahead of his upper right canine.

The third was also over six feet, and wearing a muscle shirt, but his shoulders and biceps were corded and wiry instead of bulging. He wore Rastafarian dreadlocks. He didn't look at Wolfe until the last clanging of the last door.

Wolfe smiled at them. They smiled back.

"We've only got a few seconds," said Wolfe in an almost silent whisper. "When he gets here, let's give it a minute for the deputies to get absorbed in something else, and then let's make it good."

The one in the dreadlocks snickered. "We know the background," he whispered back, "and we've been looking forward to it. Only thing is, you got to make it real, too. We heard you done it a little too real at the bar a little while ago. You know PPCT?"

Wolfe nodded. The method of stunning opponents by applying pressure to certain points allowed an opponent to be overpowered without injury of the bone-breaking kind.

"Good," said the lean man in the dreadlocks. "Use that."

Down the corridor a steel door slid open with a warning clang.

In moments Fat Phil was there, looking like a giant pumpkin in his tight orange jumpsuit. The chain belt barely went around him to hold the handcuffs at the midline of his huge stomach. Four uniformed deputies, three armed with PR-24s, surrounded him. As the pointman worked one of the keys on his huge ring into the door, another deputy slid his baton into the ring that hung from his belt on a leather strap and reached into his pocket for a handcuff key. He was beginning to unlock the huge biker when Fat Phil said, "Wait a fuckin' minute!"

Time seemed to stop. "Gimme another cell. I ain't going in there with them—with *him!* I ain't going in no cell with that asshole!"

The deputy with the key looked at him mockingly. "Shit, Phil, you're scared of that dude? He's half your size, man."

The outlaw bike gang leader glared at the deputy. "Awright, then. You know what I mean. Gimme one with my people in it."

The deputy grinned. "Sorry, Phil. It's against the sheriff's policy to let gang members fraternize."

Newell looked nervously at the three black men, who were now looking at him like wolves assessing a lamb. "You know what I fucking mean!" Newell's voice was rising slightly as he repeated his demand.

The deputy with the key nodded as he finished removing the belt chains and handcuffs. He let his eyes widen with mock understanding. "Oh," he said. "*That!* Well, gee, Phil, I hate to be the one to bring you into the current century, but the Sheriff's had his holding tanks and his jails integrated for a long time now."

The deputy tossed his head curtly, and the two deputies behind Newell shoved the big man into the cell. The first, the one with the large key ring, slammed the door shut and locked it.

"Behave now, gentlemen," he said.

Then the deputies walked down the hall and disappeared behind the ominous-sounding steel doors.

Fat Phil instantly put his back to the barred door of the steel cage. He could not remember the last time he had felt this terrifyingly alone.

He gauged them as the trio sauntered slowly around him. He figured he'd try any of them one on one. But Rasta looked whipcord tough and fast, the worst type for a man his size to fight, the bearded one was damn near his own size, at least, what his own size would be if he worked out, and the short one was built like a tank.

Rasta spoke first. "Well, well, well," he said with deceptively menacing softness. "I do believe our new roomie here has some problem being here with us."

Beard said then, with an evil grin that flashed his gold tooth, "I believe you be right, Rasta. I believe he don't feel like he with his own kind, you know?"

It was the broad-shouldered Tank's turn. "What kind you figure that be, bro? You figure he want a special wing, special cell block, just got *fat* fucks in it?" The powerfully built black man was smiling with his mouth, but not with his eyes, which were boring into the bike gang leader.

"Nah, man, but I think you gettin' closer," said Rasta, stretching his arms and legs like a boxer warming up. "Needs a special cell block with fat pussies in it, that's what he needs."

"That right, fat boy?" Beard's grin was still wide. "That what you mean by your own kind? Fat pussies?"

"Nah, nah, you way off base," said Tank, cracking his knuckles and flexing his huge biceps. "I do believe what this fat pussy mean is, his own kind be fat *white* pussy! Yeah! That the deal, man?" Tank was snarling now.

Newell finally spoke. "Don't fuck with me," he said. He tried to make his voice hard and cursed himself as the dry-throated fear made it crack at the last moment. "I'm telling you, man. I called from booking, and my lawyer's on his way down here already, and anybody screws around with me in here is gonna get paid back hard from me and my bros!"

The three black men burst into mocking laughter. "Whoo-ee," crowed Rasta. "Your bros? They're gonna come kick our poor lil' black asses, right? Shee-it, what you an' your bros call your gang, anyway? Fuckin' Weight Watchers?''

Newell glanced desperately at Wolfe. But the undercover agent was leaning against the far corner of the holding cell, his arms folded, watching impassively.

"Ooh, baby, don't be lookin' at him," said Tank. "He be mindin' his own business, not makin' nobody feel like no nigger, you catch my drift. He ain't in no trouble. You think he give a rat's ass 'bout helpin' you?"

Beard, still grinning, turned toward Wolfe. "Hey, you gonna help this fat tub?"

Wolfe looked at the black man without changing expression. "Last time I saw him, he set his whole damn gang on me. I don't see where I owe him shit."

The bearded black man turned back toward the bike gang leader. "See? Your kind ain't blood, man! He don't give a damn what happen to you. He probably gonna take the sloppy seconds after we done with you, fat boy!"

Newell's anger gave him courage. "You ain't doing nothin' with me," he growled.

"Ooh," said Rasta in a mock falsetto, going up on his toes. "Mercy me! He ain't gonna let us do nothin' to him!"

Beard laughed out loud. "Think he's got balls. You got balls, fat boy?"

"Thinks he ain't no pussy," Tank chimed in. "That true, fat fuck? You ain't no pussy?"

Fat Phil was sputtering now. His fists were clenched, his bulky back hard against the cell door. He'd be damned if he'd let them get behind him. "Yeah, I got balls. I ain't no fucking pussy."

Suddenly the steel-and-concrete room was very silent and no one was smiling anymore.

"You wrong, white racist pig," Rasta said softly. "We gonna turn you out. We gonna make a pussy outa you right quick."

"Wrong about havin' balls, too," said Tank in guttural anger. "Maybe you got your little white balls now, but you ain't gonna have 'em no more when we done with you!"

Fat Phil's body tightened almost spasmodically at the threat. "Well, well," said Beard. "I do believe he's gonna try that bullshit all them white fish try. He gonna try an' hit one of us first, show us what a big strong guy he is."

Facing Fat Phil straight on, Tank said, "Go ahead, hit me. Gimme your best shot!"

On Phil's left Beard said, "Yeah, do it. Show us you ain't no pussy. Show us you got balls."

And Rasta, on the right, just hit him.

He saw Phil turn away from him to glance at the one with the beard, and he came in with a long, looping left hook that struck the big biker flush on the cheek. The beard cushioned the blow, but the impact still snapped Fat Phil around.

On animal reflex, Phil lunged forward. He ripped a hard right fist full power into Tank's gut, but the muscular man just grunted with the impact and drove his own right fist deep into the big biker's abdomen. It sank wrist deep, and Phil went "Wuff!" as the blow expelled air from inside him in a spray of spittle.

The fight was on.

Wolfe leaned against the wall and watched. Timing, he knew, was critical. Big men, hitting full force, exerted terrible damage. If he let it go on too long, Fat Phil would lose consciousness, even die, and the whole thing would have gone too far to do any good. But interfere too soon, and Fat Phil could still have the illusion that he'd won the fight himself, just with a little help.

And the big man was a fighter all right. With his back to the wall, he lashed out with a powerful kick that would have crushed Rasta's testicles if the wiry man hadn't gracefully glided his lower body out of the way at the last second and thrown a counterpunch that made a sickening crunch as it connected with Fat Phil's face. Still leaning against the bars, Phil swung a desperate left that caught Tank on the jaw. Only the massive muscles in the squat black man's neck kept the powerful punch from spinning his head hard enough for a knockout. Instead, Tank counterpunched, sinking his fist deep into Fat Phil's belly again. Wolfe saw the big man's knees buckle.

So did the three blacks. Beard pivoted at the hips and threw a right hook into Fat Phil's kidney area, and Rasta at the same time kicked the biker hard in the the right thigh. Fat Phil went down heavily.

Phil grabbed at the nearest leg, Beard's. Tank kicked him viciously in the armpit, and Fat Phil let go.

He knew he was losing. He brought his arms in to cover his ribs, tried to curl his legs up in a fetal position to protect his belly and testicles. Harry could see blood flowing from his nose, and from a split lip that was already swelling, and from a gash that had opened on the big man's forehead. Blinking through the blood, Fat Phil's eyes were still open, still alert and almost crazed with fear.

The time had come.

Wolfe shouted one loud syllable. "Enough!!"

He swung into motion.

He saw Phil turn toward the sound, look past the legs of Beard and see him coming, and then Harry swung his right fist down like a club onto the point where the bearded black man's neck met his shoulder. From where Phil lay, it must have looked like a rabbit punch to the cervical spine.

Beard grunted hard and loud and buckled forward, his jaw going slack and his eyes rolling up in his head. The unconsciousness had been instantaneous. He fell past the prostrate form of Fat Phil, into the arms of Tank.

Rasta lunged at him. Wolfe parried the charge and, as the lean, fast opponent moved past him, Harry brought his knee up viciously into the man's thigh. Rasta cried out involuntarily as the sickening thud of the powerful impact filled the tiny cell. The blow had crushed his common peroneal nerve against the femur, the heavy thigh bone. The impact sent a shock wave of distress to the man's brain, and it made the leg collapse like jelly beneath him. From the floor Fat Phil saw the lean black man go down on his back, clutching at his leg, his face contorted in a rictus of agony.

Now Tank was on Harry Wolfe, his hands clutching at the white man's throat, forcing him back against the iron bars of the cell wall. Wolfe's fist came down on the man's thickly muscled forearm, once, again, a third time. Then the radial nerve in Tank's forearm no longer worked, and the arm fell away.

Tank had time to say, "What the fu—"

And Wolfe was on him.

He grabbed the man's useless left arm, spun him clockwise and came in from behind Tank's back, his own left arm looping around the black man's throat until his elbow was under his chin. Wolfe's biceps now pressed against Tank's left carotid artery, the rigid bone of his forearm against the right. Bringing up his other hand for support, Wolfe tightened the scissors lock around the man's neck.

Wrestlers called it the sleeper hold. Cops called it the choke-out. The judo *sensei* who had taught it to Wolfe called it *shime-waza*.

Helpless, in agony, out of breath, Fat Phil Newell watched from the floor as Tank's eyes rolled desperately in their sockets. The heavyset black man's left arm was still stunned from the blows to the radial nerve. He tried to claw at Wolfe's face with his right hand, but the white man with the nearly shaven head was too far behind him. Tank's right hand seemed to flutter, then dropped heavily to his side as his whole body went slack.

Wolfe eased the unconscious man to the floor. Down the hall he could hear a clanging of doors and the sound of running feet.

Just before the deputies reached the door, a gasping Phil Newell looked up at Harry Wolfe from the floor and managed to say four words in a strangled voice.

"Bro... Thanks, bro. Thanks."

THEY BROUGHT Fat Phil Newell to the desk. One eye was swelling shut, and blood crusted over his swollen split lip and from the coagulating cuts on his forehead and both cheeks. He had to lean heavily against the booking desk to stand.

"My God," said the tall white-haired man in the thousand-dollar suit who stood at the booking desk. "What have you done to my client?"

"Shut up," wheezed Fat Phil. "You got me bonded out?"

"Yes, of course," sputtered his attorney. "But what—"

"Never mind," grated Phil, cutting him off abruptly. "Guy in my cell. Dunno his name. White guy, skinhead. Bond him out, too."

"You don't know his name?" The lawyer was aghast. "Then he's not one of—"

Fat Phil shut him off again, this time with a hard slap on the booking desk that sounded like a pistol shot. "Don't ask me no more questions," he growled. "Just bond him out, and take him with us. I owe him, all right?"

16

The big blue Cadillac pulled up at the Princes of Hell clubhouse. Harry stepped out from the right rear door, Fat Phil from the left. Phil leaned into the driver's window and told his lawyer, "Okay. The other guys'll make it back their own way. I want you to call the hospital, find out how everybody's doing."

The distinguished man at the wheel sputtered, "For God's sake, Phil, I'm your attorney, not—"

Phil cut him off sharply. "Don't gimme that crap! They ain't gonna release no information to me, and you know it. You, they'll figure you're just another ambulance chaser. You're a lawyer, you know how to get it. Get down there and call me here as soon as you can."

The attorney's shoulders sagged in compliance. He put the big car in gear and drove slowly off into the breaking dawn.

"C'mon," said Phil. "You can crash here for a while. Lemme show ya the joint."

He bulldozed through the door of the double-wide trailer. Klaus Richter and a couple of the others were waiting for him. One of the bikers—lean, shifty-eyed Snake—blurted, "That's him, Klaus! That's the guy that laid out Rax an' Thumper an' Big Henry!"

Richter stiffened. Fat Phil raised his hand. "Chill out," he said. "Chill out. Fight was fair an' square. This is Johnny Parker. He covered my ass in jail last night when a bunch of niggers jumped me. He's cool."

Richter coldly extended his hand. He was surprised at the strength of Harry's handshake. "How you doing, Parker?"

"I been better," answered Wolfe.

Fat Phil lumbered over to an antique Coca-Cola cooler from the fifties. He threw open the lid, reached down and pulled two long-neck bottles of Budweiser from the icy water. He popped them both in the built-in opener, and handed one over. Harry Wolfe's hand closed over it gratefully. "Thanks," he said. "It's been a long night."

Phil grinned. Reaching up to a shelf above the Coke machine, he grabbed a plastic bottle of tablets. Setting down his beer, he shook a fistful of the tabs into one huge hand.

"Time to speed up," he said with a laugh, tossing half the pills into his mouth and washing them down with a long pull that drained half his bottle of beer. Flecks of foam glittered on his beard and the edges of his swollen lips, encrusted with dried blood. He extended the bottle toward Harry. "Want some?"

Wolfe was conscious of Snake and Klaus staring at him intently. "Maybe one," he shrugged. "I'm still kinda 'up.'" Wolfe reached over and plucked one tablet from the big man's palm, opened his mouth wide and threw it down the back of his throat. He washed it down with a swig of Bud.

"Make yourself comfortable," said Phil with a suddenly wide grin. "Snake, keep our guest company. Klaus, I gotta see you back in my office. Oh, one little thing, Johnny."

Wolfe looked at him inquisitively.

"We got, ah, real strict security who we let in here. Mind if I see your license for a minute?"

Wolfe tensed up a minute, to stay in character, then said, "What the hell." He pulled out the wide leather biker wallet with its chain that looped over his belt, plucked out the driver's license he'd been furnished by the Marshal's Service and handed it to the big man. "Just make sure I get it back. It's my real one."

THE BACK ROOM of the clubhouse looked like a small businessman's office: computers, modems, typewriters, files. Phil dropped into the oversize chair behind the big desk. The furious Klaus stayed standing.

"Phil, who is this guy? I can't believe you'd bring a stranger here after what we've just been through."

"Be cool," said Phil. "You just seen him drop methamphetamine, didn't you? I saw it go down his throat, man! He didn't stick it under his tongue like some stupid narc. We got busted, all our lawyer'd have to do is have him take a polygraph test. Any fucking UC ever did dope with a suspect is off the witness stand and out of a job. You ever see a narc actually take dope like he just did?''

"Not UCs," Klaus admitted, "undercover narcs just pretend to take stuff. But, Phil, after the asshole we just had to do in Colorado, after that DEA guy that blew his brains out—man, I thought you said you were going to play it careful for a while.''

Phil slammed his beer bottle down on the desk. "Shit, Klaus, lemme tell ya what it is, playing careful. That's when three jive-ass jigaboos are gonna do ya on the floor of the county jail while the deputies that hate yer guts are outside twiddling their thumbs and somebody comes along and helps you. Okay, he fucked up some of our guys last night, but it was righteous. Fair's fair.''

Klaus shook his head. "Then let's at least— Wait a minute. There's a car coming up the road." Klaus went to the window. "Taxicab. It's your wife, and some woman. Looks Hispanic.''

Phil rocked the chair forward and came to his feet, grunting with the pain of his bruises. He lumbered to the window, looked and said, "Doreen's got Johnny's bitch with her. Man, you shoulda seen that little hellcat fight. She kicked the hell out of this little hanger-on who's been trying to get in with us. Two of them got outa the bar together, looks like. C'mon.''

Klaus and Phil came back into the main room just as Doreen and Carmelita entered. Carmelita cried, "Honey," and threw herself into Harry Wolfe's arms. Fat Phil waddled forward and hugged his wife. Doreen forced herself to smile. Phil stank of sweat and blood.

"Phil," said Doreen, "this is Elita Suarez. She's Johnny's gal.''

"How ya doin', honey?" Phil's voice was syrupy sweet. "Hey, was it you that lit off that round last night?''

Carmelita looked at Harry as if asking permission to answer, and Harry nodded. "Yeah," said Carmelita. "I don't like seeing my guy get outnumbered.'' She slid her shoulder bag closer to Harry.

"It's okay, babe," laughed Wolfe. "I don't need my piece right now. We're among friends."

Phil laughed with him. "Good thing she was packing it for ya. County cops caught one of us with a piece, we'd all still be there. Whaddya carry?"

"Forty-five," said Wolfe.

"My kinda guy," said Phil. "Honey, gimme my stuff."

Doreen handed him her voluminous purse. Phil reached in and withdrew his shiny Smith & Wesson revolver. He tossed it to Harry. Wolfe caught the gun easily and thumbed the latch that opened the cylinder. He could see it was loaded with five .38 Special cartridges.

"Hammerless," said Wolfe. "Nice. I figured you for something bigger, though."

Phil chuckled, still rooting in the purse. "That's just for when I ain't carrying a gun. This is my baby." The big man withdrew a gleaming stainless-steel automatic, its hammer locked back on a live round. He tossed the loaded pistol to Wolfe, who caught it with his free hand. Harry set down the .38 and expertly stripped the cartridge clip out of the .45's butt. Tucking the magazine under the little finger of his right hand on the pistol, he drew back the slide with his left, taking the chambered round into his left palm as his thumb hit the latch that locked the slide open. "Hollowpoints," said Wolfe. "You don't screw around."

Behind him he felt rather than heard the movement as Snake picked up an M-16 and leveled it at him. But Phil glared at Snake. "Be cool, man. The dude's okay. So, Johnny, what kinda .45 you carry?"

Wolfe set down Phil's guns and reached slowly into Carmelita's bag. "Regular Colt, nowhere near as fancy as yours. And Elita's got her own little .38 here." He unloaded both guns and opened them before passing them to Fat Phil Newell.

Beginning narcs, he knew, carried tiny .25 automatics and derringers so they wouldn't be seen to be armed. Wolfe had worked enough undercover in his DEA days to know that in an armed subculture, the examination of one another's weapons was almost a ritual, like strange dogs sniffing each other.

"Good little basic gun," Newell observed. "You oughta get it tricked out like mine, though."

Wolfe nodded in agreement, working the action of Newell's big automatic. "Helluva gun. Great trigger, night sights . . . who did the work?"

"Fella named Middlebrooks, place called the Combat Shop in Virginia," the outlaw biker answered. "Son of a gun wouldn't do the work for me. Only works for straights, ya know? Had a front man get it into his shop. Check out those grips, man. Brazilian rosewood."

As Wolfe examined the customized pistol, he saw Newell surreptitiously glance at the side frame of his pistol and the butt of Carmelita's revolver. He knew the gang leader was memorizing the serial numbers. The men who'd briefed him had been right, then; the gang had a line to law-enforcement computers and was going to run the numbers to see if they were cop guns.

"Hey, listen," Phil said abruptly, "Klaus and me gotta take care of some stuff. Everybody thinks it's fat city being the prez. They don't know what it takes to clean up after a bar fight. I gotta get my guys outa the hospital, make sure all the bonds and shit are taken care of . . . you guys just have a few brews or whatever and chill out."

Klaus followed Phil back into the office. Phil said, "You talk. Enough people at the sheriff's office know my voice, and they record incoming. Ask for Wanda, leave a message tell her to call her mom. She'll get back to us on a secure phone." He handed the receiver to Klaus Richter, who still wasn't smiling at all.

WANDA WILSON WAS filing arrest reports in the records room of the San Diego Sheriff's Office when the message came over the intercom for her to call her mother. It was 7:00 a.m., and she'd barely come on.

Suppressing a smile, she hurried to the pay telephone near the ladies' room. Wanda lived alone. Calling her mother was a code that meant she should call the clubhouse of the Princes of Hell. Twenty-four, gangly, her face riddled with acne, she considered herself the most undesirable woman alive. Only with the Princes had she ever found acceptance, importance.

When the phone was picked up, she asked for Phil. In a moment she was talking to the prez. She'd never spoken a word to her "big boss," the High Sheriff of Los Angeles County, but with the Princes she was a member of the inner circle. The knowledge filled her with some of the only pride she'd ever felt in her life.

"Okay," she whispered, writing furiously on a notepad. "Got the date of birth and the Social Security number? Smith model 49. And the rest? Yes, go on . . . Colt Government .45, stainless, serial 5505904. Got it. Back to you soon. Love ya."

She hung up with a blissful smile on her face.

PHIL'S PHONE RANG. He took a weary swig from a fresh Bud and answered. "Yeah?"

"It's me," said the familiar voice of his attorney. "You guys had some battle last night. Big Henry's the worst—crushing comminuted fracture of the left elbow. That means the joint is just dust and shards. He's got a fractured skull and a shattered orbital socket. There is some damage to the left eye, and they aren't sure they can save it. He's conscious. They've got him in the neurological-injury recovery ward.

"Thumper's got a severe dislocation of the left shoulder. The rotator cuff was completely torn out. They say they can discharge him today, but he's going to need some heavy therapy and probably microsurgery to try to get it working again. He won't come back to a hundred per cent, though.

"Rax has a shattered left elbow, too. He's in a cast all the way to his shoulder. Bad sprain in the left knee, nose all busted to hell and a bruised larynx. They want him to stay for a day or two for observation in case the throat thing swells up.

"Corey Lane's just got a concussion. He—"

"Fuck him," Phil interrupted gruffly. "Goddman little wannabe got his ass kicked by a broad. I never wanna see that little pussy as long as I live."

"George Doolittle, broken jaw, broken finger, broken—"

"Forget him, too," said Phil decisively. "Just another wannabe. Look, get in there and tell *my* guys the club'll take care of the hospital bills and shit, and we'll be down to see them this afternoon. Yeah. Bye."

Phil set the phone in the cradle and shook his head. "That Johnny's gonna cost the club a few thou in medicals. Too fucking bad Blue Cross don't wanna insure the Princes of Hell."

The phone rang again. Phil grabbed it. "Yeah? Hey, babe, that was quick. Watcha got for me?" He grabbed a notepad and a pencil.

Newell wrote furiously. "John Hamilton Parker...yeah, that's about the right age...Methuen, Massachusetts? Is that a fuckin' *place?* Iron Horsemen? Hang on."

Phil covered the mouthpiece and asked Klaus, "Iron Horsemen? They a Big Four club?"

The huge muscleman nodded. "They're hooked up with the Outlaws, more or less."

Newell smiled with satisfaction and returned to the phone. "Good. What else? Served time for armed robbery...suspicion of murder, not enough evidence for indictment...disappeared, that's last June, right? Thought he was working extortion on the fucking Boston Mafia? He's got some balls...yeah, right, .38 and .45...stolen in a suitcase from Delta baggage handling, flight from LaGuardia to Boston? '87? Love it. C'mon over tonight, honey, we gonna party! You and me and everybody. Yeah, you bet yer my best girl. Love ya. Bye."

Newell set down the phone with finality. "You catch that? This dude's a heavy hitter, man. Why don't ya call Berea, check him out from your end? He's club material, my opinion." Fat Phil's expression was triumphant.

Klaus Richter still looked doubtful. "I'll call," he said reluctantly. "But I still think we're taking too much of a chance, this soon after the other stuff."

WANDA WILSON WAS humming to herself when she returned to the records section. A new sheaf of arrest reports from the night before waited on her desk. She picked them up and, when she saw the names, she had to suppress a gasp.

Rax...Thumper...Big Henry...and the name the Prez had asked her about, Johnny Parker. It had been one hell of a night.

A sergeant from the detective squad entered the room. He seemed in a hurry. "Wanda," he asked, "can I take you away from that for a minute? We've got a warrant we need you to type up. I want to get it to the judge before noon, so we can make the hit early this afternoon."

"You bet, Sarge," she said with a smile.

He turned and left. In a moment she was glad he'd turned away so quickly, so he couldn't pick up her involuntary gasp as she read the draft sheet for the warrant.

"Richard Higgins, Long Beach...suspicion of murder of a federal officer and a suspect in custody...at request of Denver, Colorado, Police and U.S. Marshal's Service..."

Richard Higgins. *Rax!* They were going to bust Rax for murder!

She spun toward the desk where last night's arrest reports lay. She rifled through until she found one that said, "Higgins, Richard, a.k.a. 'Rax,' transported to County General by fire service ambulance." She hugged it to her chest and glanced furtively around her. Sure no one had seen her, she scurried once more down the hall to the pay phone near the ladies' room.

SNAKE SAT in a corner, curing his sulkiness with a huge reefer of marijuana. Doreen Newell had curled up and drifted off to sleep on a leatherette couch under the display of upside-down police and bike club patches. For the moment Carmelita and Harry were alone.

Leaving Fat Phil's guns on the table, Harry handed Carmelita her blue Smith & Wesson snubnose with the hump-backed hammer shroud, and reloaded his own stainless .45 automatic. Leaving the hammer cocked and the safety locked on, he shoved it into his waistband behind his hip, Mexican style. It was the way an outlaw in an armed sub-culture would be expected to behave: the woman carrying his gun in public, but he carrying his own ostentatiously in the secure company of his brothers. Snake made no move to stop him. Harry took Carmelita by the hand and they walked out into the morning sun.

They had walked several yards into the desert before Carmelita whispered, "Doreen and I got out together. She's practically accepted me as a sister. She's a neat lady, really. There's something unbelievably innocent about her."

"For Christ's sake, she's killed three men."

"In self-defense," noted Carmelita.

"Okay," conceded Harry. "I've got no problem with her. Tell me about you and her."

"Well . . . the one thing she and I agreed on, you'll, ah, have to be involved in. But we can get to that later. What's with you and Phil?"

"It was perfect, Carmelita. I always thought the director was just a suit—too far removed from the realities of law enforcement in the street. I'll tell you, though, he set this up like a street agent. Phil and I were put in a cell with three black guys, ours, who looked like they came out of central casting for the official Ku Klux Klan nightmare. They slapped the stuffing out of Fat Phil, and I 'saved' him. We're bosom buddies."

Carmelita said, "Is the big white guy Klaus, the one with all the muscles? He was looking at you like you'd come out of the pit. He doesn't trust you at all."

"No," agreed Harry, "but just about now, they're finding out that the guns we're carrying were genuinely ripped off. They were taken out of an airport, from a suitcase on a flight going New York to Boston, and that all fits with the real Johnny Parker. Only the Marshal's Service knows that the real Parker's dead. Well, Marshal's Service and the

Boston Mafia, but they're not talking to the bikers lately. Seems the real Johnny was trying to pull a fast one on the Boston family, and they took him out in the bogs and shot him in the back of the head. Halloran got it from one of his other organized crime snitches, a genuine Boston mafioso. Parker was a member of the Iron Horsemen, a genuine killer outlaw, and from what Halloran can find out the Horsemen just figure things got too warm for Johnny and he split. We're physically similar, a year apart in age, and the Marshal's Service duplicated the ID so well only someone who knew the real Johnny Parker could ever say I wasn't him."

"Cool so far."

"Now," said Harry, "you said I've got to be involved in something you agreed on with Fat Phil's wife."

"Yes," said Carmelita calmly. "I told her you'd sleep with her."

"*What?*"

"She's married to one of the most repulsive human beings on the planet. He hasn't made love to her in so long, she's got cobwebs down there. You turn her on."

Wolfe was without words.

"Come on," said Carmelita. "She's a good-looking woman. Beautiful, really. And bright. I'd think she'd turn you on."

"I didn't think of her that way," Wolfe said dryly.

"Come on," Carmelita said again. "She asked me how you were in bed. I told her you were terrific. Gentle, and caring, and good for all night. You're not going to make me look like a liar, are you?"

"How the hell would *you* know how I am in bed?"

"I know you," Carmelita smiled, showing all her white teeth. "I can extrapolate. I'll set up the whole thing. Like Cupid."

"Very funny," said Wolfe glumly.

"Give me a break," said Carmelita. "When did you ever have a partner that set you up for an all-nighter with a beautiful woman? You should be grateful. Besides, think of all the inside information you can pump out of her."

"I'm just thrilled," muttered Wolfe. "Come on, let's head back in, see what the hell's happening in there."

PHIL WAS ON THE PHONE. "Thanks, honey. Wanda, we're gonna have a special party night just for you. Go ahead and do what you said with the papers. I'll take care of the rest. Love ya, babe."

Fat Phil dropped his office telephone into its cradle and looked at Klaus Richter. "Son of a bitch," he said. "I thought you were running the Colorado hit clean!"

"I ran it perfect," Klaus snapped defensively. "What the hell is going on?"

"That was my inside bitch at the sheriff's office. They're writing up a warrant for Rax. Murder of a federal marshal and a snitch, out of Denver. That sound fuckin' *familiar?*"

Klaus's whole body tightened with rage, the muscles cording, the tense stricture in his throat turning his voice into a growl. "Damn him! I told him to drive back with me, Phil! But he's got a real big ego thing. He thinks I'm a real threat. He insisted on flying back out of Denver."

Fat Phil's jaw dropped. "You never told me that! Fuck, do I have to nursemaid you guys through everything? I never gave him no fake ID! Sure, he's got the money, anybody in my inner circle has. He must have flown out under his own name. Hit in Denver, naturally they'd check the airports, run everybody through the computers. Jesus Christ!"

Klaus had control of his voice now. "He's vulnerable, Phil. Your new buddy in the other room beat the shit out of him last night. And Rax hates my guts—he thinks I'm trying to push him out of the club. If the cops get to him . . ."

Klaus didn't have to finish the sentence. Fat Phil nodded his head decisively. "I been losing faith in Rax lately anyway. He goes. Today. We gotta get him out of that hospital."

"But the cops must be there already," protested Klaus.

Fat Phil grinned. "You Big Four guys keep forgetting who runs this fucking outfit. I got my sources. I got my powers. We just stalled the warrant. The dicks serving the warrant don't know Rax got busted last night, don't know he's in County General, and right about now, that paper on him is disappearing. They're gonna serve the warrant at his house. Ain't gonna be nobody there but his common-law wife and his rug rats. And they ain't used to him being there, and they're the last people he'd call from the hospital anyway. We're his family, not them. That buys us a few hours."

"Who are we going to use to take him? Your 'inner circle' is pretty much *at* the hospital, thanks to your new friend," Klaus observed.

"Snake is here. I'll call Mongo. He's probably crashed out at home, shit-faced as usual. And you and me." Fat Phil paused, then leered. "And one more."

Klaus looked at Phil for a moment, and then said, "You can't be serious."

"Fuck, yes, I'm serious," snarled Fat Phil. "You questioned my judgment. You thought I was a shithead 'cause I brought Johnny in here. Now, correct me if I'm wrong, but when I was in the shitcan a few minutes ago, you called Berea and had 'em check on Johnny, didn't ya?"

Klaus looked downward, defeated. "Yes, I did. They confirmed. Johnny Parker fits the description, and the whole bit that you got from your insider at the sheriff's office is right. Got too big for his britches, fucked with the Mafia in Boston and disappeared. Iron Horsemen figured he was dead. My guy at Berea called his connection at Horsemen, and the guy on the other end said, 'Johnny's *alive?* All fuckin' *right!*' But Phil, I still don't trust him."

Fat Phil looked at the muscular Aryan with a triumphant look. "So," he asked Klaus, "what's it gonna take for you to believe I was right in bringin' him in?"

Klaus looked at the gang leader icily. He didn't say a word. Instead, he raised his right hand with the first and second fingers extended, and traced twin lightning bolts in the air.

Fat Phil chuckled. "Lightning bolts. Filthy Few. You'll admit I was right if Johnny kills this dude right in front of us?"

Klaus nodded.

"Okay, then," said Phil. "We go now. I'll have Snake call Cindy, get her all dressed up, have her check Rax out of the hospital. They gotta have guards on him after the fight last night, 'cause he's still under arrest. I'll call the lawyer and get it squared away for bail bond and everything. We'll pick up Rax from Cindy, and go for a little walk in the desert. I want you to be there when my man Johnny does Rax. And when he does that, you can damn well gimme an apology. Agreed?"

Klaus Richter stood coldly for a moment before he bit off one reluctant word. "Agreed."

17

When Harry and Carmelita walked back into the Princes of Hell clubhouse, Fat Phil and Klaus were waiting, looming huge in the doorway.

"Got any plans for the day, bro?" Fat Phil's voice dripped with sincerity as he asked the question.

"Yeah," said Harry. "Matter of fact, I was gonna find a place to crash, and jock my ol' lady when I wake up." Carmelita put her head on his shoulder and smiled affirmatively.

"Yeah, well, tell ya what," said Phil. "Looks to me like you got too much talent to be free-floating, like you are. I want you in with me, and I pay big. You interested?"

Harry played it cool. "Interested? Yeah, I'm interested, but I ain't committed."

"Good," said Fat Phil. "I want you to run with me for a while. I'll have ya back this afternoon."

Doreen, awake now, came up to the door to join them. "Honey," she said sweetly, "Elita and her guy are my guests. Our guests. You and Johnny can burn the candle as long as you want, but Elita and I have been up all night. Can't we find someplace for them to crash?"

Fat Phil glowered and shook his head as if to get away from a mosquito. He hated details. "Yeah, sure, sure. Take one of my credit cards, get them into some nice hotel for a while. You take Elita there, I'll call ya this afternoon, find out where she's at and I'll drop Johnny there when we're done doing business. 'Kay?"

"Okay," said Doreen in a syrupy voice, hugging the huge bearded man. "Honey, you wanna shower or change or anything?"

"Hell, no," answered Phil. "Anybody I deal with today's gonna know I'm a man, so if I smell like a man, it ain't gonna bother them none, awright?"

Snake came running up. His voice was nervous as he said, "Prez? I just got off the phone with the auto pound. They won't release none of yer sleds. They said it's a hundred per to get 'em out. Remember last time. They don't take our checks."

Fat Phil shook his head in irritation. "Shit! Doreen, dig him out the cash, have someone round up a trailer, and get somebody down there. I want my trike and every other Prince's sled back here by the time I get back."

"I'll take care of it, honey," said Doreen softly.

"C'mon," said Fat Phil to Harry. "We're going for a ride. Lemme get some fucking pills an' a cooler of brew. We'll take one of the vans."

KLAUS, PHIL, SNAKE and Harry had picked up Mongo at the ramshackle adobe house Mongo rented on the edge of Long Beach. When the dirt-encrusted fat man got into the van, Wolfe could see where he'd gotten his name. Prematurely bald, with the fringe of hair shaven off into a total bullet-head, and with a Fu Manchu mustache, Mongo had a vaguely Oriental look.

Before leaving the clubhouse, Wolfe had looked at Carmelita as if to grab her pocketbook to deposit his .45. Fat Phil had caught the gesture and said, "No. Keep it. Might be a long day, ya know?" Wolfe had just pulled his sweat-soaked T-shirt over the gun in the waistband. Even though the Colt automatic was big, it was flat in silhouette, and it concealed easily under the dark shirt in the hollow of his hip. Anyone who looked at it was less likely to see a bulge than the ostentatious letters that read, Friends Don't Let Friends Ride Rice-Burners.

Now the nondescript GMC van was parked a block away from County General Hospital. They sat in silence, sipping beer, as they waited for the brown Dodge they'd given Cindy to pull out of the parking lot marked Admissions And Discharges.

"There it is," said Klaus. The compact brown sedan wasn't hard to spot. Cindy had flashed her headlights twice as she turned onto the main road. Snake, at the wheel, hit the ignition and sent the van out after her.

They followed her for two blocks before she turned. The whole time Fat Phil and the others were watching for pickup cars, tails. There were none. No one but the outlaws knew that the wanted murderer had just been checked out of the hospital. Thanks to Wanda, the task force assembling now at the sheriff's substation only knew that Richard "Rax" Higgins dwelt at 1246 Carson Boulevard in Long Beach, and that's where they were going to get him. Dead or alive. That's why they were donning bulletproof vests and checking the chambers of their Remington 12-gauge shotguns and their H&K MP-5 submachine guns even now.

Two more turns down obscure side streets, and Cindy's car pulled over. The Princes of Hell van swept in behind it. They waited in the vehicle as Rax laboriously climbed out of the little sedan, his left arm in a cast to the shoulder and his jeans bulging with the heavy bandages that bound his left knee.

Cindy got out and helped him to the van.

"Thanks, honey," said Fat Phil from the front seat. "That'll do it, babe. I'm gonna call ya. We got a special party coming up for you foxes that been helping us out this week." Cindy's chubby face rippled with a thankful smile before she turned and walked back to her car.

Klaus, the nearest to the van's side door, swung the panel back and open. He reached down to help Rax inside. The movement hurt the chunky power-lifter, and Rax was gasping when he said, "Geez, Phil, it's good to see you guys—"

Rax's grin disappeared suddenly. He'd seen Harry in the back seat. Harry let the smile spread across his face, exposing his canine teeth.

"Phil," blurted Rax. "That's the guy! That's the mother—"

Phil shut him off with a curt gesture. "Be cool, Rax. This is Johnny. He's running with us now. Long story. We'll fill you in."

Klaus reached over, and the van door closed behind Rax with a decisively final clang.

IT TOOK ALMOST an hour to reach the high canyons. The barren wasteland was only dirt blown through scrub bushes, the land eroded in deep gullies. They passed a sign that said State Forest. It was hard not to laugh. There were almost no trees.

But there was almost nothing else, either. Soon the van pulled off on a deserted narrow pathway, and Fat Phil said, "Everybody out."

They piled out of the van, most of them with beers in their hands. Klaus and Snake and Mongo and Phil stood by the van. Wolfe and Rax got a couple of steps before they realized no one was going with them, and they were standing alone. They turned toward the van.

Fat Phil reached into his pocket and drew his gleaming hammerless revolver. He aimed it, from the hip, at Wolfe. The others also drew their guns. Snake and Mongo had .45 automatics. In Klaus's hand was a huge, ugly .44 Magnum revolver.

All the guns were leveled at Harry.

The effect of the methamphetamine had been almost nonexistent. It had just kept him awake, against the exhaustion and the beer. But now he felt the proverbial cold chill down his spine.

They've found me out, Wolfe thought. And they're going to kill me.

For an instant he thought of Carmelita. And then survival brought him back. He was acutely aware of the loaded pistol behind his hip. He braced himself to go for it, wondering how many of these bastards he could take with him before the firestorm from their handguns tore his body apart.

"All *right*," blurted Rax. "Righteous, Phil, righteous! This damn bastard deserves it! You shoulda seen Big Henry n the hospital, man! This bastard fucked him up bad!"

"I know," said Fat Phil. "But that ain't why we're here."

Rax didn't understand. He furrowed his eyebrows quiz-zically. He turned to Fat Phil.

Phil's gun was pointed at Rax's belly now. So were the pistols of Mongo and Snake.

It took Wolfe a second to see what was happening. When it came together, the sense of relief was small. Klaus's heavy revolver was still pointing at Harry Wolfe's belly, and the icy blue eyes had never left his face.

"You fucked up, Rax," Fat Phil told him sadly. "Fucked up big-time. You were like my number-two man.

"Goddamn, man, you know how embarrassing it is for me? You got that position, you speak for me, you stand for me, and in front of Klaus you make me look bad to the Big Four? You make the Princes of Hell look like a bunch of stupid assholes?"

Rax's face suddenly seemed removed, unrelated to the power-lifter's huge body. It was the face of a desperate child. "Phil," he bleated. "What'd I do, man? I done everything for you, Phil. I killed for you, man!"

Fat Phil hawked and and spit into the dirt. "Yeah, you killed for me, all right. You got into your damn ego trip with Klaus and had to fuck up all the plans I laid out!

"They know what you did in Denver, Rax!" Fat Phil was yelling now. "They're coming for ya right goddamn now! You just had to be mister big shit and do it your way, not mine!"

The big man's face crumpled. Rax was sobbing like a child. It was grotesque.

"I'm sorry, man," he blubbered. "I done it for you, Phil! I done it for the Princes! The Princes is all, man!" Rax broke down into sobs.

Fat Phil's lip curled in contempt. "Johnny," he barked. "C'mere!"

Wolfe moved cautiously forward, his eyes not leaving the ugly, squat revolver in Klaus's hand. The muzzle of Klaus's .44 Magnum followed Wolfe as he moved forward.

"Two fingers, Johnny," said Phil. "Reach down and take out your gun with two fingers and hand it to me."

They had the drop on him, and he knew it. There was no choice but to play along. With his thumb and forefinger, Harry slowly drew the Colt .45 automatic from inside his belt and extended the gun to Fat Phil.

The gang leader took the pistol slowly and carefully with his left hand, his right still curled around the snub-nosed revolver that looked like a toy in his enormous fist. With his left index finger, Phil touched the magazine release button behind the trigger of Harry's pistol. The clip, with its seven gleaming copper-jacketed bullets, fell into the dirt.

"Down to one, Johnny, the one in the chamber," Phil said loud and clear. He thrust the pistol toward Wolfe. "Take it, Johnny."

Wolfe obeyed and took the gun.

"We're the Princes of Hell, Johnny," Fat Phil said. "We're a million miles beyond the Iron Horsemen. If you'd been running with us when you took on the Mafia, we woulda had the balls and the horsepower to back you up.

"You got balls, brother. You're where you belong. Rax had balls, but he never had no brains. He's gonna send us all to prison.

"Do him, Johnny. Be one of us. Ride with the best, forever. Do him!"

Wolfe stood, the pistol in his hand, knowing there was only the one bullet in the firing chamber. He was facing four men. Snake and Mongo had now turned their .45s toward him. Klaus's Magnum had never left its aim, dead center on Wolfe's body. Fat Phil, looking very tired, let his hand with the little revolver in it slide down until it was pointed harmlessly at the ground.

When Wolfe spoke, he was surprised at the calmness of his own voice. "Phil," he said, "Rax never did anything to me but fight me. I took care of it, me and him. That's why his arm's in a cast. He didn't do anything to me worth killing for."

Phil looked back at him, eyes wild. "It ain't just you, Johnny," he said with a crazy urgency in his voice. "The Princes are all you got left. Rax is gonna die here. Only choice you got now is whether you die, too. Shoot him, and you ride out of here beside me like my brother. Don't shoot him, you die here next to him. There ain't no choice no more, man. You gotta kill him.

"Kill him!"

18

In the searing heat of the canyon, Harry Wolfe stood alone. He was surrounded by men with guns, but in his mind he was alone. Alone except for Rax.

He turned and looked at the bearded biker he'd been told to kill. The powerful man's lips were quivering, and his whole body was shaking. Rax was trying to talk, and no words would come out.

Time stood still.

Wolfe was Code Zero. He had come here to kill. He was a licensed executioner and he could count on his fingers the number of people in the world who knew who and what he was. None of these men did.

They were ordering him to commit murder. Once, Harry Wolfe *had* committed murder. There was a part of him that would do it again and a part that never let him forgive himself for the act that had brought him over the edge and given him the choice of Code Zero or prison.

None of these men understood what was happening. They were going to kill today. That was what they had come for, too. And the two parts of Harry Wolfe fought each other for dominance.

You're not one of them, said his more self-sacrificing part. It's better to die than to commit murder on the command of an animal.

But then the other part said, He's going to die anyway. Your only choice is whether you die with him or not. If you kill him, you survive.

But the other side cried, You didn't become a cop for this. You became a cop to protect people from murderers, not to become one yourself!

The second part of Wolfe answered, Rax is one of the ones you came to get! Remember what Brian Voit said in his tortured last words! It was Rax who held that little girl down while they tried to make Voit rape her! It was probably Rax who killed her afterward, or helped to!

The harsh voice of Fat Phil Newell interrupted Wolfe's thoughts. "Do him, man! Do him! Don't make me kill you, too!"

The fat man is right, the prompting came again from Wolfe's mind. *Rax will die today anyway. If I don't pull the trigger, I'll die, too. And then they'll murder Carmelita. They'll have to. But if I kill him... I'll be able to make the case that avenges Voit.*

"Do it, man!" Fat Phil was screaming now. "Do it, Johnny! *Do it!*"

Harry Wolfe shook his head, trying to clear it of the opposing thoughts. He knew what he had to do. His eyes focused on the face of Rax Higgins. The man's jaw was quivering, drool running into his beard. Rax was trying to talk, but only small animal noises came out.

Wolfe took a deep breath. He raised the stainless automatic, unconscious of its heavy weight at the end of his arm. His hand did not tremble at all, and that surprised him. He changed his visual focus from Rax's face to the sights of the gun. They were lined up at the bridge of Rax's nose. Wolfe and the big biker were about ten feet apart.

Wolfe's finger lightly touched the trigger. His thumb pressed the safety down. There was an audible snick as the lever went into the Fire position.

The cold feeling lay in Wolfe's belly like lead. It was a point of no return. The first part of himself was falling away, asking its last distant question: *Are you sure?*

Wolfe took a deep breath. He thought of the dead fifteen-year-old girl that the man in front of his gun had held down for the rape. He thought about the murdered marshal in Denver.

His trigger finger tightened.

Rax Higgins blurted one last word. "No!"

"Yes," said Harry Wolfe, clearly and coldly.

He pulled the trigger.

19

The blast of the .45 automatic was explosive, but Wolfe never actually heard it. He was only aware that the sights were in line in the center of Rax's face as the gun bucked, and suddenly Rax's face was not there anymore.

The bullet had entered barely below the bridge of Rax Higgins's nose, traveling at just under the speed of sound. Nearly a half inch in diameter, the heavy slug had driven through the soft cartilage of the nose and into the brain of the outlaw biker, tearing apart the medulla oblongata and killing the entire central nervous system instantly before it crashed out through the base of the skull in a spray of bloody mist that stood the dirty dark hair on end for a moment in the bullet's jet-stream wake.

Like a puppet with its strings cut, the corpse of Richard Higgins dropped heavily to the dirt floor of the canyon. The big man lay like a sack of laundry.

Wolfe lowered the pistol and looked down on the man he had killed. He could see the stains spreading over Rax's jeans as the sphincters relaxed in death. The eyes stared vacantly. Blood flowed lazily from the hole where the nose had been, pooling in the orbital sockets and obscuring the eyes whose pupils were already dilating in instant death.

Everyone stood very still for a long moment.

The pistol's mechanism had cocked itself on an empty chamber from the recoil. Wolfe brought his thumb to the hammer, brought it back to trip the grip safety and then held the trigger back with his index finger as he eased the hammer down. He turned the gun in his hand and held it out to Fat Phil Newell, butt first.

They looked at each other, the undercover agent and the outlaw bike gang leader. Wolfe's eyes were cold and dead. Newell's eyes brimmed with tears.

Fat Phil shoved his own revolver into his trouser pocket. He brushed angrily at the gun Wolfe offered him, and the pistol fell to the dirt of the canyon floor.

Phil reached forward, extended his arms and hugged Harry close to him. "Goddamn, man," he said emotionally. "Goddamn! I *knew* you were cool. I knew it!"

He turned defiantly to the muscular blond giant with the .44 Magnum. "Whaddya say now, Klaus? Now do ya fucking trust my judgment?"

Slowly Klaus Richter lowered his revolver. After a long moment he said, "Johnny, I owe you an apology. Phil too. We just had a couple of bad times here recently, people who ratted us out, and—well, never mind. You passed the test. I'm sorry."

Klaus Richter extended his hand. Harry Wolfe waited a moment before he reached out and took it. The power of the man's handshake was crushing. But Wolfe had done his hundreds of reps a day with the grip squeezers, and he crushed back. He couldn't crush the bigger man's hand, but Klaus couldn't hurt him, either. He saw a new glow of respect in the blond man's eye.

Fat Phil spun toward Klaus Richter triumphantly. "I bet you never had an initiation like this in the Big Four," he said.

Klaus nodded slowly. "You're right," he said. "At least, not this fast." He turned back to Wolfe. "Welcome, my brother."

Fat Phil turned to Snake. "Pick up his gun and give it to him," he barked. "And give him the clip. Here. Lock and load, Johnny. You're one of us now."

Fat Phil paused, and then laughed giddily. "Hey, Johnny! 'Johnny?' It sounds like a kid's name! You gotta have a real name, like a real Prince of Hell! Listen, I remember what it sounded like when you was fighting at the Red Wing! Remember all them crunchin' sounds? Hey, Klaus, remember when I said we gotta sign up with fuckin' Blue Cross, pay for all the bones my man here busted last night?

"From now on, you ain't just Johnny no more! I'm gonna christen you right now into the Princes of Hell. From now on, you got a new name.

"Welcome to the brotherhood, Bonebreaker!"

Klaus and Snake went through Rax's clothing while Harry stood by the van reloading his .45 automatic. There was nothing, not even a driver's license or a gun. Cindy, the biker mama, had taken it all with her. Klaus made a mental note to pick it up later and destroy it. He wondered if he shouldn't destroy Cindy, too. But that was something he could deal with another time. Klaus picked up the ejected shell casing and slipped it into his pocket. He spent a minute kicking sand over the footprints they'd left behind. The van had been parked on a gravel road, and there were no tire tracks to worry about.

They all climbed into the van. Snake drove. Wolfe sat in the middle seat next to Fat Phil. Klaus was sitting behind him, but he didn't worry about that anymore.

"Here," said Fat Phil reaching under the seat, pulling out the fancy .45 he'd shown Harry earlier that morning. "My gun. My baby. It's loaded, cocked and locked. Take it. Gimme yours. I'm gonna drop it off with some guys that work for me. By tomorrow it's gonna be back with you, with a new barrel in case they ever find the bullet. Don't worry about the extractor marks or anything like that. We're gonna melt the spent shell tonight. They'll never connect it."

Dully Harry went through the motions of swapping guns, pausing only to check the magazine and the firing chamber of Phil's fancy .45 combat pistol. "Thanks," he said absently, shoving the pistol into his belt.

"If you're half as tired as me, you're ready to crash," Phil said jovially. "Snake, gimme my cellular phone. I'm gonna call Doreen, see where she put the Bonebreaker's lady. We'll drop him off there. Bonebreaker, m'man, I'll give you a few hours and then I'll call ya tonight and we'll party. It's gonna take me a coupla days, but I'm gonna bring ya up to speed in the best fuckin' outfit in this country!"

Wolfe forced a wan smile. That second, the practical part of him was beginning to realize that he'd just set a speed record for infiltrating an organized crime gang. But that nagging first half was reminding him that he was a murderer.

So what, thought Wolfe as he reached to the cooler for another beer. I was technically a murderer before I came here. Maybe I'm where I belong after all.

As they drove down the canyon toward greater Los Angeles, the sun was high in the sky and the colors were vivid. But to Wolfe the landscape seemed washed out, as if it was worn away and dead, the way a part of himself seemed to be.

20

The hotel Doreen had picked for her new friends was the Holiday Inn at LAX, Los Angeles International Airport, on Century and La Cienega. The choice had been almost reflexive. It was an hour from the club, but an hour for Angelenos was like driving down the street. Besides, it was the hotel where Phil had her put up the dealers who came to buy methamphetamines from his speed laboratory. Dealers were nervous and liked to be close to the airport. In any case, it was easy to facilitate; the Princes of Hell had a regular account with the LAX Holiday Inn, under their corporate name, PHI. The hotel keepers had no idea who they were dealing with. Doreen had remembered the time when a couple of Phil's clients had turned pale with horror, learning that they were in the hotel at the same time the Police Marksmen Association was holding an advanced officer-survival seminar there. It was the only time any of Phil's customers had requested a change of hotel.

The van dropped him off brazenly out front. Wolfe drew a few sidelong glances when he walked up to the desk and said simply, "Parker." The man behind the desk gave him the punched-out plastic key with a disdainful look. Skinheads with filthy T-shirts weren't the standard Holiday Inn clientele. On the other hand, anybody seemed able to fly in and out of LAX these days. For all the desk man knew, he'd see this dirty, sweat-soaked customer on MTV that night.

Wolfe made his way to room 1128. He knocked before he entered. He knew what Carmelita Morales's reflexes would be if she was suddenly intruded open, and in any case, she was smart enough to have the door double-locked from inside.

The familiar voice from inside said, "Yes?"

"Me," he answered simply, surprised to hear the exhaustion in his own voice.

After a moment of snicking and snacking, the bolts were undone from the inside, and the door seemed to open by itself. There was no one visible. Wolfe stepped slowly inside.

Carmelita was behind the door. She closed it and double-locked it. Wolfe saw the snub-nosed .38 revolver was in her right hand.

She was wearing panties and a cutoff T-shirt. Her hair was mussed from sleep. Even without makeup, Wolfe saw, she was striking.

He'd never touched her sexually, never even made a move on her. When they'd met, she had been going through something incredibly hard. It had been near-rape. Wolfe was acutely conscious of not forcing anything sexual with her. Their relationship had evolved into a brother-sister thing. Still...

She looked up at him. "Jesus, Harry," she breathed, "what happened?"

He shook his head, forced himself to smile. "Nothing," he heard himself say. "I'm okay. Just a ride in the canyon, shooting the shit. Looks like I'm in with them."

He was spent. He sagged against the wall.

Reflexively Carmelita reached out to him, hugged him. He clung to her fiercely. He felt her stiffen for a moment, and then, like a warm flow, she was together with him.

He didn't kiss her, just buried his face in her long black hair. "God," he said, "it's good to be back with you." They stood like that for a long moment.

Wolfe could feel something invisible, electrical, between them. He had wanted her since the first moment he'd seen her. But not now, not like this. Not with blood on his hands.

"I need a shower," he said. "I'm spent."

Reluctantly Carmelita stepped away from him.

"I'll wait for you," she said softly.

The shower and the closet area were an anteroom away from the rest of the semisuite. Carmelita heard him set his pistol on the sink, heard the soft sounds of his clothing dropping to the floor. Their clothes, what there were of them, had been in a duffel bag on the back of the bike. Doreen had made sure that the retrieved motorcycle was dropped off that afternoon. It was parked outside, and fresh undershorts, socks, jeans and T-shirts were hanging up in the closet for him.

She heard him turn on the shower. Why did I tell Doreen he'd be kind and gentle and a great lover? She answered her own mental question. Because I know him. I've seen him hard and I've seen him tender. I've been with him when I was vulnerable and I was with him the first time I killed a man in the line of duty. I've had to keep myself remote from every male agent I ever worked with, because I knew how hard I fought to be where I am and I knew what their locker-room bragging would do to my reputation. But I also know that he won't brag. I know I am safe with him. And I know I want him.

The shower was still running. How long was he going to take?

Carmelita looked in the mirror, assessed herself. No makeup, but she didn't think that would matter. Hair all frizzy from sleeping on it. She'd awakened when he came to the door. Wait! Morning mouth! Yech! When he came out, she'd do her teeth, perhaps a fast shower....

But he was still in there. What was taking him so long? When had *she* ever taken that long a shower? They joked about women taking so long in the bathroom....

Then she remembered. The last time she'd taken an interminable shower was after she'd been held hostage. It wasn't just that her body stank. It was as if she was washing the filth and the helplessness away from her. She knew that rape victims did the same thing, stood under the hot shower forever and scrubbed themselves raw, trying to rub away the filth of the predators who'd touched them.

She remembered the way he looked when he'd come in. He had actually sagged against the wall. She didn't think it was just tiredness. Oh, God, what had he been through today? What was he trying to wash away?

After a while the rush of water stopped. A minute later Wolfe came out of the shower, a towel wrapped around his waist. He walked past her like a zombie and dropped onto one of the two queen-size beds.

"Give me a minute," Carmelita said.

Her shower was fast. She brushed her teeth furiously, rinsed out her mouth with a mouthwash. She realized she was naked. Towel? T-Shirt?

The hell with it, she thought. She took one proud glance in the mirror. What she saw was an exquisitely formed woman, firm breasts tipped with hard brown flesh, the body marred only by the three dark scars where bullets had stopped on her ballistic vest but left their brutal marks beneath. And the scar on her forehead. Quickly she brushed her hair over it. She didn't know why. Harry had seen it when it was fairly fresh.

She wondered for a moment if she could do this. She was Mexican Catholic. Her mother had brought her up to believe that her body belonged only to her husband.

Mother, she thought silently, he's closer than a husband could be, and I think I trust him more.

Carmelita Morales took a deep breath. Then, naked, she stepped out of the foyer and walked toward Harry Wolfe's bed.

Wolfe did not move. He was facedown. His arm hung down to the floor, and his eyes were closed. His back rose and fell with his breathing, gently, rhythmically.

Carmelita looked down at him. She saw that while she'd been in the shower, he'd gotten up and gone back to the sink and taken his .45 to put next to the bed. She looked down at it again. That wasn't Harry's gun, the one she'd fired to cover him in the bar fight last night. She recognized it now. The fancy wood grips, the recurved grip safety, the plastic warning strip the government made gunsmiths put on the side of the frame when they installed radioactive night sights. It was the gun Fat Phil had been showing off to them this morning.

She sighed. Harry had indeed had one hell of a day, and she'd be damned if she'd wake him up to ask him about it. Or for anything else.

She smiled ruefully. Before she went to the other bed, she traced one slender finger down her sleeping partner's spine to his buttocks. The flesh was smooth but firm. He did not react. She felt herself smile, and she said one word, softly and warmly. "Sleep."

21

The dreams tortured Wolfe. The men he had killed were back to exact vengeance in swirling red mists.

"You had no right," said the yuppie drug dealer, his hands dripping blood and his expensive leather jacket puckered from the bullets from Harry's gun.

"You had no right," echoed the wasted young Latino man, his automatic rifle still hanging on its sling across his chest and the black haft of Harry's knife still protruding from what used to be his eye.

"You had no right," shrieked the dark-faced killer, his features huge in the cross hairs of Harry's rifle scope just before his head exploded again, the way it had the first time.

Rax didn't say anything at all. He just stood there, waving his arm in the cast from where Harry had shattered it, the blood pouring from the black hole in this face that had been made when Harry's .45 slug had sucked his nose into his brain, the eyes still crying and the lips still quivering.

They all came toward him. Harry felt a gun in his hand. It wasn't the .45 but his own pistol, the Glock 9 mm, and he pulled the trigger. But instead of the crash of a high-powered gunshot there was only a soft thud. He could see the bullet hitting Rax in slow motion and bouncing off. He kept firing, but instead of shots, there were only muted knocking sounds, and the walking corpses of the men he had killed kept coming toward him. He fired madly, and the pistol only went knock, knock, knock.

Knock, knock, knock.

Wolfe shot bolt upright in the bed. From the other bed, nearer the hotel room door, he saw a flash of brown skin as Carmelita Morales came to her feet, a small blue revolver in her hand. Wolfe's reaction was instinctive. His right hand dived to the side of the bed and closed on the checkered grips of the Colt .45 automatic.

She was at the door now. He saw her turn toward him. "It's all right," she whispered. "It's Doreen. I told her to come."

Wolfe brought the shiny automatic under the covers. Carmelita opened the door, stepping behind it the way she had when she'd let him in hours ago. Wolfe glanced at the LED clock on the TV complex. It was almost 10:00 p.m. He had slept for seven hours.

"You guys know each other," Carmelita said slyly. She slipped into the alcove where the closet and shower were located.

The tall woman moved forward confidently, toward the bed. Wolfe smiled. It wasn't something he had to force. In the soft light Doreen Newell was strikingly beautiful.

"We haven't exactly been introduced," she said, extending her hand. "I'm Doreen."

"H-" Wolfe caught himself. "Hi. Johnny."

"Bonebreaker, you mean. Phil didn't stop talking about you till he passed out an hour ago." Her hand was as strong as a man's as they shook, but soft and feminine. That was a new experience for Harry.

Doreen sat down on the bed. Carmelita came back into the room, wearing jeans and a plain black French-cut T-shirt. She picked up her shoulder bag and inserted her .38.

"I'm going to go down and have a drink or two. Or three. I'll be in the lounge. Johnny, Doreen is my very *special* friend, and I've promised her great things. Don't disappoint me."

Wolfe could only manage a silly grin.

Carmelita looked at Doreen and smiled. "Enjoy," she said, and there was something poignant in her voice that Wolfe couldn't quite catch. Then she was gone, the door locking shut behind her.

Doreen Newell stood up. "This is gonna surprise you," she said, the nervousness clear in her voice. "But I'm awfully damn new to this."

"That's okay," said Wolfe gently. "I'm not."

Doreen shook her long hair. Then, with just a moment of hesitation, she unzipped her green dress. It fell away. She was wearing nothing underneath.

Wolfe looked at her admiringly. She was big without being fat. Her breasts stood firm, the light pink nipples hard. She kicked away her shoes. Her pubic hair was natural, untrimmed.

She was a strong woman, but Wolfe sensed fear, like a startled doe in the forest. This, he thought, is a biker bitch who killed three men?

Slowly he lifted the .45 and put it on the far side of the bed, on the floor. Then he peeled back the sheets, leaving an open space on his left. He reached his hand out to her.

She took it. Her own hand was trembling. She came into the bed with him, and suddenly grabbed the cover and pulled it up over herself. It was the gesture of a frightened child.

"You've been hurt," he said.

"Yes."

"I won't hurt you."

"I know," she said, and suddenly she was against him, strong but soft, hard but innocent, a beautiful paradox. Wolfe felt himself responding. He tasted her, and she responded, too.

FORTY MINUTES LATER they lay in each other's arms, exhausted, covered with a sheen of sweat. Doreen's long brown hair felt silky soft against his shoulder as she nuzzled him. "That was so good," she murmured.

"Mmm," Harry said. He was thinking, they told me biker women were scuzzy and filthy. This woman is fresh and clean and sweet.

Her fingers traced over the hair on his belly. "It's so good to touch a stomach that doesn't feel like Jell-O." She sighed. Her hand went down farther. "Ooh! That doesn't feel like Jell-O, either. Can I take that as a compliment?"

Wolfe kissed her gently and said, "What do you think?"

"I don't know what to think. Johnny, I've only been with two men. One was my stepfather. The only time he was good to me was when he was doing it to me, and after I was fifteen and as tall as he was, he said I was big and ugly and he didn't want me around anymore. Phil says I'm an old fat frigid cow."

Wolfe held her close. "I think they're both full of shit. I think you're young and you're beautiful."

"I'm twenty-six, Johnny. That's not young. And you didn't address 'frigid.'"

Wolfe laughed. "Twenty-six qualifies as 'baby fox' as far as I'm concerned. And anybody who thinks you're frigid hasn't seen the kind of wet spot you leave."

Doreen giggled nervously. "You *like* that?"

Wolfe kissed her gently again. "You kidding? You climaxed like a warm flood. If I don't wash off, it's going to dry and my crotch is going to look like a glazed doughnut."

They laughed together. "Christ," she said, "the one and only time I climaxed with Phil, he said I pissed on him and he slapped me damn near unconscious."

Harry hugged her close with a protective reflex. "Doesn't know piss from come," he muttered. "That's Bartholin's fluid. Comes from your Bartholin's gland inside your vagina. When you get that wet, it means you're really turned on. What it means is, you're one hell of a responsive woman."

Doreen giggled and hugged him back. She reached down and touched him and said, "You're no slouch yourself."

The invitation was in her words. She backed it up as she pulled him onto her, into her.

IT WAS nearly eleven-thirty. Doreen Newell lay back blissfully, her pretty face surrounded by the cascade of brown hair. Harry moved slowly down her body, kissing her everywhere. Suddenly he stopped.

"What's that?"

He felt her tense. "Phil did it," she said tightly. "When I was sixteen, the first year we were married. I wouldn't take him in my mouth that night. I don't remember why. He had a cigarette. He did . . . that."

The dark, round discolorations tracked from her abdomen to her thighs. He touched them with his fingers.

"Don't," she cried out, ashamed.

"I'm sorry," he said.

She started to sob. "Don't be sorry. Please. It's been so good...."

He held her close. She buried her face in his chest, and he felt the tears rolling down his pectorals. "He doesn't deserve you," Wolfe said softly.

"I had to get out," she said in a tiny voice. "My stepfather would have killed me. Phil took me away, married me. It was better. For a while. Now...I don't know. Something happened, never mind what, but Phil doesn't hurt me anymore. There's no love. There's no caring. But at least I survive."

She looked up at him. In the dim light Wolfe could see that unbelievable innocence in her azure eyes, an innocence that dwelt within strength and survival. He had come here to destroy her husband. Now, more than ever, he knew he was right.

He held her close.

"It's never been like this," she said.

He kissed her, deep. Her strong hands pressed him, rolled him onto his back. She reached down, found him hard and slid on top of him. "I need you so much," she breathed as she began her violent movement, pulling him deep inside her.

IT WAS ALMOST ONE when the phone rang. Doreen reflexed like a startled cat, her back arching.

"It's all right," Harry whispered soothingly. "I'll get it." In the dim light he could see fear in her face.

He picked up the phone. "Yuh," he said.

"Yuh, yourself," answered Carmelita Morales. "They're closing the bar and I'm too young to be a bag lady. Can I come back up?"

Wolfe looked at Doreen and smiled. "Elita," he said, and he watched the relief flood the biker woman's face. "Come on up, sweetheart," he said.

By the time Carmelita entered the room, Doreen's dress was back on and Harry had pulled on his jeans, the .45 tuck nonchalantly in the waistband behind his hip.

Doreen reached out impulsively and hugged Carmelita. "Thank you," she breathed. "I've dreamed of a night like this. I hope you know how lucky you are."

Carmelita forced a smile. "No problem. Leave any for me?"

"Elita." Doreen laughed. "You weren't kidding. He goes on forever. He is a renewable resource. But if I were you two, I'd get some sleep. Phil has plans for the Bone-breaker."

She turned to Harry. "He's going to take you around, show you everything he does. He told me he wants you to be his new right-hand man. Says he's fed up with the pussies the Princes have been turning into. Even Klaus accepts you, and that's something."

"What," Harry asked casually, "is the big deal with Klaus?"

Doreen laughed scornfully. "Klaus is Phil's entry to the Big Four, the big time, or so he thinks. It's like the Princes are Jeep, and Phil wants to be General Motors, and he thinks Klaus is the way to get there. But, hey, Jeep's good enough. We make a lot of money, Johnny, and you'll get a good piece of it, you and Elita. God, it's going to be good to have a woman there that I can relate with!"

She turned to Carmelita. "Elita," she said, "are you really sure...?"

Carmelita hugged her spontaneously. "Really sure," she said, laughing. "Now do you believe me?"

"Yes," said Doreen. "I believe you. And I love you both."

She pecked Elita on the cheek. Doreen said, "Can I...?"

Carmelita nodded, smiling impishly.

Doreen was in his arms then, her tongue deep in his mouth. Harry held her close. After a long moment they separated.

"I love you both," Doreen repeated breathlessly, and then she swirled through the door.

After a long moment Carmelita said, "You give a whole new meaning to the term 'undercover.'"

"Hey," protested Wolfe, "this was your idea."

Carmelita sighed. Perhaps, she thought, her mother was right about all this after all.

"Just one thing," she said.

Wolfe followed her glance to his rumpled bed. "Yeah?"

"I get the dry bed," Carmelita said.

22

The days passed in a way that didn't relate to real time, after the killing of Rax Higgins.

Wolfe had known in his life days that never seemed to end, sometimes long with pleasure and sometimes interminable with pain. The deaths of his mother and father were timeless-pain days. And the day he'd found his fiancée dead.

But there had been good long days, too. His first karate tournament, the fighting that had begun at nine in the morning and ended just short of midnight, when no one was left to stand against him anymore and the *sensei* was beside him, glowing with pride. The first day with Master Burline, the aikido *sensei,* who had opened a new world to him where it wasn't necessary to punch or kick, and technique had flowed into technique as he learned to use the force of the *uke,* the opponent, against him without spending his own effort. Or his first whole day with the first woman he loved.

And then there were days that mixed. The day of Rax, the day of Doreen. A long and timeless day. The confrontation with the horrifying fact that he could be a cold-blooded murderer, and the reassurance of knowing that Carmelita had guessed right, that he could be a gentle lover, and that he could enjoy a beautiful woman long and deep like a fine wine. That he could give, as well as take.

Then there were the days that went by like nothing, not because they were forgettable, but because there was nothing deep in them, either way. Those were the days he had spent with Fat Phil and the other members of the Princes of Hell this past week. The tour of the submachine gun factory in Long Beach, the visit to the methamphetamine laboratory in the mountains of San Juan Capistrano inland from San Diego. Wolfe's trained mind had recorded everything he saw, and within a day he'd managed to get to a random pay phone to call in his mental notes to the secured line at Centac headquarters. He saw it, recorded it, repeated it where it had to be repeated and then erased his mind. He had done the same as a young college student before law school. The law-school things, he still remembered. What he hadn't needed, he'd kept only long enough to repeat and then wiped away.

The Princes of Hell dwelt in a drugged and boozy world. Wolfe sipped the beer and took the occasional toke on a reefer. He was accepted and he had nothing to prove. He took the days as they came, accepting what he had become, building the evidence. He didn't know why—he would never testify, because his goal was to destroy these men, not to try them in a court of law. It was as if each bit of evidence he gathered had to be stored somewhere to prove the righteousness of what he had done and what he was going to do, and once that was done, he needed it no more.

He existed to punish murderers, yet he had committed murder himself. He could still see the pathetic face of Rax, so hard on the outside and so soft and weak on the inside, disappearing from in front of the gun sights when he had pulled the trigger of the Colt .45 pistol. But he still felt the animal warmth of Doreen Newell. Almost every night, sometimes deep into the morning, always waiting for Phil to crash out first, she would come to him at the hotel.

He rode now with the panhead Harley throbbing between his legs, Carmelita behind him, her soft warm breasts pressing against his back and her firm arms tight around his waist. Beside them, riding in tandem, would be Fat Phil on his trike. Phil's thirty-thousand-dollar custom machine needed the three wheels to balance his weight. Doreen would ride pillion behind Phil on runs, her long brown hair straight in the wind behind her. Harry wondered what she was thinking.

Wolfe had begun to understand why motorcycles captivated these people. They referred to the ride as being "in the wind." The countryside would rush past them, more speed only a twist of the throttle away. Freedom. Power. Probably the same reason so many people liked guns.

But, as with guns, a fraction of one percent of people couldn't handle the power. It took them over, changed their life-styles, their values. That was what had happened to Phil and the Princes.

It had been ten days since the bar fight at the Red Wing. Nine days since the death of Rax. Wolfe found himself beginning to like the life-style, beginning to relish sleeping with the outlaw chief's woman.

He knew it had to end. Soon. And he knew he had to be the one to end it. He could see it in Carmelita's eyes. He was the senior partner and she looked to him for leadership, but he knew that in some ways she was the wiser one, the one who better understood timing.

Time was something he didn't seem to understand as well as he used to.

23

On the twelfth day after the bar fight at the Red Wing, Klaus and Fat Phil were in Doreen's car, the new yellow Lincoln Continental, driving back from the collecting for a shipment of submachine guns out of the Long Beach machine shop.

"I still don't trust him," Klaus said suddenly as he drove. "I know what you're going to say, and I can't tell you why, but I still don't trust him."

Fat Phil, popping the tab on a can of beer from the back seat cooler, snorted. "Look," he said in exasperation. "First, you seen him drop fucking dope. Second, you checked him out yourself, through *Berea!* Third, I checked him out through the *Los Angeles County Sheriff's Office!* And fourth, for chrissakes, you and I both saw him—well, you know!"

Klaus nodded, frustration on his face. "I know, I know. He checks out. Still, there's something there, Phil, you know? Look, I want to go back to Berea next month and tell them, 'Guys, Princes of Hell are what Hell's Angels used to be.' I want to do that, Phil!

"But I'm telling you, man, I swear by these lightning bolts tattooed on my body, there is something about this guy that just makes me break out in a cold sweat. You know?"

"No," burped the huge man next to him. "I don't know. All I know is you got a paranoid trip on the Bonebreaker." He finished his Bud with a long swallow, tossed the empty into the back seat and reached for another from the cooler.

"Shit," said Phil angrily, "I'm outa fuckin' beer. Pull in at the next joint ya see. There's one."

They were passing through a *barrio,* a Mexican-American enclave. Ahead on the right was a *bodega.* The neon signs in the window of the little grocery said Corona Cerveza on one side and Budweiser Beer on the other.

"My kinda place," said Fat Phil as his designated driver wheeled the big vehicle to a stop in front of the tiny store. "Look," he said before he got out of the car, "Klaus, what is there that's gonna bury this shit, make it right with you that Bonebreaker's one of us?"

Klaus thought for a moment. "He never went through the initiation," he said.

"Initiation," blurted Fat Phil incredulously. "He murdered a guy in front of both of us. What the fuck you want for an initiation?"

Klaus knew he was on to something. "Think about it, Phil," he said. "Okay, from when he shot Rax I knew he couldn't be a pig. But look back at what he did before he got here. When Johnny Parker was with the Horsemen, he took on the Mafia. Got his own club in trouble. Then ran out on them, left them to deal with the Mafia by themselves. Now, when you think about it, a guy who's arrogant enough to do that has got to be arrogant enough to take on his own brothers. Maybe that's why I'm worried about him."

Phil shook his head in disgust. "So what would a regular initiation make any different?"

"The way you do it," said Klaus with careful emphasis, "you got something on him he can't go to another club with. You initiate him *your* way, the way you did me, he's the club's forever."

Fat Phil couldn't argue the point. "Maybe," he grunted. "Hey, I'm gonna get me some brew. Cover me, here."

He waddled into the *bodega*. The only beer he saw was in a cooler behind the counter. A dark and slender female stood there with her back to him.

"Hey," said Fat Phil.

The girl turned. She was about fifteen, of mixed Mexican and black descent, with long dark hair and small breasts. She was barely five feet tall.

"Can I help you, *señor?*" Her voice was sweetly accented.

Fat Phil's lips came away from his teeth in an involuntary leer. He felt hardness begin in his groin.

"Yeah, honey, I need some Budweiser."

"*Por favor, señor,* I am too young to sell beer. But I will get my father, and he can sell it to you."

She scampered into the back room. Phil stared lasciviously at the small buttocks moving under the white linen of the dress. Old enough to bleat, he thought, old enough to shear.

When a swarthy-looking man his own age came out and asked pleasantly if he could help, Phil gruffly ordered a 12-pack. He dropped a bill on the counter and said, "Keep the fuckin' change," and turned on his heel and left.

Dropping onto the front seat of the car, Phil said, "I been thinking about it in there. Tell ya what, Klaus, you might be right. I can't pull no special favors for nobody. We'll take a few guys from the inner circle and run Bonebreaker through the regular initiation."

Klaus asked, "When?"

Phil popped the top of the first can and said, "What the hell? Why not tonight?"

AT TEN THAT NIGHT Harry and Carmelita were strolling up La Cienega Boulevard.

"It's stagnating, Harry. You know that."

"I know," sighed Wolfe. "It seems like we spent all our plans on how to infiltrate them and not enough time figuring out what to do once we were inside."

"Like dogs chasing a car." Carmelita nodded grimly. "Once we catch it, we don't know what to do with it."

"We want the ones who were at the core of what happened to Brian Voit and his family, and that girl," said Wolfe. "Fat Phil. Big Henry. Thumper. Klaus. Snake. Mongo. Rax is dead already."

"You're sure of that?"

"I'm sure," said Harry. He hated not confiding in Carmelita about the death of Rax Higgins. But it would have been an admission of murder. "I'm convinced they killed him. We know the warrants went down for Rax, we know the cops didn't find him and we know we haven't seen him since. Safe to assume they did him."

Carmelita shrugged. "I guess we can go with that, for now at least. You know the one I want? Mongo. I can still hear Brian Voit on the videotape, talking about watching Mongo cut the Princes of Hell brand into that young girl's leg before they killed her."

Wolfe smiled grimly. "If we can possibly arrange it, I'll make sure he's one of your targets."

"Hey, don't be sarcastic," snapped Carmelita. "I was kidnapped once, remember? I know what that little girl felt. No, I don't, because I wasn't raped and I wasn't murdered, but I can guess what she felt. You have a problem with me doing Mongo? Bearing in mind what both of us are here for?"

Wolfe took a long moment before he said, "No, no problem. I'm sorry, Carmelita. Maybe I'm getting too old for this kind of life. I wish we could put them all in one goddamn room and set it on fire and be done with it, and out of here and gone."

"That sounds like a plan," said Carmelita. It was her turn to be sarcastic. "I think I saw it in *The Howling, Part I*. But we can't lock all the werewolves in a barn and set it on fire, Harry. We have to come up with something."

"Give it time," said Wolfe. "I'm too damn tired to think. Let's go back, get some sleep, see what we can come up with tomorrow."

"We'd better," said Carmelita urgently. "We're dealing with the Princes of Hell, not the Boy Scouts. If we don't come up with something, I've got this awful feeling they will. Remember, you're the one who's sleeping with their president's wife."

IT WAS ELEVEN O'CLOCK, and Ortega's Grocery was closing. Hector Ortega wearily locked the cash register and the front door and shut off the lights. "Maria," he called to his daughter in Spanish, "have you got the back?"

"In a moment, Papa," a girlish voice responded. "The kitty got out the back. I'll get him in a—aaiiee!"

Hearing his daughter's scream, Hector Ortega froze for a moment. Then he lunged forward, grabbing at his cash register where he kept his .38 revolver. *Hijo de puta!* He had locked the damn register!

There was no time left. He heard scuffling at the back door. He ran down the narrow corridor that led to the rear portal.

"Maria! Maria!"

Then he was at the back door. It was open. Across the murky dark of the parking lot, he could see a maroon van, and big men and the white-dressed form of his daughter.

"Maria!"

"Papa!"

Hector was moving forward when he saw one of the men turn toward him, saw the flicker of orange flame at the end of his arm. He never heard the shot. He only felt the impact, like a sledgehammer, into his left shoulder, spinning him around. Then his face was pressed against the rough wood of the back-room floor near the alley door. He couldn't remember falling.

The doors were slamming shut on the van. There were no more people outside it.

"Maria," he cried again.

And the muted answer came back one last time, "Papa!" Then the wheels of the van spun and squealed, and the vehicle was gone. Hector Ortega could only clutch the bloody, burning pain in his shoulder and scream, *"Mi querida. Mi querida!* My baby girl. My baby girl!"

THE PHONE RANG in room 1128 of the Holiday Inn, and Wolfe reached for it. "Yeah?"

"Bonebreaker," said the familiar voice of Phil Newell. "I need you, bro. Now! At the clubhouse. Bring Elita. It's important!"

The phone went dead.

In the bed across from him, Carmelita Morales was up and alert, the covers tight to her throat.

"You said we should do it before they did it for us," said Wolfe. "We may be too late."

Grim-faced, they were out of the room in minutes, and by twelve o'clock Wolfe's panhead was crunching the gravel on the lane that led to the canyon clubhouse of the Princes of Hell. The lights were on inside. Several motorcycles, all Harleys, were parked outside.

"Might be just a party," said Wolfe as he killed the ignition. He left the keys in place. "You ready?"

"Ready as ever," said Carmelita tensely as she slid gracefully off the back of the chopper.

They rapped on the door. "Come on in," said a voice from inside.

Harry and Carmelita walked in.

Arrayed in chairs and on sofas were the inner circle of the Princes of Hell. Snake was almost hopping up and down as he fondled his M-16. Thumper, sitting glumly, looked as if he was scratching his right shoulder with his left hand, but it was only that his dislocated left arm was still held that way in a gauze sling.

Big Henry sprawled in a rocking chair, his crooked left arm in a cast from shoulder to wrist, and his head bound like a mummy's. The bandages covered where his left eye had been. Harry's blow almost two weeks before with the flashlight had caused too much damage, and the doctors had been forced to remove the ruptured eyeball this past week.

Mongo stood leaning against the wall, his shoulders hunched, cracking his knuckles. Klaus was nowhere to be seen.

In the farther corner loomed the bulk of Fat Phil, his arm possessively around Doreen's shoulders. He made her look tiny.

Carmelita was the one who forced a smile and broke the silence.

"Is this a party, or what?"

"Kind of," said Fat Phil.

He let go of Doreen and walked forward. "Bonebreaker, my man," Fat Phil began, "I got some people in my inner circle that still don't accept you like I do. So, here's the deal. This is initiation night. You're coming out with me and my guys here, and we're gonna make you a righteous Prince for once and for all."

Wolfe saw the leers on the men's faces, the uncertainty on Doreen's. "Look," said Harry, "if this is the bullshit about you giving me the colors, I been through that already. If you don't mind, you do the colors without me and I'll wear them later, Phil, okay?"

Fat Phil Newell laughed. It was a forced laugh, loud and false. "Gotta do it, bro. Stand real still for a second. Look at Snake and you'll know why."

Wolfe stood motionless, turning only his eyes. He glanced to the side. Snake was leveling his M-16 machine gun at him and Carmelita.

Wolfe couldn't control his voice. Some men under stress had their voices crack or rise several octaves. When it happened to Wolfe, it was something different, an animal growl. "What the fuck is this, Phil?"

Fat Phil giggled, his voice high-pitched, the way Harry had first heard it that night in the Red Wing bar. "Gotta be done, Bonebreaker. Gotta make things right with the troops, make everybody happy, you know? Let everybody know I made the right decision, let them all know I didn't fuck up when I picked the Bonebreaker to ride beside me!"

Harry shook his head. "Phil . . ."

He didn't get to finish. Snake slid forward, as if on roller skates, and thrust the muzzle of his M-16 against Harry's head. "Don't you move, Mr. *Bone*breaker," Snake sneered. "Put up your hands. Yeah. That's good." Snake reached out and took Harry's .45 from his waistband.

"Elita," said Phil, "you been great for my old lady. No shit. She's like glowin' since she's been hanging around you. She thinks biker women ain't good enough for her to associate with, till you come along."

Phil sneered. "I got mixed feelings about that. I like that she ain't on my case no more. But I ain't too sure you're a good role model. Kickin' the shit outa guys in a bar, like I seen you do, that ain't ladylike, ya know, Elita?

"But, hey, I don't give a shit. I'm what you call a modern guy. My old lady wants to hang out with ya, that's cool.

But tell ya what, honey—I want you to slip that bag right off your shoulder, right now, and let it fall. And I'm gonna go over there and pick it up and take your little .38, 'cause if I don't do that, Snake here is gonna blow your pretty little brown butt all over the clubhouse.''

Carmelita glanced over at Snake. If he's focused on me, she thought, Harry can take him with his hands and get the M-16. But as she turned, she saw that Mongo and Big Henry were also holding guns, blue-steel .45 automatics.

It was hopeless. She flexed her shoulder and let her bag fall to the floor. Phil lumbered forward and picked it up. He extracted the Smith & Wesson Bodyguard .38 and tossed it to Mongo, who caught it in his left hand and shoved it into his hip pocket. Carmelita fixed that in her mind. My gun, she thought. Mongo's hip pocket.

Doreen had to speak. "Phil, she's my friend. My best friend. For—"

Fat Phil spun and cut Doreen off with a backhand slap across the face. She staggered back, blood trickling from her lower lip. She fixed Fat Phil with a look of absolute hatred.

"You son of a bitch!" She swung at him with her fist and caught him a glancing blow on the cheek. It was just enough to knock Fat Phil off balance. He caught himself and, furious, launched a right cross with his whole body weight behind it. The blow caught Doreen on the side of the face with a sickening impact and sent her flying against the nearest wall. She slid down to the floor, unconscious.

Fat Phil rubbed his knuckles. "Can't take shit from bitches, no matter how much you love 'em. Take that as a lesson from me, Bonebreaker. I shouldn't have let your bitch hang out so much with my bitch. Made her too high and mighty. When she wakes up, I'll come back and remind her just who the hell is in charge here."

The big man chortled. "But, hey, I got an interesting night planned for us. It's initiation time! Oh, yeah! C'mon, Bonebreaker, let's go! To the range!"

Snake prodded Harry hard with the muzzle of the M-16, pushing him out the door. Wolfe looked over his shoulder.

He caught a glance from Carmelita that told him she'd be all right. Then he was outside into the night.

Snake pushed Harry forward with the muzzle of the M-16 toward the door of the van. It was open. Harry pulled himself up inside.

"Hello, Bonebreaker," said Klaus Richter.

The big blond man was straddling the form of a small, slender girl. She was wearing a torn white dress that was stark against her dark skin. A strip of the fabric had been used to gag her. Another had been used to tie her wrists cruelly tight behind her.

"Jesus—" Harry couldn't stop himself from saying it.

"Religious, are we? Well," said Klaus solicitously, "don't worry about it. After all, she's only a spic nigger."

Wolfe felt the M-16 muzzle in his back. He choked down the deadly rage that welled inside him.

Fat Phil pulled himself into the driver's seat. The automatic he'd lent Harry and taken back tonight was stuffed in the right front of his capacious waistband. Its sharp hammer dug into the rolls of fat that spilled over his belt, but Fat Phil pretended not to notice.

While Klaus held the girl down in the back seat, Snake got into the middle seat with Harry, pushing him over with the point of the black machine gun. Klaus pulled the door shut behind them.

"To the range," cried Fat Phil, putting the van in gear.

THE VAN HAD LEFT. As soon as the sound of its engine had disappeared, Mongo rushed forward and locked the door. Big Henry shoved his .45 into the front of his belt. Thumper did the same, and hauled himself to his feet.

"Well, well, well," said Thumper. "I do believe it's a choo-choo night."

The lack of understanding must have shown on Carmelita's face. "Choo-choo, baby," he said mockingly. "You know, like train? Like pulling a fucking train?"

Carmelita felt cold. She remembered the term. "Pulling a train" was biker lingo for a gang rape.

"My man is Fat Phil's right-hand guy," she said defiantly. She herself was surprised that her voice did not waver. "You know what's going to happen to you if you gangbang his old lady?"

Big Henry burst out laughing. "Honey," he said, "how long you been around? Last night, we touched you, we'd be dead. That's 'cause last night your man was Fat Phil's asshole buddy. But tonight he is going out for an initiation. That means tonight he ain't nothin' but a wannabe, an' his ol' lady's up for grabs. An' that bastard you been sleepin' with owes me for my eye, you understand?"

"Come on," pleaded Carmelita, groping desperately to buy time. "What about Doreen?"

"The prez put her there. She's his problem, not ours," sneered Thumper.

One word went through Carmelita Morales's mind. "Damn . . . damn!"

24

There was no moon, only starlight, as the van drove into the gravel pit at the edge of the Princes of Hell property. It was what Fat Phil grandiosely called the range. A few wooden slats held target frames against a dune, and there were shards of bottles that had been broken by bullets, and beer cans torn apart by gunfire. Now it was going to be the ground for child rape.

It struck Wolfe as blasphemous. When he was a kid, a range was a place the cops and the soldiers and the town fathers had set aside for decent people to practice shooting in. Kids learned there to be safe with the powerful accoutrements of adulthood. For someone like Phil to use a range at all, let alone for this—it was an obscenity.

"Outa the car, Bonebreaker," Snake sneered sarcastically.

Wolfe stepped out. He was joined by Fat Phil and Klaus, who dragged the sobbing young girl out of the van, dumping her unceremoniously to the ground.

"I don't see the point, Phil," Wolfe said coldly.

"Then you don't understand the point, Bonebreaker," Phil answered. "I told you, man. We all gotta know we got a hundred percent loyalty. Rax is still rotting out there, and I know you're loyal, and I knew from the first you weren't no narc or no DEA or nothing. But we gotta have a bond, man, a bond nobody can cut."

"You're talking about this girl," said Wolfe, looking at the slight figure that curled in on itself, sobbing.

"Yeah, you wanna put it that way," said Fat Phil. "To me, she's just a niglet, you know? We was all born a hundred fifty years or so too late. There was a time in this country when white men were *white* men, *ran* things, you know?"

"Shit, Phil, I guess we had a misunderstanding," said Harry. "I thought you were bringing me into the Princes of Hell, not the Ku Klux Klan."

Fat Phil emitted a high-pitched giggle. "Not all that much different, is it? The Klan, they had their heyday, they rode free and wore their colors and all the straights hated 'em but everybody feared 'em. That's a description of us, Bonebreaker. That's what we are. This is just a part of it. A small part."

"Enough," snapped Klaus Richter, his .44 Magnum in his hand. "Put up or shut up, Johnny. Get it done."

There was a long moment of silence. Wolfe looked down at the child in the tattered dress. "Stand up," he said softly, reaching down his hand. She took hold tentatively, then let him pull her up.

She stood, shaking all over, afraid. "I'm not going to hurt you," Wolfe said.

His sight was adjusting to the darkness, and he could see her eyes. They looked at his, and for a moment they were bold and unafraid. He knew he would have to keep that moment.

Fat Phil laughed. "Oh, honey, he done fucking lied to you," he said.

Wolfe turned, slowly, coldly. He felt himself going into fighting mode, the automatic pilot he'd learned the hard way in those many days and nights on the dojo floor in karate competition. He mentally gauged where his opponents were.

The voice he spoke with was not his own. It was deep, guttural, an out-of-control voice, an animal growl.

"No, motherfucker. I didn't lie."

And then Harry Wolfe moved....

INSIDE THE CLUBHOUSE, things were deadly still for a long moment. Doreen Newell lay unconscious on the floor. The three men loomed around Carmelita. All of them were bigger, much bigger.

Carmelita surrendered.

She threw her hands up. "Hey, guys, I may be able to slap around a wannabe in a bar, but there isn't a one of you I'd dare take on. Now, I know Johnny's gonna come back a righteous member, and I don't want to be the one who causes a problem."

She nodded significantly at Doreen, sprawled unconscious on the floor. "I mean," Carmelita continued, "I know whatever happens later, you're going to blame it on me. So, here's the deal."

The three men stopped moving forward. They stood watching her intently.

"I see that room over there," Carmelita continued, nodding toward the lounge on the other side of the main room. "Now, tell you what. If you promise not to tell Johnny, the fact is, I kind of like big men, you know?" She glanced meaningfully at Mongo's crotch, and was rewarded with a mindless grin from the hulking bald man.

"Now, honey," she said soothingly to Mongo, "I know you and I are going to have a special time together. But this guy here, what's your name, Big Henry? I think I kinda owe him, you know? I mean, my guy cost him his eye and all, and I think Big Henry should get the first crack. You know?"

Big Henry grinned triumphantly, but Thumper wasn't happy.

"Wait a minute," he snarled. "I think she's tryin' to set us up!"

Carmelita smiled her beautiful smile. "Set up? You think so? Then consider...this!"

Carmelita began to undress.

There wasn't much to remove. She kicked off her shoes and started backing slowly toward the door of the adjoining room, working her jeans down her hips. There were only black panties underneath. She peeled the denims off and threw them aside.

Still moving slowly backward, she wriggled sexily out of her black French-cut T-shirt. Her large, firm breasts came free. She saw the men's mouths open involuntarily as they saw her soft, dark nipples.

She was almost to the door now. Carmelita slid gracefully out of her black panties, and the three big men stared openmouthed at her full black thatch of pubic hair. She suggestively touched herself between her legs.

"Big Henry," she said in a soft, cooing voice. And then, lowering the voice deep in her throat as she looked straight at the blond man's crotch, she continued, "*Big* Henry. Oh, baby, you first. You first."

She had almost disappeared into the darkness. The man with the arm in a cast and a skullcap around his head and over one eye cried, "Get back. This one's mine!"

"Gimme yer gun," blurted Thumper. "Remember what she done in the bar!"

Angrily Big Henry jerked his blue-steel Colt .45 automatic out of his belt and threw it behind him. It sailed past Thumper's reaching hand and landed on the sofa. Then he was inside the door.

Thumper and Mongo stood outside. They heard the grunts and the sounds of flesh on flesh.

"Oh, man," Mongo said. "Listen to that! That is some piece of ass!"

Then there was a crunching sound, and no more noise.

Crunch? Mongo and Thumper looked at each other. *Crunch?* What the hell was that?

"I'm goin' in there," said Thumper suddenly. He threw himself at the door and flung it open.

ALL HELL had broken loose in a fraction of a second.

Harry Wolfe had moved, surging like a barracuda striking in deep blue water. They'd had him in a semicircle, Phil in the middle and Snake on the left and Klaus on the right, and suddenly he had spun around like a whirlwind and his foot had lashed out, driving his heel into Snake's chest as he grabbed the young girl and pulled her down to the ground.

His heel had pistoned into Snake's chest, breaking the ribs, and Snake had screamed and convulsed on the M-16, jerking back the trigger. The night exploded into an orange firestorm. The thunder of the 5.56 mm machine gun rendered Phil instantly if temporarily deaf, and the concussion of the fireballs of the gun muzzle in front of his face was like a slap across his open eyes. He cried out involuntarily, shoving his .45 automatic out in front of him and firing one shot.

He never knew that as the M-16 went off Klaus had gone involuntarily to the ground—thus saving himself from death, because the hail of copper-jacketed, high-velocity bullets had streamed through the place where he'd been standing. Klaus had reflexively pulled the trigger of his .44 Magnum twice. The heavy magnum bullets went harmlessly into the air, but the shots triggered two more flaring fireballs that effectively blinded everyone there.

Everyone, that is, but Bonebreaker and the girl.

The spinning wheel-kick had turned Harry Wolfe away from the gunfire. The bullets missed him, and because he was facing away in that moment, so did the muzzle-flashes. He grabbed at Fat Phil, hoping to take him hostage, but his hands missed their purchase. Instead of grabbing Fat Phil's throat, they closed over his pistol.

The reflex had been inborn, in hours of training in the dojo. When Wolfe's hands recognized the cold steel of the automatic, they reverted to long-term muscle memory, to the technique he had practiced for so many hours under Chin Ho Lee, the master *sensei* at the DEA Academy.

His right hand closed first on the slide and barrel of the pistol. Instinctively his body drove his left hand forward in a palm-heel strike that had all his weight behind it.

This was the movement that jammed the trigger guard against the base joint of Fat Phil Newell's finger so hard that it shattered the joint and cut through the soft cartilage that was left. Before Phil could scream, Wolfe had completed the movement and pivoted away into the darkness taking the girl with him.

Snake opened fire, raking the night with a fully automatic burst of high-powered bullets. Klaus Richter fired a third shot and would have fired a fourth if the fireball from the last one had not blinded him.

Phil Newell tried to pull the trigger to fire again. Nothing happened. His hand was numb. He reached over with the other hand to take the gun to shoot. But he felt no gun.

He felt only his own empty right hand. It was wet and slick. He pawed at the hand.

His right index finger was gone.

Phil Newell, for the first time in his life, screamed into the darkness.

WHEN CARMELITA MOVED backward into the room, she saw Big Henry moving toward her like a freight train, his casted arm sticking out to the side like a flag. He came in on her in a rush.

She flitted to the side.

Big Henry's momentum kept him going past her. He landed facedown on the bed. "Unnh!"

She pivoted and dived on him, coming down in a knee drop to his kidney. She felt tissue give way as she landed on him with a slap of flesh. "Unnh!"

He tried to roll over and use his weight. Carmelita was too fast and limber. In an instant she was up and swarming on top of him, driving her knee into his throat. "Whump... Unnh."

He reached out with his one good arm to grab her. He caught her by the throat. He was down on his back on the bed, and she was on her knees. She grabbed his wrist with both hands, locked it against her throat, then threw herself up and came back down, her knee landing with her full hundred twenty-five pounds of body weight on his elbow.

It was the same thing Harry had done to Big Henry's other arm, and this arm gave way with the same sickening crunch. Big Henry would have screamed except her blow to the throat had already caved in his larynx. No sound came out.

She threw the arm down. She knew he had discarded his pistol, but she knew they all carried knives. She groped at his belt, found a knife, pulled it free and opened it.

She ran toward the door. The blood lust was high in Carmelita Morales. The last time she had been naked, she had been helpless. This time she was naked and armed, and therefore not naked at all.

As she rushed silently toward the door, she heard a gruff voice say, "I'm goin' in there!"

The door swung open just as she reached it, and she burst through with the full power of her hurtling body, the blade point down and edge forward in her hand the way her master instructors had taught her, her thumb locking the pommel of the knife in position.

Thumper was opening the door when the hurtling light brown missile passed through it. He was in the wrong place at the wrong time. With all her rage and survival instinct behind it, Carmelita's forward slash drove the knife through Thumper's throat, through his carotid artery and jugular vein, until the sharpened edge touched and gouged the forward edge of his cervical vertebrae.

Paralyzed by the impact shock to the spinal cord, Thumper's body went numb and collapsed. Instantly quadriplegic, Thumper saw the blood jet outward in a power spray from his own throat and knew he was helpless to stop it.

He died in stark, silent-screaming terror, not knowing or caring that the naked woman with the knife had gone past him, homing in on the killer Mongo, her mind and body locking into a lethal killing mode.

WOLFE GRABBED the young girl and jerked her away from the bikers, rolling in the darkness toward the edge of the sand dune that marked the outer boundary of the shooting range.

They fired at him. Reflexively Wolfe fired back, raking a burst of .45 slugs across the area where he'd last seen them. In the cacophony of the gunfire, he heard two wet thuds. Then there was a grunt and a scream.

Wolfe knew what that meant. Two of his bullets had taken flesh.

Harry and the young girl skidded, rolled. He pulled her to him and tried to curl himself around her so his body could take the impacts instead of hers. On automatic pilot now, he'd pulled his finger out away from the trigger, and thumbed the safety latch to the no-shoot position.

She fought him, savagely and blindly and instinctively. He felt the blows and finally he grabbed her and pulled her even closer.

"It's all right," he hissed. "I won't hurt you. I'm trying to protect you, dammit."

She stopped fighting. They were still. They were alone amid darkness and silence.

Then Wolfe heard Klaus's voice. "That motherfucker! I'll blow him away!"

Wolfe pulled her head close to his. "Don't be afraid," he whispered very softly. "I'm not one of them. I'll get you out of this. But you have to be absolutely silent."

He felt her nod against him.

Above him in the darkness of the sands, he heard Fat Phil squeal, "Klaus! He's got my gun, Klaus! He ripped my fuckin' finger off, man! And—" there was a pause before the voice went to a higher pitch "—and he shot me, man!"

Another voice came from the darkness, above and to the left. "Me, too!" It was a falsetto shriek. "He shot me, too!"

From the right came an angry roar. "Shut up, you weaklings! The bastard's still out there! If he survives, we're all worse than dead. Finish him!"

That was the voice Wolfe homed in on. Klaus's voice.

Wolfe fell back into primal survival. He became a creature of his training. *Focus on the deadliest threat first.* They'd taught him that at the DEA Academy. He tuned himself in to Klaus's position.

Create distance! Time and distance favor the trained defender! They'd taught him that in advanced officer survival. He rolled toward the left, taking the girl with him...away from the deadliest threat, toward the weakest and already wounded one. Moving straight back was not an option. Even in the starlight he could see the cliff behind them. And forward was not an option for a man with a half-empty gun, and with a child to protect.

He heard them moving around on the cliff. "Down there," came Snake's choking cry, and Wolfe heard the thunder of the M-16 and saw the muzzle-flashes, star shaped in the darkness.

He raised the pistol. It was Fat Phil's, the custom gun with the night sights that glowed green in the dark, the same Trijicon sights that were on his own long-lost 9 mm.

He raised the weapon, lined up the dots. The small one between the two large ones. He aimed at where he'd seen the muzzle-flashes. He felt the girl's arms wrapping around him clutching his belly, and Harry knew something he had never felt before: a terrible and dominating parental instinct, something lupine, something that told him to kill whatever it was that threatened this child.

"Where is he?" It was Klaus Richter's voice in the dark.

"Down there somewhere. He's got my .45, Klaus," he heard Fat Phil whine.

"If he's got your gun, get out of the way," Klaus yelled in the darkness.

"I can fight," shouted Fat Phil. "I got my backup! I got my hammerless!"

As Phil struggled to pull the gun from his pocket with a hand that only had three fingers left, he stood up. Wolfe's eyes had adjusted to the darkness. He saw the shape of Phil's pearlike body against the dark blue skyline.

"Take the target of opportunity," he'd been told by Paul Vunak, a second-generation student of Bruce Lee. The training followed. Wolfe turned the gun, lined up the three green dots of the Trijicon night sights and squeezed the trigger.

An orange flash the size of a grapefruit appeared at the muzzle of the gun. It silhouetted a front sight in perfect alignment with a rear sight. There was a smacking sound He saw the shape of Fat Phil twist in the starlight and fall.

Once you've fired in the dark, move from where you left those muzzle-flashes. Wolfe had paid out of his own pocket to go to Josh Hooper's gunfighting school, and he remembered the Marine colonel's lesson. He grabbed the young girl and rolled violently sideways.

They barely made it. Automatic fire came roaring down from Snake's M-16, farther to the left than it had been before—a clear indication that he was moving, too—and the bullets chewed up the sand where Wolfe and the child had been a moment ago.

There was a clicking sound above him.

Focus on the danger, world-champion pistolero Ron Chappick had taught Wolfe when he took the master's course at his own expense. *If you've practiced your technique deeply enough, the long-term muscle memory will carry you to even a target that you hear but do not see, so long as you have truly identified it as a target that must be shot.*

Wolfe rolled silently through the sand, carrying the fifteen-year-old girl with him. He brought up the gun. He heard the sound of the M-16's bolt clicking home.

Wolfe stroked the trigger back.

The .45's blast split the night. Even as he rolled away, taking the girl with him, he heard the strangled scream of a man and the sound of a human body plunging downhill through the sand. To the far right there was a giant bloom of flame, and he felt something sing over him like a bumblebee. It was a .44 Magnum bullet fired by Klaus. It did not touch him or the girl.

Trust your perceptions, the survival master had told him. *Laymen call it premonition, but a master calls it precognition. You sense things your subconscious has learned to recognize, and if you don't face it on the reactive level, and instead wait for your conscious to confirm it, you will die.*

Wolfe couldn't see Klaus Richter, couldn't hear him, but he had coordinated the muzzle-flash and sensed a movement, and he fired.

There was the slap of a bullet hitting flesh, followed by a shout and a flare that lanced skyward as the .44 Magnum went off again. Wolfe heard the sound of a heavy man hitting the ground thirty feet away.

Something told Wolfe to stay still. He did. The girl was clutching him tightly, and he shifted himself so his body would be between her and the incoming fire.

Slowly and carefully, enveloped in the darkness, he pressed the button behind the trigger guard and dropped the magazine into his left hand. Harry ran his thumb over the top of the clip. It touched only the flat sheet metal of the follower, not the roundness of a live cartridge. There were no rounds left in the magazine.

But the slide was forward, and that meant that there was one cartridge left in the firing chamber. He had to be sure. He brought the slide back and probed with his index finger, and felt the cartridge halfway into the chamber. One shot left. He eased the operating slide forward so the one last shot would be ready to go. Behind him, against him, the child quivered in the darkness.

MONGO SAW the naked woman come toward him over Thumper's falling body, saw the geyser of blood jet up behind her and felt a coldness to his quick. He clawed at his .45.

He didn't make it. The Buck knife slashed down across his forearm, severing the radial nerve, and back forward again, cutting up across the ulnar nerve. The arm went dead, the hand flopping down, turning into a dead and useless flipper.

Mongo lashed out blindly with his good arm. He was lucky. His fist caught Carmelita Morales on the cheek, and the blow sent her to the floor. Her head smashed against the edge of a coffee table, and for three or four seconds, she was unconscious.

During those seconds her right hand opened, and the Buck knife fell away.

It was time enough for Mongo to regain his courage. It was only a woman, after all. Women were things he destroyed for his pleasure, like hunters shooting deer. He was ashamed that he'd been afraid of her. She was helpless now and small, half his size.

He moved toward her, the fear that he'd felt a moment before fueling his anger. Hurt him? Hurt Mongo? No! He would crush this bitch!

He lumbered forward. He was bending down to reach for her when she came awake and saw him.

Her legs thrashed like a shark striking.

One light brown foot hooked him behind the left ankle. The other drove straight forward in a piston kick. With the leg locked in place, he couldn't roll with the blow, and Mongo couldn't help but scream when Carmelita's heel smashed his kneecap.

He went down as his leg buckled with the agony of the blow. The woman, cat quick, was on her feet already. Mongo pulled himself after her, dragging his half-dead lower body.

She was unarmed, naked, helpless. She was outside now, but she was unarmed. Mongo pulled himself to his feet, throwing his weight onto his good leg, ignoring the screaming pain from his shattered kneecap on the other side. His gun was gone, somewhere on the floor. It had slipped out of his waistband when he'd fallen.

But he still had his knife.

He leaned against the wall to free his hands to open it. The blade locked open, gleaming and deadly. He threw himself forward, hopping on the one good leg.

The woman was on the motorcycle, trying to get it started. Whose bike was it, anyway? Bonebreaker's? In the haze of the pain from his shattered leg, Mongo couldn't think it out and remember. All that filled his mind was the red haze of anger. She had hurt him. She had hurt the others.

She would pay.

Mongo lurched forward. He uttered an inarticulate animal sound of triumph. She was almost within reach. She turned on the bike, looked at him and brought her hand to the gasoline cap.

He frowned through the pain that twisted his face. Gas cap? Stupid bitch. This was no time to gas up.

The lithe, naked woman pivoted toward him, her hand suddenly coming away from the gas tank and thrusting toward him palm forward, like the gesture that says Stop. Mongo felt a sudden impact in his chest, and beneath the impact, a terrible burning pain.

Carmelita Morales had released the gas cap of the motorcycle and thrust forward the push dagger that was brazed to it. The blade entered Mongo's right chest, impaling and instantly deflating his right lung. As her hand came away, the flat-ended dagger remained in place.

Mongo was suddenly very short of breath.

"Aargh," he snarled, lashing out with both fists. Carmelita blocked one punch but not the other. The blow knocked her backward, and the weight carried her against the Harley, throwing it back off the kickstand. The bike went down heavily, with Carmelita beneath it.

"Kill you, bitch," Mongo growled. A bubble of blood grew and burst between his lips as he spoke. He tottered forward, the knife upraised.

The sissy bars on the back of the bike loomed over Carmelita. She grabbed one, pulled it loose. Its spear point was hidden in the darkness.

Mongo lunged.

Carmelita thrust.

Mongo screamed as the spear went through his left chest. His body-alarm reaction made him writhe away from her. He fell away from her, past the rear wheel of the downed motorcycle.

Carmelita tried to pull herself free. She couldn't. One leg was trapped under the weight of the bike.

Behind the bike, Mongo pulled himself to his hands and knees. A rattling wheeze escaped his chest and his throat. The chrome sissy bar hung from the front of him, still embedded in his chest. Even in the darkness, Carmelita could see that the push dagger with the gas-cap handle was still stuck in his chest on the other side.

No! He couldn't still be going! But how long could a man hold his breath underwater? Minutes? That was how long Mongo could still fight, still kill, she realized, even with both his lungs torn apart.

He came upright on his knees, tottering toward her. The knife was still in his hand, and her leg was still trapped beneath the crushing weight of the Harley.

Then she remembered. Carmelita threw herself to her back, beneath the handlebars that lay askew above her. She grabbed the right handlebar, shoved as hard as she could, pointed the end of it toward the man who was inching closer, the blood foaming at his mouth and out of his chest.

She grabbed the handlebar as tight as she could and twisted with all her strength.

She had despised Don McAllister when she first met him, the sexist son of a bitch, but he was the one who had given them the money to rig the bike outlaw style, with all the hidden weaponry, and in this last terrible second she thanked him.

She twisted the handlebar as Mongo lunged forward with the knife, and she felt the heat under her hands and heard the deafening blast of the 12-gauge buckshot shell that had been rigged inside. The concussion was like a slap in the face.

The nine double-ought buckshot pellets, each a third of an inch in diameter, caught Mongo full in the upper chest. The impact slammed him backward like a giant, unseen club. There was a hollow sound as his head smashed against the gravel. A spray of blood shot into the air from the ragged hole that reached into the aorta. It pumped in spurts, splashing on Carmelita.

She put the heel of her free foot on the motorcycle and pushed. She felt flesh tear as her leg finally came free. Carmelita scrambled to her feet.

The thing on the ground still moved. The blood jets were slowing down now, barely bubbling from the huge hole in his chest. The sissy-bar spear was still protruding from his left chest, the gas-cap dagger still embedded in his right.

Yet he looked up at her, the eyes glazed with hate and tried to move. She remembered Brian Voit's words. *Avenge me!*

She saw in her mind this monster carving the initials in the leg of the teenage girl.

The fury gave her strength. Carmelita ripped the other sissy bar loose from the motorcycle, its sharpened tip gleaming in the starlight.

"Die, you inhuman monster!"

She drove it down with all her weight.

The hollow steel spear plunged through Mongo's throat and out the back of his neck. Carmelita drove her weight down until the spear point dug into the gravel, impaling Mongo like a vampire on a wooden stake.

He made a gurgling sound. The hatred that blazed in his eyes seemed to flare out. Under the light of the stars, Carmelita saw the pupils of his eyes widen as his body thrashed one last time and then relaxed in death.

There was a sound from the door. Carmelita pivoted, dropping low in a cat stance, her hands rising to claw and kill.

Doreen stood in the doorway. She swayed slightly, the blood oozing from the massive bruise on her cheek where her husband had punched her. In her left hand was a flashlight. In her right was a .38 Colt Detective Special.

"Elita," she shouted. "Elita!"

Carmelita relaxed from her stance. "Doreen," she said, hearing the breathlessness in her own voice. "I'm here."

Doreen came forward. "Jesus. What happened?"

"They were going to pull a train on me. They paid for it. Do you understand?"

"Oh, God," said Doreen after a moment. "Oh, God, do I understand."

"They've got my guy, Doreen. At the range. Do you know where that is?"

Doreen nodded.

"Give me a second," said Carmelita. She reached down to Mongo's body and pulled her Smith & Wesson from his hip pocket. The stupid bastard had forgotten he'd had her gun. He could have killed her if he'd remembered it. But he had victimized women for so long he no longer associated them with power and had forgotten it as soon as she was disarmed. He'd paid the price.

Carmelita ran inside long enough to pull on her jeans and T-shirt. When she came back out, Doreen had already started up the Continental. "Come on," the big woman said impatiently. Carmelita threw herself into the car.

"Doreen," she said as the big car lurched down the gravel road toward the range, "we've got to talk. Our guys are going against each other right now, I think . . . and . . ."

Doreen raised her hand to silence Carmelita. "Don't say it, Elita. I know. I know."

AN INSTRUCTOR HAD TOLD Harry Wolfe, "Expect to lose count of your own shots if it goes past two or three fired, but expect the other guy to be able to keep count of the rounds you fire."

Harry had already learned the truth of that. He'd had to check the pistol he'd ripped out of Fat Phil's hand, only to find out that there was a single bullet left.

He hadn't been able to keep count of Snake's shots—who could count full-automatic fire?—but he also wasn't worried about Snake much anymore.

Klaus had a revolver. Harry counted five distinctive Magnum rounds fired, from a 6-shot weapon. But he had to assume that Klaus was smart enough to reload during one of the lulls in the firefight.

The young girl still clung to him, her breathing panicky. He didn't dare speak for fear of giving their position away. He reached down with his left hand and stroked her hair softly.

It was the gesture of a parent caressing a child. It struck a primal chord. He felt the girl relax, felt her breathing slow. Good.

Above him, on the sandbank, there was movement.

The protective instinct surged again. Intellectually, Wolfe understood that there were two of them, and he had only one bullet left, and Klaus was the most dangerous one that he had to take first. But the father instinct told him, *Kill what attacks the young one! Kill it now!*

A shape loomed over the hill. Wolfe's night vision was in gear now. The shape had a gun.

Wolfe raised the pistol. The three green dots aligned themselves. He pressed the trigger.

The .45's blast split the night.

The figure above him jerked violently and fell backward, and there was a deafening blast as a turnip-shaped fireball exploded in the darkness, pointing upward. It was the .44 Magnum.

And, Wolfe prayed, the last bullet.

He felt his own slide lock to the rear, his automatic empty. He dropped the gun and lunged forward, crying out to the girl behind him, "Stay down!" Wolfe lunged toward the fallen figure.

It rose to meet him.

They had told Wolfe that nineteen times out of twenty a .45 automatic would put a man down with one shot. They had lied. Snake hadn't been heard from since Harry shot him with the .45, but Fat Phil had been shot twice with it, and Harry wasn't sure yet that he was neutralized. Klaus Richter, the most dangerous of all, had been shot twice with it, and now he was rising again.

Their bodies collided. Wolfe felt the impact of the big man's muscular body driving him back. Suddenly the dirt was under him, and the bulk of Klaus was above him, stifling his breath. He felt an acrid wetness in his face.

"Goddamn you, I'll kill you!" The voice above him was guttural, bubbling. Wolfe realized why. His bullet had gone through one of Richter's lungs.

A fist smashed into his face. Wolfe saw stars. Again a violent blow smashed into his head, and he almost passed out from the pain and shock, but it was followed by another incredibly powerful blow.

His mind wanted to leave his body, to seek peace in the darkness. But then he heard the wordless cry of the young girl behind him, a cry of unspeakable fear, and that feeling rose in him again.

The feeling of the protective father. The feeling he would have had for his own child if his fiancée hadn't been killed by drugs, if that death hadn't thrown him headlong into the mission that Centac called Code Zero. If drug dealers hadn't killed the woman he had loved, and murdered their children yet unborn along with her, and made him a sanctioned murderer.

The rage welled up inside him, the terrible red killing fury, and Wolfe in that moment remembered the *sensei* who had told him, "Turn the fear to anger, and the anger to strength, and the strength to purpose." Then the memory was lost in the crimson haze of his homicidal fury.

Wolfe struck back. All the teaching, all the training of years past brought his body to automatic pilot, driving his total weight behind the punches and kicks, again and again. He felt bone crumble and give way beneath his fists. He felt the bigger man fall back, felt Klaus's fear, but he didn't stop. Wolfe struck again and again, driving in close now, hammering his elbows into the man's body.

He heard sounds, gurgling wet noises that sounded like "stop...I give..." but he ignored them. He thought of the child, and hit it again, harder.

He felt Klaus Richter's body slump down to the knees, felt the arms go around his waist in a final beseeching gesture of surrender. And then the image came to his mind of this same man, looming huge and indomitable over the helpless young girl, saying "only a nigger."

The rage reached a white-hot nova.

Wolfe's arm snaked down under the kneeling man's throat, his forearm creating the leverage for the inescapable judo hold that *sensei* only taught the black belts, the terrible *hakimi-waza*.

He grabbed his own hand as it came through into the hold, and lifted, straightening his exhausted legs with his last bit of strength, throwing every ounce of power that remained to him into the technique.

"Noo...aahhhkkk!"

Klaus Richter's last utterance on earth was futile. Harry Wolfe completed the movement. He felt Richter's larynx cave in like a stepped-on hornet's nest against his forearm in the last instant before the irresistible leverage snapped Klaus Richter's neck at the seventh cervical vertebra. The sharp edge of the vertebra sheared through the spinal cord like a knife through cheese.

Richter's body went dead. His mind screamed, "No. No! No!"

But it was only his mind that could scream. Wolfe let go and the living husk that was Klaus Richter fell to the ground.

Richter felt no pain, no impact. His eyes were in the sand and he couldn't move them. They were still wide with horror.

"No," he still screamed inside his own mind. "No!" Then the darkness overwhelmed his consciousness forever.

Klaus Richter was dead.

Wolfe took a moment to breathe. Then he stood up. The girl . . . where was the girl?

Then, with a voice colder than death, the man behind him said, "Don't move! I got this little bitch!"

PHIL NEWELL had reconciled himself to the loss of his finger in the first minute of the encounter. He knew his trigger finger had been torn away by the man he'd named the Bonebreaker. He also knew he wouldn't bleed to death from it.

After the Bonebreaker's first surge of movement, Fat Phil had been thrown against the van and had felt the hot shock waves of the gunshot concussions. He knew he was in deep shit. He still had the presence of mind to claw in his pocket for his backup gun, the Smith & Wesson 5-shot .38 hammerless.

Then, when he realized that the Bonebreaker and the girl had gone down the hill, he knew he had to move to cover. He started to go around to the other side of the van—and fell on his face.

His right leg had just given out from under him. He'd reached down and felt the wetness. When that bastard opened fire, he'd put a bullet through Fat Phil's leg.

The firefight had gone on around him for a while. Phil had pulled himself to his feet, seeking a target for his .38, and the next thing he knew, there had been the hardest punch he'd ever taken to his gut. It had sent him sprawling in the dirt, and when he reached down to touch his stomach and make sure it was all right, he had felt a slimy wetness.

Fear scurried down his spine in chilling waves. Oh, Jesus. Slimy wetness? Those are my intestines. This is *bad!*

He couldn't remember how long he had contemplated his mortality, with his Smith & Wesson in one hand and his intestines in the other. Then there had been the last flurry of two shots, and the sickening struggle between the two men down the hill and that crunching sound that he knew too well. The Bonebreaker had done it again.

Then there had been the warm movement to his side. Fat Phil instinctively lunged out, grabbing. He caught the slender arm of the girl, then he lost his balance and fell. She went down with him, under his enormous weight.

The Bonebreaker was moving up the hill now. But shit had changed real quick. The price of poker had just gone up. His guts might be hanging out, and he might be ready to die, but Fat Phil still held a loaded .38 Special *and* a hostage.

He felt himself weakening from loss of blood. Still, he had no fear of pain. No fear of death, even. And Fat Phil heard himself shout, "Don't move! I got this little bitch!"

WOLFE WAS ALONE, and he knew it, and he knew Fat Phil knew it. No loaded gun. No nothing. Barely enough strength left to talk, after fighting and killing the huge muscleman who lay dead at his feet.

"It didn't have to be like this, Phil," Wolfe yelled at the shadowy figure in the darkness. "There's still time!"

"Time for what?" Fat Phil was screaming now. "You got me good, you rat fuck. You think a lot of this little niglet? Come on up now! I don't give a damn if she lives or dies. I just give a damn if *you* live or die! Come up where I can see you! Come into my sights, you son of a bitch!"

It was then that the headlights bathed them all as Doreen Newell's Continental swung into the gravel pit that the Princes of Hell used for a shooting range.

BEFORE SHE THREW the Continental into Park, Doreen Newell asked only one thing from Carmelita Morales, the woman she knew as Elita Suarez. "Are we together?"

"Yes," Carmelita answered curtly before she bailed out of the car with the Smith & Wesson revolver in her hand.

There were only the stars and the headlights to carve the darkness. They saw Fat Phil, down on his knees in front of the van, holding the young girl hostage. His gun was to her head. Only a few steps away from him, on the edge of the sandy incline, was Harry Wolfe, his hands empty.

Doreen stepped out of the car purposefully. Her Colt Detective Special was in her right hand. In the darkness the long-stemmed rose engraved on its side was not visible.

"Phil," she called. "It's me. You okay?"

"Doreen!" She could hear the relief in his voice. "Doreen, honey, come help me! Fucking Bonebreaker went nuts. He killed Klaus. I think he killed Snake, too!"

The tall woman moved behind him. "It's okay, Phil. Who's the girl?"

"Some niglet bitch. Doreen, you gotta help me here!"

Fat Phil coughed. Blood came to his lips.

"Cover this bastard in front of me, Doreen," he screamed. "Cover this goddamn Johnny! He set me up!"

Doreen raised her gun, somewhere between Phil and Harry. She wasn't sure where to point.

Behind her Carmelita reflexively raised her own .38, level with Doreen's head. Don't do it, she thought. Please, Doreen, don't do it! Carmelita lined up the sights, and she began taking up the slack from the trigger.

"Doreen," bleated Phil. "Get me outa here, babe!"

"It's okay, honey," Doreen said softly. "Send the girl over to me. I'll cover her here, and we'll take care of the rest."

"You stupid bitch! I'm holding this little niglet hostage!"

The girl let out a pathetic sob.

"Oh, Jesus," said Doreen very softly. "Phil, let her go. I'll take her here."

"Will you fuckin' listen to me?" Phil screamed. "Shoot the Bonebreaker! Shoot Johnny! Shoot him! Then I'll let her go!"

Doreen began to cry. "Phil, please. If you care for me at all, if you remember us at all when I was her age, let her go!"

A blood bubble expanded and popped at the corner of Fat Phil's mouth. "Kill him, Doreen! Don't you listen to me at all? Kill him, or I'll kill her!"

One last sob choked itself back into Doreen Newell's throat. She brought the gun up, and Carmelita came a quarter inch back on her own trigger before she realized where the biker woman's gun was pointing.

Doreen cried one last time, "Phil!"

In that shout there was an emotion that spoke of time once cherished, now lost and gone forever. It was a cry of pain, a cry for forgiveness. It even made Fat Phil turn and look. For an instant his stainless .38 came away from Maria's head.

In that last unearthly moment, Fat Phil Newell saw the pain he had wrought, saw his hopes and dreams that had risen and fallen, and saw it all pass away into a life he could have had, but didn't.

"No," he screamed, trying to turn with the gun in his hand.

The last thing he saw was his wife, with tears in her eyes, standing behind the nickel-plated revolver. Then the world exploded into a giant orange ball of flame that coalesced into an inky darkness that started from the outside in, inexorably filling up everything in front of Phil and obliterating all.

WOLFE SAW PHIL try to turn the gun toward the child, saw the sheet of orange flame leap from the front of Doreen's revolver, saw Phil slammed back to the ground as if slapped down by a giant, invisible hand. He saw the young girl run forward and clutch the tall white woman, and saw Doreen bend forward to hold her safe, instinctively turning her and putting her own body between the child and Phil.

But there was no need of that any more.

Wolfe moved forward. Doreen Newell was convulsing with sobs. So was the girl. "It's all right, honey," Doreen was saying. "He can't hurt you anymore." There was no resistance when Wolfe took the revolver out of Doreen's hand.

Carmelita finally let her breath out and lowered her revolver. She moved in behind Wolfe, who checked the Colt he'd taken from Doreen and confirmed that there were five bullets left in it, and then moved forward to check out the situation.

Snake was sprawled on his back, his jaw locked open in the rictus of death. The first slug Harry had struck him with had apparently creased his leg. The second had killed him outright.

Klaus Richter was dead, his tongue protruding from his mouth, his blue eyes locked forever open in a look of horror, his eyes wide and blank and covered with granules of sand.

At last Wolfe came up behind the body of Fat Phil Newell, just to be sure. Phil lay on his side. Wolfe didn't have to move the heavy corpse to see that the entry hole in the forehead was rimmed with gray brain matter, and that the exit hole above the back of the neck was covered with more brain tissue blown outward by the departing bullet.

He moved toward the cars, the halo of light that came from the Continental. He asked one thing of Morales, "The others?"

She answered in a single word. "Dead."

Wolfe nodded. He and Carmelita Morales looked at Doreen Newell. The tall woman was hugging the sobbing child close to her chest, her head bent over the girl's.

Carmelita looked at Wolfe. "I won't turn her in, Harry."

"Me neither."

"She saved your— You neither?"

"No way."

Morales cocked an eyebrow. "Sleeping with her has nothing to do with it?"

"Partner," said Wolfe, "every second person I meet is the owner of female genitalia. That doesn't mean I let them all get away with shit. The fact is, it would be tough for you and I to explain why we killed these people without making any effort to arrest them."

"Also true," said Carmelita with an absolutely straight face. "So, what do you think we should do?"

"Well, if we were CIA, we'd kill Doreen. If we were straight DEA, we'd arrest Doreen and then blow the case for not having arrested them when we could have, instead of doing them when we did."

Carmelita smiled. "So, senior partner?"

Wolfe smiled back. "Trust me," he said, and walked toward Doreen.

The tall woman looked at him. She wasn't crying anymore, but she was still holding the girl protectively. She looked at Wolfe, defiance in her eyes.

"You're cops," Doreen said. It wasn't accusatory, just a flat statement. "So I'm in jail for life if I don't get the gas chamber."

"Actually," said Wolfe, "given the fact that you saved this kid's life, we were thinking of letting you go."

Doreen looked at him for a long moment and said, "My God, you're serious."

"We didn't mean just walking away," said Carmelita. "Would you have a problem with giving us some names, some dates, some addresses, things like that?"

"Would you need me to testify?"

"Nah. We can work that out," said Carmelita cheerfully.

"And you want the stuff on the gun factory and the meth factory?"

"We've got all that," said Harry.

"But," said Doreen, "you want all the money."

"Actually," Carmelita told her, "that would be a problem."

"We'd have to testify to things we haven't seen and things that happened in places we haven't been," Wolfe added.

"The easiest thing," said Carmelita, "would be if tomorrow, when the raid teams hit at about noon, you had already taken what you needed and left."

"That makes sense to me, too," said Wolfe.

For a moment in the darkness, they hugged each other: the tall biker woman and the male and female Centac agents and the young girl who only knew that she was going to live after all.

When they separated, Doreen Newell looked at Harry and said wistfully, "It's over."

Wolfe just nodded in mute agreement.

Epilogue

The day after the shoot-out, "anonymous but credible" information was furnished to the Bureau of Alcohol, Tobacco, and Firearms that resulted in a raid taking place in Long Beach, California, within twenty-four hours. Eighty-six submachine guns were seized, along with parts to manufacture over two hundred more, and twenty-two people were arrested. No resistance was offered by the suspects. However, they did become extremely agitated when, upon incarceration in the Los Angeles County Jail, they learned that Fat Phil Newell was not coming to bail them out.

On the same day a combined task force of the San Diego County Sheriff's Department and the U.S. Department of Justice Drug Enforcement Administration swept down on the Princes of Hell methamphetamine factory in San Juan Capistrano, California. One employee grabbed a shotgun and attempted to aim it at the officers. He was killed instantly by the submachine gun fire of DEA agents.

Simultaneously a captain of the Organized Crime Bureau of the Los Angeles County Sheriff's Department arrested clerk Wanda Wilson of the San Diego Sheriff's Office on charges of obstruction of justice, falsification and destruction of legal documents, and conspiracy to perpetuate organized crime under the federal RICO statutes.

Before that day was over, deputies from the felony warrant squads of the Los Angeles County and San Diego County sheriff's departments, in concert with the special reaction teams of the same agencies, arrested eighty-six sworn members of the Princes of Hell Motorcycle Club, Inc. Only two members resisted arrest. They regretted it deeply.

Four days later investigators from the United States Internal Revenue Service swept into three Los Angeles and San

Diego banks with warrants to seize certain safe-deposit boxes registered in the names of Phillip Newell, Doreen Newell and PHI. All safe-deposit boxes were found empty by the agents.

THE TALL brown-haired woman had driven aimlessly for days across the country. When she stopped for lunch in Remington, Indiana, across from the railroad station, she was reminded of the village where she had grown up. On the spur of the moment, she decided this was as good a place as any.

When she paid for her lunch, leaving a generous tip, she walked across the street to a telephone booth. She picked up the phone book and, in the front pages under community services, she found the number for the county crisis hotline.

She dropped coins in the machine and dialed. The woman she reached seemed genuinely concerned about the anonymous caller.

"I want to know," the tall woman asked, "if you have a shelter for battered women and abused children."

There was a long pause on the other end. "Ma'am," the volunteer said at length, "if you'll tell me what your problem is, I'll do the best we can do to help you. But, no, we don't have a shelter. There just isn't enough money in this county for a shelter."

"You have a shelter," the tall woman said.

"No, ma'am, you don't understand," said the volunteer on the phone. "I wish we did, but we don't have a shelter. We don't have the money, and we don't have a shelter."

In the phone booth Doreen Newell turned and glanced across the street. She looked at the two-year-old Audi she'd bought before leaving California, still with the ten-day plates, and registered in the name of Erma Eldridge. It was the name that was now listed on her driver's license, her Social Security card and her passport.

"No," the tall woman said, wiping a tear from her eye and thinking about the one-point-eight million dollars in cash that reposed in her luggage in the car's trunk, money that formerly belonged to the Princes of Hell Motorcycle Club, Incorporated.

"No, miss," the tall woman said, "*you* don't understand. You have your money. And you have your shelter—as of right now."

IT WAS two and a half weeks after the shootings. The Princes of Hell Motorcycle Club had ceased to exist. The summer sun shone down on the Potomac River.

Aboard the sumptuous cabin cruiser were three people: a heavyset black man, a slim and beautiful Latino woman and an average-looking white guy with close-cropped hair. They all wore bathing suits.

The woman said to the black man, "I'm going to say it one last time, Director—Harry and I really appreciate this. We need a winding down."

The older man smiled. "Carmelita," he said, "in the office, I'm the boss, and it's nice for you to call me Director. But on my boat you're my friends, and my friends call me Skip."

She smiled at him. They were alone at the bow, he sitting and she supine, enjoying the warmth of the sun. The white guy was at the rear of the boat, staring glumly at the white foam wake.

"Thanks...Skip. That's going to take some getting used to. I just want you to know, it means something to know that you understand about winding down after something like this."

The director smiled back. "You and Harry did a great job," he said in his soft rumble of a voice. "It was your first Code Zero. I was curious how it affected you."

Carmelita lifted her sunglasses. Her frank brown eyes stared into the director's. "I knew I could do it. I did it. One of them felt good to do, knowing what he'd done. If feeling good about it means you can't do it anymore, that's up to you."

The director shook his head. "Would it surprise you to know that *I* felt good about it? I think you know what it meant to me, after...after the way it started."

She reached out and touched his hand. "My sister is a nurse," Carmelita said. "She spends a lot of time in the terminal ward. I asked her once, how could she stand to deal with all that death and grief? She told me that the death and grief were going to be there whether she was there or not. The difference was, if she was there, she could relieve some of the grief, some of the suffering. I guess that's why I bought into Code Zero, Skip."

He watched her eyes as she spoke. He was a trained interrogator. Her eyes had not flickered, her voice had not faltered, and he knew she was telling the truth.

"I appreciate that," he said. "I appreciate you."

She smiled. A gust of wind came across the bow and blew her hair to the side. She felt it happen, and she reached up to brush her hair back. The director caught her hand.

"Don't," he said. "Don't worry about the scar. That scar is honor. It's a medal."

She smiled back and took her hand away. The wind blew her hair away again, leaving the scar on the edge of her forehead exposed. She let it go. She squeezed his hand. "Thank you," she whispered.

The director stood and made his way to the rear of the boat. He came up behind the man with the close-cropped hair.

"Good job," the director said simply.

"Thanks," said Harry Wolfe.

"Having second thoughts?"

Wolfe looked into the distance before he answered. He remembered Rax's face being blasted back away from the muzzle of his .45 automatic. Harry had not put that in his verbal report. The only other people who knew it had happened were all dead now.

The director looked out at the water. "It looks like a clean wrap. Your lady informant confirms that Fat Phil's copy of the Voit tape, which we recovered from his desk at the clubhouse, hadn't been copied. You said the informant's out clean. Still worried about the Princes getting at her mother in Visalia?"

"No," said Wolfe. "She knew where all the money's buried. She doesn't owe her mom a whole lot, but blood is blood. She's moving her to the East Coast."

Wolfe sipped his beer. He'd developed a taste for Budweiser lately. "I don't think it's that clean a wrap," he said. "There were ten made members involved in the thing with Voit. We accounted for eight."

"You did better than that," said the director placidly. "Once they knew Fat Phil wasn't there to take care of them anymore, and no one to inherit the mantle of prez, some of the Princes in custody seemed to start talking awfully quick. Remember the two you dropped at the Red Wing, the guy whose neck you snapped and the one with all the broken ribs? They were the other two who'd been to the Voit house."

"Then I'll have to go back," said Wolfe flatly.

"No need," the director told him. "They both died last night, the one at home and the other still at the hospital. Complications."

"That was convenient," said Wolfe.

"You and Carmelita aren't our only Code Zero personnel. The efficiency frightens me sometimes."

"There are always going to be second thoughts after a Code Zero," Wolfe said. "You must have known that when you created us, Director."

"Skip," said the director. "On the boat, when we're alone, I'd rather you called me Skip. And, yes, I did know that would happen when I unleashed Code Zero. That's why I asked you."

Harry looked out over the water, felt the cool breeze lashing his face and head. "Sure, I've got second thoughts. Code Zero means committing murder. It's like a Mickey Spillane novel. We're the judge, we're the jury and we're the executioner."

"We're also the appellate court. We review our own actions and pass judgment upon ourselves. We have to. Did you pass the appellate hearing?"

"Yes," Wolfe sighed. "I ran it all the way up to my own Supreme Court before I pulled the trigger. I hated myself for doing it. But I'll never know how many decent people saved by pulling that trigger. I can live with it.''

After a long moment the director said, ''I want to than you, Harry, you and Carmelita. I know it was hard for you I just want you to know that it meant a very great deal to m personally. Remember, we talked about your thing with th post-shooting trauma? Well, I think it's time. I'd like yo to implement that program before the end of the next fisca year.''

''Is that my next assignment?''

''Unless a Code Zero comes along. If it does, are you sti ready for it?''

Wolfe crumpled his empty beer can and threw it into th stern. He thought of the men he had killed. He asked him self for the thousandth time if their deaths were warranted The answer was the same as always.

He turned and looked the director of Centac square in th eye.

''When I'm not ready for it anymore,'' said Agent Harr Wolfe, ''I'll let you know.''

GLOSSARY

a.k.a.—An alias, literally meaning Also Known As.

BATF—Federal Bureau of Alcohol, Tobacco and Firearms, the primary repository of gun registration lists.

blue and blond—Law-enforcement terminology for blue eyes, blond hair.

Centac—A special group within the Drug Enforcement Administration, empowered to investigate major drug offenders and to bring to justice the murderers of DEA agents outside the legal system. The name originated as a contraction of "central tactical" group.

CI—Confidential Informant. Law-enforcement shorthand for what criminals call a fink or a stool pigeon.

Code Zero—"License to execute" priority code of Centac.

DEA—Drug Enforcement Administration.

DOB—Acronym for Date of Birth.

DT—Defensive Tactics. Police terminology for unarmed combat.

ETA—Estimated Time of Arrival.

FI—Field Interview. Casual interrogation of suspect by officers.

fish—Prison jargon for new inmates.

lone wolf—Outlaw biker terminology for a hard man who, though following the biker life-style, chooses not to belong to a club.

MAGLOCLEN—The Mid-Atlantic/Great Lakes Organized Crime Law Enforcement Network. Functions as an information-gathering center and data bank on criminal suspects and gangs.

NAACP—The National Association for the Advancement of Colored People is the oldest and most respected black citizens' rights lobby group in the U.S.

NCIC—National Crime Information Centre.

op—Abbreviation of "operation."

PPCT—Pressure Point Control Tactics. This is a police fighting method developed by a former police officer with the St. Louis county sheriff's office to allow individuals to be stunned out without suffering serious or permanent injury.

RICO statutes—The Rico statutes—Racketeer Influenced Corrupt Organization—are U.S. federal laws designed to fight organized crime.

righteous—In the outlaw biker culture, a man who defeats another in an open fight is "righteous," that is, he is not usually the subject of gang vengeance, which is reserved for traitors, informants and those who openly challenge the gang itself.

sally port—Secured entrance through which police vehicles pass to discharge their prisoners for direct processing through booking and jailing.

SAND—A contraction for Search and Destroy operation.

sheep—Outlaw biker terminology for a woman who has voluntary sex indiscriminately with gang members. She will often wear a tattoo stating the name of the club whose "property" she is. They are also commonly known as "mamas."

sleds—Outlaw biker terminology for motorcycles.

suits—FBI and DEA terminology for a bureaucrat who doesn't understand street law enforcement.

terminate with extreme prejudice—CIA terminology for assassination.

toke—An inhalation from a marijuana cigarette. Outdated hippie slang from the 1960s, still in use by outlaw biker gangs.

U/C—This stands for "You-See," the term used by both police and the underworld for undercover law-enforcement agents.

VIN—Vehicle Identification Number.

wannabe—A probationary member who "wants to be" a "made" member, that is, a full-fledged member of an outlaw gang.

These heroes can't be beat!
Celebrate the American hero with this collection of never-before-published installments of America's finest action teams—ABLE TEAM, PHOENIX FORCE and VIETNAM: GROUND ZERO—only in Gold Eagle's

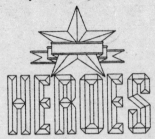

Available for the first time in print, eight new hard-hitting and complete episodes of America's favorite heroes are contained in three action-packed volumes:

In **HEROES: Book I**   July $5.99   592 pages

ABLE TEAM: Razorback by Dick Stivers
PHOENIX FORCE: Survival Run by Gar Wilson
VIETNAM: GROUND ZERO: Zebra Cube by Robert Baxter

In **HEROES: Book II**   August $5.99   592 pages

PHOENIX FORCE: Hell Quest by Gar Wilson
ABLE TEAM: Death Lash by Dick Stivers
PHOENIX FORCE: Dirty Mission by Gar Wilson

In **HEROES: Book III**   September $4.99   448 pages

ABLE TEAM: Secret Justice by Dick Stivers
PHOENIX FORCE: Terror in Warsaw by Gar Wilson

Celebrate the finest hour of the American hero with your copy of the Gold Eagle HEROES collection.

Available in retail stores in the coming months.   HEROES

For the eternal soldier, Dan Samson, the battle has shifted to the Mexican-American war in Book 2 of the time-travel miniseries...

TIMERAIDER

John Barnes

Dan Samson, a hero for all time, is thrown back to the past to fight on the battlefields of history.

In Book 2: BATTLECRY, Dan Samson faces off against deadly enemies on both sides of the conflict—ready to forfeit his life to ensure the course of destiny.

Available in August at your favorite retail outlet.

To order your copy of Book 1: WARTIDE, or Book 2: BATTLECRY, please send your name, address, zip or postal code, along with a check or money order (please do not send cash) for $3.50 for each book ordered, plus 75¢ postage and handling ($1.00 in Canada), payable to Gold Eagle Books to:

In the U.S.	In Canada
Gold Eagle Books	Gold Eagle Books
3010 Walden Avenue	P.O. Box 609
P.O. Box 1325	Fort Erie, Ontario
Buffalo, NY 14269-1325	L2A 5X3

Please specify book title(s) with your order.
Canadian residents add applicable federal and provincial taxes.

GOLD EAGLE

TR2

**In the Deathlands, the only
thing that gets easier is dying.**

JAMES AXLER

DEATH LANDS.
Moon Fate

Out of the ruins of nuclear-torn America emerges a band of warrior-
survivalists, led by a one-eyed man called Ryan Cawdor. In their quest
to find a better life, they embark on a perilous odyssey across the ravaged wasteland known as Deathlands.

An ambush by a roving group of mutant Stickies puts Ryan in the clutches
of a tyrant who plans a human sacrifice as a symbol of his power. With
the rise of the new moon, Ryan Cawdor must meet his fate or chance
an escape through a deadly maze of uncharted canyons.

Justice Marshall Cade and his partner, Janek,
continue to bring home the law in Book 2 of the
exciting new future-law-enforcement
miniseries...

MIKE LINAKER

It takes a new breed of cop to deliver justice in tomorrow's
America—a ravaged world gone mad.

In Book 2: HARDCASE, a series of seemingly random murders
puts Cade and Janek on to a far-reaching conspiracy
orchestrated by a ruthless money manipulator and military
renegades with visions of taking over the U.S. government and
military.

Available in September at your favorite retail outlet.

Play by the
the Dieting Game!

Who says dieting must be dull? It's as exciting as you make it with the handy pocket-size book that proves that you *can* eat your cake and have your shape too! Portion control is the key to healthy eating and successful weight loss, and here's the book that shows you how much of your favorite foods you can enjoy—guilt-free!

Dine on steamed crab (4 oz.) at the finest restaurants for a waist-whittling 110 calories!

Dying for pizza? A *Lean Cuisine* deluxe (6 1/8 oz. package) will set you back only 350 calories. If you're out on the town, you can shoot the works with a *Pizza Hut Personal Pan Pizza* supreme (1 pie, 9.3 oz.) at 647 calories.

You're in control with the book that puts the power back where it belongs: in your own hands. Discover *real* satisfaction with dieting you can live with. *Use it* and you'll lose it!

The Corinne T. Netzer 1993 Calorie Counter

Also by Corinne T. Netzer

THE BRAND-NAME CALORIE COUNTER
THE BRAND-NAME CARBOHYDRATE GRAM COUNTER
THE CHOLESTEROL CONTENT OF FOOD
THE COMPLETE BOOK OF FOOD COUNTS
THE CORINNE T. NETZER DIETER'S DIARY
THE CORINNE T. NETZER ENCYCLOPEDIA OF FOOD VALUES
THE CORINNE T. NETZER GOOD EATING SERIES:

101 Low Fat Recipes
101 High Fiber Recipes
101 Low Cholesterol Recipes*
101 Low Calorie Recipes*
101 Low Sodium Recipes*
THE DIETER'S CALORIE COUNTER
THE CORINNE T. NETZER FAT GRAM COUNTER
*coming soon

QUANTITY SALES

Most Dell books are available at special quantity discounts when purchased in bulk by corporations, organizations, or groups. Special imprints, messages, and excerpts can be produced to meet your needs. For more information, write to: Dell Publishing, 666 Fifth Avenue, New York, NY 10103. Attention: Director, Diversified Sales.

Please specify how you intend to use the books (e.g., promotion, resale, etc.).

INDIVIDUAL SALES

Are there any Dell books you want but cannot find in your local stores? If so, you can order them directly from us. You can get any Dell book currently in print. For a complete up-to-date listing of our books and information on how to order, write to: Dell Readers Service, Box DR, 666 Fifth Avenue, New York, NY 10103.

THE
Corinne T. Netzer
1993
Calorie
Counter

Corinne T. Netzer

A Dell Book

Published by
Dell Publishing
a division of
Bantam Doubleday Dell Publishing Group, Inc.
666 Fifth Avenue
New York, New York 10103

The trademark Dell® is registered in the U.S. Patent and Trademark Office.

ISBN: 0-440-21228-6

Printed in the United States of America

Published simultaneously in Canada

February 1993

10 9 8 7 6 5 4 3 2 1

OPM

Introduction

The Corinne T. Netzer 1993 Calorie Counter has been compiled with a twofold purpose: as an annual, to keep you up-to-date with many of the changes made by the food industry, and to provide a slim, handy, put-in-purse-or-pocket volume.

My books *The Brand-Name Calorie Counter, The Complete Book of Food Counts,* and *The Encyclopedia of Food Values* are much larger in size and scope, and are therefore much less portable. However, *THIS BOOK CONTAINS MORE PRODUCTS THAN ANY OTHER BOOK OF ITS SIZE!*

To keep this book concise yet comprehensive, I have grouped together listings of the same manufacturer whenever possible. Many brand-name yogurts, for example, are listed as "all fruit flavors." Therefore, instead of three pages filled with individual flavors of yogurt, all with identical calorie counts, I have been able to use the extra space for many other products. And for many basic foods and beverages (such as butter, oil, and alcoholic beverages) I have used the generic listing, rather than include the numerous brands with the same or similar caloric values. Also in the interest of saving space, you will generally find only one description of a food—usually in the form it is most commonly eaten.

Finally, in the process of updating this edition without adding pages, it was necessary to eliminate many previous listings to accommodate new products; therefore, if you do not find a specific brand-name food that was listed in a previous edition of this book, this does not necessarily mean that the food product is no longer available. Also, since food producers are constantly revising and improving products, the caloric counts of your favorite food may have changed even if the description of the product hasn't. Be sure to check for any revised entries.

This book contains data derived from individual producers and manufacturers and from the United States government. It contains the most current information available as we go to press.

Good luck—and good eating.

C.T.N.

Abbreviations

approx. . . . . approximately
diam. . . . . diameter
fl. . . . . fluid
lb. . . . . pound(s)
oz. . . . . ounce(s)
pkg. . . . . package
pkt. . . . . packet
tbsp. . . . . tablespoon(s)
tsp. . . . . teaspoon(s)

Symbols

" . . . . inch
< . . . . less than
* . . . prepared according to basic package directions

A

Abalone, fresh, meat only, raw, 4 oz. 119
Acorn squash:
baked, 4 oz. 64
boiled, mashed, 1/2 cup 41
Alfalfa sprouts, raw, 1/2 cup 5
Alfredo sauce (see also "Pasta dishes, mix"):
(*Contadina Fresh*), 6 oz. 540
(*Progresso* Authentic Pasta Sauces), 1/2 cup 340
Allspice, ground (*McCormick/Schilling*), 1 tsp. 6
Almond, shelled:
raw (*Fisher*), 1 oz. 170
dried, sliced or diced, 1 cup 554
Almond butter:
raw (*Hain*), 2 tbsp. 190
toasted, blanched (*Hain*), 2 tbsp. 220
Almond extract, pure (*McCormick/Schilling*), 1 tsp. 10
Almond paste, 1 oz. 127
Amaranth, whole grain, 1 oz. 106
Anchovies, canned, drained, 5 medium, approx. .7 oz. 42
Anise extract, pure (*McCormick/Schilling*), 1 tsp. 23
Anise seed, 1 tsp. 7
Apple:
fresh, with peel, 1 medium, 2³/4″ diam. — 81
fresh, peeled, 1 medium, 2³/4″ diam. 72
fresh, peeled, sliced, 1/2 cup 31
canned, diced or sliced (*Lucky Leaf/Musselman's*), 4 oz. . . . 50
canned, rings, spiced (*White House*), 3.5 oz. 180
dried, slices (*Del Monte*), 2 oz. 140
Apple, escalloped, frozen (*Stouffer's*), 4 oz. 130
Apple butter, all varieties (*Smucker's*), 1 tbsp. 36
Apple chips, all varieties (*Nature's Favorite*), 1 oz. . . . 120
Apple cider:
sparkling (*Lucky Leaf*), 6 fl. oz. 80

Apple cider (cont.)
canned or frozen* (*Tree Top*), 6 fl. oz. 90
spiced, instant (*Alpine*), 1 pkt. 16
Apple crisp, frozen (*Pepperidge Farm* Classic), 1 piece 240
Apple Danish, see "Danish"
Apple drink (*Hi-C* Jammin' Apple), 6 fl. oz. 90
Apple dumpling, frozen (*Pepperidge Farm*), 3 oz. 260
Apple juice:
(*Welch's* 100% Pure), 6 fl. oz. 80
blend (*Libby's Juicy Juice*), 6 fl. oz. 90
chilled or frozen* (*Sunkist*), 8 fl. oz. 79
cocktail (*Welch's Orchard*), 10 fl. oz. 170
Apple pastry pocket (*Tastykake*), 3-oz. piece 323
Apple pie, see "Pie"
Apple-cherry juice (*Del Monte*), 6 fl. oz. 100
Apple-cranberry juice:
(*Smucker's* 100%), 8 fl. oz. 120
cocktail (*Welch's* Juice Cocktail), 6 fl. oz. 110
Apple-grape juice:
(*Mott's*), 6 fl. oz. 86
canned or frozen* (*Tree Top*), 6 fl. oz. 100
cocktail (*Welch's Orchard*), 6 fl. oz. 110
drink (*Apple & Eve*), 8.45 fl. oz. 120
Apple-orange-pineapple juice drink (*Welch's Orchard* Juice
   Cocktail), 6 fl. oz. 110
Applesauce:
(*Del Monte Lite*), 1/2 cup 50
(*Mott's* Natural), 6 oz. 80
(*Stokely*), 1/2 cup 90
cinnamon (*Mott's*), 6 oz. 152
Apricot:
fresh, 3 medium, approx. 12 per lb. 51
fresh, pitted, halves, 1/2 cup 37
canned, in juice (*Libby Lite*), 1/2 cup 60
canned, halves, unpeeled, heavy syrup (*Del Monte*), 1/2 cup . . . 100
dried (*Del Monte*), 2 oz. 140
Apricot fruit syrup:
(*Knott's Berry Farm*), 1 fl. oz. 100
(*Polaner's* Pourable Fruit), 1 fl. oz. 72
Apricot nectar (*Del Monte*), 6 fl. oz. 100
Arby's:
breakfast, 1 serving:
   biscuit, plain, 2.9 oz. 280
   biscuit, bacon, 3.1 oz. 318
   biscuit, ham, 4.4 oz. 323
   biscuit, sausage, 4.2 oz. 460

croissant, plain, 2.2 oz.   260
croissant, bacon and egg, 4.3 oz.   430
croissant, ham and cheese, 4.2 oz.   345
croissant, mushroom and cheese, 5.2 oz.   493
croissant, sausage and egg, 5 oz.   519
Danish, cinnamon nut, 3.5 oz.   360
muffin, blueberry, 2.7 oz.   240
scrambled egg platter, 7.1 oz.   460
scrambled egg and bacon platter, 7.8 oz.   593
scrambled egg and ham platter, 9.1 oz.   518
scrambled egg and sausage platter, 8.4 oz.   640
Toastix, 3.5 oz.   420
sandwiches, 1 serving:
   Arby Q, 6.7 oz.   389
   bac'N cheddar deluxe, 8.1 oz.   512
   beef'N cheddar, 6.9 oz.   509
   chicken breast fillet, 7.2 oz.   445
   chicken Cordon Bleu, 8 oz.   518
   fish fillet, 7.8 oz.   526
   French Dip, 5.4 oz.   368
   French Dip'N Swiss, 6.3 oz.   429
   grilled chicken barbecue, 7.1 oz.   386
   grilled chicken deluxe, 8.1 oz.   430
   ham'N cheese, 6 oz.   355
   Italian sub, 10.5 oz.   671
   Philly Beef'N Swiss, 7 oz.   467
   roast beef, junior, 3.1 oz.   233
   roast beef, regular, 5.5 oz.   383
   roast beef, giant, 8.5 oz.   544
   roast beef, super, 9 oz.   552
   roast beef deluxe, light, 6.4 oz.   294
   roast beef sub, 10.8 oz.   623
   roast chicken club, 8.4 oz.   503
   roast chicken deluxe, light, 6.8 oz.   276
   roast turkey deluxe, light, 6.8 oz.   260
   tuna sub, 10 oz.   663
   turkey sub, 9.7 oz.   486
potatoes, 1 serving:
   baked, plain, 8.5 oz.   240
   baked, broccoli'N cheddar, 12 oz.   417
   baked, deluxe, 12.3 oz.   621
   baked, mushroom'N cheese, 12.3 oz.   515
   baked, sour cream, 11 oz.   463
   cakes, 3 oz.   204
   cheddar fries, 5 oz.   399
   curly fries, 3.5 oz.   337

Arby's, potatoes, 1 serving (cont.)
french fries, 2.5 oz. 246
soups, 8-oz. serving:
Boston clam chowder 193
chicken noodle, old fashioned 99
cream of broccoli 166
lumberjack mixed vegetable 89
potato with bacon 184
Wisconsin cheese 281
salads, 1 serving:
chef, 14.5 oz. 205
garden, 11.6 oz. 117
roast chicken, 14 oz. 204
side, 5.3 oz. 25
salad dressings and sauces:
Arby's sauce, .5 oz. 15
au jus, 4 oz. 7
blue cheese dressing, 2 oz. 295
buttermilk ranch dressing, 2 oz. 349
honey French dressing, 2 oz. 322
horsey sauce, .5 oz. 55
light Italian dressing, 2 oz. 23
Thousand Island dressing, 2 oz. 298
desserts, 1 serving:
apple turnover, 3 oz. 303
blueberry turnover, 3 oz. 320
cheesecake, 3 oz. 306
cherry turnover, 3 oz. 280
chocolate chip cookie, 1 oz. 130
Polar Swirl, Butterfinger, 11.6 oz. 457
Polar Swirl, Heath, 11.6 oz. 543
Polar Swirl, Oreo, 11.6 oz. 482
Polar Swirl, peanut butter cup, 11.6 oz. 517
Polar Swirl, Snickers, 11.6 oz. 511
shake, chocolate, 12 oz. 451
shake, Jamocha, 11.5 oz. 368
shake, vanilla, 11 oz. 330
Arrowroot, powdered (*Tone's*), 1 tsp. 10
Arugula, fresh, raw, 1/2 cup 2
Artichoke, globe or French:
fresh, boiled, 1 medium, approx. 11.3 oz. raw 60
fresh, boiled, hearts, 4 oz. 57
canned, hearts, drained (*Progresso*), 1/2 cup 16
canned, hearts, marinated, with liquid (*Progresso*), 1/2 cup 190
frozen, hearts (*Birds Eye* Deluxe), 3 oz. 30

Asparagus:

fresh, boiled, 4 medium, 1/2″ diam. at base	14
fresh, boiled, cuts and spears, 1/2 cup	22
canned, green, spears and tips (*Del Monte*), 1/2 cup	20
canned, white (*Green Giant*), 1/2 cup	16
frozen, spears or cuts (*Birds Eye*), 3.3 oz.	25

Asparagus pilaf (*Green Giant Garden Gourmet Right for Lunch***),**
9.5-oz. pkg.	190

Au jus gravy:

canned (*Heinz*), 2 oz. or 1/4 cup	18
mix* (*McCormick/Schilling*), 1/4 cup	20

Avocado:

California, 8 oz. or 1 medium	306
California, puree, 1 cup	407
Florida, 1 lb. or 1 medium	339
Florida, puree, 1 cup	257

Avocado dip, see "Guacamole"

B

Food and Measure	Calories

Bacon:

(*Jones Dairy Farm*), 1 unheated slice	130
(*Oscar Mayer/Oscar Mayer* Lower Salt), 1 cooked slice	35
(*Oscar Mayer* Thick Sliced), 1 cooked slice	55

Bacon, Canadian style:

(*Jones Dairy Farm*), .5-oz. slice	30
(*Oscar Mayer*), .8-oz. slice	25

Bacon, substitute, cooked:

beef (*JM*), 2 slices	100
beef and turkey (*Sizzlean*), 2 strips	70
pork (*Sizzlean*), 2 strips	90
turkey (*Butterball*), 1 slice	25
vegetarian (*Morningstar Farms* Breakfast Strips), 3 strips	80

Bacon bits, real or imitation:
(*Bac*Os*), 2 tsp. 25
(*McCormick/Schilling* Bac'N Pieces), 1 tbsp. 26
(*Oscar Mayer*), 1 tbsp. 20
Bacon-horseradish dip (*Breakstone's* Gourmet/*Sealtest*), 2 tbsp. 70
Bacon-onion dip (*Breakstone's*), 2 tbsp. 70
Bagel, 1 piece:
plain (*Thomas'*) 170
cinnamon raisin (*Thomas'*) 160
egg or onion (*Thomas'*) 180
Bagel, frozen, 1 piece:
plain (*Lender's Bagelettes*), .9 oz. 70
plain, egg, onion, or sesame seed (*Lender's*), 2 oz. 150
plain, soft (*Lender's* Original), 2.5 oz. 200
blueberry or cinnamon-raisin (*Lender's*), 2.5 oz. 190
garlic, poppy seed, pumpernickel, or rye (*Lender's*), 2 oz. 140
oat bran (*Lender's*), 2.5 oz. 170
Bagel chips:
plain or hot'n spicy (*New York Style* Bite Size), 3/4 oz. 100
onion and garlic, toasted (*Pepperidge Farm*), 1/2 oz. 60
sourdough cheese (*Pepperidge Farm*), 1/2 oz. 70
Baking mix (see also "Biscuit mix") (*Bisquik*), 1/2 cup 240
Baking powder (*Davis*), 1 tsp. 8
Baking soda, 1 tsp. 0
Bamboo shoots, canned (*La Choy*), 1/4 cup 6
Banana (see also "Plantain"):
1 medium, 83/4″ long 105
mashed, 1/2 cup 104
Banana extract, imitation (*McCormick/Schilling*), 1 tsp. 11
Banana-berry drink (*Hi-C* Stompin' Banana Berry), 6 fl. oz. 90
Barbecue loaf, pork and beef, 1 oz. 49
Barbecue sauce, 2 tbsp., except as noted:
(*Heinz* Select Original), 1 oz. 40
all varieties (*K.C. Masterpiece*) 60
all varieties, except Texas style (*Hunt's*) 40
Cajun, hickory smoke, old fashioned, or original (*Heinz* Thick &
  Rich), 1 oz. 35
chunky, mesquite, mushroom, onion, or Texas hot (*Heinz* Thick &
  Rich), 1 oz. 30
chunky, honey, or Kansas City (*Kraft* Thick'n Spicy) 60
Hawaiian style (*Hunt's* Thick & Rich), 1 oz. 40
hickory smoke (*Heinz* Select), 1 oz. 35
honey (*Hain*) 28
plain, hickory, or mesquite smoke (*Kraft* Thick 'n Spicy) 50
Oriental (*La Choy*) 32
Texas style (*Hunt's*) 50

Barbecue seasoning (*McCormick/Schilling* Spice Blends), 1 tsp.   3
Barley, pearled, dry (*Quaker Scotch*), 1/4 cup 172
Basil:
fresh, chopped, 2 tbsp. 1
dried, ground (*McCormick/Schilling*), 1 tsp. 3
Bass, fresh, meat only (see also "Sea bass"):
smallmouth and largemouth, raw, 4 oz. 118
striped, baked, broiled, or microwaved, 4 oz. 141
Bay leaves, dried, crumbled (*McCormick/Schilling*), 1 tsp. 5
Bean dip (*Eagle*), 1 oz. 35
Bean salad, canned or in jars:
four-bean (*Hanover*), 1/2 cup 80
green bean, German (*Read*), 1/2 cup 85
three-bean (*Hanover*), 1/2 cup 130
Bean sprouts:
fresh, mung, raw, 1 cup 32
fresh, soy, raw, 1 cup 90
canned (*La Choy*), 2/3 cup 8
Bean and rice mix*, Cajun red or pinto Mexicana (*Fantastic
    Foods*), 10 fl. oz. 190
Beans, adzuki, boiled, 1/2 cup 147
Beans, baked, canned (see also specific listings):
(*Grandma Brown's*), 1 cup 301
(*Green Giant/Joan of Arc*), 1/2 cup 130
(*Hunt's Big John's* Beans'n Fixin's), 4 oz. 170
barbecue (*B&M* Brick Oven), 8 oz. 280
barbecue (*Green Giant Something Special*), 1/2 cup 130
with franks (*Hormel Kid's Kitchen Micro Cup*), 7.5 oz. 290
honey, hot and spicy, or maple (*B&M* Brick Oven), 8 oz. . . . 240
pea, small, with pork (*Friends*), 8 oz. 260
with pork (*Hormel Micro Cup*), 7.5 oz. 250
with pork (*Hunt's*), 4 oz. 135
with pork, in tomato sauce (*Campbell's*), 8 oz. 190
with pork, in tomato sauce (*Green Giant/Joan of Arc*), 1/2 cup 90
red kidney (*B&M* Brick Oven), 8 oz. 240
red kidney, with pork (*Friends*), 8 oz. 270
in tomato sauce or vegetarian (*B&M* Brick Oven), 8 oz. . . . 230
in tomato sauce (*Whole Earth*), 3.9 oz. 90
western style (*Van Camp's*), 1 cup 207
yellow-eyed (*B&M* Brick Oven), 8 oz. 250
Beans, black:
boiled, 1/2 cup 113
canned (*Green Giant/Joan of Arc*), 1/2 cup 90
Beans, broad, see "Broad beans"
Beans, butter, canned (*Green Giant/Joan of Arc*), 1/2 cup 70

Beans, chili, canned:

(*Gebhardt*), 4 oz. 115

all varieties (*Green Giant/Joan of Arc*), 1/2 cup 100

Mexican style (*Van Camp's*), 1 cup 210

Beans, great northern, canned:

(*Green Giant/Joan of Arc*), 1/2 cup 80

with pork (*Allens*), 1/2 cup 100

Beans, green, 1/2 cup, except as noted:

fresh, raw, 1 lb. 123

fresh, boiled, drained 22

canned, all varieties, except Italian, cut (*Del Monte*) 20

canned, all varieties, except almondine (*Green Giant*) 16

canned, almondine (*Green Giant*) 45

canned, dilled (*S&W*) 60

canned, Italian, cut (*Del Monte*) 25

packaged (*Del Monte Vegetable Classics*) 50

frozen, all varieties, except Italian (*Seabrook*), 3 oz. 25

frozen, cut (*Green Giant Harvest Fresh*) 16

frozen, Italian (*Seabrook*), 3 oz. 30

frozen, in butter sauce (*Green Giant* One Serving), 5.5 oz. 60

Beans, green, combinations, frozen or packaged:

country, with potatoes and mushrooms, in sauce (*Del Monte
Vegetable Classics*), 1/2 cup 60

and mushrooms, creamy (*Green Giant Garden Gourmet Right for
Lunch*), 9.5-oz. pkg. 220

potatoes, mushrooms, sauce (*Green Giant Pantry Express*),
1/2 cup 60

Beans, kidney, canned:

red (*Hunt's*), 4 oz. 100

red (*Progresso*), 4 oz. 100

white (*Progresso* Cannellini), 4 oz. 80

Beans, lima:

canned (*S&W*), 1/2 cup 100

canned, green (*Del Monte*), 1/2 cup 70

frozen, baby (*Green Giant Harvest Fresh*), 1/2 cup 80

frozen, Fordhook (*Seabrook*), 3.3 oz. 100

frozen, in butter sauce (*Green Giant*), 1/2 cup 100

Beans, Mexican style, canned:

(*Green Giant Something Special*), 1/2 cup 110

(*Old El Paso* Mexe-Beans), 1/2 cup 163

Beans, navy, canned, honey (*Green Giant Something Special*),
1/2 cup 160

Beans, pinto:

canned (*Gebhardt*), 4 oz. 100

canned (*Green Giant/Joan of Arc*), 1/2 cup 90

frozen (*Seabrook*), 3.2 oz. 160

Beans, red, canned (*Green Giant/Joan of Arc*), 1/2 cup 90
Beans, refried, canned or in jars:
(*Gebhardt*), 4 oz. 100
plain or with green chilies (*Old El Paso*), 1/4 cup 50
plain, spicy, or vegetarian (*Rosarita*), 4 oz. 100
black beans (*Bearitos*), 3.2 oz. 80
jalapeño (*Gebhardt*), 4 oz. 115
vegetarian (*Old El Paso*), 4 oz. 70
Beans, yellow or wax:
fresh, see "Beans, green"
canned, golden, cut or French style (*Del Monte*), 1/2 cup 20
frozen, cut (*Seabrook*), 3 oz. 25
Beans and frankfurters dinner, frozen (*Banquet* Meals), 10 oz. 350
Bearnaise sauce (*Great Impressions*), 2 tbsp. 192
Beechnut, shelled, 4 oz. 656
Beef, choice grade, trimmed to 1/4″ fat (except as noted),
  boneless, 4 oz.:
brisket, whole, braised, lean with separable fat 437
brisket, whole, braised, lean only 274
chuck roast, arm, braised, lean with separable fat 395
chuck roast, arm, braised, lean only 255
chuck roast, blade, braised, lean with separable fat 412
chuck roast, blade, braised, lean only 298
flank steak, trimmed to 0″ fat, broiled, lean only 235
ground, lean, broiled, medium 308
ground, regular, broiled, medium 328
porterhouse steak, broiled, lean with separable fat 346
porterhouse steak, broiled, lean only 247
rib, whole, roasted, lean with separable fat 426
rib, whole, roasted, lean only 276
round:
  bottom, braised, lean with separable fat 322
  bottom, braised, lean only 249
  eye of, roasted, lean with separable fat 273
  eye of, roasted, lean only 198
  tip, roasted, lean with separable fat 280
  tip, roasted, lean only 213
  top, broiled, lean with separable fat 254
  top, broiled, lean only 214
short ribs, braised, lean with separable fat 534
short ribs, braised, lean only 335
sirloin steak, wedge bone, broiled, lean with separable fat 305
sirloin steak, wedge bone, broiled, lean only 229
T-bone steak, broiled, lean with separable fat 338
T-bone steak, broiled, lean only 243
tenderloin, broiled, lean with separable fat 345

Beef (cont.)

tenderloin, broiled, lean only	252
top loin, broiled, lean with separable fat	338
top loin, broiled, lean only	243

Beef, corned:

(*Oscar Mayer*), .6-oz. slice	15
chopped (*Carl Buddig*), 1 oz.	40
loaf, jellied (*Oscar Mayer*), 1-oz. slice	40
canned (*Dinty Moore*), 2 oz.	130

Beef, corned, hash, canned (*Libby's*), 7.5 oz. 400

Beef, corned, spread (*Hormel*), ¹/₂ oz. 35

Beef, roast, see "Beef"

Beef, roast, hash, canned (*Mary Kitchen*), 7.5 oz. 350

Beef, roast, spread, canned:

(*Underwood* Light), 2¹/₈ oz.	90
regular or mesquite smoked (*Underwood*), 2¹/₈ oz.	140

Beef dinner, frozen:

(*Banquet Extra Helping*), 15.5 oz.	430
in barbecue sauce (*Swanson*), 11 oz.	460
champignon (*Tyson* Premium Dinners), 10.5 oz.	370
chopped steak (*Swanson Hungry Man*), 16.75 oz.	640
marinated (*Le Menu New American Cuisine*), 10.25 oz.	310
pepper steak (*Armour Classics Lite*), 11.25 oz.	220
pepper steak (*Healthy Choice*), 11 oz.	290

pot roast:

(*The Budget Gourmet* Light & Healthy), 1 serving	230
old fashioned (*Le Menu New American Cuisine*), 10 oz.	250
Yankee (*The Budget Gourmet* Hearty & Healthy), 1 serving . . .	320
Yankee (*Healthy Choice*), 11 oz.	250

Salisbury steak:

(*Armour Classics*), 11.25 oz.	350
(*Banquet Extra Helping*), 16.25 oz.	590
(*Healthy Choice*), 11.5 oz.	300
char-grilled (*Le Menu New American Cuisine*), 10.5 oz.	370
parmigiana (*Armour Classics*), 11.5 oz.	410

short ribs (*Tyson* Premium Dinners), 11 oz. 470

sirloin:

(*The Budget Gourmet* Light & Healthy Special), 1 serving . . .	250
barbecue sauce (*Healthy Choice*), 11 oz.	300
chopped (*Swanson*), 11 oz.	370
roast (*Armour Classics*), 10.45 oz.	190
tips (*The Budget Gourmet* Hearty & Healthy), 1 serving	310
tips (*Healthy Choice*), 11.75 oz.	280
tips (*Le Menu New American Cuisine*), 10.25 oz.	360

sirloin and Salisbury steak (*The Budget Gourmet* Hearty & Healthy), 1 serving 350

sliced (*Swanson Hungry Man*), 15.25 oz. 450
Stroganoff (*Armour Classics Lite*), 11.25 oz. 250
Swiss steak (*Swanson*), 10 oz. 350
teriyaki (*The Budget Gourmet* Light & Healthy), 1 serving 270
Beef enchilada, see "Enchilada dinner" or "Enchilada entree"
Beef entree, canned or packaged:
chow mein (*La Choy* Bi-Pack), 3/4 cup 70
ribs, boneless (*Hormel Top Shelf*), 10 oz. 340
roast, tender (*Hormel Top Shelf*), 10 oz. 250
roast, mashed potatoes (*Dinty Moore American Classics*), 10 oz. 260
Salisbury steak (*Hormel Top Shelf*), 10 oz. 320
stew (*Healthy Choice* Microwave), 7.5 oz. 140
stew (*Hormel/Dinty Moore Micro Cup*), 7.5 oz. 190
stew (*Libby's Diner*), 7.75 oz. 240
Beef entree, frozen:
(*Banquet* Platters), 9 oz. 230
Cantonese (*The Budget Gourmet*), 1 serving 270
cheeseburger (*Hormel Quick Meal*), 1 serving 400
cheeseburger, bacon (*Hormel Quick Meal*), 1 serving 440
creamed, chipped (*Stouffer's*), 5.5 oz. 230
Dijon, with pasta and vegetables (*Right Course*), 9.5 oz. 290
fiesta, with corn pasta (*Right Course*), 87/8 oz. 270
jade garden (*Weight Watchers Ultimate 200*), 9 oz. 150
London broil (*Weight Watchers Ultimate 200*), 7.5 oz. 110
noodles, vegetable medley (*Stouffer's* Homestyle), 83/8 oz. 230
Oriental (*The Budget Gourmet* Light & Healthy), 1 serving 290
Oriental (*The Budget Gourmet Quick Stirs*), 1 serving 280
Oriental, with vegetables and rice (*Lean Cuisine*), 85/8 oz. 290
patty:
   charbroiled (*On•Cor* Deluxe Entree), 8 oz. 277
   charbroiled, mushroom gravy (*Banquet Family Entrees*), 7 oz. 260
   Italian style, sauce and (*On•Cor* Deluxe Entree), 8 oz. 316
   and mushroom gravy (*Banquet Entree Express*), 7 oz. 350
   onion gravy and (*Banquet Family Entrees*), 7 oz. 260
pepper Oriental (*Chun King*), 13 oz. 310
pepper steak (*Healthy Choice*), 9.5 oz. 250
pepper steak, with rice (*The Budget Gourmet*), 1 serving 320
pie (*Stouffer's*), 10 oz. 500
pie (*Swanson* Pot Pie), 7 oz. 370
pot roast, browned potatoes (*Stouffer's* Homestyle), 87/8 oz. . . . 280
ribs, barbecue (*Healthy Choice* Homestyle), 11 oz. 330
Salisbury steak:
   (*Banquet Healthy Balance*), 10.5 oz. 260
   (*Dining Lite*), 9 oz. 200
   (*On•Cor* Deluxe Entree), 8 oz. 281
   (*Swanson* Homestyle Recipe), 10 oz. 320

Beef entree, frozen, Salisbury steak (cont.)

sirloin (*The Budget Gourmet* Light & Healthy), 1 serving 220
sirloin (*Kraft Eating Right*), 9.5 oz. 230
and gravy (*Banquet Entree Express*), 7 oz. 300
gravy and (*Banquet Family Entrees*), 7 oz. 260
and macaroni and cheese (*Stouffer's* Homestyle), 9 5/8 oz. . . . 350
gravy and scalloped potatoes (*Lean Cuisine*), 9.5 oz. 240
with mushroom gravy (*Healthy Choice* Homestyle), 11 oz. 280

sirloin:

(*The Budget Gourmet Quick Stirs*), 1 serving 220
cheddar melt (*The Budget Gourmet*), 1 serving 380
herb sauce (*The Budget Gourmet* Light & Healthy), 1 serving . 250
roast, supreme (*The Budget Gourmet*), 1 serving 320
tips, Burgundy sauce (*Swanson* Homestyle), 7 oz. 160
tips, country vegetables (*The Budget Gourmet*), 1 serving . . . 290
tips, and noodles (*Kraft Eating Right*), 9 oz. 280
sliced (*On•Cor* Deluxe Entree), 8 oz. 90
sliced, gravy and (*Banquet Family Entrees*), 7 oz. 140
stew (*On•Cor* Deluxe Entree), 8 oz. 134
Stroganoff (*The Budget Gourmet* Light & Healthy), 1 serving . . 270
teriyaki (*Dining Lite*), 9 oz. 270

Beef entree mix*:

pepper steak (*La Choy* Dinner Classics), 3/4 cup 180
stew, hearty (*Lipton Microeasy*), 1/4 pkg. 370
Beef gravy, canned (*Franco-American*), 2 oz. 25
Beef jerky (*Hormel* Lumberjack), 1 oz. 101

Beef luncheon meat:

all varieties (*Hillshire Farm Deli Select*), 1 oz. 31
corned, see "Beef, corned"
loaf, jellied (*Hormel* Perma-Fresh), 2 slices 90
sandwich steak (*Steak-Umm*), 2 oz. 180
smoked (*Oscar Mayer*), .5-oz. slice 15
smoked, chopped (*Carl Buddig*), 1 oz. 40
Beef pie, see "Beef entree, frozen"

Beef sandwich, frozen or refrigerated:

croissant, with American cheese (*Classic Delights*), 3.8 oz. 270
pocket, and broccoli (*Lean Pockets*), 1 pkg. 250
pocket, and cheddar (*Hot Pockets*), 5 oz. 370

Beef seasoning mix:

ground, with onions (*French's*), 1/4 pkg. 25
stew (*McCormick/Schilling* Bag'n Season), 1 pkg. 87
Stroganoff (*McCormick/Schilling*), 1/4 pkg. 32
Beef stew, see "Beef entree"
Beefalo, meat only, raw, 4 oz. 162

Beer:

regular, 12 fl. oz. 150

light, 12 fl. oz. 95
Beerwurst, see "Salami, beer"
Beet:
fresh, raw, 1 medium, 2″ diam. 36
fresh, boiled, sliced, 1/2 cup 26
canned, whole, tiny or sliced (*Del Monte*), 1/2 cup 35
canned, Harvard (*Stokely*), 1/2 cup 70
canned, pickled, sliced (*Blue Boy*), 1/2 cup 90
Beet greens, fresh, boiled, drained, 1″ pieces, 1 cup 40
Berliner, pork and beef, 1 oz. 65
Berry drink (*Hi-C Boppin' Berry/Hi-C Wild Berry*), 6 fl. oz. 90
Berry juice drink:
mixed, with grape (*Boku*), 8 oz. 120
wild (*Tropicana Juice sparkler*), 6 fl. oz. 84
Bialy, frozen, plain (*Slim's*), 2-oz. piece 140
Biscuit, packaged or refrigerated, 1 piece:
(*Arnold Old Fashioned*) 60
(*Pillsbury Big Premium Heat'n Eat*) 140
(*Pillsbury Country*) 50
all varieties (*Ballard Extra Lights Ovenready*) 50
all varieties (*Grands!*) 190
butter or buttermilk (*Pillsbury*) 50
buttermilk (*Hungry Jack Extra Rich*) 50
buttermilk (*Pillsbury Heat'n Eat*) 85
buttermilk, fluffy (*Hungry Jack*) 90
flaky (*Hungry Jack Butter Tastin'*) 100
fluffy (*Pillsbury Good'n Buttery*) 90
Southern style, flaky (*Hungry Jack*) 80
Biscuit mix* (see also "Baking mix"):
(*Martha White BixMix*), 1 piece 100
(*Robin Hood/Gold Medal Pouch*), with skim milk, 1/8 mix 90
Blackberry, fresh, 1/2 cup 37
Blackberry fruit syrup (*Knott's Berry Farm*), 1 fl. oz. 120
Black-eyed peas:
canned (*Green Giant/Joan of Arc*), 1/2 cup 90
frozen (*Seabrook*), 3.3 oz. 130
Blintz, frozen:
apple (*Empire Kosher Foods*), 6 pieces 100
apple-raisin (*Golden*), 1 piece 152
blueberry, cheese, or cherry (*Empire Kosher Foods*), 6 pieces . . 110
blueberry, cheese, or cherry (*Golden*), 1 piece 153
pillow cheese (*Golden*), 1 piece 188
potato (*Empire Kosher Foods*), 6 pieces 130
potato (*Golden*), 1 piece 103
Blood sausage, 1 oz. 107

Blueberry:

fresh, 1 cup 82

canned, wild Maine, in heavy syrup (*S&W*), 1/2 cup 111

Blueberry fruit syrup:

(*Knott's Berry Farm*), 1 fl. oz. 120

(*Polaner's* Pourable Fruit), 1 fl. oz. 72

(*Smucker's*), 1 fl. oz. 100

Bluefish, meat only, baked, broiled, or microwaved, 4 oz. 180

Bockwurst, 1 link, approx. 2.3 oz. 200

Bologna:

(*Hillshire Farm* Large), 1 oz. 90

(*Kahn's* Thick Deluxe), 1 slice 140

(*Kahn's* Thin Sliced Deluxe), 1 slice 60

(*Oscar Mayer/Oscar Mayer* Wisconsin), 1 oz. 90

(*Oscar Mayer* Light), 1-oz. slice 60

beef:

   (*Eckrich* Thick Sliced), 1.5-oz. slice 130

   (*Hebrew National* Original Deli Style), 1 oz. 90

   (*Oscar Mayer* Light), 1-oz. slice 60

   plain or garlic (*Oscar Mayer*), 1 oz. 90

   Lebanon (*Oscar Mayer*), .8-oz. slice 45

with cheese (*Oscar Mayer*), .8-oz. slice 75

cheese or garlic (*Eckrich*), 1-oz. slice 90

garlic (*Oscar Mayer*), 1.4-oz. slice 130

pork, 1-oz. slice 70

turkey, see "Turkey bologna"

Bolognese sauce, canned or refrigerated:

(*Contadina Fresh*), 7.5 oz. 230

(*Master Choice*), 1/2 cup 90

(*Progresso* Authentic Pasta Sauces), 1/2 cup 150

Bonito, meat only, raw, 1 oz. 37

Bouillon (see also "Soup"):

beef (*Steero*), 1 tsp. or cube 6

brown or golden (*G. Washington's*), 1 pkt. 6

chicken (*Steero*), 1 tsp. or cube 8

chicken or onion (*MBT*), 1 pkt. 14

onion or vegetable (*G. Washington's*), 1 pkt. 12

Boysenberry, fresh, see "Blackberry"

Boysenberry fruit syrup (*Knott's Berry Farm*), 1 fl. oz. 120

Boysenberry juice (*Smucker's* 100%), 8 fl. oz. 120

Brains:

beef, pan-fried, 4 oz. 222

veal (calf), braised, 4 oz. 154

Bran (see also "Cereal"), unprocessed (*Quaker*), 2 tbsp. 8

Brandy extract, imitation (*McCormick/Schilling*), 1 tsp. 20

Bratwurst:

(*Hillshire Farm* Fully Cooked), 2 oz.	170
fresh or smoked (*Hillshire Farm*), 2 oz.	190
smoked (*Eckrich* Lite), 1 link	190
spicy (*Hillshire Farm*), 2 oz.	180
Braunschweiger (see also "Liverwurst") (*Oscar Mayer/Oscar Mayer* German Brand), 1 oz.	95
Brazil nut, shelled, 1 oz., 6 large or 8 medium	186
Bread (see also "Bread dough"), 1 slice, except as noted:	
apple-walnut swirl (*Pepperidge Farm*)	80
(*Arnold Bran'nola* Original)	90
bran, honey (*Pepperidge Farm* Old Fashioned)	90
bran, light (*Arnold Bakery* Country)	40
bran and oat (*Oatmeal Goodness* Light)	40
brown, canned (*S&W* New England), 2 slices	76
cinnamon oatmeal (*Oatmeal Goodness*)	90
cinnamon swirl (*Pepperidge Farm*)	90
date nut roll (*Dromedary*), 1/2" slice	80
French, twin (*Arnold Francisco*), 2 oz.	150
French twin (*Pepperidge Farm* European Bake Shoppe), 1 oz. . . .	80
garlic (*Colombo* Brand), 2 oz.	185
grain, multi (*Hearty Grains*)	80
grain, seven, light (*Pepperidge Farm* Light Style)	40
grain, twelve (*Arnold* Natural)	60
Irish potato (*Pepperidge Farm* Hearty)	95
Italian (*Pepperidge Farm* Deli Classics)	70
Italian, light (*Arnold Bakery*)	40
(*Monk's* Hi-Fibre)	70
oat (*Arnold Bran'nola* Country)	90
oatmeal, light (*Arnold* Bakery)	40
oatmeal, soft (*Pepperidge Farm*)	60
oatmeal or oatmeal raisin (*Arnold*)	60
oatmeal raisin (*Hearty Grains*)	90
oatmeal twists (*Hearty Grains* Country)	80
pita (*Sahara*), 1/2 regular or 1 mini	80
pita, large (*Sahara* Original), 1 piece	120
pita, oat bran (*Sahara*), 1/2 piece	80
pita, wheat or white (*Arnold*), 1/2 piece	71
pita, whole wheat (*Sahara*), 1 piece	130
pita, whole wheat, mini (*Sahara*), 1 piece	80
pumpernickel (*Pepperidge Farm* Party), 4 slices	60
pumpernickel, soft (*Pepperidge Farm*)	50
raisin (*Arnold/Sunmaid*)	70
raisin cinnamon swirl (*Pepperidge Farm*)	90
rye (*Pepperidge Farm* Party), 4 slices	60
rye, Dijon (*Pepperidge Farm* Thick Sliced)	70

Bread (cont.)

rye, dill (*Arnold*)	60
rye, Jewish (*Arnold* Real Melba Thin)	40
rye, Jewish, Dijon, seeded or seedless (*Arnold* Real)	70
rye, onion (*Arnold/August Bros.*)	80
rye, seedless or seeded (*Arnold/August Bros.*, 1 lb.)	80
rye, seedless, thin sliced (*Arnold/August Bros.*)	40
rye, seedless or seeded, soft (*Arnold Bakery*)	70
rye, soft, light (*Arnold Bakery*)	40
rye and pumpernickel (*Arnold/August Bros.*, 1½ lb.)	90
sourdough, French (*Boudin*), 2 oz. or 2 slices	130
sunflower and bran (*Monk's*)	70
Vienna, thick-sliced (*Pepperidge Farm* Deli Classics)	70
wheat:	
(*Arnold* Natural)	80
(*Pepperidge Farm* Light Style)	45
(*Thomas'* Lite)	40
cracked, and honey, twists (*Hearty Grains*)	80
dark (*Arnold Bran'nola*)	90
golden, light (*Arnold Bakery*)	40
hearty (*Arnold Bran'nola*)	100
honey wheatberry (*Pepperidge Farm* Hearty)	90
oatmeal (*Oatmeal Goodness*)	90
sesame (*Pepperidge Farm*)	95
whole (*Pepperidge Farm* Thin Sliced, 1 lb.)	60
whole, light (*Arnold* Brick Oven 100%)	40
whole, soft (*Pepperidge Farm*)	50
white (*Arnold* Country)	100
white (*Pepperidge Farm* Country)	95
white (*Pepperidge Farm* Sandwich), 2 slices	130
white (*Pepperidge Farm* Toasting)	90
white (*Wonder*)	70
white, extra fiber (*Arnold* Brick Oven)	50
white, light (*Arnold Bakery* Premium/Brick Oven)	40

Bread, sweet, mix*:

apple-cinnamon or blueberry (*Pillsbury* Quick), 1/12 loaf	180
banana or nut (*Pillsbury* Quick), 1/12 loaf	170
blueberry nut (*Pillsbury*), 1/12 loaf	150
cherry nut (*Pillsbury*), 1/12 loaf	180
corn bread (*Ballard*), 1/16 mix	150
corn bread, white (*Robin Hood/Gold Medal* Pouch), 1/6 mix	140
cranberry or date (*Pillsbury* Quick), 1/12 loaf	160
date nut (*Dromedary*), 1/12 loaf	183
gingerbread (*Pillsbury*), 1/9 mix	180
oatmeal raisin (*Pillsbury* Quick), 1/12 loaf	190

Bread crumbs, plain or Italian (*Arnold*), ½ oz. ... 50

Bread dough:

frozen, challah (*Kineret*), 2 oz. 150
frozen, honey walnut or white (*Bridgford*), 1 oz. 76
refrigerated, corn bread twists (*Pillsbury*), 1 twist 70
referigerated, French, crusty (*Pillsbury*), 1″ slice 60
refrigerated, wheat or white (*Pipin' Hot*), 1″ slice 70
Breadfruit, 1/4 small, approx. 3.4 oz. 99
Breadsticks, 1 piece, except as noted:
garlic or sesame seed, soft (*Pepperidge Farm*) 130
garlic and herb, pizza, or traditional (*Master Choice*) 14
plain (*Stella D'Oro*) 41
onion (*Stella D'Oro*) 40
pizza (*Fattorie & Pandea*), 3 pieces 59
sesame or sun-dried tomato, thin (*Pepperidge Farm*) 60
seven grain, soft (*Pepperidge Farm*) 120
refrigerator, soft (*Pillsbury*) 100
Broad beans, boiled, drained, 4 oz. 64
Broccoli:
fresh, raw, 1 spear, approx. 8.7 oz. 42
fresh, boiled, drained, chopped, 1/2 cup 22
frozen:
  spears (*Green Giant Harvest Fresh*), 1/2 cup 20
  spears, cuts, or chopped (*Birds Eye*), 3.3 oz. 25
  florets (*Birds Eye Deluxe*), 3.3 oz. 25
  in butter sauce, cuts (*Green Giant* One Serving), 4.5 oz. 45
  in cheese-flavored sauce (*Green Giant*), 1/2 cup 60
Broccoli combinations, frozen:
carrots and rotini, cheese sauce (*Green Giant* One Serving),
  5.5 oz. 100
cauliflower medley (*Green Giant Valley Combinations*), 1/2 cup   60
cauliflower and carrots:
  (*Green Giant* One Serving), 4 oz. 30
  in butter sauce (*Green Giant*), 1/2 cup 30
  with cheese sauce (*Birds Eye Combinations*), 4.5 oz. 110
  in cheese-flavored sauce (*Green Giant*), 1/2 cup 60
fanfare (*Green Giant Valley Combinations*), 1/2 cup 80
and red peppers (*Green Giant*), 1/2 cup 25
potatoes, cauliflower, bacon (*Birds Eye* Austrian), 3.3 oz. 70
Broccoli and cheese pastry, frozen (*Pepperidge Farm/Pepperidge
Farm* Bake-Your-Own), 1 piece 230
Brown gravy:
canned (*La Choy*), 1 tsp. 30
canned, regular or with onions (*Heinz*), 2 oz. or 1/4 cup 25
mix* (*McCormick/Schilling* Lite), 1/4 cup 10
mix* (*Pillsbury*), 1/4 cup 16

Brownie:
(*Tastykake*), 3 oz.	335
pecan fudge (*Drake's*), 3 oz.	360
regular or walnut (*Hostess Brownie Bites*), 5 pieces	260
frozen, hot fudge (*Pepperidge Farm* Classic Desserts), 1 piece	370

mix*, 1 piece:
(*Betty Crocker* Supreme Original)	140
(*Betty Crocker* Supreme Party)	150
caramel (*Betty Crocker* Supreme)	120
chocolate, double or walnut (*Pillsbury Great Additions*)	140
chocolate chip (*Betty Crocker* Supreme)	140
frosted (*Betty Crocker MicroRave*)	180
fudge (*Betty Crocker* Light)	100
fudge (*Pillsbury Lovin' Lites*), 1/24 pkg.	100
fudge (*Pillsbury* Microwave), 1/9 mix	190
fudge (*Robin Hood/Gold Medal* Pouch), 1/16 mix	100
fudge, chocolate fudge frosted (*Pillsbury* Microwave)	240
fudge, peanut butter (*Duncan Hines*)	150
Funfetti, frosted (*Pillsbury Great Additions*), 2″ square	140
walnut (*Betty Crocker MicroRave*)	160

Browning sauce (*Gravymaster*), 1 tsp.	12

Brussels sprouts:
fresh, boiled, 1/2 cup	30
frozen (*Birds Eye*), 3.3 oz.	35
frozen, in butter sauce (*Green Giant*), 1/2 cup	40
frozen, baby, in cheese sauce (*Birds Eye* Combinations), 4.5 oz.	130
frozen, with cauliflower, carrots (*Birds Eye* Farm Fresh), 4 oz.	40
Buckwheat groats, roasted (*Arrowhead Mills*), 2 oz. dry	190
Bulgur, cooked, 1 cup	152

Bun, sweet (see also "Roll, sweet"), 1 piece:
honey (*Aunt Fanny's*), 3 oz.	346
honey, glazed (*Tastykake*)	362
honey, iced (*Tastykake*)	348
orange swirl (*Hostess Breakfast Bake Shop*)	230
pecan twirl (*Tastykake*)	109
pecan caramel swirl (*Hostess Breakfast Bake Shop*)	240
Burbot, meat only, baked, broiled, or microwaved, 4 oz.	130

Burger King:
breakfast, 1 serving:
Breakfast Buddy, with egg, cheese, and sausage	255
Croissan'wich with bacon	353
Croissan'wich with ham	351
Croissan'wich with sausage	534
French toast sticks	538
hash browns	213
mini muffins, blueberry	292

burgers and sandwiches, 1 serving:

bacon double cheeseburger	507
bacon double cheeseburger deluxe, 6.9 oz.	584
BK Broiler chicken sandwich, 5.4 oz.	267
Burger Buddies, 4.6 oz.	349
cheeseburger, 4.3 oz.	318
cheeseburger, double, 6.1 oz.	483
cheeseburger deluxe, 5.3 oz.	390
chicken sandwich, 8.1 oz.	685
Chicken Tenders, 6 pieces	236
hamburger, 3.8 oz.	272
hamburger deluxe, 4.9 oz.	344
Ocean Catch fish fillet, 5.8 oz.	479
Whopper, 9.5 oz.	614
Whopper with cheese, 10.4 oz.	706
Whopper, double, 12.4 oz.	844
Whopper, double, with cheese, 13.2 oz.	935

salads and side dishes, 1 serving:

chef salad	178
chicken salad, chunky	142
french fries, medium	372
garden salad	95
onion rings	339
side salad	25

salad dressings and dipping sauces:

BK Broiler sauce, .4 oz.	37
bleu cheese, *Newman's Own,* 1 pkt.	300
Bull's Eye barbecue sauce, .5 oz.	22
Burger King A.M. Express Dip, 1 oz.	84
French or Thousand Island, *Newman's Own,* 1 pkt.	290
honey dipping sauce, 1 oz.	91
Italian, light, *Newman's Own,* 1 pkt.	170
olive oil and vinegar, *Newman's Own,* 1 pkt.	310
ranch, *Newman's Own,* 1 pkt.	350
ranch dipping sauce, 1 oz.	171
sweet and sour dipping sauce, 1 oz.	45

desserts and shakes, 1 serving:

apple pie, 4.4 oz.	311
cherry pie, 4.5 oz.	360
lemon pie, 3.2 oz.	290
shake, chocolate, 10 oz.	326
shake, strawberry, 11 oz.	394
shake, vanilla, 10 oz.	334
Snickers ice cream bar, 2 fl. oz.	220

Burrito, frozen, 1 piece, except as noted:

bean and cheese or medium beef and bean (*Old El Paso*)	330

Burrito (cont.)

beef, nacho (*Patio Britos*), 3 oz.	220
beef and bean, hot (*Old El Paso*)	310
beef and bean, medium (*Patio*), 5-oz. pkg.	370
beef and bean, mild (*Old El Paso*)	320
beef and bean, red chili, red hot (*Patio*), 5-oz. pkg.	360
beef and bean or spicy chicken and cheese (*Patio Britos*), 3 oz.	210
cheese, nacho (*Patio Britos*), 3.63 oz.	250
Burrito dinner, frozen, beef and bean (*Banquet Meals*), 9.5 oz.	390
Burrito seasoning mix (*Old El Paso*), 1/8 pkg.	17

Butter, salted or unsalted:

regular, 4 oz., 1 stick, or 1/2 cup	813
regular, 1 tbsp.	102
whipped, 1/2 cup or 1 stick	542
whipped, 1 tbsp.	67

Butter flavor seasoning:

original, garlic, or sour cream (*McCormick/Schilling Best O' Butter*), 1 tsp.	8
cheddar cheese (*McCormick/Schilling Best O' Butter*), 1 tsp.	12
Butterfish, meat only, baked, broiled, or microwaved, 4 oz.	212

Butternut squash:

fresh, baked, cubed, 1/2 cup	41
frozen (*Southland*), 3.6 oz.	80
Butterscotch baking chips (*Nestlé* Toll House Morsels), 1 oz.	150
Butterscotch topping (*Smucker's*), 2 tbsp.	140

C

Food and Measure	**Calories**

Cabbage, 1 cup, except as noted:

fresh, green, raw, shredded	16
fresh, green, boiled, drained, shredded	32
fresh, red, raw, shredded	19
fresh, red, boiled, drained, shredded	32

fresh, savoy, boiled, drained, shredded 35
canned, red, sweet-sour (*Blue Boy*), 1/2 cup 70
Cabbage, Chinese, fresh:
bok choy, boiled, drained, shredded, 1 cup 20
pe-tsai, boiled, drained, shredded, 1 cup 16
Cabbage entree, stuffed, frozen:
(*Lean Cuisine*), 10.75 oz. 210
(*On•Cor* Deluxe Entree), 8 oz. 170
Cake, frozen or refrigerated, 1 slice or piece:
Black Forest (*Sara Lee*), 1/8 cake 190
Boston cream (*Mrs. Smith's, 8"*), 1/8 cake 180
carrot, single layer, iced (*Sara Lee*), 1/8 cake 250
cheese, cream (*Sara Lee* Original), 1/6 cake 230
cheese, strawberry, French (*Sara Lee* Classic), 1/8 cake . . 240
chocolate fudge or German layer (*Pepperidge Farm*), 15/8 oz. . . . 180
chocolate mousse (*Pepperidge Farm* Supreme), 2 oz. 190
coconut layer (*Pepperidge Farm*), 15/8 oz. 180
coffee, all varieties, iced (*Pillsbury* Streusel), 1/6 cake 230
coffee, all butter pecan or streusel (*Sara Lee*), 1/8 cake 160
devil's food layer (*Pepperidge Farm*), 15/8 oz. 180
golden layer (*Pepperidge Farm*), 15/8 oz. 180
lemon coconut (*Pepperidge Farm* Supreme), 3 oz. 280
pineapple cream (*Pepperidge Farm* Supreme), 2 oz. 190
pound, all butter (*Sara Lee* Family Size Original), 1/15 cake 130
pound, chocolate or golden (*Pepperidge Farm* Fat Free), 1 oz. 70
strawberry cream (*Pepperidge Farm* Supreme), 2 oz. 190
strawberry stripe layer (*Pepperidge Farm*), 1.5 oz. 160
vanilla layer (*Pepperidge Farm*), 15/8 oz. 190
Cake, mix*, 1/12 cake, except as noted:
all varieties (*Pillsbury Streusel Swirl*), 1/16 cake 260
angel food (*Pillsbury Lovin' Loaf*), 1/8 cake 90
angel food, traditional (*Betty Crocker*) 130
apple streusel (*Betty Crocker MicroRave*), 1/6 cake 240
banana or chocolate, German (*Pillsbury Plus*) 250
Black Forest cherry (*Pillsbury* Bundt), 1/16 cake 270
Boston cream (*Betty Crocker* Classic), 1/8 cake 270
butter chocolate (*Betty Crocker SuperMoist*) 280
butter recipe or carrot (*Pillsbury Plus*) 260
butter yellow (*Betty Crocker SuperMoist*) 260
cheesecake (*Royal No-Bake*), 1/8 cake 160
cherry chip (*Betty Crocker SuperMoist*) 190
chocolate, fudge, milk, or German (*Betty Crocker SuperMoist*) 260
chocolate caramel (*Pillsbury* Bundt), 1/16 cake 290
chocolate chip (*Pillsbury Plus*) 240
chocolate chocolate chip (*Betty Crocker SuperMoist*) 260
chocolate macaroon (*Pillsbury* Bundt), 1/16 cake 280

Cake, mix* (cont.)

chocolate mousse (*Pillsbury* Bundt), 1/16 cake	260
chocolate pudding (*Betty Crocker* Classic), 1/6 cake	230
cinnamon pecan streusel (*Betty Crocker MicroRave*), 1/6 cake	280
devil's food (*Betty Crocker SuperMoist*)	260
devil's food (*Pillsbury Lovin' Lites*)	170
fudge marble (*Duncan Hines* Delights)	180
lemon or marble (*Betty Crocker SuperMoist*)	260
lemon chiffon or golden pound (*Betty Crocker* Classic)	200
lemon pudding (*Betty Crocker* Classic), 1/6 cake	230
pineapple creme (*Pillsbury* Bundt), 1/16 cake	280
pineapple upside-down (*Betty Crocker* Classic), 1/9 cake	250
sour cream chocolate or spice (*Betty Crocker SuperMoist*)	260
sour cream white (*Betty Crocker SuperMoist*)	180
vanilla sunshine or yellow (*Pillsbury Plus*)	260
white (*Betty Crocker SuperMoist*)	240
yellow (*Duncan Hines* Delights)	180

Cake, snack, 1 piece, except as noted:

apple delight (*Little Debbie*), 1.25 oz.	140
apple strudel (*Aunt Fanny's*), 3 oz.	315
applesauce (*Aunt Fanny's*), 2.5 oz.	234
banana (*Tastykake* Creamie)	165
butterscotch (*Tastykake Krimpets*)	103
cherry strudel (*Aunt Fanny's*), 3 oz.	288
chocolate:	
(*Hostess Grizzly Chomps,* 97% Fat Free)	110
(*Hostess Ho Hos*)	120
(*Little Debbie*), 2.5 oz.	320
(*Tastykake* Juniors)	341
cream filled (*Drake's Devil Dog*), 1.5 oz.	160
fudge (*Aunt Fanny's*), 2.5 oz.	222
fudge crispy (*Little Debbie*), 2.08 oz.	260
mint, cream filled (*Drake's Ring Ding*), 1.5 oz.	190
roll, cream filled (*Drake's Yodel*), 1 oz.	150
chocolate or coconut (*Tastykake* Kandy Kake)	78
chocolate chip (*Hostess* Cookie Cakes), 5 pieces	250
coconut (*Tastykake* Junior)	296
coffee (*Tastykake* Koffee Kake Junior)	261
coffee, cream filled (*Tastykake* Koffee Kake)	110
coffee, small (*Drake's*), 2 oz.	220
coffee crumb cake, chocolate (*Drake's*), 2.25 oz.	245
coffee crumb cake, cinnamon (*Drake's*), 1.3 oz.	150
coffee crumb cake, cinnamon (*Hostess* 97% Fat Free)	80
cupcake:	
chocolate (*Tastykake*)	100
chocolate (*Tastykake* Royale)	171

chocolate, cream filled (*Tastykake*) 118
chocolate, creme filled (*Hostess* Lights) 130
chocolate or vanilla, cream filled (*Tastykake Tastylight*) 100
golden, cream filled (*Drake's Sunny Doodle*), 1 oz. 100
orange (*Aunt Fanny's*), 3 oz. 334
devil's food finger (*Aunt Fanny's*), 3 oz. 288
golden or banana, creme filled (*Hostess Twinkies*) 150
lemon (*Tastykake* Junior) 306
orange (*Tastykake* Junior) 337
peanut butter (*Tastykake* Kandy Kake) 87
pound (*Aunt Fanny's*), 2.5 oz. 260
raspberry finger (*Aunt Fanny's*), 3 oz. 303
spice finger (*Aunt Fanny's*), 3 oz. 290
strawberry (*Hostess Twinkies* Fruit'n Creme), 1.8 oz. 160
vanilla (*Hostess Grizzly Chomps*, 97% Fat Free) 110
vanilla (*Tastykake* Creamie) 184
Cake, snack, frozen, 1 piece or serving:
Black Forest or carrot (*Sara Lee* Lights) 170
carrot (*Pepperidge Farm* Classic), 2.5 oz. 260
cheese, classic (*Sara Lee*) 200
cheese, strawberry (*Pepperidge Farm* Classic Desserts) 250
chocolate, German (*Pepperidge Farm* Classic Desserts) 250
chocolate mousse (*Sara Lee*), 3 oz. 180
coconut (*Pepperidge Farm* Classic), 2.25 oz. 230
coffee, apple cinnamon (*Sara Lee* Individual) 290
coffee, pecan (*Sara Lee* Individual) 280
lemon supreme (*Pepperidge Farm* Dessert Lights), 2.75 oz. . . . 170
pound, all butter (*Sara Lee*) 200
shortcake, strawberry (*Pepperidge Farm* Dessert Lights), 3 oz. . 170
vanilla fudge swirl (*Pepperidge Farm* Classic), 2.25 oz. 250
Cake, snack, mix*, devil's food or yellow (*Betty Crocker MicroRave* Singles), 1 piece 440
Candy:
almond, candy coated (*Brach's* Jordan Almonds), 1 oz. 120
(*Baby Ruth*), 2.2 oz. 300
(*Butterfinger*), 2.1 oz. 280
butterscotch (*Brach's* Disks), 1 oz. 110
caramel (*Kraft*), 1 piece 30
caramel, chocolate coated (*Pom Poms*), 1 oz. 100
caramel or coffee (*Pearson* Nip), 1 oz. 120
caramel cookie bar (*Twix*), 1 oz. 140
cherry, chocolate cream or coated (*Brach's*), 1 oz. 110
chocolate:
   with almonds (*Hershey's Golden Almond/Solitaires*), 1.6 oz. . 260
   with almonds, roasted (*Cadbury*), 1 oz. 150
   candy coated (*M&M's*), 1.69 oz. 230

Candy, chocolate (cont.)

cream (*Callard & Bowser*), 1 oz.	120
dark, sweet (*Hershey's Special Dark*), 1.45 oz.	220
milk chocolate:	
(*Hershey's Kisses*), 1.46 oz. or 9 pieces	220
(*Nestlé*), 1.45 oz.	220
with almonds (*Nestlé*), 1.45 oz.	220
creamy, almonds and toffee (*Hershey's Symphony*), 1.75 oz.	280
with crisps (*Nestlé Crunch*), 1.4 oz.	200
with crisps and peanuts (*Nestlé 100 Grand*), 1.5 oz.	200
with fruit and nuts (*Chunky*), 1.4 oz.	170
with peanuts, candy coated (*M&M's*), 1.74 oz.	250
pecan caramel (*Demet's Turtles*), 1 piece	90
mint or parfait (*Pearson*), 1 oz.	120
white chocolate, with almonds (*Nestlé Alpine*), 1.25 oz.	200
cinnamon (*Brach's* Disks/Imperials), 1 oz.	110
coconut, dark or milk chocolate coated (*Bounty*), 1 oz.	140
cough drops (*Halls* Cough Tablets), 1 piece	15
fruit-flavored chews (*Starburst*), 2.07 oz.	240
fudge (*Kraft* Fudgies), 1 piece	35
gum, 1 average piece	10
honey (*Bit-O-Honey*), 1.7 oz.	200
jellied (*Brach's* Beans/Gummi Bears/Leaves), 1 oz.	100
lemon drops (*Brach's*), 1 oz.	110
licorice (*Pearson* Nip), 1 oz.	120
(*Mars*), 1.76-oz. bar	240
marshmallow (*Campfire*), 2 large or 24 mini pieces	40
(*Milky Way*), 2.15 oz.	280
(*Milky Way* Dark), 1.76 oz.	220
mint, chocolate coated (*York Peppermint Pattie*), 1.5 oz.	180
mint, dark chocolate coated (*After Eight*), 1 piece	35
(*Munch*), 1.42 oz.	220
nonpareils, sweet chocolate (*Nestlé Sno-Caps*), 1 oz.	140
peanut, milk chocolate coated (*Nestlé Goobers*), 1 3/8 oz.	200
peanut brittle (*Kraft*), 1 oz.	130
peanut butter (*PB Max*), 1.48 oz.	240
peanut butter (*Snickers*), 1.76 oz.	280
peanut butter-chocolate, candy coated (*M&M's*), 1.63 oz.	240
peanut butter cup (*Reese's*), 1 piece	34
peanut butter parfait (*Pearson*), 1 oz.	120
raisins, milk chocolate coated (*Raisinets*), 1 3/8 oz.	180
(*Skittles*), 2.3 oz.	270
(*Snickers*), 2.07-oz. bar	280
taffy, all flavors (*Brach's* Salt Water), 1 oz.	100
toffee, English (*Bits 'O Heath*), 3.5 oz.	520

Cannelloni entree, frozen:

beef, with tomato sauce (*Lean Cuisine*), 9⅝ oz.	210
cheese (*Dining Lite*), 9 oz.	310
Cantaloupe, fresh, ½ melon, 5″ diam.	94
Capers, 1 tbsp.	6
Capocollo (*Hormel*), 1 oz.	80
Caramel topping (*Smucker's*), 2 tbsp.	140
Caraway seed (*McCormick/Schilling*), 1 tsp.	8
Cardamom seed (*McCormick/Schilling*), 1 tsp.	6
Cardoon, fresh, boiled, drained, 4 oz.	25

Carrot:

fresh, raw, 1 medium, 7½″ × 1⅛″ diam.	31
fresh, raw, baby, 1 medium, 2¾″ long	4
fresh, boiled, drained, sliced, 1 cup	70
canned, whole, sliced, or diced (*Del Monte*), ½ cup	30
frozen, baby (*Green Giant Harvest Fresh*), ½ cup	18
frozen, and peas, pearl onions (*Birds Eye* Deluxe), 3.3 oz.	50
Carrot juice, canned, (*Hain*), 6 fl. oz.	60
Carrot pâté, in jars (*Three Fold Farm*), 3.5 oz.	155
Casaba melon, cubed, 1 cup	45

Cashew, 1 oz.:

dry-roasted (*Fisher*)	160
honey-roasted or low-sodium (*Eagle*)	170
oil-roasted or pieces (*Fisher*)	170

Cashew butter:

raw (*Hain*), 2 tbsp.	190
raw, unsalted or toasted (*Hain*), 2 tbsp.	210
Catfish, fresh, channel, meat only, raw, 4 oz.	132

Catsup, 1 tbsp.:

(*Del Monte*)	15
(*Heinz* Lite)	8
(*Hunt's* No Salt Added)	20
(*Smucker's*)	24
hot (*Heinz*)	14

Cauliflower:

fresh, raw, cuts, 1 cup	24
fresh, boiled, drained, 1 cup	30
frozen (*Birds Eye*), 3.3 oz.	25
frozen, in cheese sauce (*Green Giant* One Serving), 5.5 oz.	80
frozen, baby carrots and snow pea pods (*Birds Eye*), 3.2 oz.	30
Caviar (see also "Roe"), black or red, granular, 1 oz.	71
Celeriac, raw (*Frieda* of California), 4 oz.	45

Celery, fresh:

raw, 1 stalk, 7½″ × 1¼″ diam.	6
raw, diced, ½ cup	10
boiled, drained, diced, ½ cup	13

Celery seed (*McCormick/Schilling*), 1 tsp. 11
Cereal, ready-to-eat, 1 oz., except as noted:
bran:
   (*All Bran/Bran Buds*) 70
   (*Kellogg's* Bran Flakes/40% Bran Flakes) 90
   apple and cinnamon or raisin (*Health Valley* 100% Natural) 70
   with raisins (*Total* Raisin Bran), 1.5 oz. 140
   with raisins and nuts (*General Mills Raisin Nut Bran*) 110
corn (*Nutri•Grain*) 100
corn (*Total* Corn Flakes) 110
mixed grain:
   (*Crispix*) 110
   (*Familia* Crunchy) 116
   (*Fiber One*) 60
   (*Kellogg's Fiberwise*) 90
   (*Team* Flakes) 110
   almond date (*Ralston* Müesli), 1.45 oz. 140
   almond raspberry (*Ralston* Müesli), 1.45 oz. 150
   cinnamon and raisin (*Nature Valley*) 120
   fruit and nut (*Basic 4*), 1.3 oz. 130
   fruit and nut (*Kellogg's Müeslix* Crispy Blend), 1.5 oz. . . 160
   fruit and nut (*Kellogg's Müeslix Golden Crunch*), 1.2 oz. . 120
   fruit and nut or toasted oat (*Nature Valley*) 130
   pecan, double (*Post Great Grains*) 120
   raisin date pecan (*Post Great Grains*) 130
   walnut cranberry (*Ralston* Müesli), 1.45 oz. 150
oat, all varieties (*Cheerios*) 110
oat, cinnamon or brown sugar (*Quaker Oat Squares*) 100
oat, honey bran or raisin nut (*Kellogg's Oatbake*) 110
oat bran (*Cracklin' Oat Bran*) 110
oatmeal (*General Mills* Oatmeal Crisp) 110
rice (*Kellogg's Rice Krispies/Frosted Krispies*) 110
rice bran (*Kellogg's Kenmei*) 110
wheat (*Clusters*) 110
wheat (*Total*) 100
wheat, with apple (*Fruit Wheats*) 90
wheat, shredded (*Nabisco*), 1 biscuit 80
wheat, shredded, mini (*Nabisco* Spoon Size) 90
wheat, shredded, with oat bran (*Nabisco*) 100
Cereal, cooking:
farina (*Pillsbury*), 2/3 cup cooked 80
oat bran:
   banana pecan, instant (*Casbah Breakfast Cup*), 6 oz.* 190
   blueberry nut, peach macadamia, or rasberry nut, instant
   (*Casbah Breakfast Cup*), 6 oz.* 160
   honey (*Wholesome 'N Hearty* Instant), 1 pkt. 110

raisin hazelnut, instant (*Casbah Breakfast Cup*), 6 oz.*	165
strawberry almond, instant (*Casbah Breakfast Cup*), 6 oz.*	150

oatmeal and oats:

(*Quaker* Quick/Old Fashioned), 1/3 cup dry	99
(*Total* Instant), 1.2 oz.	110
cinnamon raisin (*Total* Instant), 1.8 oz.	170
cinnamon and spice (*Instant Quaker*), 1 pkt.	164
plain or extra fiber (*H-O Brand* Instant), 1 pkt.	110
maple brown sugar (*Total* Instant), 1.6 oz.	160
rice (*Cream of Rice*), 1 oz.	100
rye, cream of (*Roman Meal*), 1/3 cup dry	110
wheat (Quick *Cream of Wheat*), 1 oz.	100
wheat, all flavors (*Mix'n Eat Cream of Wheat* Instant), 1 pkt.	130

Cervelat, see "Thuringer cervelat"

Champagne, see "Wine"

Chard, Swiss, fresh, boiled, drained, chopped, 1 cup	35
Cheddarwurst (*Hillshire Farm* Bun Size), 2 oz.	200

Cheese (see also "Cheese food"), 1 oz., except as noted:

all varieties, except Swiss (*Kraft Light Naturals*)	80
American, processed (*Land O' Lakes*)	110
American, processed, hot pepper (*Sargento*)	110
American, processed, sharp or with Swiss (*Land O' Lakes*)	100
asiago, wheel (*Frigo*)	110
(*Bel Paese* Domestic Traditional)	101
blue, crumbled, 1/2 cup not packed	239
blue (*Frigo*)	100
bonbino (*Laughing Cow*)	103
brick (*Land O' Lakes*)	110
Brie (*Dorman's*)	81
Camembert (*Dorman's* 50%)	89
cheddar (*Frigo*)	110
cheddar (*Frigo* Lite)	80
cheddar, extra sharp, processed (*Land O' Lakes*)	100
cheddar, shredded, 1/2 cup not packed	228
cheddar, cheddar and bacon, or colby (*Land O' Lakes*)	110

cottage cheese, 4 oz., except as noted:

(*Light n'Lively* Nonfat)	90
creamed, low fat 2% (*Breakstone's/Sealtest*)	100
creamed, low fat 2% with peach or pineapple (*Knudsen*)	170
creamed, low fat 1%, plain or garden salad (*Light n'Lively*)	80
dry curd, unsalted (*Breakstone's*)	90
pot style, large curd, low-fat 2% (*Friendship*), 1/2 cup	100

cream cheese:

plain, regular, soft, or whipped (*Philadelphia Brand*)	100
with chives or pimientos (*Philadelphia Brand*)	90

Cheese, cream cheese (cont.)

soft, all varieties, except plain, chives and onion, or honey (*Philadelphia Brand*)	90
soft, chives and onion, or honey (*Philadelphia Brand*)	100
whipped (*Temp-Tee*)	100
whipped, all varieties, except plain (*Philadelphia Brand*)	90
Edam or Gouda (*Land O' Lakes*)	100
farmer (*Friendship*), 1/2 cup	160
feta (*Frigo*)	100
fontina (*Sargento*)	110
gjetost (*Sargento*)	130
goat, hard type	128
goat, semisoft type	103
goat, soft type	76
Gruyère	117
havarti (*Sargento*)	120
impastata (*Frigo*)	60
jalapeño jack (*Land O' Lakes*)	90
Jarlsberg (*Norseland*)	97
Limburger (*Mohawk Valley* Little Gem)	90
mascarpone (*Galbani* Imported)	128
Monterey Jack, plain or hot pepper (*Land O' Lakes*)	110
mozzarella, whole milk (*Frigo*)	90
mozzarella, part skim, low moisture (*Land O' Lakes*)	80
mozzarella, reduced fat (*Frigo* Lite)	60
mozzarella, fat-free (*Polly-O* Free)	40
Muenster (*Land O' Lakes*)	100
Neufchâtel, all flavors (*Kaukauna*)	80
Parmesan (*Frigo Parmazest*)	120
Parmesan, reduced fat (*Frigo* Lite)	100
Parmesan and Romano, fresh grated (*Frigo*)	110
Parmesan or Romano, grated (*Progresso*), 1 tbsp.	23
pizza, shredded (*Frigo*)	65
Port du Salut	100
pot cheese (*Sargento*)	25
provolone (*Frigo* Lite)	70
provolone (*Land O' Lakes*)	100
ricotta, whole milk (*Breakstone's*)	50
ricotta, part skim (*Frigo*)	40
ricotta, reduced fat, low-salt (*Frigo*)	30
ricotta, fat-free (*Frigo*)	20
Romano (*Kraft* Natural)	100
Romano, fresh grated or wheel (*Frigo*)	110
Roquefort	105
string (*Frigo*)	80
string, reduced fat (*Frigo* Lite)	60

Swiss (*Kraft* Light Naturals) 90
Swiss (*Land O' Lakes*) 110
Swiss, smoked (*Dorman's*) 100
taco, shredded (*Frigo*) 110
Tilsit (*Sargento*) 100
Cheese, substitute:
cheddar or mozzarella (*Frigo*), 1 oz. 90
soy, jalapeño or mozzarella style (*Soya Kaas*), 1 oz. 80
Cheese dip:
blue (*Kraft* Premium), 2 tbsp. 50
cheddar (*Bachman* Premium), 1 oz. 45
nacho (*Kraft* Premium), 2 tbsp. . . . . : 55
Cheese food (see also "Cheese product" and "Cheese spread"):
all varieties (*Land O' Lakes*), 1 oz. 90
all varieties (*Velveeta*), 1 oz. 100
all varieties, except port wine or sharp (*Cracker Barrel*), 1 oz. . . 90
cheddar, port wine or sharp (*Cracker Barrel*), 1 oz. 100
Cheese nuggets, frozen (*Banquet* Cheese Hot Bites), 2.63 oz. 240
Cheese pastry pocket (*Tastykake*), 3-oz. piece 332
Cheese product, all varieties (*Kraft* Light/Spreadery/Velveeta
  Light), 1 oz. 70
Cheese sauce:
mix (*McCormick/Schilling*), 1/4 pkg. 35
mix, nacho (*McCormick/Schilling*), 1/4 pkg. 42
Cheese spread, 1 oz.:
all varieties (*Nabisco Easy Cheese*) 80
all varieties (*Shedd's Country Crock* Fresh) 70
American, bacon, or jalapeño cheese (*Kraft*) 80
blue (*Roka Brand*) 70
jalapeño pepper, pimiento, or pineapple (*Kraft*) 70
limburger (*Mohawk Valley*) 70
Cheese sticks, breaded, frozen, mozzarella (*Farm Rich*), 2 pieces 89
Cheesecake mousse mix* (*Sans Sucre* of Paris), 1/2 cup 70
Cherimoya, fresh, 1 medium, approx. 1.9 lb. 515
Cherry:
fresh, sour, trimmed, 1/2 cup 39
fresh, sweet, trimmed, 1/2 cup 52
fresh, sweet, 10 medium, approx. 2.6 oz. 49
canned, sour, red, in water (*Stokely*), 1/2 cup 45
canned, sweet, dark, with pits or pitted (*Del Monte*), 1/2 cup . . . 90
canned, sweet, light, pitted (*Del Monte*), 1/2 cup 90
frozen, sweet, sweetened (*Lucky Leaf*), 4 oz. 130
Cherry, maraschino, in jars, with liquid, 1 oz. 33
Cherry fruit concentrate, black (*Hain*), 2 tbsp. 70
Cherry fruit syrup, black (*Polaner's* Pourable Fruit), 2 tbsp. . . . 72
Cherry juice, black (*Smucker's* 100%), 8 fl. oz. 130

Cherry pastry pocket (*Tastykake*), 3-oz. piece 325
Cherry-grape juice drink, black cherry-white grape (*Boku*),
  8 fl. oz. 120
Chestnut:
Chinese, boiled or steamed, shelled, 4 oz. 176
Chinese, dried, peeled, 1 oz. 105
European, boiled or steamed, peeled, 4 oz. 148
European, dried, peeled, 1 oz. 105
European, roasted, 4 oz. 280
Japanese, boiled or steamed, 4 oz. 64
Japanese, dried, 1 oz. 102
Chestnut, Chinese water, see "Water chestnut"
Chestnut pâté, in jars (*Three Fold Farm*), 3.5 oz. 130
Chicken, fresh, 4 oz., except as noted:
broilers or fryers, roasted:
  meat with skin 271
  meat only 215
  skin only, 1 oz. 129
  breast, meat with skin 223
  breast, meat only 187
  drumstick, meat with skin 245
  drumstick, meat only 195
  leg, meat with skin (5.7 oz. leg with bone) 265
  leg, meat only 217
  thigh, meat with skin 280
  thigh, meat only 237
  wing, meat with skin (2.3 oz. wing with bone) 99
capon, roasted, meat with skin 260
roaster, roasted:
  meat with skin 253
  meat only 189
  dark meat only 202
  light meat only 174
stewing, stewed:
  meat with skin 323
  meat only 269
  dark meat only 293
  light meat only 242
Chicken, boneless and luncheon meat:
bologna, see "Chicken bologna"
breast, hickory smoked or oven-roasted (*Louis Rich*), 1 oz. . . . 30
breast, hickory, honey, mesquite, or roasted (*Tyson*), 1 slice . . . 25
breast, oven-roasted (*Oscar Mayer Healthy Favorites*), 1 slice . . . 12
breast, oven-roasted or smoked (*Oscar Mayer*), 1-oz. slice 25
breast, roast (*Oscar Mayer Deli-Thin*), .4-oz. slice 14
breast, smoked (*Hillshire Farm Deli Select*), 1 oz. 31

roll *(Tyson)*, 1 slice 26
white meat, oven-roasted *(Louis Rich)*, 1-oz. slice 35
Chicken, canned, white or white and dark *(Swanson)*, 2.5 oz.   100
Chicken bologna:
(Health Valley), 1 slice 85
(Tyson), 1 slice 44
Chicken dinner, frozen:
à la king *(Armour Classics Lite)*, 11.25 oz. 290
baked *(Swanson Hungry Man)*, 15 oz. 740
barbecue *(Tyson Healthy Portions)*, 12.5 oz. 470
breast:
   mesquite *(The Budget Gourmet Light & Healthy)*, 1 serving   280
   Parmesan *(The Budget Gourmet Light & Healthy)*, 1 serving   250
   parmigiana *(Le Menu New American Cuisine)*, 10.25 oz. 340
   roast *(The Budget Gourmet Hearty & Healthy)*, 1 serving . . . 290
   teriyaki *(The Budget Gourmet Light & Healthy)*, 1 serving . . . 300
Burgundy *(Armour Classics Lite)*, 10 oz. 210
Cordon bleu, grilled *(Le Menu New American Cuisine)*, 10.5 oz.   390
Dijon *(Healthy Choice)*, 11 oz. 260
Français *(Tyson Premium Dinner)*, 9.5 oz. 280
fried *(Banquet Extra Helping)*, 14.25 oz. 790
fried, barbecue flavored *(Swanson)*, 10 oz. 520
fried, Southern *(Banquet Extra Helping)*, 13.25 oz. 790
fried, white meat *(Swanson Hungry-Man)*, 14.25 oz. 870
garlic *(Swanson Hungry Man)*, 16.5 oz. 500
glazed *(Armour Classics)*, 10.75 oz. 300
glazed, with sauce *(Tyson Premium Dinner)*, 9.25 oz. 240
grilled *(Tyson Premium Dinner)*, 7.75 oz. 220
grilled, Italian *(Tyson Premium Dinner)*, 9 oz. 210
herb *(Tyson Healthy Portion)*, 13.75 oz. 340
herb roasted *(Healthy Choice)*, 12.3 oz. 290
honey mustard *(Le Menu New American Cuisine)*, 11 oz. 290
honey mustard *(Tyson Healthy Portion)*, 13.75 oz. 380
honey-roasted *(Tyson Premium Dinner)*, 9 oz. 220
Italian style *(Tyson Healthy Portion)*, 13.75 oz. 320
Kiev *(Tyson Premium Dinner)*, 9.25 oz. 450
marinara *(Tyson Healthy Portion)*, 13.75 oz. 330
Marsala *(Tyson Premium Dinner)*, 9 oz. 200
mesquite *(Armour Classics)*, 9.5 oz. 370
mesquite *(Tyson Healthy Portion)*, 13.25 oz. 330
and noodles *(Armour Classics)*, 11 oz. 230
nuggets, barbecue or sweet and sour sauce *(Banquet Extra
   Helping)*, 10 oz. 540
Oriental *(Healthy Choice)*, 11.25 oz. 230
parmigiana *(Armour Classics)*, 11.5 oz. 370
parmigiana *(Tyson Premium Dinner)*, 11.25 oz. 380

Chicken dinner (cont.)

and pasta divan (*Healthy Choice*), 11.5 oz.	310
picante (*Tyson* Premium Dinner), 9 oz.	250
picatta (*Tyson* Premium Dinner), 9 oz.	200
roasted (*Tyson* Premium Dinner), 9 oz.	200
salsa (*Tyson Healthy Portions*), 13.75 oz.	370
Santa Fe, grilled (*Le Menu New American Cuisine*), 10 oz.	320
sesame (*Tyson Healthy Portion*), 13.5 oz.	390
supreme (*Tyson* Premium Dinner), 9 oz.	230
sweet and sour (*Le Menu New American Cuisine*), 11.25 oz.	360
sweet and sour (*Tyson* Premium Dinner), 11 oz.	420
tomato garden (*Le Menu New American Cuisine*), 9 oz.	390
with wine and mushroom sauce (*Armour Classics*), 10.75 oz.	280

Chicken entree, canned or packaged:

à la king (*Hormel Top Shelf*), 10 oz.	340
breast, glazed (*Hormel Top Shelf*), 10 oz.	170
breast, with Spanish rice (*Hormel Top Shelf*), 10 oz.	400
cacciatore (*Hormel Top Shelf*), 10 oz.	200
Oriental (*La Choy* Bi-Pack), 3/4 cup	240
sweet and sour (*La Choy* Bi-Pack), 3/4 cup	120
teriyaki (*La Choy* Bi-Pack), 3/4 cup	85

Chicken entree, frozen:

à la king, over baked potato (*Stouffer's* Homestyle Favorites), 12.25 oz.	350
à l'orange, with almond rice (*Lean Cuisine*), 8 oz.	280
à l'orange (*Tyson Gourmet Selection*), 9.5 oz.	300
au gratin (*The Budget Gourmet* Light & Healthy), 1 serving	230
barbecue sauce, rice pilaf (*Lean Cuisine*), 8.75 oz.	260
breast:	
baked, whipped potatoes (*Stouffer's* Homestyle), 87/8 oz.	230
barbecue marinated (*Tyson*), 3.75 oz.	120
battered (*Weaver* Batter Dipped), 4.4 oz.	310
butter garlic or Italian marinated (*Tyson*), 3.75 oz.	120
fried (*Weaver* Crispy Dutch Frye), 4.5 oz.	350
fried, whipped potatoes (*Stouffer's* Homestyle), 71/8 oz.	350
grilled, barbecue sauce (*Stouffer's* Homestyle), 75/8 oz.	210
in herb cream sauce (*Lean Cuisine*), 9.5 oz.	260
and Italian vegetables (*The Budget Gourmet Quick Stirs*), 1 serving	270
lemon pepper or teriyaki marinated (*Tyson*), 3.75 oz.	130
Marsala, with vegetables (*Lean Cuisine*), 81/8 oz.	190
Parmesan, breaded (*Lean Cuisine*), 107/8 oz.	270
patties or tenders (*Banquet Healthy Balance*), 2.25 oz.	120
patties (*Weaver*), 3 oz.	205
portions, fried (*Banquet*), 5.75 oz.	220
strips (*Weaver*), 3.3 oz.	200

tenders, O'Brien potatoes (*Stouffer's* Homestyle), 8³/8 oz. . . .	430
tenders, spaghetti swirls (*On•Cor* Deluxe Entree), 8 oz.	209
cacciatore (*Healthy Choice* Homestyle), 12.5 oz.	310
cacciatorie (*Swanson* Homestyle), 10.95 oz.	260
chow mein (*Healthy Choice*), 8.5 oz.	220
chow mein (*Lean Cuisine*), 9 oz.	240
chunks (*Country Skillet*), 3 oz.	260
chunks, Southern fried (*Country Skillet*), 3 oz.	270
creamed (*Stouffer's*), 6.5 oz.	300
creamed, with biscuit (*Stouffer's* Homestyle Favorites), 9 oz. . . .	470
croquettes (*Weaver*), 2 pieces, ¹/2 cup gravy	280
drumsticks, crispy (*Weaver* Mini Drums), 3 oz.	210
drumsticks, herb and spice (*Weaver* Mini Drums), 3 oz.	200
drumsticks and thighs (*Weaver* Crispy Dutch Frye), 3.5 oz.	290
drumsticks and thighs, battered (*Weaver* Batter Dipped), 3 oz. .	210
and egg noodles (*The Budget Gourmet*), 1 serving	440
with fettuccine (*The Budget Gourmet*), 1 serving	400
fiesta (*Lean Cuisine*), 8.5 oz.	240
French recipe (*The Budget Gourmet* Light & Healthy), 1 serving	210
fried, Southern (*Banquet* Platters), 8.75 oz.	400
glazed (*Healthy Choice*), 8.5 oz.	220
herb, French vegetables (*The Budget Gourmet Quick Stirs*),	
1 serving	270
imperial (*Chun King*), 13 oz.	300
Italiano, fettuccine and vegetables (*Lean Cuisine*), 9 oz.	290
Mandarin (*Healthy Choice*), 11 oz.	260
Marsala (*The Budget Gourmet*), 1 serving	260
mesquite (*Banquet Healthy Balance*), 10.5 oz.	310
and noodles (*Banquet Entree Express*), 8.5 oz.	240
and noodles (*Stouffer's* Homestyle), 10 oz.	290
nuggets (*Banquet Healthy Balance*), 2.25 oz.	120
nuggets (*Country Skillet*), 3 oz.	250
nuggets (*Weaver*), 2.6 oz.	190
orange glazed (*The Budget Gourmet* Light & Healthy), 1 serving	290
Oriental, vegetables and noodles (*The Budget Gourmet Quick*	
Stirs), 1 serving	270
Oriental, vegetables and vermicelli (*Lean Cuisine*), 9 oz.	280
Parmesan (*Banquet Healthy Balance*), 10.8 oz.	300
parmigiana (*On•Cor* Deluxe Entree), 8 oz.	343
parmigiana, and pasta Alfredo (*Stouffer's* Homestyle), 9⁷/8 oz.	360
patties (*Country Skillet*), 3 oz.	230
patties, Southern fried (*Banquet*), 2.5 oz.	200
pie (*Stouffer's*), 10 oz.	530
pie (*Swanson*), 7 oz.	390
pie (*Tyson* Premium), 9 oz.	390
pie, white meat (*Tyson* Premium), 9 oz.	400

Chicken entree, frozen (cont.)

rondolet, cheese or Italian (*Weaver*), 2.6 oz.	190
skinless, crispy (*Weaver* Light), 2.9 oz.	170
sticks (*Banquet*), 2.5 oz.	210
sweet and sour (*Banquet Healthy Balance*), 10.25 oz.	270
sweet and sour (*The Budget Gourmet*), 1 serving	340
tenderloins, in herb cream sauce (*Lean Cuisine*), 9.5 oz.	240
tenderloins, in peanut sauce (*Lean Cuisine*), 9 oz.	290
tenders, honey batter (*Weaver*), 3 oz.	220
and vegetables primavera (*Banquet Family Entrees*), 7 oz.	140
wings, all varieties (*Tyson*), 3.5 oz.	218
wings, battered (*Weaver* Batter Dipped), 4 oz.	400
wings, hot (*Weaver*), 2.7 oz.	170

Chicken entree mix*:

broccoli, cheesy (*Skillet Chicken Helper*), 7.5 oz.	270
creamy (*Skillet Chicken Helper*), 8.25 oz.	290
fettuccine Alfredo (*Skillet Chicken Helper*), 7.5 oz.	270
mushroom, creamy (*Skillet Chicken Helper*), 8 oz.	280
stir-fry (*Skillet Chicken Helper*), 7 oz.	330
sweet and sour (*La Choy* Dinner Classics), 3/4 cup	310

Chicken frankfurter:

(*Hygrades* Grillmaster), 1 link	130
(*Tyson*), 1 link	115
cheese (*Tyson*), 1 link	145

Chicken gravy:

canned (*Heinz*), 2 oz. or 1/4 cup	35
canned, giblet (*Franco-American*), 2 oz.	30
mix* (*McCormick/Schilling* Lite), 1/4 cup	12
mix* (*Pillsbury*), 1/4 cup	25
Chicken ham (*Pilgrim's Pride*), 1-oz. slice	35

Chicken luncheon meat, see "Chicken, boneless and luncheon meat"

Chicken pie, see "Chicken entree, frozen"

Chicken sandwich, frozen:

barbecue (*Tyson* Microwave), 4 oz.	230
breast, grilled (*Tyson*), 3.5 oz.	150
with broccoli and cheddar (*Quaker Oven Stuffs*), 1 piece	340
with country vegetables (*Quaker Oven Stuffs*), 1 piece	270
grilled (*Tyson*), 3.5 oz.	200
pocket, and cheddar (*Hot Pockets*), 5 oz.	310

Chicken sauce:

cacciatore (*Betty Crocker* Recipe Sauces), 3.9 oz.	40
cacciatore or Oriental (*Ragú Chicken Tonight*), 4 oz.	70
country French (*Ragú Chicken Tonight*), 4 oz.	140
creamy, with mushrooms (*Ragú Chicken Tonight*), 4 oz.	110
pepper steak (*Betty Crocker* Recipe Sauces), 3.8 oz.	45

salsa (*Ragú Chicken Tonight*), 4 oz.	35
Spanish (*Ragú Chicken Tonight*), 4 oz.	70
teriyaki (*Betty Crocker* Recipe Sauces), 3.9 oz.	60
mix*, 1 serving:	
cacciatore (*McCormick/Schilling* Sauce Blends)	575
creole (*McCormick/Schilling* Sauce Blends)	229
curry, creamy (*McCormick/Schilling* Sauce Blends)	237
mesquite (*McCormick/Schilling* Sauce Blends)	545
Parmesan (*McCormick/Schilling* Sauce Blends)	366
Southwest style (*McCormick/Schilling* Sauce Blends)	359
teriyaki (*McCormick/Schilling* Sauce Blends)	202

Chicken seasoning and coating mix:

(*McCormick/Schilling* Bag'n Season), 1 pkg.	122
country (*McCormick/Schilling* Bag'n Season), 1 pkg.	134

Chicken spread, canned:

chunky (*Underwood* Light), 2¹/8 oz.	100
chunky, regular, or smoky flavor (*Underwood*), 2¹/8 oz.	150

Chick-peas (garbanzos):

boiled, 1/2 cup	134
canned, all varieties (*Green Giant/Joan of Arc*), 1/2 cup	90
Chicory, witloof, raw, trimmed, 1/2 cup	7
Chicory greens, raw, untrimmed, 1 lb.	87
Chicory root, raw, 1 root, approx. 2.6 oz.	44

Chili, canned or packaged:

with beans (see also "Beans, chili"):

(*Gebhardt*), 1 cup	495
(*Libby's Diner*), 7.75 oz.	280
(*Old El Paso*), 1 cup	217
hot (*Gebhardt*), 1 cup	470
hot (*Just Rite*), 4 oz.	195
regular or hot (*Hormel Micro Cup*), 7³/8 oz.	250
spicy, and ground turkey (*Healthy Choice* Microwave), 7.5 oz.	210
vegetarian, mild or spicy (*Health Valley*), 4 oz.	130
without beans (*Gebhardt*), 1 cup	530
without beans (*Hormel Micro Cup*), 7³/8 oz.	380
without beans (*Just Rite*), 4 oz.	180
with chicken, spicy (*Hain*), 7.5 oz.	130
and franks (*Van Camp's Chilee Weenee*), 1 cup	309
with macaroni (*Hormel Chili Mac Micro Cup*), 7.5 oz.	200
vegetarian, with lentils, mild (*Health Valley*), 4 oz.	130

Chili entree, frozen:

with beans, over baked potato (*Stouffer's* Homestyle Favorites), 11³/8 oz.	390
con carne, with beans (*Stouffer's*), 8.75 oz.	260
Chili pepper, see "Pepper, hot"	
Chili powder (*Gebhardt*), 1 tsp.	15

Chili sauce:
(*Del Monte*), 1/4 cup 70
(*Heinz*), 1 oz. 30
(*Hunt's Manwich* Chili Fixin's), 5.3 oz. 110
green, mild (*El Molino*), 2 tbsp. 10
hot dog (*Gebhardt*), 2 tbsp. 30
red (*Las Palmas*), 1/2 cup 25
Chili seasoning mix:
(*Gebhardt* Chili Quik), 1 tsp. 10
(*Old El Paso*), 1/5 pkg. 21
Chimichanga, frozen:
beef (*Old El Paso* Individual), 1 piece 370
chicken (*Old El Paso* Individual), 1 piece 360
Chimichanga entree, frozen:
bean and cheese, or beef (*Old El Paso*), 1 pkg. 380
beef and pork (*Old El Paso*), 1 pkg. 340
chicken (*Old El Paso*), 1 pkg. 370
Chives, fresh or freeze-dried, chopped, 1 tbsp. 1
Chocolate, see "Candy"
Chocolate, baking:
bars, semisweet (*Nestlé*), 1 oz. 160
bars, sweet (*Baker's German*), 1 oz. 140
bars, unsweetened (*Nestlé*), 1 oz. 180
chips:
  (*Nestlé* Toll House Merry/Rainbow Morsels), 1 oz. . . . 140
  milk (*Nestlé* Toll House Morsels), 1 oz. 150
  mint (*Nestlé* Toll House), 1 oz. 140
  semisweet, regular or mini (*Nestlé* Toll House), 1 oz. . . 140
chunks, milk or semisweet (*Nestlé Treasures*), 1 oz. 150
chunks, white (*Nestlé Premier Treasures*), 1 oz. 160
premelted, unsweetened (*Nestlé Choco Bake*), 1 oz. 190
Chocolate extract, imitation (*McCormick/Schilling*), 1 tsp. . . 8
Chocolate milk:
(*Borden*), 8 fl. oz. 210
low-fat 2% (*Borden* Light/*Viva*), 8 fl. oz. 130
Chocolate mousse mix*:
(*Jell-O* Rich & Luscious), 1/2 cup 150
(*Oetker* Mousse Light), 1/2 cup 62
fudge (*Jell-O* Rich & Luscious), 1/2 cup 140
Chocolate syrup and topping:
(*Hershey's* Syrup), 2 tbsp. or 1 oz. 80
regular or fudge (*Smucker's*), 2 tbsp. 130
fudge, hot (*Smucker's* Light), 2 tbsp. 70
fudge, hot, regular or toffee (*Smucker's*), 2 tbsp. 110
fudge, Swiss milk (*Smucker's*), 2 tbsp. 140
Cilantro, see "Coriander leaf"

Cinnamon, ground (*McCormick/Schilling*), 1 tsp.   6
Cisco, meat only, smoked, 4 oz.   201
Citrus juice drink, all varieties (*Five Alive*), 6 fl. oz.   90
Clam, meat only:
fresh, mixed species, raw, 9 large or 20 small, 6.3 oz.   133
fresh, mixed species, raw, 4 oz.   84
canned, minced, drained (*Progresso*), 1/2 cup   90
frozen, battered, fried (*Mrs. Paul's*), 2.5 oz.   240
frozen, strips (*Gorton's* Microwave Specialty), 2.9 oz.   270
Clam dip (*Breakstone's/Breakstone's* Chesapeake), 2 tbsp.   50
Clam juice (*Snow's*), 3 fl. oz.   4
Clam sauce:
canned, red (*Progresso*), 1/2 cup   70
canned, white (*Progresso*), 1/2 cup   110
refrigerated, red (*Contadina Fresh*), 7.5 oz.   120
refrigerated, white (*Contadina Fresh*), 6 oz.   290
Cloves, ground (*McCormick/Schilling*), 1 tsp.   7
Cocktail sauce, seafood (*Del Monte*), 1/4 cup   70
Cocoa, powder (*Hershey's*), 1 oz. or 1/3 cup   120
Cocoa mix:
(*Hershey's*), 1 oz. or 1/3 cup   120
(*Swiss Miss*), 1-oz. pkt.   110
(*Swiss Miss* Sugar Free), .53-oz. pkt.   60
chocolate, all varieties (*Carnation*), 1-oz. pkt.   110
Coconut:
fresh, meat only, 1 piece, 2″ × 2″ × 2 1/2″   159
fresh, shredded or grated, 1 cup   283
(*Baker's Angel Flake*), 1/3 cup   120
toasted (*Baker's Angel Flake*), 1/3 cup   200
Coconut cream, canned (*Holland House*), 1 fl. oz.   81
Coconut extract, imitation (*McCormick/Schilling*), 1 tsp.   7
Cod, Atlantic or Pacific:
fresh, baked, broiled, or microwaved, 4 oz.   119
dried, Atlantic, salted, 1 oz.   81
frozen, Atlantic (*Van de Kamp's* Natural), 4 oz.   90
Cod entree, frozen, breaded (*Van de Kamp's Light*), 1 piece   250
Cod liver oil, all flavors (*Hain*), 1 tbsp.   120
Coffee, brewed, 6 fl. oz.   4
Collards:
fresh, boiled, drained, chopped, 1/2 cup   17
canned, chopped (*Allens*), 1/2 cup   20
frozen, chopped (*Seabrook*), 3.3 oz.   25
Cookie, 1 piece, except as noted:
animal crackers (*Barnum's*), 5 pieces   60
apple bar (*Apple Newtons*)   70
apple-oatmeal tart (*Pepperidge Farm Wholesome Choice*)   70

Cookie (cont.)

apricot-raspberry (*Pepperidge Farm* Fruit Cookies)	50
arrowroot biscuit (*National*)	20
banana-nut (*My Goodness*)	90
butter (*Pepperidge Farm* Chessmen)	45
butter, fudge creme filled (*Keebler Elfkins*), 4 pieces	70
carrot-walnut (*Pepperidge Farm Wholesome Choice*)	60
chocolate (*Nabisco* Snaps), 4 pieces	70

chocolate chip:

(*Almost Home* Real)	60
(*Chips Ahoy!*)	50
(*Drake's*)	70
(*Nabisco* Snaps), 3 pieces	70
bar (*Tastykake*)	193
candy coated (*Keebler Rainbow Chips Deluxe*)	80
candy coated, mini (*Rainbow Chips Deluxe* Bite Size)	20
chewy (*Chips Ahoy!*)	60
chocolate (*Drake's*)	65
chocolate (*Tastykake* Soft 'n Chewy)	171
chocolate, chocolate chunk (*Chips Ahoy!* Selections)	90
chocolate, chocolate walnut (*Pepperidge Farm Soft Baked*) . . .	130
chunk (*Pepperidge Farm Soft Baked*)	130
chunk, pecan (*Pepperidge Farm Chesapeake*)	120
pure or sprinkled (*Chips Ahoy!*)	50
milk, macadamia (*Pepperidge Farm Soft Baked*)	130
with raisins (*My Goodness*)	90
sprinkled (*Chips Ahoy!*)	60

chocolate peanut bar (*Ideal*)	90

chocolate sandwich:

(*Pepperidge Farm* Brussels)	55
creme filled (*Oreo*)	50
creme filled (*Oreo Big Stuf*)	200
creme filled (*Sunshine Bavarian Fingers*)	70
creme filled, fudge or white fudge covered (*Oreo*)	110
creme filled, mini (*Oreo*), 5 pieces	70
fudge creme filled (*Keebler Elfkins*), 4 pieces	70
peanut butter and creme filled (*Hydrox*)	60
mint or orange (*Pepperidge Farm* Milano)	75
vanilla creme filled (*Keebler Elfkins*), 4 pieces	70

coconut macaroon (*Drake's*)	135
cranberry-honey (*Pepperidge Farm Wholesome Choice*)	60
date-walnut (*Pepperidge Farm Wholesome Choice*)	60
devil's food cakes (*Nabisco*)	70
fig bar (*Fig Newtons*)	60
fudge bar (*Tastykake*)	205
gingersnaps (*Archway*, 54/pkg.)	35

graham crackers:

(*Nabisco*)	30
all varieties (*Honey Maid* Graham Bites), 11 pieces	60
all varieties (*Teddy Grahams*), 11 pieces	60
all varieties (*Teddy Graham Bearwich's*), 4 pieces	70
chocolate (*Nabisco*)	50
cinnamon (*Keebler Cinnamon Crisp*), 4 pieces	70
crispy (*Pepperidge Farm* Wholesome), 4 pieces	70
fudge (*Nabisco Cookies'N Fudge*)	45
hazelnut or lemon nut crunch (*Pepperidge Farm*)	55
hazelnut crunch (*Master Choice* Pâtisserie)	90
Heath toffee chunk (*Chips Ahoy!* Selections)	90
hermit (*Drake's*)	230
jelly tarts (*FFV*)	60
lemon butter finger (*Master Choice* Pâtisserie)	70
marshmallow, chocolate fudge cake (*Pinwheels*)	130
marshmallow, coconut covered (*Sunshine Mallowpuffs*)	70
marshmallow, fudge cake (*Nabisco* Puffs)	90
mint sandwich (*Mystic Mint*)	90
molasses (*Nabisco Pantry*)	80

oatmeal:

(*Baker's Bonus*)	80
(*Drake's*)	60
(*Pepperidge Farm* Old Fashioned Irish)	45
with chocolate middle (*Keebler Magic Middles*)	80
chocolate chunk (*Chips Ahoy!* Selections)	90
creme (*Drake's*)	240
raisin (*My Goodness*)	90
raisin (*Pepperidge Farm Wholesome Choice*)	60
raisin bar (*Tastykake*)	212
orange butter finger (*Master Choice* Pâtisserie)	70
peanut butter (*Delicious Skippy*)	80
peanut butter, chocolate chunk (*Pepperidge Farm* Cheyenne)	110
peanut butter sandwich (*Nutter Butter*)	70
peanut butter wafer (*Drake's*)	324
peanut creme pattie (*Nutter Butter*)	80
pecan chip (*Pecan Chips Deluxe*)	70
raisin bar, iced (*Keebler*)	80
raspberry bar (*Raspberry Newtons*)	70
raspberry filled, chocolate (*Pepperidge Farm* Chantilly)	90
raspberry tart (*Pepperidge Farm Wholesome Choice*)	60

shortbread:

(*Pepperidge Farm* Old Fashioned)	75
chocolate cream center (*Keebler Magic Middles*)	80
with chocolate drops (*Keebler Sweet Spots*), 2 pieces	50
fudge striped (*Nabisco Cookies'n Fudge*)	60

Cookie, shortbread (cont.)
pecan (*Nabisco Pecan Shortbread*) 80
toffee fudge covered (*Keebler Toffee Toppers*) 35
vanilla (*Tastykake*) 55
strawberry (*Pepperidge Farm* Fruit Cookies) 50
strawberry bar (*Strawberry Newtons*) 70
sugar (*Pepperidge Farm* Old Fashioned) 50
sugar wafer (*Biscos*), 4 pieces 70
tea biscuit (*Social Tea*), 3 pieces 70
toffee, English (*Delicious Heath*) 70
vanilla, chocolate coated (*Pepperidge Farm* Orleans) 30
vanilla, yogurt iced (*Sunshine Sea Flappers*), 3 pieces 60
vanilla creme sandwich (*Cameo*) 70
wafer, brown edge or chocolate (*Nabisco/Nabisco* Famous),
1/2 oz. 70
wafer, fudge striped (*Nabisco Cookies 'n Fudge*) 70
wafer, vanilla (*Nilla*), 1/2 oz. 60
waffle cremes (*Biscos*) 40
Cookie, refrigerator, 1 piece:
all varieties (*Pillsbury Oven Lovin'*) 70
all varieties, except oatmeal raisin (*Pillsbury's Best*) 70
oatmeal raisin (*Pillsbury's Best*) 60
Cookie mix*:
caramel oatmeal, chocolate peanut butter, chocolate toffee, or
Sunkist lemon (*Betty Crocker* Bar Mix), 1 piece 110
chocolate (*Betty Crocker Big Batch*), 2 pieces 120
Coriander leaf:
fresh, raw, 1/4 cup 1
dried, 1 tsp. 2
Coriander seed (*McCormick/Schilling*), 1 tsp. 6
Corn:
fresh, boiled, kernels from 1 medium ear, approx. 2.7 oz. 83
fresh, boiled, drained, 1/2 cup 89
canned or packaged, 1/2 cup:
(*Green Giant Delicorn*) 80
(*Green Giant Sweet Select*) 60
kernel, golden or white (*Del Monte*) 70
kernel, with peppers (*Green Giant Mexicorn*) 70
cream style, golden (*Del Monte*) 80
cream style, white (*Del Monte*) 90
Santa Fe style (*Del Monte Vegetable Classics*) 90
frozen:
on cob (*Green Giant Niblet Ears*), 1 ear 120
on cob (*Green Giant Sweet Select*), 1 whole or 2 half ears . . . 90
on cob (*Ore-Ida*), 1 ear 190
on cob, miniature (*Ore-Ida Mini-Gold*), 1 ear 90

kernel (*Birds Eye/Birds Eye* Deluxe), 3.3 oz. 80
kernel (*Green Giant Niblets* Supersweet), 1/2 cup 60
kernel, white shoepeg (*Green Giant*), 1/2 cup 90
cream style (*Green Giant*), 1/2 cup 110
in butter sauce (*Green Giant Niblets*/Shoepeg), 1/2 cup 100
Corn, combinations, frozen or packaged:
with green beans, carrots and pasta, tomato sauce (*Green Giant
Pantry Express*), 1/2 cup 80
and carrots, herb sauce (*Del Monte Vegetable Classics*), 1/2 cup 70
Corn chips and similar snacks, 1 oz.:
plain 153
all varieties (*Doritos* Light) 120
all varieties (*Pringles* Light) 130
barbecue (*Bachman* BBQ) 150
barbecue, Cheez-ums, original, or sour cream and onion
(*Pringles*) 160
cheese flavor (*Chee•tos* Crunchy) 150
cheese flavor (*Jax* Crunchy) 160
nacho, roasted, or popcorn (*Pringles*) 140
ranch (*Bearitos* Organic Ranch Rounds) 120
tortilla, all varieties (*Tyson* Mexican Original) 140
tortilla, blue corn (*Bearitos* Organic) 146
tortilla, ranch (*Eagle*) 140
Corn flake crumbs (*Kellogg's*), 1 oz. 100
Corn grits, cooked, 1 cup 146
Corn soufflé, frozen (*Stouffer's*), 4 oz. 160
Corn syrup, dark or light (*Karo*), 1 tbsp. 60
Cornish game hen, frozen, with skin (*Tyson*), 3.5 oz. 250
Cornmeal:
dry, white or yellow (*Albers*), 1 oz. 100
mix, yellow, bolted (*Aunt Jemima*), 1 oz. 97
Cornstarch (*Argo/Kingsford's*), 1 tbsp. 30
Country gravy mix*:
(*McCormick/Schilling*), 1/4 cup 40
sausage (*McCormick/Schilling*), 1/4 cup 41
Couscous, mix*:
(*Fantastic Foods*), 1/2 cup 105
pilaf, savory (*Quick Pilaf*), 1/2 cup 94
Cowpeas, boiled, drained, 1/2 cup 79
Crab, meat only:
fresh, Alaska King, steamed, 4 oz. 110
fresh, blue, steamed, 4 oz. 116
fresh, Dungeness, steamed, 4 oz. 125
fresh, queen, steamed, 4 oz. 130
fresh, soft shell, breaded, fried in vegetable oil, 4.4 oz. 334
canned, blue, 1 cup, approx. 4.75 oz. 133

Crab (cont.)
canned, Dungeness (*S&W*), 3.25 oz. 81
frozen, snow (*Wakefield*), 3 oz. 60
Crab, imitation (*Icicle Brand*), 3.5 oz. 99
Crab cake seasoning mix (*Old Bay Crab Cake Classic*), 1 pkg. 133
Crab cakes, deviled, frozen:
breaded (*Mrs. Paul's*), 3-oz. piece 170
breaded (*Mrs. Paul's* Miniatures), 3.5 oz. 250
Crab and shrimp, frozen (*Wakefield*), 3 oz. 60
Crabapple:
fresh, with skin, sliced, 1/2 cup 42
canned, spiced (*Lucky Leaf/Musselman's*), 4 oz. 110
Cracker (see also "Cracker crumbs and meal"):
all varieties:
  (*Nabisco American Classic*), 4 pieces 70
  except cheese or peanut butter sandwich (*Ritz/Ritz Bits*), 1/2 oz. 70
bacon flavor (*Nabisco Bacon Flavored Thins*), 7 pieces 70
bacon cheese (*Eagle*), 1 oz. 140
with bacon and cheese (*Handi-Snacks*), 1 pkg. 120
butter flavor (*Escort*), 3 pieces 70
cheese or cheese flavor:
  (*Eagle*), 1 oz. 130
  (*Hain*), 6 pieces 70
  (*Nabisco Nips*), 13 pieces or 1/2 oz. 70
  (*Tid-Bits*), 15 pieces or 1/2 oz. 70
  cheddar (*Nabisco Cheddar Wedges*), 31 pieces or 1/2 oz. 70
  Swiss (*Nabisco Swiss Cheese*), 7 pieces 70
  three (*Pepperidge Farm* Snack Sticks), 8 pieces 130
cheese sandwich (*Ritz Bits*), 6 pieces 80
cheese sandwich, and peanut butter (*Eagle*), 1.8 oz. 280
(*Chicken in a Biskit*), 7 pieces 80
crispbread (see also specific grains):
  (*Kavli* Norwegian), 2 thin pieces 40
  dark, regular or caraway (*Finn Crisp*), 2 pieces 38
flatbread, all varieties (*Lavosh Hawaii*), 1 piece 20
grain, multi (*Pepperidge Farm* Wholesome), 4 pieces 70
matzo (*Manischewitz* Daily Unsalted), 1-oz. board 110
matzo (*Manischewitz* Passover), 1.1-oz. board 129
matzo, egg (*Manischewitz*), 1.2-oz. board 132
matzo, miniature (*Manischewitz*), 10 pieces 90
melba toast:
  all varieties (*Old London* Melba Toast), 1/2 oz. 50
  all varieties (*Old London* Rounds), 1/2 oz. 60
  onion (*Devonsheer* Rounds), 1/2 oz. 51
  plain, rye, vegetable, or whole wheat (*Devonsheer*), 1 piece 16
oat (*Harvest Crisps*), 6 pieces 60

(*Oat Thins*), 8 pieces	70
onion (*Hain No Salt Added*), 6 pieces	70
peanut butter sandwich (*Ritz Bits*), 6 pieces	80
pretzel (*Pepperidge Farm* Snack Sticks), 8 pieces	120
pumpernickel (*Pepperidge Farm* Snack Sticks), 8 pieces	140
rice (*Harvest Crisps*), 6 pieces	60
rich (*Hain/Hain No Salt Added*), 4 pieces	70
rye (*Hain*), 6 pieces	70
rye, original (*Finn Crisp* Hi-Fiber), 1 piece	40
saltine:	
(*Premium* Bits), 16 pieces	70
(*Premium* Fat Free), 5 pieces	50
all varieties, except bits or fat free (*Premium*), 5 pieces	60
whole wheat (*Premium Plus*), 5 pieces	60
seasoned (*Munch'ems* Original), 14 pieces	60
sesame (*Hain/Hain No Salt Added*), 6 pieces	70
sesame (*Pepperidge Farm* Snack Sticks), 8 pieces	140
sesame wafer (*Meal Mates*), 3 pieces	70
sesame wheat (*Wasa* Crispbread), 1 piece	50
sesame and cheese (*Nabisco Twigs*), 7 pieces	70
soda or water (*Pepperidge Farm* Distinctive English), 4 pieces	70
soup and oyster (*Premium*), 20 pieces or 1/2 oz.	60
sour cream and chives (*Hain*), 5 pieces	60
sour cream and onion (*Munch'ems*), 14 pieces	60
sourdough (*Hain/Hain No Salt Added*), 6 pieces	70
vegetable, garden (*Pepperidge Farm*), 5 pieces	60
(*Vegetable Thins*), 7 pieces	70
wheat:	
(*Keebler Wheatables*), 12 pieces	70
(*Sociables*), 6 pieces	70
all varieties (*Triscuit/Triscuit* Bits), 1/2 oz.	60
all varieties (*Wheat Thins*), 7 pieces or 1/2 oz.	70
cheddar or ranch (*Keebler Wheatables*), 11 pieces	70
hearty (*Pepperidge Farm* Distinctive), 4 pieces	100
sesame (*Health Valley* Stoned Wheat), 13 pieces	130
Cracker crumbs and meal:	
matzo (*Manischewitz Farfel*), 1 cup	180
matzo meal (*Manischewitz*), 1 cup	514
Cranberry, fresh, raw (*Ocean Spray*), 2 oz. or 1/2 cup	25
Cranberry fruit concentrate (*Hain*), 2 tbsp.	40
Cranberry juice, 6 fl. oz.:	
(*Lucky Leaf*)	110
cocktail (*Ocean Spray*)	110
cocktail, blend (*Ocean Spray Crantastic*)	110
cocktail, bottled or frozen* (*Sunkist*)	110
drink (*Tropicana* Cranberry Orchard Juice Sparkler)	96

Cranberry sauce, canned, whole or jelled (*Ocean Spray*), 2 oz. 90
Crayfish, meat only, steamed, 4 oz. 129
Cream:
half-and-half, 1 tbsp. 20
heavy, 1 tbsp., approx. 2 tbsp. whipped 52
light, coffee or table, 1 tbsp. 29
light, whipping, 1 tbsp., approx. 2 tbsp. whipped 44
sour, 1 tbsp. 26
sour, half-and-half (*Sealtest Light*), 1 tbsp. 25
sour, imitation (*Pet/Dairymate*), 1 tbsp. 25
sour, light, regular or with chive (*Land O' Lakes*), 2 tbsp. .. 40
sour, nonfat, imitation (*Light n'Lively* Alternative), 1 tbsp. 10
Cream gravy, canned (*Franco-American*), 2 oz. 35
Cream of tartar (*Tone's*), 1 tsp. 2
Cream topping, whipped:
(*Kraft* Real Cream), 1/4 cup 30
pressurized (*Crowley*), 1 tbsp. 20
pressurized (*Reddi Wip* Lite), 1 tbsp. 6
nondairy (*Birds Eye Cool Whip* Dairy Recipe), 1 tbsp. 14
nondairy, mix* (*Dream Whip*), 1 tbsp. 10
Creamer, nondairy:
Amaretto, hazelnut, or Irish creme (*Coffee-mate*), 1 tbsp. 40
frozen (*Rich's Coffee Rich/Rich's Farm Rich*), 1/2 oz. 20
powdered (*Cremora*), 1 tsp. 10
Cress, garden, raw, 1/2 cup 8
Cress, water, see "Watercress"
Croaker, fresh, Atlantic, meat only, raw, 4 oz. 118
Croissant, 1 piece:
(*Pepperidge Farm* Sandwich Quartet) 170
frozen, all butter (*Sara Lee*), 1.5-oz. roll 170
Crookneck or straightneck squash, fresh:
boiled, drained, sliced, 1/2 cup 18
canned, yellow, cut (*Allens*), 1/2 cup 16
frozen, yellow (*Seabrook*), 3.3 oz. 18
Croutons, 1/2 oz.:
all varieties (*Pepperidge Farm* Homestyle) 70
all varieties, except fine herbs (*Arnold* Crispy Croutons) 60
fine herbs (*Arnold* Crispy Croutons) 50
Italian style (*Progresso*) 30
seasoned (*Reese*) 60
Cucumber, with peel, raw:
1 medium, untrimmed, 81/4" long, approx. 10.9 oz. 39
ends trimmed, sliced, 1/2 cup 7
Cumin seed (*McCormick/Schilling*), 1 tsp. 7
Currant, Zante, dried (*Del Monte*), 1/2 cup 200

Curry powder, 1 tsp.   92
Cusk, fresh, baked, broiled, or microwaved, 4 oz.   127
Cuttlefish, mixed species, meat only, steamed, 4 oz.   179

D

Food and Measure   Calories

Daiquiri mixer, frozen*:
banana, with rum (*Bacardi*), 7 fl. oz.   210
peach or strawberry, with rum (*Bacardi*), 7 fl. oz.   200
Dairy Queen/Brazier:
sandwiches, chicken, and side dishes, 1 serving:
  BBQ beef, 4.5 oz.   225
  chicken fillet, breaded, 6.7 oz.   430
  chicken fillet, breaded, with cheese, 7.2 oz.   480
  chicken fillet, grilled, 6.5 oz.   300
  DQ Homestyle Ultimate burger, 9.7 oz.   700
  fish fillet, 6 oz.   370
  fish fillet, with cheese, 6.5 oz.   420
  french fries, regular, 3.5 oz.   300
  hamburger, single, 5 oz.   310
  hamburger, double, 7 oz.   460
  hamburger with cheese, single, 5.5 oz.   365
  hamburger with cheese, double, 8 oz.   570
  hot dog, plain, 3.5 oz.   280
  hot dog, with cheese, 4 oz.   330
  hot dog, with chili, 4.5 oz.   320
  hot dog, 1/4 pound Super Dog   590
onion rings, regular, 3 oz.   240
desserts and shakes, 1 serving:
  banana split, 13 oz.   510
  Blizzard, Heath, regular, 14.3 oz.   820
  Blizzard, strawberry, regular, 13.5 oz.   740
  Breeze, Heath, regular, 13.4 oz.   680

Dairy Queen/Brazier, desserts and shakes (cont.)

Breeze, strawberry, regular, 12.5 oz.	590
Buster Bar, 5.3 oz.	450
cone, chocolate or vanilla, regular, 5 oz.	230
cone, chocolate dipped, regular, 5.5 oz.	330
cone, yogurt, regular, 5 oz.	180
cup, yogurt, regular, 5 oz.	170
DQ frozen cake slice, undecorated, 5.8 oz.	380
DQ Sandwich, 2.2 oz.	140
Dilly Bar, 3 oz.	210
Hot Fudge Brownie Delight, 10.8 oz.	710
malt, vanilla, regular, 14.7 oz.	610
Mr. Misty, regular, 11.6 oz.	250
Nutty Double Fudge, 9.7 oz.	580
Peanut Buster Parfait, 10.8 oz.	710
QC Big Scoop, chocolate, 4.5 oz.	310
QC Big Scoop, vanilla, 4.5 oz.	300
shake, chocolate, regular, 14 oz.	540
shake, vanilla, regular, 14 oz.	520
sundae, chocolate, regular, 6.2 oz.	300
sundae, yogurt, strawberry, regular, 6 oz.	200
Waffle Cone Sundae, strawberry, 6.1 oz.	350
Dandelion greens, boiled, drained, chopped, 1 cup	35

Danish, frozen or refrigerator, 1 piece:

apple or raspberry (*Pepperidge Farm*)	220
cheese (*Pepperidge Farm*)	240
cinnamon-raisin (*Pepperidge Farm*)	250
cinnamon-raisin or orange, iced (*Pillsbury*)	150
Date, pitted, whole or chopped (*Dole*), 1/2 cup	280

Dill:

seasoning (*McCormick/Schilling Parsley Patch* It's a Dilly), 1 tsp.	11
seed (*McCormick/Schilling*), 1 tsp.	9
weed, fresh, sprigs, 1/4 cup	1
weed, dried, 1 tsp.	3
Dock, raw, trimmed, chopped, 1/2 cup	15
Dolphin fish, meat only, baked, broiled, or microwaved, 4 oz.	124

Domino's Pizza, 2 slices of large (16") pie:

cheese	376
deluxe	498
double cheese and pepperoni	545
ham	417
pepperoni	460
sausage and mushroom	430
veggie	498

Donut, 1 piece, except as noted:

(*Drake's* Old Fashion)	182

plain (*Tastykake* Assorted) 185
plain, cinnamon, or powdered sugar (*Hostess Breakfast Bake
   Shop Donette Gems*) 60
cinnamon (*Tastykake* Assorted) 179
cinnamon, mini (*Tastykake*) 48
cinnamon apple (*Hostess Breakfast Bake Shop Donette Gems*) 70
crumb (*Hostess Breakfast Bake Shop*) 160
frosted (*Tastykake* Rich Frosted) 258
frosted, mini (*Tastykake* Rich Frosted) 61
glazed, old fashioned (*Hostess Breakfast Bake Shop*) 250
honey wheat (*Tastykake*) 209
honey wheat, mini (*Tastykake*) 40
orange glazed (*Tastykake*) 219
powdered sugar (*Drake's Donut Delites*), 7 pieces 300
powdered sugar (*Tastykake* Assorted) 183
powdered sugar, mini (*Tastykake*) 42
Drum, freshwater, meat only, baked, broiled, or microwaved,
   4 oz. 174
Duck, domesticated:
roasted, meat with skin, 4 oz. 382
roasted, meat only, 4 oz. 228
Dunkin' Donuts:
apple filled, with cinnamon sugar, 2.8 oz. 250
Bavarian filled, with chocolate frosting, 2.8 oz. 240
blueberry filled, 2.4 oz. 210
buttermilk ring, glazed, 2.6 oz. 290
cake ring, plain, 2.2 oz. 270
cake ring, chocolate, glazed, 2.5 oz. 324
cake ring, mini, .9 oz. 100
chocolate, glazed, mini, 1.1 oz. 122
chocolate chunk cookie, 1.5 oz. 200
chocolate chunk cookie, with nuts, 1.5 oz. 210
cinnamon cake, mini, 1 oz. 116
coconut, mini, 1.2 oz. 140
coffee roll, glazed, 2.9 oz. 280
coffee roll, mini, .8 oz. 78
croissant, 2.5 oz. 310
croissant, almond, 3.7 oz. 420
croissant, chocolate, 3.3 oz. 440
cruller, French, glazed, 1.3 oz. 140
eclair, mini, 1.3 oz. 114
jelly filled, 2.4 oz. 220
lemon filled, 2.8 oz. 260
muffin:
   apple and spice, 3.5 oz. 300
   banana nut, 3.6 oz. 310

Dunkin' Donuts, muffin (cont.)

blueberry, 3.6 oz.	280
bran with raisins, 3.7 oz.	310
corn, 3.4 oz.	340
cranberry nut, 3.5 oz.	290
oat bran, 3.4 oz.	330
oatmeal pecan raisin cookie, 1.6 oz.	200
whole wheat ring, glazed, 2.9 oz.	330
yeast ring, chocolate frosted or glazed, 1.9 oz.	200
Dutch brand loaf (*Kahn's*), 1 slice	80

E

Food and Measure	Calories

Eclair, chocolate, frozen (*Rich's*), 1 piece	210
Egg, chicken, fresh:	
raw, whole, 1 large, approx. 1.75 oz.	75
raw, white from 1 large egg	17
raw, yolk from 1 large egg	59
hard-cooked in shell, 1 large egg	77
Egg, substitute:	
frozen or refrigerated:	
(*Fleischmann's Egg Beaters*), 1/4 cup	25
(*Healthy Choice*), 1/4 cup	30
(*Second Nature*), 2 oz.	60
omelet, cheese (*Fleischmann's Egg Beaters*), 1/2 cup	110
omelet, ham and cheese (*Weight Watchers* Handy Omelet), 4 oz.	180
omelet, vegetable (*Fleischmann's Egg Beaters*), 1/2 container	50
omelet, vegetable (*Second Nature* Omelet Blend), 2.75 oz.	60
mix (*Lite-Egg*), 1 heaping tsp.	18
Egg breakfast, frozen:	
omelet, cheese sauce and ham (*Swanson Great Starts*), 7 oz.	390

scrambled:
with cheese (*Golden*), 1 serving	140
with cheese, cinnamon pancakes (*Swanson Great Starts*), 3.4 oz.	290
with ham, hash browns (*Downyflake*), 6.25 oz.	360
with hash browns, sausage (*Downyflake*), 6.25 oz.	420
with home fries (*Swanson Budget Breakfast*), 4³/₈ oz.	250
Mexican style (*Golden*), 1 serving	120
with sausage, hash browns (*Swanson Great Starts*), 6.5 oz.	430
with waffle, sausage, bacon (*Swanson Great Starts Big Start*), 6.75 oz.	590

Egg breakfast sandwich:
biscuit, Canadian bacon, cheese (*Swanson Great Starts*), 5.2 oz.	420
biscuit, sausage and cheese (*Swanson Great Starts*), 5.5 oz. . . .	460
English muffin (*Healthy Choice*), 4.25 oz.	200
English muffin, turkey sausage omelet (*Healthy Choice*), 4.75 oz.	210
English muffin, western omelet (*Healthy Choice*), 4.75 oz.	200
muffin, Canadian bacon, cheese (*Swanson Great Starts*), 4.1 oz.	290
omelet, garden vegetable (*Weight Watchers*), 3.6 oz.	210

Egg foo young entree mix* (*La Choy* Dinner Classics), 2 patties,
3 oz. sauce	170

Egg roll, frozen:
chicken, almond (*La Choy*), 3 oz.	120
chicken, snack (*La Choy*), 1.45 oz.	90
chicken, sweet and sour (*La Choy*), 3 oz.	150
chicken, meat and shrimp, or shrimp (*Chun King*), 3.6 oz.	220
lobster or shrimp, snack (*La Choy*), 1.45 oz.	75
meat and shrimp, snack (*La Choy*), 1.45 oz.	80
pork (*Chun King* Restaurant Style), 3 oz.	180
pork (*La Choy* Restaurant Style), 3 oz.	150
shrimp (*La Choy* Restaurant Style), 3 oz.	130

Egg roll wrapper (*Nasoya*), 1 wrapper	23
Eggnog, nonalcoholic, chilled (*Crowley*), 6 fl. oz.	270
Eggplant, fresh, boiled, drained, cubed, ¹/₂ cup	13
Eggplant appetizer (*Progresso* Caponata), ¹/₂ can	70
Eggplant entree, frozen, parmigiana (*Celentano*), 8 oz.	280
Elderberry, fresh, ¹/₂ cup	53
Enchilada, canned (*Gebhardt*), 2 pieces	310

Enchilada dinner, frozen:
beef (*Banquet* Meals), 11 oz.	370
beef (*Healthy Choice*), 12.75 oz.	350
beef (*Patio*), 13.25 oz.	520
cheese (*Patio*), 12 oz.	370
cheese or chicken (*Banquet* Meals), 11 oz.	340
chicken (*Healthy Choice*), 12.75 oz.	330

Enchilada entree, frozen:

beef (*Old El Paso*), 1 pkg. 210

beef, chili gravy and (*Banquet Family Entrees*), 7 oz. 270

beef, sirloin ranchero (*The Budget Gourmet* Light & Healthy), 1

    serving 270

beef and bean (*Lean Cuisine* Enchanadas), 9.25 oz. 240

cheese (*Old El Paso*), 1 pkg. 250

chicken (*Banquet Healthy Balance*), 11 oz. 300

chicken (*Healthy Choice*), 9.5 oz. 280

chicken (*Lean Cuisine* Enchanadas), 9⁷/₈ oz. 290

chicken (*Old El Paso*), 1 pkg. 220

chicken, with sour cream sauce (*Old El Paso*), 1 pkg. 280

chicken Suiza (*The Budget Gourmet* Light & Healthy), 1 serving   290

vegetable, with tofu and sauce (*Legume* Mexican), 11 oz. 270

Enchilada mix* (*Old El Paso* Dinner), 1 piece 145

Enchilada sauce (see also "Salsa"):

(*Gebhardt*), 3 tbsp. 25

green (*Old El Paso*), 2 tbsp. 11

hot (*Las Palmas*), 1/2 cup 25

mild (*Rosarita*), 2.5 oz. 25

Enchilada seasoning mix (*Old El Paso*), 1/18 pkg. 6

Endive:

1 head, approx. 1.3 lb. 86

trimmed, chopped, 1/2 cup 4

Endive, French or Belgian, raw, trimmed, 1.9-oz. head 8

Escarole, see "Endive"

F

Food and Measure   **Calories**

Fajita entree, frozen:

beef (*Healthy Choice*), 7 oz. 210

chicken (*Healthy Choice*), 7 oz. 200

Fajita marinade (*Old El Paso*), 1 oz. 14

Falafel, mix* (*Near East*), 3 patties 270
Fat, see specific listings
Feijoa, fresh, raw, 2.3-oz. fruit 25
Fennel, bulb, fresh, raw, sliced, 1 cup 27
Fennel seed (*McCormick/Schilling*), 1 tsp. 8
Fettuccini entree, frozen:
(*Dining Lite*), 9 oz. 290
Alfredo (*Healthy Choice*), 8 oz. 240
chicken (*Armour Classics*), 11 oz. 260
chicken (*Healthy Choice*), 8.5 oz. 240
chicken (*Lean Cuisine*), 9 oz. 280
chicken, herb sauce (*The Budget Gourmet Quick Stirs*), 1 serving 280
chicken, vegetable medley (*Stouffer's* Homestyle), 9.5 oz. 350
primavera (*Green Giant Garden Gourmet Right for Lunch*), 1 pkg. 230
with turkey, vegetables (*Healthy Choice* Pasta Classics), 12.5 oz. 350
Figs:
fresh, 1 medium, approx. 1.8 oz. 37
canned, whole kadota (*S&W* Fancy), 1/2 cup 100
dried, uncooked, 10 figs, approx. 6.6 oz. 477
Filbert, shelled:
dried, unblanched, 1 oz. 191
dry-roasted, 1 oz. 188
oil-roasted, 1 oz. 187
Finnan haddie, see "Haddock, smoked"
Fish, see specific listings
Fish dinner, frozen (see also specific fish listings):
'n' chips (*Swanson*), 10 oz. 500
lemon pepper (*Healthy Choice*), 10.7 oz. 300
Fish entree, frozen (see also specific fish listings):
in butter sauce, fillets (*Mrs. Paul's* Light), 1 piece 140
cakes (*Mrs. Paul's*), 2 pieces 190
Dijon (*Mrs. Paul's* Light), 8.75 oz. 200
fillet, battered:
(*Gorton's* Crispy Batter), 2 pieces 290
(*Gorton's* Crunchy Microwave Portions), 2 pieces 300
(*Gorton's* Potato Crisp), 2 pieces 300
(*Gorton's* Value Pack Portions), 1 piece 180
(*Mrs. Paul's* Crunchy), 2 pieces 280
(*Van de Kamp's*), 1 piece 170
fillet, breaded:
(*Mrs. Paul's* Crispy Crunchy), 2 pieces 220
(*Mrs. Paul's* Healthy Treasures), 1 piece 170
(*Van de Kamp's*), 2 pieces 280
(*Van de Kamp's* Snack Pack), 2 pieces 220
baked (*Van de Kamp's* Crisp & Hearty), 2 pieces 150
crispy (*Van de Kamp's* Microwave), 1 piece 140

Fish entree, fillet, breaded (cont.)

crispy, large (*Van de Kamp's* Microwave), 1 piece	290
fillet of, divan (*Lean Cuisine*), 10⅜ oz.	210
fillet of, Florentine (*Lean Cuisine*), 9⅝ oz.	220
gems, fancy style (*Wakefield*), 4 oz.	80
Mornay (*Mrs. Paul's Light*), 9 oz.	230
oven-baked (*Weight Watchers Ultimate 200*), 6.64 oz.	120

sticks, battered:

(*Gorton's* Crunchy), 4 pieces	200
(*Gorton's* Crunchy Microwave), 6 pieces	360
(*Gorton's* Potato Crisp), 4 pieces	220
(*Gorton's* Value Pack), 4 pieces	190
(*Mrs. Paul's* Crunchy), 4 pieces	180
(*Van de Kamp's*), 4 pieces	160

sticks, breaded:

(*Mrs. Paul's* Crispy Crunchy), 4 pieces	140
(*Mrs. Paul's Healthy Treasures*), 4 pieces	150
(*Van de Kamp's*), 4 pieces	200
(*Van de Kamp's* Value Pack), 4 pieces	170
baked (*Van de Kamp's Crisp & Healthy*), 4 pieces	120
crispy (*Van de Kamp's* Microwave), 3 pieces	130

Fish seasoning and coating mix:

batter, fish and chips (*Golden Dipt*), 1.25 oz.	120
fish fry, plain or Cajun (*Golden Dipt*), ⅔ oz.	60
Italian herb (*McCormick/Schilling* Bag'n Season), 1 pkg.	94
lemon and dill (*McCormick/Schilling* Bag'n Season), 1 pkg.	161

Fish sticks, see "Fish entree"

Flatfish, meat only, baked, broiled, or microwaved, 4 oz.	133

Flounder:

fresh, see "Flatfish"

frozen (*Gorton's Fishmarket Fresh*), 5 oz.	110
frozen (*Van de Kamp's* Natural), 4 oz.	100

Flounder entree, frozen:

battered (*Gorton's* Crispy Batter), 2 pieces	280
breaded (*Van de Kamp's Light*), 1 piece	260

Flour (see also specific listings):

barley (*Arrowhead Mills*), 2 oz.	200
bread (*Gold Medal Better for Bread*), 1 cup	400
buckwheat, 1 cup	402
cake (*Swans Down*), ¼ cup	100
carob (St.-John's bread), 4 oz.	204
corn, 4 oz.	417
gluten, 45%, 4 oz.	429
millet, whole grain (*Arrowhead Mills*), 2 oz.	185
oat, blend (*Gold Medal*), 4 oz. or 1 cup	390
(*Quaker Masa Harina*), ⅓ cup	140

(*Quaker Masa Trigo*), 1/3 cup   150
rye, dark, 1 cup   415
rye, light, 1 cup   374
rye, stone-ground (*Robin Hood*), 1 cup   360
rye and wheat (*Pillsbury's Best* Bohemian Style), 1 cup . . .   400
self-rising (*Gold Medal*), 1 cup   380
soybean, low-fat, 4 oz.   404
wheat, whole (*Gold Medal*), 1 cup   350
wheat, whole, blend (*Gold Medal*), 1 cup   380
white, all-purpose or unbleached (*Gold Medal*), 1 cup   400
white, presifted (*Pillsbury* Shake & Blend), 2 tbsp.   50
Frankfurter:
(*Gwaltney* Choice Franks), 1 link   140
(*Hillshire Farm* Natural Casing Wieners), 2 oz.   180
(*Hormel Light & Lean*), 1 link   45
(*Kahn's* Wieners), 1 link   140
(*Oscar Mayer* Light Wieners), 2-oz. link   130
(*Oscar Mayer* Wieners), 1.6-oz. link   145
(*Oscar Mayer Bun-Length* Wieners), 2-oz. link   185
(*Tobins First Prize* Lite Franks), 1 link   90
bacon and cheddar (*Oscar Mayer* Hot Dogs), 1.6-oz. link . . .   145
beef (*Eckrich* Bunsize or Jumbo), 1 link   190
beef (*Hebrew National*), 1.7-oz. link   150
beef (*Hebrew National* Lite Franks), 1.7-oz. link   120
beef (*Hormel* 12 oz.), 1 link   100
beef (*Kahn's*), 1 link   140
beef (*Oscar Mayer* Franks), 1.6-oz. link   145
beef (*Oscar Mayer Bun-Length* Franks), 2-oz. link   185
beef (*Oscar Mayer Bun-Length* 1/4 Pound), 4 oz.   360
beef with cheddar (*Oscar Mayer* Franks), 1.6-oz. link   130
cheese (*Oscar Mayer* Hot Dogs), 1.6-oz. link   145
chicken, see "Chicken frankfurter"
smoked (*Kahn's* Big Red Smokey)   170
smoked, beef (*Kahn's* Bun Size Beef Smokey), 1 link   190
smoked, with cheese (*Hormel Wranglers*), 1 link   180
turkey, see "Turkey frankfurter"
"Frankfurter," vegetarian, frozen (*Not Dogs*), 1.5-oz. link   120
French toast, frozen:
(*Downyflake*), 2 slices   270
cinnamon swirl (*Aunt Jemima*), 3 oz.   171
sticks (*Farm Rich* Original), 3 oz.   300
French toast breakfast, frozen:
cinnamon swirl, sausage (*Swanson Great Starts*), 5.5 oz.   390
with sausages (*Swanson Great Starts*), 5.5 oz.   380
with scrambled eggs, bacon (*Swanson Great Starts Big Start*),
   8.75 oz.   650

French toast breakfast (cont.)

Texas style, with sausage (*Downyflake*), 4.25 oz.	400

Frosting and cake topping, 1/12 can, except as noted:

all flavors (*Betty Crocker Creamy Deluxe* Party)	160
all flavors (*Pillsbury Bake Tops/Pillsbury Lovin' Lites*)	130
all flavors, except butter pecan, chocolate chip, cream cheese, lemon, and rainbow chip (*Betty Crocker Creamy Deluxe*)	160
all flavors, except chocolate (*Betty Crocker Creamy Deluxe* Light)	140
all flavors, except chocolate fudge (*Pillsbury Funfetti*)	150
caramel pecan or chocolate fudge (*Pillsbury Frosting Supreme*)	150
chocolate:	
(*Betty Crocker Creamy Deluxe* Light)	130
double Dutch or butter fudge (*Pillsbury Frosting Supreme*)	140
fudge (*Pillsbury Funfetti*)	140
milk, fudge swirl (*Pillsbury* Swirl Frosting)	150
chocolate chip (*Pillsbury Frosting Supreme*)	150
chocolate chip (*Betty Crocker Creamy Deluxe*)	170
chocolate mocha or coconut almond (*Pillsbury Frosting Supreme*)	150
coconut pecan or cream cheese (*Pillsbury Frosting Supreme*)	160
decorator, all flavors (*Pillsbury*), 1 tbsp.	60
lemon, strawberry, or vanilla (*Pillsbury Frosting Supreme*)	160
lemon or rainbow chip (*Betty Crocker Creamy Deluxe*)	170
vanilla fudge swirl (*Pillsbury* Swirl Frosting)	150

Fruit and fruit juices, see specific listings

Fruit, mixed:

canned (*Del Monte Fruit Naturals/Lite* Fruit Cup), 4.5 oz.	60
canned (*Orchard Naturals*), 4 oz.	60
canned, in heavy syrup (*Del Monte* Fruit Cup), 4.5 oz.	100
canned, tropical, fruit salad (*Dole*), 1/2 cup	70
chilled, salad (*Kraft Pure*), 1/2 cup	80
dried (*Del Monte*), 2 oz.	130
dried, with raisins (*Sunsweet Fruit Morsels*) 2 oz.	150
frozen, in syrup (*Birds Eye* Quick Thaw Pouch), 5 oz.	120
cocktail, canned (*Hunt's*), 4 oz.	90
cocktail, canned, in heavy syrup (*Del Monte*), 1/2 cup	90

Fruit bar, frozen, 1 bar:

all flavors (*Welch's* Fruit Juice Bars)	80
all flavors (*Welch's* Fruit Juice Bars No Sugar Added)	25
all flavors, except chocolate chip (*Dole Fresh Lites*)	25
all flavors, except raspberry (*Dole Fruit & Juice*)	70
banana or coconut, creamy (*Frozfruit*)	120
chocolate chip (*Dole Fresh Lites*)	60
lemon or chunky strawberry (*Frozfruit*)	70
raspberry (*Dole Fruit & Juice*)	60
and cream, all flavors (*Welch's* Fruit Juice Bars No Sugar Added)	45
and cream, all flavors (*Dole* Fruit & Cream)	90

and yogurt, chocolate (*Dole* Fruit & Yogurt) 70
and yogurt, strawberry-banana (*Dole* Fruit & Yogurt) 60
Fruit cocktail, see "Fruit, mixed"
Fruit juice, blend, chilled:
(*Chiquita Calypso Breeze/Hawaiian Sunrise*), 6 fl. oz. 100
(*Chiquita Caribbean Splash/Tropical Squeeze*), 6 fl. oz. 90
Fruit juice drink, seven fruit (*Boku*), 8 fl. oz. 120
Fruit punch, canned or bottled:
(*Veryfine* 100% Juice Punch), 8 fl. oz. 122
blend (*Libby's Juicy Juice*), 6 fl. oz. 100
cocktail, island fruit (*Hawaiian Punch*), 6 fl. oz. 90
Fruit punch drink:
(*Shasta*), 12 fl. oz. 196
(*Shasta Plus*), 12 fl. oz. 168
(*Welch's* Juice Cocktail), 6 fl. oz. 110
mix*, mountain berry (*Wylers* Crystals), 8 fl. oz. 85
Fruit roll, see "Fruit snack"
Fruit snack (see also specific fruit listings), all flavors:
(*Fruit by the Foot*), 1 roll 80
(*Fruit Roll-Ups*), .5-oz. roll 50
(*Fruit Wrinkles*), 1 pouch 100
(*Sunkist Fruit Flippits*), .8-oz. pouch 107
all varieties (*Sunkist Fun Fruits*), .9-oz. pouch 100
Fruit spread (see also "Jam, jelly, and preserves"):
all flavors (*Smucker's* Extra Fruit), 1 tsp. 15
all flavors (*Smucker's* Simply Fruit), 1 tsp. 16
all flavors (*Welch's* Totally Fruit), 1 tsp. 14
Fudge topping, see "Chocolate syrup and topping"

G

Food and Measure	Calories

Garbanzos, see "Chick-peas"
Garden salad (*Read*), 1/2 cup 80
Garlic:
fresh, raw, 1 clove, approx. .1 oz. 4
in jars, crushed (*Gilroy*), 1 tsp. 8
in jars, minced (*Gilroy*), 1 tsp. 23
in jars, puree (*Progresso*), 1 tsp. 4
Garlic pepper (*McCormick/Schilling* California Style), 1 tsp. . . . 8
Garlic powder (*McCormick/Schilling* California Style), 1 tsp. . . . 12
Garlic salt (*McCormick/Schilling* California Style), 1 tsp. 12
Garlic seasoning:
(*McCormick/Schilling* Garlic Bread Sprinkle), 1 tsp. 20
(*McCormick/Schilling Season All*), 1 tsp. 8
Gefilte fish, 1 ball:
sweet (*Mother's* Old World) 54
whitefish and pike, jelled broth (*Rokeach*, 12 oz.), 2 oz. 46
Gelatin, unflavored (*Knox*), 1 pkt. 25
Gelatin dessert mix*, all flavors (*Royal*), 1/2 cup 80
Ginger, root, sliced, 1 tbsp. 4
Ginger, ground (*McCormick/Schilling*), 1 tsp. 6
Ginger, pickled, Japanese, 1 oz. 10
Goose, domesticated, roasted:
meat with skin, 4 oz. 346
meat only, 4 oz. 270
Goose liver pâté, see "Pâté"
Gooseberry, fresh, 1/2 cup 34
Granola and cereal bars or squares, 1 piece, except as noted:
all flavors (*Kellogg's Nutri•Grain* Cereal Bars) 150
all flavors, except strawberry (*Fibar*) 110

apple oatmeal spice, raisin nut bran, or strawberry oatmeal almond (*Fibar AM*)	150
apple raisin (*Kudos Pan Squares*)	160
chocolate chip (*Quaker Chewy*), 1 oz.	128
cinnamon (*Nature Valley*), .8 oz.	120
cranberry and wild berry or raspberry (*Fibar AM*)	120
honey nut, bite size (*Nature Valley Granola Bites*), 1 pouch . . .	170
honey and oats (*Quaker Chewy*), 1 oz.	125
nut and raisin, chunky (*Quaker Chewy*), 1 oz.	131
oat bran-honey graham (*Nature Valley*), .8 oz.	110
oats and honey or peanut butter (*Nature Valley*), .8 oz.	120
peaches and cream or strawberry and cream cheese (*Kudos Pan Squares*)	170
peanut butter, chocolate coated (*Kudos*), 1.3 oz.	190
peanut butter and chocolate chip (*Kudos Pan Squares*)	190
raisin and cinnamon (*Quaker Chewy*), 1 oz.	128
rice bran-cinnamon graham (*Nature Valley*), .6 oz.	90
strawberry (*Fibar*)	120
Grape, seedless or seeded:	
fresh:	
American type (slipskin), 1/2 cup	29
American type (slipskin), 10 medium, 1.4 oz.	15
European type (adherent skin), 1/2 cup	57
European type (adherent skin), 10 medium, 1.75 oz.	36
canned, Thompson seedless, in heavy syrup (*S&W* Premium), 1/2 cup	100
Grape drink (*Tropicana*), 6 fl. oz.	90
Grape juice:	
(*Welch's* 100% Pure), 6 fl. oz.	120
frozen* (*Sunkist*), 6 fl. oz.	69
cocktail, bottled (*Welch's Orchard*), 6 fl. oz.	110
Grape juice drink:	
canned (*Shasta Plus*), 12 fl. oz.	176
canned (*Welch's/Welch's Orchard*), 6 fl. oz.	110
frozen* (*Sunkist*), 6 fl. oz.	69
Grape-apple drink (*Welch's* Juice Cocktail), 6 fl. oz.	110
Grape-raspberry juice drink, white grape (*Boku*), 8 fl. oz.	120
Grapefruit:	
fresh, pink or red:	
California or Arizona, 1/2 medium, 33/4″ diam.	46
California or Arizona, sections with juice, 1/2 cup	43
Florida, 1/2 medium, 33/4″ diam.	37
Florida, sections with juice, 1/2 cup	34
fresh, white:	
California, 1/2 medium, 33/4″ diam.	43
California, sections with juice, 1/2 cup	42

Grapefruit (cont.)
Florida, 1/2 medium, 33/4" diam. 38
Florida, sections with juice, 1/2 cup 38
canned (*S&W* Unsweetened) 40
canned, in light syrup (*Stokely*) 90
chilled (*Kraft* Pure), 1/2 cup 50
Grapefruit juice, 6 fl. oz., except as noted:
fresh 72
canned, bottled, or chilled:
(*Del Monte*) 70
(*Sunkist* Fresh Squeezed), 8 fl. oz. 96
(*Welch's* 100% Pure) 70
pink (*Ocean Spray Pink Premium*) 60
white or ruby red (*Tropicana* 100% Pure) 70
frozen* (*Minute Maid*) 83
cocktail, pink (*Tropicana Twister*) 80
cocktail, pink (*Topicana Twister* Light) 30
Grapefruit juice drink:
(*Citrus Hill*), 6 fl. oz. 70
golden (*Tropicana* Juice Sparkler), 6 fl. oz. 84
Gravy, see specific listings
Green pepper, see "Pepper, sweet"
Grouper, meat only, baked, broiled, or microwaved, 4 oz. 134
Guacamole (*Sonora Valley*), 1 oz. 36
Guacamole seasoning mix (*Old El Paso*), 1/7 pkg. 7
Guava:
common, trimmed, 1/2 cup 42
strawberry, trimmed, 1/2 cup 85
Guava juice (*Welch's Orchard Tropicals*), 6 fl. oz. 100
Guinea hen, fresh, raw:
meat with skin, 4 oz. 180
meat only, 4 oz. 124

H

Food and Measure	Calories

Häagen-Dazs **Ice Cream Shops,** 4 fl. oz. serving:
ice cream:

cherry, brandied	250
chocolate, regular or Belgian, or maple walnut	330
chocolate Swiss almond	300
pralines and cream	290
sorbet, lemon or orange	140
sorbet, raspberry	110
yogurt, frozen, nonfat, chocolate, coffee, or strawberry	120
yogurt, frozen, nonfat, vanilla	110

Haddock, meat only:

fresh, baked, broiled, or microwaved, 4 oz.	127
smoked (finnan haddie), 4 oz.	132
frozen (*Van de Kamp's Natural*), 4 oz.	90

Haddock entree, frozen:

battered (*Gorton's* Crispy Batter), 2 pieces	300
battered (*Mrs. Paul's* Crunchy), 2 pieces	280
battered (*Van de Kamp's*), 2 pieces	250
breaded (*Mrs. Paul's* Crispy Crunchy), 2 pieces	280
breaded (*Van de Kamp's*), 2 pieces	270
breaded (*Van de Kamp's* Light), 1 piece	240

Halibut, meat only:

fresh, Atlantic and Pacific, baked, broiled, or microwaved, 4 oz.	159
fresh, Greenland, baked, broiled, or microwaved, 4 oz.	271
frozen, steaks, without seasoning mix (*SeaPak*), 6-oz. pkg.	160
Halibut entree, frozen, battered (*Van de Kamp's*), 2 pieces	150
Halvah (*Fantastic Foods*), 1.5-oz. bar	232

Ham, fresh (see also "Ham, cured"), boneless, roasted:
whole leg:

lean with separable fat, 4 oz.	333

Ham, fresh, whole leg (cont.)
lean with separable fat, chopped or diced, 1 cup 411
lean only, 4 oz. 249
lean only, chopped or diced, 1 cup 309
rump half, lean with separable fat, 4 oz. 311
rump half, lean only, 4 oz. 251
rump half, lean only, chopped or diced, 1 cup 309
shank half, lean with separable fat, 4 oz. 344
shank half, lean only, 4 oz. 244
shank half, lean only, chopped or diced, 1 cup 301
Ham, cured, whole, boneless:
lean with separable fat, unheated, 1 oz. 70
lean only, unheated, 1 oz. 42
lean with separable fat, roasted, 4 oz. 276
lean only, roasted, 4 oz. 178
lean with separable fat, roasted, chopped or diced, 1 cup 341
lean only, roasted, chopped or diced, 1 cup 219
Ham, cured, boneless (see also "Ham luncheon meat"):
center slice, lean with separable fat, unheated, 1 oz. 57
country style, lean only, raw, 1 oz. 55
regular (11% fat), unheated, 1 oz. 52
regular, roasted, 4 oz. 202
regular, roasted, chopped or diced, 1 cup 249
extra lean (5% fat), unheated, 1 oz. 37
extra lean, roasted, 4 oz. 164
extra lean, roasted, chopped or diced, 1 cup 203
(*Jones Dairy Farm*), 1 oz. 40
slice (*Oscar Mayer* Jubilee), 1 oz. 30
steak (*Oscar Mayer* Jubilee), 2-oz. steak 55
Ham, canned:
(*Black Label,* 5 lb. or 3 lb.), 4 oz. 140
(*Holiday Glaze,* 3 lb.), 4 oz. 130
(*Hormel Curemaster*), 4 oz. 140
(*Light & Lean* Boneless), 2 oz. 60
(*Oscar Mayer* Jubilee), 1 oz. 30
hickory smoked (*Rath Black Hawk*), 2 oz. 60
Ham entree, frozen:
(*Banquet* Platters), 8.25 oz. 200
and asparagus au gratin (*The Budget Gourmet* Light & Healthy),
  1 serving 300
and asparagus bake (*Stouffer's*), 9.5 oz. 510
scalloped potatoes and (*Swanson* Homestyle Recipe), 9 oz. 340
Ham luncheon meat:
(*Jones Dairy Farm*), 1 oz. 30
(*Kahn's* Low Salt), 1 slice 30
(*Oscar Mayer* Breakfast Ham, 95% Fat Free), 1.5-oz. slice 45

all varieties (*Hillshire Farm Deli Select*), 1 oz. 31
baked (*Healthy Choice*), 1-oz. slice 30
baked (*Oscar Mayer* 97% Fat Free), .7-oz. slice 20
Black Forest (*Healthy Deli*), 1 oz. 32
boiled (*Oscar Mayer*), .7-oz. slice 25
boiled (*Oscar Mayer Deli-Thin/Healthy Favorites*), .4-oz. slice . . . 12
chopped (*Oscar Mayer* 90% Fat Free), 1-oz. slice 40
chopped, regular or peppered (*Oscar Mayer*), 1-oz. slice 55
cooked, sliced (*Kahn's*), 1 slice 30
glazed (*Light & Lean*), 2 slices 50
honey (*Oscar Mayer Deli-Thin/Healthy Favorites*), .4-oz. slice . . . 14
honey or smoked, cooked (*Oscar Mayer*), .7-oz. slice 20
peppered, black, cracked (*Oscar Mayer*), .7-oz. slice 20
smoked, cooked (*Oscar Mayer Deli-Thin*), .4-oz. slice 12
smoked, cooked (*Oscar Mayer Healthy Favorites*), .4-oz. slice . . 14
turkey, see "Turkey ham"
Ham spread, deviled, canned:
(*Underwood*), 2 1/8 oz. 220
(*Underwood* Light), 2 1/8 oz. 120
smoked (*Underwood*), 2 1/8 oz. 190
Ham and cheese breakfast bagel, frozen:
(*Swanson Great Starts*), 3 oz. 240
(*Weight Watchers*), 3 oz. 210
Ham and cheese loaf:
(*Hormel* Perma-Fresh), 2 slices 110
(*Light & Lean*), 2 slices 90
(*Oscar Mayer*), 1-oz. slice 70
Ham and cheese pocket sandwich, frozen:
(*Hot Pockets*), 5 oz. 360
(*Weight Watchers Ultimate 200*), 4 oz. 200
Hamburger entree mix*, 1 cup, except as noted:
beef noodle or chili macaroni (*Hamburger Helper*) 330
beef Romanoff (*Hamburger Helper*) 350
cheddar and bacon (*Hamburger Helper*) 380
cheeseburger macaroni or cheesy Italian (*Hamburger Helper*) . . . 370
hamburger hash (*Hamburger Helper*) 320
hamburger pizza dish (*Hamburger Helper*) 360
hamburger stew (*Hamburger Helper*) 300
Italian, zesty, or lasagne (*Hamburger Helper*) 340
meat loaf or nacho cheese (*Hamburger Helper*) 360
pizza (*Hamburger Helper Pizzabake*), 4.5 oz. 320
potato au gratin (*Hamburger Helper*) 350
potato Stroganoff or beef taco (*Hamburger Helper*) 330
rice Oriental or spaghetti (*Hamburger Helper*) 340
sloppy Joe (*Hamburger Helper Sloppy Joe Bake*), 5 oz. 340
Stroganoff (*Hamburger Helper*) 390

Hamburger entree mix* (cont.)
taco (*Hamburger Helper Tacobake*), 5.75 oz. 320
Hamburger seasoning mix (*McCormick/Schilling*), 1/4 pkg. 33
Hardee's:
breakfast, 1 serving:
    bacon biscuit, 3.3 oz. 360
    bacon and egg biscuit, 4.4 oz. 410
    bacon, egg, and cheese biscuit, 4.8 oz. 460
    Big Country Breakfast, bacon, 7.7 oz. 660
    Big Country Breakfast, country ham, 9 oz. 670
    Big Country Breakfast, ham, 8.9 oz. 620
    Big Country Breakfast, sausage, 9.7 oz. 850
    Biscuit 'N' Gravy, 7.8 oz. 440
    Canadian Rise 'N' Shine biscuit, 5.7 oz. 470
    chicken biscuit, 5.1 oz. 430
    Cinnamon 'N' Raisin biscuit, 2.8 oz. 320
    country ham biscuit, 3.8 oz. 350
    country ham and egg biscuit, 4.9 oz. 400
    ham biscuit, 3.7 oz. 320
    ham and egg biscuit, 4.9 oz. 370
    ham, egg, and cheese biscuit, 5.3 oz. 420
    Hash Rounds, 2.8 oz. 230
    muffin, blueberry, 4 oz. 400
    muffin, oat bran-raisin, 4.3 oz. 410
    pancakes, three, 4.8 oz. 280
    pancakes, three, with bacon, 5.3 oz. 350
    pancakes, three, with 1 sausage pattie, 6.2 oz. 430
    Rise 'N' Shine biscuit, 2.9 oz. 320
    sausage biscuit, 4.2 oz. 440
    sausage and egg biscuit, 5.3 oz. 490
    steak biscuit, 5.2 oz. 500
    steak and egg biscuit, 6.3 oz. 550
burgers and sandwiches, 1 serving:
    Big Deluxe burger, 7.6 oz. 500
    Big Roast Beef, 6 oz. 380
    Big Twin, 6.1 oz. 450
    cheeseburger, 4 oz. 300
    cheeseburger, bacon, 7.7 oz. 610
    cheeseburger, quarter pound, 6.4 oz. 500
    chicken breast sandwich, grilled, 6.8 oz. 310
    Chicken Fillet, 6.1 oz. 370
    combo sub, 9.1 oz. 380
    Fisherman's Fillet, 7.3 oz. 470
    ham sub, 8.6 oz. 370
    hamburger, 3.5 oz. 260
    hot dog, 4.2 oz. 290

Hot Ham 'N' Cheese, 5.3 oz. 330
Mushroom 'N' Swiss burger, 6.6 oz. 490
roast beef, regular, 4.4 oz. 280
roast beef sub, 9.1 oz. 370
Turkey Club, 7.3 oz. 390
turkey sub, 9.3 oz. 390
chicken, 1 serving:
  breast, 4 oz. 340
  Chicken Stix, 6 piece, 3.5 oz. 210
  Chicken Stix, 9 piece, 5.3 oz. 310
  leg, 2 oz. 152
  thigh, 3.8 oz. 370
  wing, 1.9 oz. 205
salads and side dishes, 1 serving:
  cole slaw, 4 oz. 240
  Crispy Curls, 3 oz. 300
  fries, regular, 2.5 oz. 230
  fries, Big Fry, 5.5 oz. 500
  gravy, 1.5 oz. 20
  mashed potatoes, 4 oz. 70
  salad, chef, 9.5 oz. 214
  salad, garden, 7.9 oz. 184
  salad, side, 4 oz. 20
desserts, 1 serving:
  apple turnover, 3.2 oz. 270
  Big Cookie, 1.7 oz. 250
  Cool Twist ice cream:
    cone, chocolate or vanilla, 4.2 oz. 180
    cone, vanilla/chocolate twist, 4.2 oz. 170
    sundae, caramel, 6 oz. 330
    sundae, hot fudge, 5.9 oz. 320
    sundae, strawberry, 5.9 oz. 260
  shake, chocolate or strawberry 390
  shake, vanilla 370
Hazelnut, see "Filbert"
Hazelnut pâté, in jars (*Three Fold Farm*), 3.5 oz. 195
Head cheese (*Oscar Mayer*), 1-oz. slice 55
Herb and garlic sauce, with lemon juice (*Lawry's*), 1/4 cup . . . 36
Herb gravy mix* (*McCormick/Schilling*), 1/4 cup 20
Herb side dish mix* (*Hain* 3-Grain), 1/2 cup 120
Herbs, see specific listings
Herbs, mixed (*Lawry's* Pinch of Herbs), 1 tsp. 9
Herring, fresh, meat only:
Atlantic, baked, broiled, or microwaved, 4 oz. 230
Atlantic, kippered, 4 oz. 246
Atlantic, pickled, 4 oz. 297

Herring, fresh (cont.)
Pacific, baked, broiled, or microwaved, 4 oz. 284
Herring, canned, see "Sardine"
Hollandaise sauce:
(*Great Impressions*), 2 tbsp. 192
mix* (*McCormick/Schilling McCormick Collection*), 1/4 cup 137
Homestyle gravy mix*:
(*McCormick/Schilling*), 1/4 cup 24
(*Pillsbury*), 1/4 cup 16
Hominy, canned (see also "Corn grits"):
golden or Mexican (*Allens*), 1/2 cup 80
white (*Van Camp's*), 1 cup 138
Honey (*Sioux Honey*), 1 tbsp. 60
Honey loaf (*Oscar Mayer*), 1-oz. slice 35
Honeydew melon:
1/10 melon, 7" × 2" wedge 46
pulp, cubed, 1/2 cup 30
Horseradish, prepared, hot, red, or white (*Gold's*), 1 tsp. 4
Horseradish sauce (*Heinz*), 1 tbsp. 80
Hot dog, see "Frankfurter"
Hot sauce, see "Pepper sauce" and specific listings
Hubbard squash:
baked, cubed, 1/2 cup 51
boiled, drained, mashed, 1/2 cup 35
Hummus, mix (*Casbah*), 1 oz. dry 110
Hunter sauce mix* (*McCormick/Schilling McCormick Collection*),
1/4 cup 104
Hush puppy, mix, all varieties (*Golden Dipt*), 1 1/4 oz. 120

I

Food and Measure	Calories
Ice, cherry, Italian (*Good Humor*), 6 fl. oz.	138
Ice bar, all flavors (*Borden* Ice Pop), 1 bar	40
Ice cream, 1/2 cup, except as noted:	
butter almond (*Breyers*)	170
butter crunch (*Sealtest*)	150
butter pecan (*Frusen Glädjé*)	280
butter pecan (*Häagen-Dazs*)	290
butter pecan, roasted (*Lady Borden*)	160
caramel nut sundae (*Häagen-Dazs*)	310
cherry, chocolate coated (*Rondos* Chicago Cherry), .75-oz. piece	60
cherry vanilla (*Breyers*)	150
chocolate:	
(*Breyers*)	160
(*Frusen Glädjé*)	240
(*Häagen-Dazs*)	270
chocolate coated (*Rondos*), .75-oz. piece	60
chocolate-crisp coated (*Nestlé Crunch Nuggets*), 2.25 fl. oz.	180
chocolate mint or deep fudge (*Häagen-Dazs*)	300
deep (*Häagen-Dazs*)	290
Dutch or swirl (*Borden/Borden Olde Fashioned Recipe*)	130
marshmallow sundae (*Sealtest*)	150
milk chocolate coated (*Nestlé Bon Bons*), 2.25 fl. oz.	190
plain or triple (*Sealtest*)	140
chocolate, deep, and peanut butter (*Häagen-Dazs*)	330
chocolate almond, Swiss (*Frusen Glädjé*)	270
chocolate chip:	
chocolate (*Breyers*)	180
chocolate (*Frusen Glädjé*)	270
chocolate (*Häagen-Dazs*)	290
chocolate coated (*Rondos*), .75-oz. piece	80

Ice cream, chocolate chip (cont.)

mint (*Lady Borden*)	160
regular or mint (*Breyers*)	170
vanilla (*Frusen Glädjé*)	280
chocolate or coffee (*Häagen-Dazs*)	270
chocolate elegance or coffee almond (*Lady Borden*)	160
coffee (*Breyers*)	150
coffee (*Frusen Glädjé*)	260
coffee toffee crunch (*Häagen-Dazs*)	300
cookies and cream or macadamia brittle (*Häagen-Dazs*)	280
cookies and cream or heavenly hash (*Sealtest*)	150
cookies and cream, chocolate coated (*Rondos*), .75-oz. piece	70
fudge royale or peanut fudge sundae (*Sealtest*)	140
maple walnut (*Sealtest*)	160
mocha chip or pralines and cream (*Frusen Glädjé*)	280
Neapolitan supreme (*Lady Borden*)	160
peach, natural (*Breyers*)	130
rum raisin or strawberry (*Häagen-Dazs*)	250
strawberry (*Frusen Glädjé*)	230
strawberry (*Lady Borden*)	160
strawberry cream (*Borden Olde Fashioned Recipe*)	130
toffee chunk (*Frusen Glädjé*)	270

vanilla:

(*Frusen Glädjé*)	230
(*Häagen-Dazs*)	260
French (*Sealtest*)	140
honey (*Häagen-Dazs*)	250
natural (*Breyers*)	150
chocolate-crisp coated (*Nestlé Crunch Nuggets*), 2.25 fl. oz.	190
classic or French, chocolate coated (*Rondos*), .75-oz. piece	60
dark chocolate coated (*Nestlé Bon Bons*), 2.25 fl. oz.	190
milk chocolate coated (*Nestlé Bon Bons*), 2.25 fl. oz.	160
Swiss almond (*Frusen Glädjé*)	270
Swiss almond (*Häagen-Dazs*)	290
vanilla fudge (*Häagen-Dazs*)	270
vanilla fudge (*Sealtest*)	140
vanilla fudge twirl or vanilla-chocolate (*Breyers*)	160
vanilla-chocolate (*Sealtest Cubic Scoops*)	140
vanilla-chocolate-strawberry (*Breyers*)	150
vanilla-peanut butter swirl (*Häagen-Dazs*)	280
vanilla-red raspberry (*Frusen Glädjé*)	230

Ice cream, substitute and imitation, 1/2 cup, except as noted:

all flavors (*Lite-Lite Tofutti*)	90
all flavors (*Sealtest Free*)	100
all flavors, except chocolate, cookies and cream, praline and caramel, or rocky road (*Healthy Choice*)	120

chocolate (*Simple Pleasures*), 4 oz. 140
chocolate supreme (*Tofutti*) 210
chocolate or cookies and cream (*Healthy Choice*) 130
coffee (*Simple Pleasures*), 4 oz. 120
peach (*Simple Pleasures*), 4 oz. 135
praline and caramel (*Healthy Choice*) 130
rocky road (*Healthy Choice*) 160
rum raisin (*Simple Pleasures*), 4 oz. 130
strawberry (*Simple Pleasures*), 4 oz. 120
vanilla (*Tofutti*) 200
wildberry (*Tofutti*) 210
Ice cream bar (see also "Sherbet bar" and "Yogurt bar"), 1 bar:
(*Borden* Dream Bar) 70
(*Klondike*), 5 fl. oz. 280
(*Nestlé Butterfinger*), 2.5 fl. oz. 130
all varieties (*Milky Way*), 2 fl. oz. 190
all varieties (*Milky Way* Snack Size), .72-fl. oz. 70
all varieties (*3 Musketeers*), 2 fl. oz. 170
all varieties (*3 Musketeers* Snack Size), .72-fl. oz. 60
almond (*Dove*), 3.67 fl. oz. 350
caramel almond crunch (*Häagen-Dazs*) 240
chocolate (*Klondike*), 5 fl. oz. 270
chocolate, chocolate-crisp coated (*Nestlé Crunch*), 3 fl. oz. . . . 230
chocolate, dark chocolate coated (*Dove*), 3.8 fl. oz. 350
chocolate, milk chocolate coated (*Dove*), 3.8 fl. oz. 340
chocolate or vanilla, dark chocolate coated (*Häagen-Dazs*) 380
coffee almond crunch (*Häagen-Dazs*) 360
crunchy cookies (*Dove*), 3.8 fl. oz. 330
(*Mars* Almond Bar), 1.85 fl. oz. 210
peanut bar (*Dove*), 3.67 fl. oz. 350
peanut butter crunch (*Häagen-Dazs*) 270
(*Snickers*), 2 fl. oz. 220
(*Snickers* Snack Size), 1 fl. oz. 110
strawberry shortcake (*Good Humor*), 3 fl. oz. 176
vanilla crunch (*Häagen-Dazs* Vanilla Crisp) 220
vanilla, chocolate-crisp coated (*Nestlé Crunch*), 3 fl. oz. 180
vanilla, dark or milk chocolate coated (*Dove*), 3.8 fl. oz. 340
vanilla, milk chocolate coated (*Häagen-Dazs*) 330
vanilla, milk chocolate almond coated (*Häagen-Dazs*) 370
vanilla, milk chocolate almond coated (*Klondike* Sensation) 190
vanilla, milk chocolate brittle coated (*Häagen-Dazs*) 370
vanilla, milk chocolate crisp coated (*Nestlé Crunch*) 180
Ice cream bar, substitute and imitation, 1 bar:
(*Borden* Light/*Viva* Dream Bar) 30
(*Good Humor* Light), 3 fl. oz. 170
(*Nestlé Crunch* Lite), 2.5 fl. oz. 140

Ice cream bar, substitute and imitation (cont.)

chocolate fudge swirl (*Sealtest Free*)	90
raspberry, nondairy (*Tofutti Frutti*), 2 fl. oz.	55
strawberry swirl or vanilla fudge swirl (*Sealtest Free*)	80

Ice cream cone, 1 piece:

(*Comet*)	18
sugar (*Keebler*)	45
waffle (*Comet*)	70
waffle, giant (*Keebler*)	100

Ice cream sandwich, 1 piece:

(*Borden* Dessert Sandwich)	180
(*Viva* Sugar Free)	130
chocolate, chocolate chip cookie (*Good Humor*), 4 fl. oz.	246
chocolate, nondairy, chocolate wafer (*Tofutti Cuties*)	140
vanilla (*Klondike*), 5 fl. oz.	230
vanilla, chocolate chip cookie (*Chipwich* Light)	175
vanilla, nondairy, chocolate wafer (*Tofutti Cuties*)	130

Ice cream and sorbet, see "Sorbet"

Ice milk, 1/2 cup:

caramel nut or chocolate chip (*Light n'Lively*)	120
chocolate or vanilla (*Breyers* Light)	120
chocolate fudge or praline almond (*Breyers* Light)	130
coffee (*Light n'Lively*)	100
cookies and cream (*Light n'Lively*)	110
heavenly hash (*Light n'Lively*)	120
heavenly hash (*Breyers* Light)	150
strawberry (*Breyers* Light)	110
toffee fudge parfait (*Breyers Light*)	140
vanilla or vanilla-chocolate-strawberry (*Light n'Lively*)	100
vanilla chocolate almond (*Light n'Lively*)	120
vanilla fudge or vanilla raspberry swirl (*Light n'Lively*)	110
vanilla raspberry (*Breyers* Light)	130

Ice milk cone (*Gold Bond* Olde Nut Sundae), 3 fl. oz. 230

Iowa brand loaf (*Hormel* Perma-Fresh), 2 slices 90

Italian sausage:

(*Jones Dairy Farm*), 2-oz. link	160
hot (*Hillshire Farm* Links), 2 oz.	180
mild (*Hillshire Farm* Links), 2 oz.	190

Italian seasoning (*McCormick/Schilling* Spice Blends), 1 tsp. . . 4

J

Food and Measure	Calories

Jack-in-the-Box:
breakfast, 1 serving:
    Breakfast Jack, 4.4 oz. 307
    hash browns, 2 oz. 156
    pancake platter, 8.1 oz. 612
    pancake syrup, 1.5 oz. 121
    sausage crescent, 5.5 oz. 584
    scrambled egg platter, 7.5 oz. 559
    scrambled egg pocket, 6.5 oz. 431
    sourdough breakfast sandwich, 5.2 oz. 381
    supreme crescent, 5.2 oz. 547
burgers and sandwiches, 1 serving:
    bacon cheeseburger, 8.5 oz. 705
    cheeseburger, 4 oz. 315
    cheeseburger, double, 5.3 oz. 467
    cheeseburger, ultimate, 9.9 oz. 942
    chicken fajita pita, 6.7 oz. 292
    chicken fillet, grilled, 7.4 oz. 431
    chicken and mushroom sandwich, 7.8 oz. 438
    chicken supreme, 8.6 oz. 641
    fish supreme, 7.7 oz. 510
    ham and turkey melt, 7.7 oz. 592
    hamburger, 3.4 oz. 267
    Jumbo Jack, 7.8 oz. 584
    Jumbo Jack, with cheese, 8.5 oz. 677
    old-fashioned patty melt, 7.6 oz. 713
    pastrami melt, 8.1 oz. 556
    sirloin steak sandwich, 8.4 oz. 517
    sirloin steak sandwich, with cheese, 9.2 oz. 608
    sourdough burger, grilled, 7.9 oz. 712

Jack-in-the-Box (cont.)

Mexican food, 1 serving:

guacamole, .9 oz.	55
salsa, 1 oz.	8
taco, 2.8 oz.	187
taco, super, 4.4 oz.	281

finger foods and side dishes, 1 serving:

chicken strips, 4 pieces, 4 oz.	285
chicken strips, 6 pieces, 6.2 oz.	451
chicken wings, spicy, 6 pieces, 7.3 oz.	846
chicken wings, spicy, 9 pieces, 10.9 oz.	1270
chimichangas, mini, 4 pieces, 7.3 oz.	571
chimichangas, mini, 6 pieces, 10.9 oz.	856
egg rolls, 3 pieces, 5.8 oz.	437
egg rolls, 5 pieces, 10.1 oz.	753
fries, small, 2.4 oz.	219
fries, regular, 3.8 oz.	351
fries, jumbo, 4.3 oz.	396
fries, curly, seasoned, 3.8 oz.	358
onion rings, 3.6 oz.	380
ravioli, toasted, 7 pieces, 5.8 oz.	537
ravioli, toasted, 10 pieces, 8.3 oz.	768
sesame breadsticks, .6 oz.	70
taquitos, 5 pieces, 4.7 oz.	362
taquitos, 7 pieces, 6.7 oz.	511
tortilla chips, 1 oz.	139

salads, 1 serving:

chef, 11.7 oz.	325
side, 3.9 oz.	51
taco, 14.2 oz.	503

dressings and sauces:

BBQ sauce, 1 oz.	44
bleu cheese dressing, 2.5 oz.	262
buttermilk house dressing, 2.5 oz.	362
Italian dressing, low-calorie, 2.5 oz.	25
sweet and sour sauce, 1 oz.	40
Thousand Island dressing, 2.5 oz.	312

desserts and shakes, 1 serving:

apple turnover, hot, 3.9 oz.	354
cheesecake, 3.5 oz.	309
double fudge cake, 3 oz.	288
shake, chocolate	330
shake, strawberry or vanilla	320

Jalapeño dip:

bean (*Old El Paso*), 1 tbsp.	14
cheddar (*Breakstone's* Gourmet), 2 tbsp.	70

pepper, nacho (*Price's*), 1 oz.	80
Jalapeño loaf (*Kahn's*), 1 slice	70
Jalapeño pepper, see "Pepper, hot"	
Jam, jelly, and preserves (see also "Fruit spread"):	
all flavors (*Knott's Berry Farm*), 1 tsp.	18
all flavors (*Polaner*), 2 tsp.	35
all flavors (*Smucker's*), 1 tsp.	18
grape, raspberry-apple, or strawberry (*Welch's*), 2 tsp.	35
jalapeño jelly (*Great Impressions*), 1 tbsp.	58
Java plum, fresh, seeded, 1/2 cup	41
Jerusalem artichoke, sliced, 1/2 cup	57
Jicama, see "Yam bean tuber"	
Jujube, dried, 1 oz.	81

K

Food and Measure	**Calories**

Kale:	
fresh, raw, chopped, 1/2 cup	17
fresh, boiled, drained, chopped, 1/2 cup	21
canned, chopped (*Allens*), 1/2 cup	25
frozen, chopped (*Seabrook*), 3.3 oz.	25
Kale, Scotch, fresh, boiled, drained, chopped, 1/2 cup	18
Kasha, see "Buckwheat groats"	
Kentucky Fried Chicken, 1 serving:	
chicken, *Original Recipe:*	
breast, center, 3.6 oz.	260
breast, side, 2.9 oz.	245
drumstick, 2 oz.	152
thigh, 3.4 oz.	287
wing, 1.9 oz.	172
chicken, *Extra Tasty Crispy:*	
breast, center, 3.9 oz.	344
breast, side, 3.7 oz.	379

Kentucky Fried Chicken, chicken, *Extra Tasty Crispy* (cont.)
drumstick, 2.4 oz.	205
thigh, 4.2 oz.	414
wing, 2 oz.	231
chicken, *Kentucky Nuggets,* 6 pieces	284

chicken, *Skinfree Crispy:*
breast, center, 3.9 oz.	296
breast, side, 3.7 oz.	293
drumstick, 2 oz.	166
thigh, 3 oz.	256
chicken, *Hot Wings,* 6 pieces, 4.8 oz.	471
Chicken Littles sandwich, 1.7 oz.	169
Colonel's chicken sandwich, 5.9 oz.	482

Kentucky Nuggets sauces:
barbecue, 1 oz.	35
honey, .5 oz.	49
mustard, 1 oz.	36
sweet and sour, 1 oz.	58

side dishes:
buttermilk biscuit, 2.3 oz.	235
cole slaw, 3.2 oz.	114
corn-on-the-cob, 2.6 oz.	90
french fries, crispy, 3.1 oz.	294
french fries, regular, 2.7 oz.	244
mashed potatoes and gravy, 3.5 oz.	71

Ketchup, see "Catsup"

Kidneys:
lamb, braised, 4 oz.	155
pork, braised, 4 oz.	171
veal, braised, 4 oz.	185

Kielbasa (see also "Polish sausage"):
(*Hillshire Farm* Bun Size), 2 oz.	180
(*Tobins First Prize* Lite Polska), 2 oz.	140
all varieties (*Hillshire Farm* Polska Flavorseal or Links), 2 oz.	190
turkey, see "Turkey kielbasa"	
Kiwifruit, 1 large, approx. 3.7 oz.	55

Knockwurst:
(*Hillshire Farm* Links), 2 oz.	180
beef (*Hebrew National*), 3-oz. link	260

Kohlrabi:
raw, sliced, 1/2 cup	19
boiled, drained, sliced, 1/2 cup	24
Kumquat, 1 medium, approx. .7 oz.	12

L

Food and Measure — Calories

Lamb, domestic, choice grade, boneless, 4 oz.:
cubed (leg and shoulder), braised or stewed	253
cubed (leg and shoulder), broiled	211
foreshank, braised or stewed, lean with separable fat	276
foreshank, braised or stewed, lean only	212
ground, broiled	321
leg, roasted:	
whole, lean with separable fat	293
whole, lean only	217
shank half, lean with separable fat	255
shank half, lean only	204
sirloin half, lean with separable fat	331
sirloin half, lean only	231
loin, broiled, lean with separable fat	358
loin, broiled, lean only	245
loin, roasted, lean with separable fat	350
loin, roasted, lean only	229
rib, broiled, lean with separable fat	409
rib, broiled, lean only	266
rib, roasted, lean with separable fat	407
rib, roasted, lean only	263
shoulder:	
whole, braised or stewed, lean with separable fat	390
whole, braised or stewed, lean only	321
whole, roasted, lean with separable fat	313
whole, roasted, lean only	231
arm, braised or stewed, lean with separable fat	392
arm, braised or stewed, lean only	316
arm, roasted, lean with separable fat	316
arm, roasted, lean only	218

Lamb, shoulder (cont.)
blade, braised or stewed, lean with separable fat 391
blade, braised or stewed, lean only 327
blade, roasted, lean with separable fat 319
blade, roasted, lean only 237
Lamb, New Zealand, frozen, 4 oz.:
foreshank, braised or stewed, lean with separable fat 293
foreshank, braised or stewed, lean only 211
leg, whole, roasted, lean with separable fat 279
leg, whole, roasted, lean only 205
loin, broiled, lean with separable fat 357
loin, broiled, lean only 226
rib, roasted, lean with separable fat 386
rib, roasted, lean only 222
shoulder, whole, braised or stewed, lean with separable fat 405
shoulder, whole, braised or stewed, lean only 323
Lamb's quarters, boiled, drained, chopped, 1/2 cup 29
Lard, pork, 1 tbsp. 115
Lasagna, canned or packaged:
(*Dinty Moore American Classics*), 10 oz. 334
(*Hormel Micro Cup*), 7.5 oz. 250
Italian style (*Hormel Top Shelf*), 10 oz. 350
with meat sauce (*Healthy Choice* Microwave), 7.5 oz. 220
vegetable (*Hormel Top Shelf*), 10 oz. 280
Lasagna entree, frozen:
(*Dining Lite*), 9 oz. 240
(*On•Cor* Deluxe Entrees), 8 oz. 232
(*Stouffer's*), 10.5-oz. pkg. 360
cheese, three (*The Budget Gourmet*), 1 serving 390
with meat sauce:
(*The Budget Gourmet* Light & Healthy), 1 serving 290
(*Healthy Choice*), 10 oz. 260
(*Kraft Eating Right*), 10 oz. 270
(*Lean Cuisine*), 10.25 oz. 260
(*Swanson* Homestyle Recipe), 10.5 oz. 400
primavera (*Celentano*), 11 oz. 330
sausage, Italian (*The Budget Gourmet*), 1 serving 430
tuna, spinach noodles and vegetables (*Lean Cuisine*), 9.75 oz. . . 240
vegetable (*The Budget Gourmet* Light & Healthy), 1 serving . . . 290
vegetable (*On•Cor* Deluxe Entrees), 8 oz. 229
vegetable, with tofu and sauce (*Legume*), 12 oz. 240
zucchini (*Healthy Choice*), 11.5 oz. 240
Leek:
boiled, drained, 1 medium, approx. 4.4 oz. 38
boiled, drained, chopped, 1/2 cup 16
Lemon, whole, 1 medium, 2 1/8″ diam. 22

Lemon butter dill cooking sauce (*Golden Dipt*), 1 fl. oz.   110
Lemon extract, pure (*McCormick/Schilling*), 1 tsp.   35
Lemon herb marinade (*Golden Dipt*), 1 fl. oz.   130
Lemon juice:
fresh, 1/2 cup   30
canned or bottled (*Minute Maid* 100% Pure), 1 tbsp.   4
refrigerated (*ReaLemon* 100%), 1 fl. oz.   6
Lemon mousse mix* (*Sans Sucre* of Paris), 1/2 cup   70
Lemon and pepper (*McCormick/Schilling* Spice Blends), 1 tsp.   8
Lemonade:
(*Shasta*), 12 fl. oz.   168
(*Shasta Plus*), 12 fl. oz.   172
(*Tropicana*), 6 fl. oz.   90
(*Welch's*), 6 fl. oz.   100
chilled, all styles (*Minute Maid*), 6 fl. oz.   81
frozen* (*Sunkist*), 8 fl. oz.   92
drink mix*, pink (*Wylers*), 8 fl. oz.   78
Lentil, boiled, 1/2 cup   115
Lentil, sprouted, raw, 1/2 cup   40
Lettuce:
bibb, Boston, or butterhead, 1 head, 5″ diam.   21
cos or romaine, shredded, 1/2 cup   4
iceberg, 6″ diam. head   70
iceberg, 1 leaf, approx. .7 oz.   3
looseleaf, 1/2 cup shredded   5
Lime, 1 medium, 2″ diam.   20
Lime juice:
fresh, 1/2 cup   33
bottled, sweetened (*Rose's*), 1 fl. oz.   48
reconstituted (*ReaLime*), 1 fl. oz.   6
Ling, meat only, baked, broiled, or microwaved, 4 oz.   126
Lingcod, meat only, baked, broiled, or microwaved, 4 oz.   124
Linguine entree, frozen:
with clam sauce (*Lean Cuisine*), 95/8 oz.   280
with scallops and clams (*The Budget Gourmet* Light & Healthy),
   1 serving   280
with shrimp (*Healthy Choice*), 9.5 oz.   230
with shrimp and clams (*The Budget Gourmet*), 1 serving   270
Liquor, pure distilled (bourbon, gin, rye, vodka, etc.):
80 proof   65
90 proof   74
100 proof   83
Little Caesars:
Baby Pan! Pan!, 1 serving   525
Crazy Bread, 1 piece   98
Crazy Sauce, 1 serving   63

Little Caesars (cont.)
Pizza! Pizza!, one slice:

cheese, round, small	138
cheese, round, medium	154
cheese, round, large	169
cheese, square, small or large	188
cheese, square, medium	185
cheese and pepperoni, round, small	151
cheese and pepperoni, round, medium	168
cheese and pepperoni, round, large	185
cheese and pepperoni, square, small or large	204
cheese and pepperoni, square, medium	201
Slice! Slice!, 1 serving	756

salads and sandwiches, 1 serving:

greek salad, small	85
tossed salad, small	37
ham and cheese sandwich	553
Italian sandwich	615
tuna sandwich	610
turkey sandwich	450
veggie sandwich	784

Liver:

beef, pan-fried, 4 oz.	246
chicken, broiler-fryer, simmered, 4 oz.	180
chicken, broiler-fryer, simmered, chopped or diced, 1 cup	219
duck, domesticated, raw, 1 oz.	39
goose, domesticated, raw, 1 oz.	38
lamb, braised, 4 oz.	249
pork, braised, 4 oz.	187
turkey, simmered, 4 oz.	192
veal (calf), braised, 4 oz.	187
veal (calf), pan-fried, 4 oz.	278

Liver cheese, pork fat-wrapped (*Oscar Mayer*), 1.34-oz. slice — 115
Liver loaf (*Kahn's*), 1 slice — 170
Liver pâté, see "Pâté"
Liverwurst (see also "Braunschweiger"):

(*Jones Dairy Farm*), 1-oz. slice	80
(*Oscar Mayer* Liver Sausage), 1 oz.	95
low-fat (*Jones Dairy Farm*), 1-oz. slice	55

Liverwurst spread, canned (*Underwood*), 2 1/8 oz. — 190
Lobster, northern, meat only, boiled, poached, or steamed, 4 oz. — 111
Lobster sauce, rock (*Progresso*), 1/2 cup — 120
Loganberry, fresh, trimmed, 1/2 cup — 45
Loquat, 1 medium, approx. .6 oz. — 5
Luncheon meat (see also specific listings):
loaf (*Oscar Mayer*), 1-oz. slice — 75

spiced (*Kahn's* Luncheon Loaf), 1 slice   80
canned, all varieties, except deviled (*Spam*), 2 oz.   170
canned, deviled (*Spam*), 1 tbsp.   35
canned, deviled (*Spam Lite*), 2 oz.   140
Luxury loaf, pork, 1-oz. slice   40
Lychee nut, raw, shelled and seeded, 1/2 cup   63

M

Food and Measure	Calories

Macadamia nut (*Mauna Loa*), 1 oz.   210
Macaroni (see also "Noodles" and "Pasta"):
dry, 2 oz.   210
cooked, elbows, 1 cup   197
cooked, spirals, 1 cup   189
cooked, rainbow or tri-color, spirals, 1 cup   171
cooked, whole wheat, elbows, 1 cup   174
Macaroni and cheese dinner, frozen (*Banquet* Meals), 9 oz.   240
Macaroni and cheese mix*:
(*Kraft* Dinner/Family Size Dinner), 3/4 cup   290
cheddar (*Fantastic Foods* Traditional), 1/2 cup*   112
Parmesan and herbs (*Fantastic Foods*), 1/2 cup*   109
shells (*Velveeta/Velveeta* Touch of Mexico), 1/2 cup   210
shells and cheddar (*Prince*), 3/4 cup   300
shells and curry, with tofu (*Tofu Classics*), 1/2 cup   103
twists and cheddar (*Prince*), 1/2 cup   230
Macaroni dishes, canned or packaged:
and beef (*Chef Boyardee Beefaroni* Microwave Meals), 7.5 oz.   220
and beef (*Hormel Kid's Kitchen Micro Cup*), 7.5 oz.   200
and beef (*Libby's Diner*), 7.75 oz.   230
and cheese (*Hormel Kid's Kitchen Micro Cup*), 7.5 oz.   260
shells and cheddar (*Lipton Hearty Ones*), 11 oz.   367
shells in meat sauce (*Chef Boyardee* Microwave), 7.5 oz.   210
shells in mushroom sauce (*Chef Boyardee* Microwave), 7.5 oz.   170

Macaroni entree, frozen:

and beef, in tomato sauce (*Lean Cuisine*), 10 oz. 240

and cheese:

(*Banquet* Casserole), 6.5 oz. 290

(*Banquet Family Entrees*), 7 oz. 260

(*Green Giant* One Serving), 5.7 oz. 220

(*Healthy Choice*), 9 oz. 280

(*Kraft Eating Right*), 9 oz. 270

(*Lean Cuisine*), 9 oz. 290

(*On•Cor* Deluxe Entree), 8 oz. 161

(*Swanson* Homestyle Recipe), 10 oz. 390

Mace, ground (*McCormick/Schilling*), 1 tsp. 10

Mackerel, meat only:

fresh, Atlantic, baked, broiled, or microwaved, 4 oz. 297

fresh, king, baked, broiled, or microwaved, 4 oz. 152

fresh, Pacific and Jack, baked, broiled, or microwaved, 4 oz. . . . 228

fresh, Spanish, baked, broiled, or microwaved, 4 oz. 179

canned, Atlantic, with liquid, 8 oz. 415

canned, Jack, drained, 4 oz. 177

Mahi mahi, see "Dolphin fish"

Mai tai mix, bottled (*Holland House*), 1 fl. oz. 32

Malted milk mix:

chocolate (*Carnation*), 3 heaping tsp. 80

natural (*Carnation*), 3 heaping tsp. 90

Mammy apple, peeled and seeded, 1 oz. 14

Mandarin orange, see "Tangerine"

Mango:

1 medium, approx. 10.6 oz. 135

peeled, sliced, 1/2 cup 54

Mango nectar (*Libby's*), 6 fl. oz. 110

Manicotti entree, frozen:

(*Celentano*), 10 oz. 380

cheese (*The Budget Gourmet*), 1 serving 440

cheese (*Healthy Choice*), 9.25 oz. 230

with tofu and sauce (*Legume* Classic), 8 oz. 220

vegetable marinara (*On•Cor* Deluxe Entree), 8 oz. 200

Maple flavoring, imitation (*McCormick/Schilling*), 1 tsp. 8

Maple sugar, 1 oz. 99

Maple syrup (see also "Pancake syrup"), 1 tbsp. 50

Margarine, 1 tbsp.:

(*Country Morning* Light) 60

(Diet *Fleischmann's*) 50

(*Fleischmann's*) 100

(*Land O'Lakes* Stick or Tub) 105

all varieties (*Hain* Safflower) 100

stick or soft (*Blue Bonnet*) 100

stick or soft (*Fleischmann's*) 100
spread (*Blue Bonnet Better Blend*) 90
spread (*Fleischmann's* Extra Light Corn Oil) 50
spread (*Fleischmann's* Light Corn Oil) 80
spread (*Kraft* "Touch of Butter" Bowl) 50
spread, squeeze (*Parkay*) 90
spread, sweet cream (*Land O'Lakes* Stick) 90
spread, whipped (*Blue Bonnet*) 80
whipped (*Fleischmann's*) 70
Margarita mixer, frozen*, with rum (*Bacardi*), 7 fl. oz. . . . 160
Marjoram, dried (*McCormick/Schilling*), 1 tsp. 4
Marmalade, orange (*Welch's* Totally Fruit), 1 tsp. 14
Marshmallow topping (*Smucker's*), 2 tbsp. 120
Mayonnaise (see also "Salad dressings"), 1 tbsp.:
(*Bama* Light) 45
(*Hain* Canola) 100
(*Hain* Canola Reduced Calorie/Light Low Sodium) 60
(*Hain* Cold Pressed/Real/Safflower) 110
(*Hellmann's/Best Foods*) 100
(*Hellmann's/Best Foods* Light) 50
(*Hollywood* Safflower Kosher) 110
(*Kraft* Light) 50
eggless (*Hain* No Salt Added) 110
fresh garlic, lemon dill, or tarragon onion (*Chalif*) 100
imitation (*Hellmann's* Cholesterol Free) 50
tofu (*Nasoya Naoynaise*) 40
McDonald's:
breakfast, 1 serving:
apple bran muffin, fat-free 180
apple Danish, 4.1 oz. 390
biscuit, plain, with spread, 2.6 oz. 260
biscuit, with bacon, egg, and cheese, 5.4 oz. 440
biscuit, with sausage, 4.2 oz. 420
biscuit, with sausage and egg, 6.2 oz. 505
burrito, 3.7 oz. 280
cheese Danish, iced, 3.9 oz. 390
cinnamon raisin Danish, 3.9 oz. 440
Egg McMuffin, 4.8 oz. 280
eggs, scrambled, 3.5 oz. 140
English muffin, with spread, 2 oz. 170
hash brown potatoes, 1.9 oz. 130
hotcakes with margarine and syrup, 6.1 oz. 440
raspberry Danish, 4.1 oz. 410
sausage, pork, 1.5 oz. 160
Sausage McMuffin, 4.8 oz. 345
Sausage McMuffin, with egg, 5.6 oz. 430

McDonald's (cont.)

sandwiches, chicken, and ribs, 1 serving:

Big Mac, 7.6 oz.	500
cheeseburger, 4.1 oz.	305
chicken fajitas, 2.9 oz.	185
Chicken McNuggets, 6 pieces	270
Filet-O-Fish, 5 oz.	370
hamburger, 3.6 oz.	255
McChicken, 6.6 oz.	415
McLean Deluxe, 7.3 oz.	320
McLean Deluxe, with cheese, 7.7 oz.	370
McRib, 6.7 oz.	460
Quarter Pounder, 5.9 oz.	410
Quarter Pounder, with cheese, 6.8 oz.	510

Chicken McNuggets sauces:

barbecue, 1.12 oz.	50
honey, .5 oz.	45
hot mustard, 1.05 oz.	70
sweet and sour, 1.12 oz.	60
french fries, large, 4.3 oz.	400
french fries, medium, 3.4 oz.	320

salads, 1 serving:

chef salad, 9.3 oz.	170
chunky chicken salad, 9 oz.	150
garden salad, 6.7 oz.	50
side salad, 3.7 oz.	30

salad dressings, 1 tbsp.:

bleu cheese	50
French, red, reduced calorie	40
ranch	55
Thousand Island	45
vinaigrette, lite	12

desserts and shakes, 1 serving:

apple pie, 3 oz.	260
cookies, chocolaty chip, 2 oz.	330
cookies, *McDonaldland*, 2 oz.	290
milk shake, low-fat, chocolate, or strawberry, 10.4 oz.	320
milk shake, low-fat, vanilla, 10.4 oz.	290

yogurt, lowfat, frozen:

cone, vanilla, 3 oz.	105
sundae, hot caramel, 6 oz.	270
sundae, hot fudge, 6 oz.	240
sundae, strawberry, 6 oz.	210

Meat, see specific listings

Meat loaf dinner, frozen:

(*Armour Classics*), 11.25 oz.	360

(*Banquet Extra Helping*), 16.25 oz. 640
Meat loaf entree, frozen:
(*Banquet Healthy Balance*), 11 oz. 270
(*On·Cor* Deluxe Entree), 8 oz. 518
in gravy, and whipped potatoes (*Stouffer's* Homestyle), 9⅞ oz. 360
Italian style (*The Budget Gourmet* Hearty & Healthy), 1 serving 270
with tomato sauce (*Banquet Entree Express*), 7 oz. 330
Meat loaf entree mix, homestyle (*Lipton Microeasy*), ¼ pkg. 390
Meat loaf seasoning mix:
(*McCormick/Schilling*), ¼ pkg. 38
(*McCormick/Schilling* Bag'n Season), 1 pkg. 111
Meat marinade mix (*McCormick/Schilling*), ¼ pkg. 28
Meatball dinner, frozen, Swedish (*Armour Classics*), 11.25 oz. 330
Meatball entree, frozen:
beef sirloin, and gravy (*The Budget Gourmet* Hearty & Healthy),
  1 serving 330
Italian (*The Budget Gourmet* Hot Lunch), 8.25 oz. 470
Swedish (*Swanson* Homestyle Recipe), 8.5 oz. 360
Swedish, in gravy, with pasta (*Lean Cuisine*), 9⅛ oz. 290
Swedish, with noodles (*The Budget Gourmet*), 1 serving 590
Swedish, sauce and (*Dining Lite*), 9 oz. 280
Swedish, sauce and (*On·Cor* Deluxe Entree), 8 oz. 295
Meatball seasoning mix, Swedish (*McCormick/Schilling*), ¼ pkg. 57
Menudo:
canned (*Old El Paso*), ½ can 476
mix (*Gebhardt*), 1 tsp. 5
Mexican dinner, frozen (see also specific listings):
(*Swanson Hungry Man*), 20.25 oz. 820
fiesta (*Patio*), 12 oz. 460
style (*Banquet Meals*), 11 oz. 410
style (*Banquet Extra Helping*), 19 oz. 680
style (*Patio*), 13.25 oz. 540
style combination (*Banquet Meals*), 11 oz. 360
Milk, cow, fluid:
buttermilk (*Crowley/Crowley* Unsalted), 1 cup 110
buttermilk, low-fat 2% (*Knudsen*), 1 cup 120
buttermilk, low-fat 1.5%, (*Borden* Golden Churn), 1 cup 120
low-fat 2% (*Viva*), 1 cup 120
low-fat 1% (*Borden*), 1 cup 100
skim (*Borden*), 1 cup 90
whole (*Borden/Borden* Hi-Calcium), 1 cup 150
Milk, canned:
condensed, sweetened (*Pet/Dairymate*), ½ cup 170
evaporated:
  (*Carnation*), ½ cup 170
  filled (*Pet/Dairymate*), ½ cup 150

Milk, canned, evaporated (cont.)
low-fat (*Carnation*), 1/2 cup 110
skim (*Pet* Light), 1/2 cup 100
Milk, chocolate, see "Chocolate milk"
Milk, dry:
buttermilk, sweet cream, 1/2 cup 232
whole, 1/2 cup 318
nonfat, instant, 1/2 cup 163
nonfat, instant (*Sanalac*), .8-oz. pkt. 80
Milk, goat:
whole, 1 cup 168
powdered (*Meyenberg*), 1 cup* 150
Milk, sheep, whole, 1 cup 264
Milkfish, meat only, baked, broiled, or microwaved, 4 oz. 215
Milkshake, frozen (*Milky Way*), 10 fl. oz. 380
Millet, cooked, 1 cup 287
Mint extract, pure (*McCormick/Schilling*), 1 tsp. 20
Miso, 1/2 cup 284
Molasses:
bead (*La Choy*), 1 tsp. 14
dark or light (*Brer Rabbit*), 1 tbsp. 55
Monkfish, meat only, baked, broiled, or microwaved, 4 oz. 110
Monosodium glutamate (*Tone's*), 1 tsp. 0
Mortadella, beef and pork, 1 oz. 88
Mostaccioli entree, frozen, and meatballs (*On•Cor* Deluxe
Entree), 8 oz. 220
Mousse, see specific listings
Muffin, 1 piece, except as noted:
(*Arnold Bran'nola*) 160
(*Arnold* Extra Crisp) 130
apple streusel or blueberry (*Hostess Breakfast Bake Shop* 99%
Fat Free) 100
banana nut, mini (*Tastykake*) 55
blueberry, mini (*Tastykake*) 51
carrot-raisin-nut, mini (*Tastykake*) 58
cinnamon apple, mini (*Hostess Breakfast Bake Shop*), 5 pieces . 260
English:
(*Pepperidge Farm*) 140
(*Thomas'*) 130
all varieties (*Oatmeal Goodness*) 140
bran nut (*Thomas'*) 140
cinnamon raisin (*Pepperidge Farm*) 150
honey wheat (*Thomas'*) 120
oat bran (*Thomas'*) 120
raisin (*Arnold*) 160
rye (*Thomas'*) 120

sourdough (*Arnold*) 130
sourdough (*Thomas'*) 130
oat bran (*Hostess Breakfast Bake Shop*) 160
oat bran banana nut (*Hostess Breakfast Bake Shop*) 140
Muffin, frozen, 1 piece:
apple oatmeal (*Pepperidge Farm Wholesome Choice*) 120
apple spice or blueberry (*Healthy Choice*) 190
banana nut (*Healthy Choice*) 180
banana nut or blueberry (*Weight Watchers*) 170
blueberry (*Pepperidge Farm Wholesome Choice*) 130
bran with raisins (*Pepperidge Farm Wholesome Choice*) 140
cheese streusel or chocolate chunk (*Sara Lee*) 220
corn (*Pepperidge Farm Wholesome Choice*) 150
oat bran (*Sara Lee*) 210
raisin bran (*Sara Lee*), 2.5 oz. 220
Muffin mix*, 1 piece:
apple cinnamon or banana nut (*Betty Crocker*) 120
applesauce (*Robin Hood/Gold Medal* Pouch), 1/6 pkg. 160
banana (*Robin Hood/Gold Medal* Pouch), 1/6 pkg. 150
blueberry (*Betty Crocker* Twice the Blueberries) 120
blueberry (*Pillsbury Lovin' Lites*) 100
blueberry streusel (*Betty Crocker* Bake Shop) 210
bran (*Martha White*), 1/6 pkg. 150
caramel (*Robin Hood/Gold Medal* Pouch), 1/6 pkg. 150
cinnamon streusel (*Betty Crocker*) 200
corn (*Dromedary*) 120
honey bran (*Robin Hood/Gold Medal* Pouch), 1/6 pkg. 170
oat bran (*Betty Crocker*) 190
oat bran, double blueberry (*Martha White*) 120
Mulberry, fresh, 1/2 cup 31
Mullet, striped, meat only, baked, broiled, or microwaved, 4 oz. 170
Mushroom:
fresh, raw, pieces, 1/2 cup 9
fresh, boiled, drained, pieces, 1/2 cup 21
canned, plain or with garlic (*B in B*), 1/4 cup 12
canned, pieces and stems, sliced (*Green Giant*), 1/4 cup 12
canned, marinated, with liquid (*Progresso*), 1/4 cup 160
frozen, whole (*Birds Eye* Deluxe), 2.6 oz. 20
frozen, sliced (*Giorgio*), 2 oz. 16
frozen, breaded (*Ore-Ida*), 2.67 oz. 120
enoki, fresh, raw, 1 medium, 3 3/8" long 1
oyster, fresh, raw (*Frieda* of California), 2 oz. 14
shiitake, fresh cooked, 4 medium or 1/2 cup pieces 40
shiitake, dried, 4 medium, approx. .5 oz. 44
straw, canned, whole (*Green Giant*), 2 oz. 12

Mushroom gravy:

canned (*Heinz*), 2 oz. or 1/4 cup 25
mix* (*McCormick/Schilling*), 1/4 cup 19
Mushroom pâté, in jars (*Three Fold Farm*), 3.5 oz. 85
Mushroom and herb dip (*Breakstone's* Gourmet), 2 tbsp. 50
Mussel, blue, fresh, meat only, boiled or steamed, 4 oz. 195
Mustard, prepared, 1 tbsp.:

(*Kraft* Pure) 11
brown, spicy (*Heinz*) 14
country, Dijon, or Parisian (*Grey Poupon*) 18
with horseradish (*French's*) 16
yellow, mild (*Heinz*) 8
Mustard greens:

fresh, boiled, drained, chopped, 1/2 cup 11
canned, chopped (*Allens*), 1/2 cup 20
frozen, chopped (*Seabrook*), 3.3 oz. 20
Mustard powder (*McCormick/Schilling*), 1 tsp. 9
Mustard sauce, hot (*Sauceworks*), 1 tbsp. 35
Mustard spinach, fresh, boiled, drained, chopped, 1/2 cup 14

N

Food and Measure

Calories

Nacho seasoning (*Lawry's* Seasoning Blends), 1 pkg. 141
Natto, 1/2 cup 187
Nectarine, fresh:

1 medium, 2 1/2" diam., approx. 5.3 oz. 67
pitted, sliced, 1/2 cup 34
New England brand sausage (*Oscar Mayer*), .8-oz. slice 30
Newberg sauce, with sherry, canned (*Snow's*), 1/3 cup 120
Noodle, egg:

plain, dry (*San Giorgio*), 2 oz. 220
plain, cooked, 1 cup 212
spinach, cooked, 1 cup 211

Noodle, Chinese:

cellophane or long rice, dehydrated, 2 oz. 199

chow mein, 1 cup 237

Noodle, Japanese:

soba (buckwheat), cooked, 1 cup, approx. 4 oz. 113

somen (wheat), cooked, 1 cup 230

udon (wheat), cooked, 4 oz. 115

Noodle and chicken dinner, frozen (*Swanson*), 10.5 oz. 280

Noodle dishes, canned or packaged:

and chicken (*Dinty Moore American Classics*), 10 oz. 260

and chicken, with vegetables (*Nalley's*), 7³/8 oz. 160

with franks (*Van Camp's Noodle Weenee*), 1 cup 245

Noodle dishes, mix*, 1/2 cup:

Alfredo or carbonara Alfredo (*Lipton* Noodles and Sauce) 200

beef (*Lipton* Noodles and Sauce) 180

butter, butter and herb, or cheese (*Lipton* Noodles and Sauce) . . 190

chicken (*Minute* Microwave Family/Single Size) 160

chicken, creamy or chicken broccoli (*Lipton* Noodles and Sauce) . 190

garlic, creamy (*Lipton* Noodles and Sauce) 220

Oriental (*Noodle Roni*) 200

Parmesan or Romanoff (*Lipton* Noodles and Sauce) 210

Parmesan (*Minute* Microwave Family Size) 170

shells and white cheddar (*Noodle Roni*) 180

sour cream and chives (*Lipton* Noodles and Sauce) 190

Stroganoff or tomato herb Alfredo (*Lipton* Noodles and Sauce) . . 200

Noodle entree, frozen:

and beef, with gravy (*Banquet Family Entrees*), 7 oz. 180

Romanoff (*Stouffer's*), 4-oz. serving 170

Nut topping (*Fisher*), 1 oz. 160

Nutmeg, ground (*McCormick/Schilling*), 1 tsp. 11

Nuts, see specific listings

Nuts, mixed, 1 oz.:

all varieties (*Eagle*) 180

dry or oil-roasted (*Fisher*) 170

almonds and cashews, oil-roasted (*Fisher*) 170

cashews and peanuts, honey-roasted (*Fisher*) 170

peanuts and cashews, honey-roasted (*Fisher*) 150

O

Food and Measure	Calories

Oat bran: (see also "Cereal"):
raw, 1/2 cup	116
cooked, 1/2 cup	44

Oats (see also "Cereal"):
whole grain, 1 cup	607
rolled or oatmeal, dry, 1 cup	311
rolled or oatmeal, cooked, 1 cup	145

Ocean perch, meat only:
fresh, Atlantic, baked, broiled, or microwaved, 4 oz.	137
frozen (*Van de Kamp's* Natural), 4 oz.	130

Ocean perch entree, frozen:
battered (*Gorton's* Crispy Batter), 2 pieces	300
breaded (*Van de Kamp's* Light), 1 piece	280

Octopus, common, meat only, steamed, 4 oz.	186

Oil:
corn, cottonseed, safflower, sesame, or soybean, 1 tbsp.	120
olive or peanut, 1 tbsp.	119
olive, spray (*Pam*), 1/3 of 10″ skillet	2

Okra:
fresh, boiled, drained, 8 pods, 3″ × 5/8″	27
fresh, boiled, drained, sliced, 1/2 cup	25
frozen, whole (*Ardsley*), 3.3 oz.	30
frozen, cut (*Ardsley*), 3.3 oz.	25
frozen, breaded (*Ore-Ida*), 3 oz.	170

Old-fashioned drink mix, bottled (*Holland House*), 1 fl. oz.	33
Old-fashioned loaf (*Oscar Mayer*), 1-oz. slice	65

Olive, pickled, canned or bottled:
green, with pits, 10 small, approx. 1.2 oz.	33
green, with pits, 10 large, approx. 1.6 oz.	45
green, with pits, 10 giant, approx. 2.75 oz.	76

green, pitted, 1 oz.	33
ripe, Manzanillo or Mission, pitted:	
(*Lindsay*), 10 small	37
(*Lindsay*), 10 medium	44
(*Lindsay*), 10 large	50
(*Lindsay*), 10 extra large	63
ripe, mixed varieties, sliced (*Lindsay*), 1/2 cup	70
ripe, oil-cured (*Progresso*), 5 medium	60
ripe, salt-cured, oil-coated, Greek style, 10 medium	65
ripe, Sevillano and Ascolano, pitted (*Lindsay*), 10 jumbo	66
ripe, Sevillano and Ascolano, pitted (*Lindsay*), 10 colossal	90
Olive appetizer:	
(*Progresso*), 1/2 cup	180
salad (*Progresso*), 1/2 cup	130
Olive loaf (*Oscar Mayer*), 1-oz. slice	60
Olive oil, see "Oil"	
Onion, mature:	
raw, chopped, 1/2 cup	30
boiled, drained, chopped, 1/2 cup	47
canned, whole, small (*S&W*), 1/2 cup	35
canned, cocktail, lightly spiced (*Vlasic*), 1 oz.	4
canned, french-fried (*Durkee*), 1 oz.	160
canned, sweet (*Heinz*), 1 oz.	40
dried, flakes, 1 tbsp.	16
dried, minced, with green onion (*Lawry's*), 1 tsp.	7
frozen, whole, small (*Seabrook*), 3.3 oz.	35
frozen, chopped (*Ore-Ida*), 2 oz.	20
frozen, with cream sauce, small (*Birds Eye* Combinations), 5 oz.	140
frozen, rings (*Ore-Ida Onion Ringers*), 2 oz.	150
Onion, green (scallion), with top, chopped, 1/2 cup	16
Onion dip:	
bean (*Hain*), 4 tbsp.	70
creamy or French (*Kraft* Premium), 2 tbsp.	45
toasted (*Breakstone's* Gourmet), 2 tbsp.	50
Onion gravy mix* (*McCormick/Schilling*), 1/4 cup	22
Onion pâté (*Three Fold Farm*), 3.5 oz.	100
Onion powder (*McCormick/Schilling*), 1 tsp.	8
Onion ring batter mix (*Golden Dipt*), 1 oz.	100
Orange:	
California navel, 1 medium, 2 7/8" diam.	65
California navel, sections, 1/2 cup	38
California Valencia, 1 medium, 2 5/8" diam.	59
California Valencia, sections, 1/2 cup	44
Florida, 1 medium, 2 11/16" diam.	69
Florida, sections, 1/2 cup	42
Orange, canned, Mandarin, see "Tangerine"	

Orange drink (see also "Orange juice drink"):

(*Tropicana*), 6 fl. oz.	90
chilled or frozen*, breakfast (*Bright & Early*), 6 fl. oz.	90
Orange extract, pure (*McCormick/Schilling*), 1 tsp.	23

Orange juice:

fresh, 6 fl. oz.	83
canned or bottled:	
(*Del Monte*), 6 fl. oz.	80
(*Tropicana* 100% Pure), 6 fl. oz.	80
(*Veryfine* 100%), 8 fl. oz.	121
pure or blend (*Welch's* 100%), 6 fl. oz.	90
chilled (*Citrus Hill* Select/Plus Calcium), 6 fl. oz.	90
chilled (*Minute Maid* Premium Choice), 6 fl. oz.	90
chilled, regular, country style, pulp free, or calcium fortified (*Minute Maid*), 6 fl. oz.	80
frozen* (*Sunkist*), 8 fl. oz.	112

Orange juice drink:

(*Citrus Hill* Lite Premium), 6 fl. oz.	60
(*Shasta Plus*), 12 fl. oz.	184
tropical (*Tropicana* Juice Sparkler), 6 fl. oz.	84

Orange juice drink blend, 6 fl. oz.:

with cranberry (*Tropicana Twister*)	100
with cranberry (*Tropicana Twister* Light)	20
with mango, peach, raspberry, strawberry-guava, or strawberry-banana (*Tropicana Twister*)	90
with passion fruit (*Tropicana Twister*)	80
with raspberry (*Tropicana Twister* Light)	30
with strawberry-banana (*Tropicana Twister* Light)	25
Mandarin, with papaya (*Tropicana Twister*)	90
Orange-banana juice (*Chiquita*), 6 fl. oz.	100
Orange-grapefruit juice, chilled (*Kraft* Pure 100%), 6 fl. oz.	80
Orange-kiwi-passion fruit juice (*Tropicana* 100% Pure), 6 fl. oz.	80
Orange-peach-mango juice (*Tropicana* 100% Pure), 6 fl. oz.	80

Orange-pineapple juice:

chilled (*Tropicana* 100% Pure), 6 fl. oz.	80
cocktail (*Musselman's* Breakfast), 6 fl. oz.	90
Orange-strawberry-banana juice (*Tropicana* 100% Pure), 6 fl. oz.	80
Oregano, dried (*McCormick/Schilling*), 1 tsp.	6
Oriental seasoning mix (*McCormick/Schilling* Bag'n Season), 1 pkg.	152

Oyster, meat only:

fresh, Eastern, raw or steamed, 6 medium (70 per qt.)	58
fresh, Pacific, raw or steamed, 1 medium (20 per qt.)	41
canned (*Bumble Bee*), 1 cup	218
Oyster plant, see "Salsify"	

P

Food and Measure   Calories

P&B loaf (*Kahn's*), 1 slice 40
Pancake, frozen, 3 pieces:
(*Hungry Jack* Original Microwave) 240
plain or buttermilk (*Downyflake*) 280
blueberry (*Downyflake*) 290
blueberry, harvest wheat, or oat bran (*Hungry Jack* Microwave) 230
buttermilk (*Aunt Jemima* Lite Microwave) 140
buttermilk (*Hungry Jack* Microwave) 260
Pancake breakfast, frozen:
with bacon (*Swanson Great Starts*), 4.5 oz. 400
with home fries, sausages, and bacon (*Swanson Great Starts Big
    Start*), 7.75 oz. 620
and sausages (*Downyflake*), 5.5 oz. 430
and sausages (*Swanson Great Starts*), 6 oz. 460
with scrambled eggs, sausages, and bacon (*Swanson Great Starts
    Big Start*), 9 oz. 750
silver dollar, and sausage (*Swanson Great Starts*), 3.75 oz. 310
whole wheat, with lite links (*Swanson Great Starts*), 5.5 oz. . . . 350
Pancake and waffle mix*, 3 pieces, 4″ each, except as noted:
(*Aunt Jemima* Original) 116
(*Bisquick Shake'N Pour* Original) 250
(*Hungry Jack Extra Lights*) 190
(*Hungry Jack Extra Lights* Complete) 180
(*Martha White FlapStax*), 1 piece 100
apple cinnamon (*Bisquick Shake'N Pour*) 240
blueberry (*Bisquick Shake'N Pour*) 270
blueberry, wild (*Hungry Jack*) 320
buckwheat (*Aunt Jemima*) 143
buttermilk (*Betty Crocker* Complete), 1/2 cup 210
buttermilk (*Bisquick Shake'N Pour*) 250

Pancake and waffle mix* (cont.)
buttermilk (*Hungry Jack* Complete) 180
buttermilk (*Robin Hood/Gold Medal* Pouch), 1/6 mix 110
whole wheat (*Aunt Jemima*) 161
Pancake syrup (see also "Maple syrup"):
(*Hungry Jack*), 2 tbsp. 100
(*Hungry Jack* Lite), 2 tbsp. 50
(*Knott's Berry Farm* Country), 2 tbsp. 110
(*Mrs. Butterworth's* Lite), 2 tbsp. 60
reduced calorie (*Cary's*), 2 tbsp. 20
Pancreas:
beef, braised, 4 oz. 307
pork, braised, 4 oz. 248
veal, braised, 4 oz. 290
Papaya:
whole, 1 lb. or 1 medium, 31/2″ × 51/8″ 117
cubed, 1/2 cup 27
Papaya nectar (*Libby's*), 6 fl. oz. 110
Papaya punch (*Veryfine*), 8 fl. oz. 120
Paprika (*McCormick/Schilling*), 1 tsp. 7
Parsley:
fresh, raw, chopped, 1/2 cup 11
dried, flakes (*McCormick/Schilling*), 1 tsp. 4
Parsley seasoning (*McCormick/Schilling Parsley Patch*), 1 tsp. 6
Parsnip, fresh, boiled, drained, sliced, 1/2 cup 63
Passion fruit, purple, 1 medium, approx. 1.2 oz. 18
Passion fruit juice drink (*Welch's Orchard Tropicals*), 6 fl. oz. 100
Pasta (spaghetti, linguine, ziti, etc.), uncooked, except as noted:
plain, 2 oz. 210
plain, cooked, 1 cup 197
amaranth (*Health Valley* Spaghetti), 2 oz. 170
with egg (*Creamette*), 2 oz. 221
spinach, cooked, 1 cup 183
spinach, with egg (*Creamette*), 2 oz. 220
whole wheat, cooked, 1 cup 174
whole wheat spinach (*Health Valley*), 2 oz. 170
Pasta dinner, frozen (see also specific listings), primavera
(*Healthy Choice*), 11 oz. 280
Pasta dishes, canned or packaged (see also specific listings):
broccoli marinara (*Del Monte Pasta Classics*), 3/4 cup 70
garden medley (*Lipton Hearty Ones*), 11 oz. 323
Italian style (*Del Monte Pasta Classics*), 3/4 cup 60
Italiano (*Lipton Hearty Ones*), 11 oz. 328
rings or twists and meatballs, in sauce (*Buitoni*), 7.5 oz. 210
spirals, and chicken (*Libby's Diner*), 7.75 oz. 120

Pasta dishes, frozen (see also "Pasta entree"):
Alfredo, with broccoli (*The Budget Gourmet* Side Dish), 1 serving   210
creamy cheddar (*Green Giant Pasta Accents*), 1/2 cup   90
Dijon (*Green Giant Garden Gourmet Right for Lunch*), 9.5 oz.   260
garden herb (*Green Giant Pasta Accents*), 1/2 cup   80
garlic seasoning (*Green Giant Pasta Accents*), 1/2 cup   100
Florentine (*Green Giant Garden Gourmet Right for Lunch*), 9.5 oz.   230
Parmesan, with sweet peas (*Green Giant* One Serving), 5.5 oz.   160
primavera (*Green Giant Pasta Accents*), 1/2 cup   110
Pasta dishes, mix*, 1/2 cup:
all varieties, except chicken and herb (*Kraft* Pasta & Cheese) . . .   180
Alfredo (*Hain* Pasta & Sauce)   350
Alfredo (*McCormick/Schilling Pasta Prima*)   253
broccoli, cheddar with fusilli (*Lipton* Pasta & Sauce)   200
cheese, cheddar (*Minute* Microwave Family/Single Size)   160
cheese, cheddar, tangy (*Hain* Pasta & Sauce)   310
chicken and herb (*Kraft* Pasta & Cheese)   170
dill, creamy, multibran (*Hain* Pasta & Sauce)   150
garlic, creamy (*McCormick/Schilling Pasta Prima*)   277
herb, Italian (*Hain* Pasta & Sauce)   180
herb and garlic (*McCormick/Schilling Pasta Prima*)   326
Italian, multibran (*Hain* Pasta & Sauce)   120
marinara (*McCormick/Schilling Pasta Prima*)   329
Parmesan, creamy (*Hain* Pasta & Sauce)   220
pesto (*McCormick/Schilling Pasta Prima*)   193
primavera (*Hain* Pasta & Sauce)   180
primavera (*McCormick/Schilling Pasta Prima*)   244
salad (*McCormick/Schilling Pasta Prima*)   390
salad, with bacon (*Kraft Light Rancher's Choice*)   250
salad, bacon vinaigrette (*Country Recipe*)   140
salad, broccoli and vegetables (*Kraft*)   210
salad, classic or Italian (*Suddenly Salad*)   160
salad, Dijon, creamy (*Country Recipe*)   190
salad, Italian, creamy (*Country Recipe*)   160
salad, Italian, robust (*Lipton*)   190
salad, Oriental, spicy (*Fantastic*)   175
salad, primavera (*Suddenly Salad*)   190
salad, ranch (*Country Recipe*)   140
salad, tortellini Italiano (*Suddenly Salad*)   160
salsa, multibran (*Hain* Pasta & Sauce)   130
seafood, creamy (*McCormick/Schilling Pasta Prima*)   209
Swiss, creamy (*Hain* Pasta & Sauce)   180
tomato basil (*McCormick/Schilling Pasta Prima*)   175
Pasta entree frozen (see also specific listings):
angel hair (*Weight Watchers*), 10 oz.   200
with shrimp (*Healthy Choice* Pasta Classics), 12.5 oz.   270

Pasta entree (cont.)

teriyaki, with chicken (*Healthy Choice* Pasta Classics), 12.6 oz.	350

Pasta sauce (see also "Tomato sauce" and specific listings):

(*Campbell's Healthy Request* Homestyle), 4 oz.	40
(*Hunt's* Chunky), 4 oz.	50
(*Pastorelli Italian Chef*), 4 oz.	81
(*Ragú*), 4 oz.	80
(*Ragú Fino Italian*) 4 oz.	90
all varieties (*Enrico's*), 4 oz.	60
all varieties (*Progresso* Spaghetti Sauce), 1/2 cup	110
all varieties (*Ragú Slow Cooked Homestyle*), 4 oz.	110
plain or with meat (*Hunt's* Homestyle), 4 oz.	60
extra garlic and onion or traditional (*Campbell's Healthy Request*), 4 oz.	50
garden harvest, mushroom, or tomato herb (*Ragú Today's Recipe*), 4 oz.	50
marinara (*Progresso*), 1/2 cup	90
with meat, mushrooms, or traditional (*Hunt's*), 4 oz.	70
with mushrooms (*Hunt's* Homestyle), 4 oz.	50
mushroom and pepper (*Master Choice* Giardino), 1/2 cup	80
sausage and green pepper (*Prego* Extra Chunky), 4 oz.	170
tomato and onion (*Prego* Extra Chunky), 4 oz.	110
with zinfandel (*Sutter Home*), 1/2 cup	100
mix, cheese-garlic or Italian (*French's Pasta Toss*), 2 tsp.	25
mix, Romanoff (*French's Pasta Toss*), 2 tsp.	30
Pasta snack chip (*Bachman Pastapazazz*), 1 oz.	150

Pastrami:

(*Hillshire Farm Deli Select*), 1 oz.	31
(*Oscar Mayer*), .6-oz. slice	15
turkey, see "Turkey pastrami"	

Pastry sheets and shells, frozen (see also "Pie crust shell"):

patty shells (*Pepperidge Farm*), 1 shell	210
puff pastry, sheets (*Pepperidge Farm*), 1/4 sheet	260
puff pastry, shells, mini (*Pepperidge Farm/Pepperidge Farm* Bake-Your-Own), 1 shell	50
tart shell (*Pet-Ritz*), 3″ shell	150

Pâté, canned or in jars (see also specific listings):

liver (*Sells*), 2.25 oz.	190
chicken liver, 1 tbsp.	26
goose liver, smoked, 1 tbsp.	60
Pea pods, Chinese, see "Peas, edible-podded"	

Peach:

fresh, 1 medium, 2 1/2″ diam. or peeled, sliced, 1/2 cup	37
canned, halves, sliced, or diced:	
(*Hunt's*), 4 oz.	90
cling (*Del Monte* Fruit Naturals/Lite Fruit Cup), 4.5 oz.	60

cling (*Del Monte* Fruit Cup), 4.5 oz.	100
cling, diced (*Orchard Naturals*), 4 oz.	60
freestone or cling, in heavy syrup (*S&W*), 1/2 cup	100
whole, spiced (*S&W*), 1/2 cup	90
dried (*Del Monte*), 2 oz.	140
frozen, sweetened, sliced, 1/2 cup	118
Peach butter (*Smucker's*), 1 tsp.	15
Peach drink (*Hi-C*), 6 fl. oz.	100
Peach juice:	
(*Dole Pure & Light*), 6 fl. oz.	100
(*Smucker's* 100%), 8 fl. oz.	120
Peach nectar (*Libby's*), 6 fl. oz.	100
Peanut, 1 oz., except as noted:	
(*Beer Nuts*)	180
all varieties, raw, shelled, 1/2 cup	414
all varieties (*Eagle*)	170
dry- or oil-roasted (*Fisher*)	160
honey-roasted (*Fisher*)	150
honey-roasted, dry-roasted (*Planters*)	160
oil-roasted, salted (*Planters/Planters* Cocktail or Redskin)	170
Spanish, raw (*Fisher*)	160
Spanish, roasted (*Fisher*)	170
Spanish, dry-roasted (*Planters*)	160
Virginia, oil-roasted	161
Peanut butter, 2 tbsp.:	
(*Health Valley* Creamy or Chunky)	180
(*JIF* Smooth or Chunky)	190
(*Peter Pan* Creamy or Crunchy)	190
(*Skippy* Creamy or Super Chunk)	190
(*Woodstock* Old Fashioned Unsalted)	200
low salt, low sugar (*Simply Jif*)	180
regular or honey-sweetened (*Smucker's* Creamy or Chunky Natural)	200
Peanut butter flavor baking chips (*Reese's*), 1/4 cup, 1.5 oz.	230
Peanut butter and jelly (*Smucker's Goober Grape*), 2 tbsp.	180
Peanut butter-caramel topping (*Smucker's*), 2 tbsp.	150
Pear:	
fresh, with skin, sliced, 1/2 cup	49
fresh, Asian, 1 medium, 2 1/2" diam. × 2 1/4"	51
fresh, Bartlett, 1 medium, 2 1/2" diam. × 3 1/2"	98
canned, Bartlett:	
halves (*Hunt's*), 4 oz.	90
diced (*Orchard Naturals*), 4 oz.	60
in extra light syrup, diced (*Del Monte* Lite Fruit Cup), 4.5 oz.	60
in heavy syrup, diced (*Del Monte* Fruit Cup), 4.5 oz.	100
in heavy syrup, halves or slices (*Del Monte*), 1/2 cup	90

Pear (cont.)

dried, uncooked, halves, 1/2 cup 236
Pear nectar, canned, 6 fl. oz. 114
Pear and apple spread (*Poiret*), 1 tsp. 34
Peas, black-eyed, see "Black-eyed peas" and "Cowpeas"
Peas, cream, canned (*Allens* Fresh), 1/2 cup 90
Peas, crowder:
canned (*Allens* Fresh), 1/2 cup 80
frozen (*Seabrook*), 3 oz. 130
Peas, edible-podded:
fresh, raw, 1/2 cup 30
fresh, boiled, drained, 1/2 cup 34
frozen, Chinese (*Chun King*), 1.5 oz. 20
frozen, snow (*La Choy*), 3 oz. 35
frozen, sugar snap (*Green Giant Harvest Fresh*), 1/2 cup 30
frozen, sugar snap, carrots, water chestnuts (*Birds Eye* Farm
    Fresh), 3.2 oz. 50
Peas, field, canned (*Allens* Fresh), 1/2 cup 100
Peas, green or sweet:
fresh, raw, shelled, 1/2 cup 58
fresh, boiled, drained, 1/2 cup 67
canned or packaged, 1/2 cup:
    all varieties (*Green Giant*) 50
    seasoned or sweet (*Del Monte*) 60
    small, sweet (*Del Monte*) 50
    sweet, with tiny pearl onions (*S&W*) 60
    and mushrooms (*Del Monte Vegetable Classics*) 70
frozen:
    sweet (*Green Giant/Green Giant Harvest Fresh*), 1/2 cup 50
    tiny (*Seabrook*), 3.3 oz. 60
    in butter sauce, *Le Sueur* or sweet (*Green Giant*), 1/2 cup . . . 80
    with cream sauce (*Birds Eye* Combinations), 5 oz. 180
Peas, green, combinations, frozen:
and carrots, see "Peas and carrots"
Le Sueur style (*Green Giant Valley Combination*), 1/2 cup 70
Le Sueur, baby, and mushrooms (*Green Giant*), 1/2 cup 60
and onions (*Seabrook*), 3.3 oz. 70
and pearl onions, cheese sauce (*Birds Eye* Combinations), 5 oz. 140
and potatoes, cream sauce (*Birds Eye* Combinations), 5 oz. . . . 190
and water chestnuts (*The Budget Gourmet* Side Dish), 1 serving 110
Peas, white acre, canned, fresh (*Allens*), 1/2 cup 90
Peas and carrots:
canned (*Del Monte*), 1/2 cup 50
packaged, in cream sauce (*Del Monte Vegetable Classics*), 1/2 cup 80
frozen (*Seabrook*), 3.3 oz. 60
Pecan topping, in syrup (*Smucker's*), 2 tbsp. 130

Pecan:

dried, in shell, 4 oz.	401
dry-roasted, 1 oz.	187
honey-roasted (*Eagle*), 1 oz.	200
oil-roasted, 1 oz.	195
raw, ground or chopped (*Fisher*), 1 oz.	190
Pepper, ground, all varieties (*McCormick/Schilling*), 1 tsp.	9
Pepper, bell, see "Pepper, sweet"	
Pepper, cherry, mild (*Vlasic*), 1 oz.	8

Pepper, hot, canned or in jars, except as noted:

raw, chili, green and red, chopped, 1/2 cup	30
whole or diced (*Ortega*), 1 oz.	8
cherry (*Progresso*), 1/2 cup	190
cherry, pickled (*Progresso*), 1/2 cup	130
chili, green (*Old El Paso*), 1 whole or 2 tbsp. chopped	8
jalapeño (*Vlasic*), 1 oz.	10
rings (*Vlasic*), 1 oz.	4

Pepper, pepperoncini:

Greek (*Vlasic*), 1 oz.	4
Tuscan (*Progresso*), 1/2 cup	20
Pepper, piccalilli (*Progresso*), 1/2 cup	190

Pepper, stuffed, entree, frozen:

(*On•Cor* Deluxe Entree), 8 oz.	168
(*Stouffer's* Single Serving), 10 oz.	230
green, with beef, in tomato sauce (*Stouffer's*), 7.75 oz.	200

Pepper, sweet, bell:

fresh, green or red, raw, 1 medium, 3 3/4″ × 3″ diam.	20
fresh, green or red, raw, chopped, 1/2 cup	13
fresh, green or red, boiled, drained, chopped, 1/2 cup	19
fresh, yellow, raw, 1 large, 5″ × 3″ diam.	50
frozen, green (*Seabrook*), 1 oz.	6
frozen, red (*Seabrook*), 1 oz.	8

Pepper, sweet, appetizer or condiment:

fried (*Progresso*), 1/2 jar	37
roasted (*Progresso*), 1/2 cup	20
Pepper sauce, hot (*Gebhardt*), 1/2 tsp.	<1
Peppercorn sauce mix*, green (*McCormick/Schilling McCormick Collection*), 1/4 cup	86
Peppered loaf (*Kahn's*), 1 slice	40

Pepperoni:

(*Hormel* Regular, Chunk, Rosa or Rosa Grande), 1 oz.	140
(*Hormel* Perma-Fresh), 2 slices	80

Perch (See also "Ocean perch"), meat only:

fresh, mixed species, baked, broiled, or microwaved, 4 oz.	133
frozen (*SeaPak*), 4 oz.	100
Perch entree, frozen, battered (*Van de Kamp's*), 2 pieces	310

Persimmon:
Japanese, fresh, 1 medium, 2½" × 3½" 118
Japanese, dried, 1 medium, approx. 1.3 oz. 93
native, fresh, 1 medium, approx. 1.1 oz. 32
Pesto sauce, refrigerated (*Contadina Fresh*), 2⅓ oz. 350
Pheasant, fresh, raw:
meat with skin, 4 oz. 204
meat only, 4 oz. 152
Picante sauce (see also "Salsa"):
all varieties (*Old El Paso*), 2 tbsp. 8
all varieties (*Old El Paso* Chunky), 2 tbsp. 7
medium (*Rosarita* Chunky), 3 tbsp. 16
mild (*Rosarita* Chunky), 3 tbsp. 25
hot (*Rosarita* Chunky), 3 tbsp. 18
Pickle, 1 oz., except as noted:
bread and butter, slices (*Claussen* Bread 'n butter) 20
bread and butter, sweet (*Vlasic* Sweet Butter Chips) 25
dill:
   (*Vlasic* Original) 4
   whole or hamburger slices (*Heinz/Heinz* Genuine) 2
   spears (*Claussen*) 4
   hamburger chips, half salt (*Vlasic*) 2
   kosher, spears, half salt or no garlic, crunchy (*Vlasic*) . . . 4
   kosher or zesty (*Vlasic* Snack Chunks), 1 piece 2
   Polish style, whole or spears (*Heinz*) 4
kosher, all varieties (*Heinz* Old Fashioned) 4
mixed, garden, hot and spicy (*Vlasic*) 4
salad cubes, sweet (*Heinz*) 30
sweet (*Heinz* Cucumber Stix) 25
sweet, gherkins (*Heinz/Heinz* Midget) 35
sweet, half salt (*Vlasic* Sweet Butter Chips) 30
Pickle loaf:
(*Hormel* Perma-Fresh), 2 slices 102
beef (*Kahn's* Family Pack), 1 slice 60
Pickle and pimiento loaf (*Oscar Mayer*), 1-oz. slice 65
Pickling spice (*Tone's*), 1 tsp. 10
Picnic loaf (*Oscar Mayer*), 1-oz. slice 60
Pie, 4 oz.:
apple, berry, cherry, or peach (*McMillin's*) 430
chocolate pudding (*McMillin's*) 420
coconut pudding or lemon (*McMillin's*) 450
strawberry (*McMillin's*) 400
Pie, frozen:
apple (*Banquet* Family Size), ⅙ pie 250
apple (*Pet-Ritz*), ⅙ pie 330
apple, Dutch (*Mrs. Smith's*, 8"), ⅛ pie 250

apple, Dutch, natural juice (*Mrs. Smith's*, 9"), 1/8 pie 380
apple-cranberry (*Mrs. Smith's*, 8"), 1/8 pie 230
banana cream (*Banquet*), 1/6 pie 180
banana cream (*Mrs. Smith's*, 8"), 1/8 pie 140
berry or blackberry (*Mrs. Smith's*, 8"), 1/8 pie 230
blueberry (*Pet-Ritz*), 1/6 pie 370
blueberry (*Mrs. Smith's*, 8"), 1/8 pie 210
blueberry, natural juice (*Mrs. Smith's*, 9"), 1/8 pie 350
cherry (*Banquet* Family Size), 1/6 pie 250
cherry (*Pet-Ritz*), 1/6 pie 300
cherry, natural juice (*Mrs. Smith's*, 9"), 1/8 pie 350
chocolate cream (*Mrs. Smith's*, 8"), 1/8 pie 150
chocolate meringue (*Mrs. Smith's*, 8"), 1/8 pie 260
chocolate or coconut cream (*Banquet*), 1/6 pie 190
coconut custard (*Mrs. Smith's*, 8"), 1/8 pie 180
egg custard (*Pet-Ritz*), 1/6 pie 200
French silk cream (*Mrs. Smith's*, 8"), 1/8 pie 280
lemon cream (*Banquet*), 1/6 pie 170
lemon cream (*Mrs. Smith's*, 8"), 1/8 pie 140
lemon meringue (*Mrs. Smith's*, 8"), 1/8 pie 210
mince (*Mrs. Smith's*, 8"), 1/8 pie 220
mincemeat (*Banquet* Family Size), 1/6 pie 260
Neopolitan cream (*Pet-Ritz*), 1/6 pie 180
peach (*Banquet* Family Size), 1/6 pie 245
peach (*Pet-Ritz*), 1/6 pie 320
peach, natural juice (*Mrs. Smith's*, 9"), 1/8 pie 330
pecan (*Mrs. Smith's*, 8"), 1/8 pie 330
pumpkin (*Banquet* Family Size), 1/6 pie 200
pumpkin, hearty (*Mrs. Smith's*, 8"), 1/8 pie 190
pumpkin custard (*Mrs. Smith's*, 8"), 1/8 pie 180
raspberry, red (*Mrs. Smith's*, 8"), 1/8 pie 220
strawberry cream (*Banquet*), 1/6 pie 170
strawberry-rhubarb (*Mrs. Smith's*, 8"), 1/8 pie 230
sweet potato (*Pet-Ritz*), 1/6 pie 150
Pie, snack, 1 piece:
apple (*Tastykake*) 296
apple, Dutch (*Little Debbie*), 2.5 oz. 270
apple, French (*Tastykake*) 353
apple or blueberry (*Drake's*) 210
banana creme (*Tastykake*) 382
blackberry or blueberry (*Hostess*) 420
blueberry (*Tastykake*) 308
cherry (*Drake's*) 220
cherry (*Tastykake*) 298
coconut creme (*Tastykake*) 377
custard creme (*Tastykake* Tasty Klair) 402

Pie, snack (cont.)
lemon (*Drake's*) 210
lemon-lime (*Tastykake*) 324
peach (*Tastykake*) 295
pecan (*Little Debbie*), 3 oz. 280
pineapple-cheese (*Tastykake*) 343
pumpkin (*Tastykake*) 324
strawberry (*Tastykake*) 342
Pie crust shell, frozen or refrigerated:
(*Mrs. Smith's,* 8″), 1/8 shell 80
(*Mrs. Smith's,* 9″), 1/8 shell 90
(*Pet-Ritz*), 1/6 shell 120
(*Pillsbury* All Ready), 1/8 of 2 crust pie 240
butter flavor (*Keebler Ready Crust*), 1/8 crust 110
chocolate or graham cracker (*Keebler Ready Crust*), 1/8 crust . . . 120
deep dish (*Pet-Ritz*), 1/6 shell, 1 oz. 130
deep dish, vegetable shortening (*Pet-Ritz*), 1/6 shell, 1 oz. 140
graham cracker or vegetable shortening (*Pet-Ritz*), 1/6 shell 110
Pie crust shell mix* (*Pillsbury*), 1/8 shell 200
Pie crust stick (*Betty Crocker*), 1/8 stick 120
Pie filling, canned, 3.5 oz., except as noted:
apple (*Comstock* Lite) 80
apricot or banana (*Comstock*) 110
blackberry or boysenberry (*Lucky Leaf/Musselman's*), 4 oz. . . . 120
blueberry (*White House*) 118
cherry (*White House*) 141
chocolate (*Comstock*) 130
coconut (*Comstock*) 120
gooseberry (*Lucky Leaf/Musselman's*), 4 oz. 180
lemon (*Comstock*) 140
mincemeat (*Comstock*) 150
mincemeat, with brandy (*S&W* Old Fashioned), 4 oz. 234
mincemeat, with brandy and rum (*Borden None Such*), 1/3 cup . . . 220
mincemeat, condensed (*Borden None Such*), 1/4 pkg. . . . 220
peach (*White House*) 117
pineapple (*Comstock*) 100
pumpkin pie mix (*Libby's*), 1 cup 260
raisin (*Comstock*) 120
raspberry, black or red (*Lucky Leaf/Musselman's*), 4 oz. 190
strawberry (*Comstock*) 100
strawberry-rhubarb (*Lucky Leaf/Musselman's*), 4 oz. 120
Pie mix, 1/8 pie:
banana cream (*Jell-O* No Bake) 240
chocolate mousse or coconut cream (*Jell-O* No Bake) . . . 260
chocolate mousse or lemon meringue (*Royal No-Bake*) 130
pumpkin (*Jell-O* No Bake) 250

Pierogy, frozen:
potato and cheddar (*Mrs. T's*), 1 piece 60
potato and cheese (*Golden*), 3 pieces 250
potato and onion (*Golden*), 3 pieces 210
potato and onion (*Mrs. T's*), 1 piece 50
Pigeon peas:
boiled, drained, 1/2 cup 86
dried, boiled, 1/2 cup 102
Pig's feet, pickled (*Penrose*), 1 piece, approx. 6 oz. 220
Pig's knuckles, pickled (*Penrose*), 1 piece, approx. 6 oz. 290
Pike, fresh, meat only:
northern, baked, broiled, or microwaved, 4 oz. 128
walleye, baked, broiled, or microwaved, 4 oz. 135
Pilaf mix*, three-grain, with butter (*Quick Pilaf*), 1/2 cup . . . 142
Pimiento, all varieties, drained (*Dromedary*), 1 oz. 10
Pimiento spread (*Price's*), 1 oz. 80
Piña colada mixer, frozen*, with rum (*Bacardi*), 7 fl. oz. 240
Pine nut, dried, shelled:
pignolia, 1 oz. 146
pignolia, 1 tbsp. 51
pignolia, imported (*Progresso*), 1 tbsp. 60
piñon, 1 oz. 161
Pineapple:
fresh, sliced, 1 slice, 31/2″ diam. × 3/4″ 42
fresh, diced, 1/2 cup 39
canned:
in juice (*Dole*), 1/2 cup 70
in juice, spears (*Del Monte*), 2 spears, 3.1 oz. 50
in juice, crushed (*Empress*), 1/2 cup 70
in syrup, all cuts (*Del Monte*), 1/2 cup 80
in heavy syrup, slices (*S&W* 100% Hawaiian), 2 slices 90
with Mandarin orange segments (*Dole*), 1/2 cup 60
frozen, chunks, 1/2 cup 104
Pineapple extract, imitation (*McCormick/Schilling*), 1 tsp. 12
Pineapple juice, canned, chilled, or frozen* (*Dole*), 6 fl. oz. . . . 100
Pineapple nectar (*Libby's*), 6 fl. oz. 110
Pineapple topping (*Smucker's*), 2 tbsp. 130
Pineapple-banana juice drink (*Welch's Orchard Tropicals*),
6 fl. oz. 100
Pineapple-grapefruit juice:
(*Dole*), 6 fl. oz. 90
with pink grapefruit (*Dole*), 6 fl. oz. 100
cocktail (*Ocean Spray*), 6 fl. oz. 110
Pineapple-grapefruit juice drink, white or pink grapefruit (*Del
Monte*), 6 fl. oz. 90

Pineapple-orange juice, regular or Mandarin (*Del Monte*),
  6 fl. oz. 100
Pistachio nut:
dried, 1 oz., approx. 47 kernels 164
dry-roasted (*Planters*), 1 oz. 170
red tint or natural (*Fisher*), 1 oz. 170
roasted (*Dole*), 1 oz. 160
Pita chips, plain, garlic, or sesame (*New York Style*), 3/4 oz. . . . 100
Pizza, frozen or refrigerated:
Canadian bacon (*Jeno's Crisp'N Tasty*), 1/2 pie 240
Canadian bacon (*Totino's Party*), 1/2 pie 330
cheese:
  (*Celeste*), 1/4 pie 317
  (*Celeste* Pizza For One), 1 pie 497
  (*Contadina Fresh*), 1/8 pie 180
  (*Ellio's Healthy Slices*), 1/6 pie 160
  (*Jeno's Crisp'N Tasty*), 1/2 pie 240
  (*Pillsbury Oven Lovin'* Microwave), 1/2 pie 250
  (*Totino's Pan Pizza*), 1/6 pie 290
  (*Totino's Party*), 1/2 pie 290
  (*Totino's Party* Family Size), 1/3 pie 320
  and hamburger (*Tombstone*), 1/4 pie 360
  and pepperoni (*Tombstone* Microwave), 7.5-oz. pkg. 530
  and sausage, Italian (*Tombstone* Thin Crust), 1/4 pie 330
  sausage and mushroom (*Tombstone*), 1/4 pie 360
  three cheese (*Pappalo's* Pan Pizza), 1/5 pie 310
  three cheese (*Pappalo's* Traditional, 12"), 1/4 pie 310
combination (*Jeno's Crisp'N Tasty*), 1/2 pie 280
combination (*Pillsbury Oven Lovin'* Microwave), 1/2 pie 310
combination (*Totino's Party*), 1/2 pie 370
combination (*Totino's Party* Family Size), 1/3 pie 400
deluxe (*Celeste*), 1/4 pie 378
hamburger (*Jeno's Crisp'N Tasty*), 1/2 pie 280
hamburger (*Totino's Party*), 1/2 pie 350
pepperoni:
  (*Celeste*), 1/4 pie 368
  (*Celeste* Pizza For One), 1 pie 546
  (*Jeno's Crisp'N Tasty*), 1/2 pie 280
  (*Pappalo's* Pan Pizza), 1/5 pie 350
  (*Pappalo's* Traditional, 12"), 1/4 pie 350
  (*Pillsbury Oven Lovin'* Microwave), 1/2 pie 300
  (*Totino's Pan Pizza*), 1/6 pie 330
  (*Totino's Party*), 1/2 pie 380
  (*Totino's Party* Family Size), 1/3 pie 410
  double cheese (*Tombstone* Double Top Deluxe), 1/4 pie 550

sausage:
(*Celeste*), 1/4 pie 376
(*Celeste* Pizza For One), 1 pie 571
(*Jeno's Crisp'N Tasty*), 1/2 pie 280
(*Pappalo's* Pan Pizza), 1/5 pie 350
(*Pappalo's* Traditional, 12"), 1/4 pie 350
(*Pillsbury Oven Lovin'* Microwave), 1/2 pie 290
(*Totino's Pan Pizza*), 1/6 pie 320
(*Totino's Party*), 1/2 pie 370
(*Totino's Party* Family Size), 1/3 pie 410
combination (*Tombstone*), 1/4 pie 370
and mushroom (*Celeste* Pizza For One), 1 pie 592
and pepperoni (*Pappalo's* Pan Pizza), 1/5 pie 360
and pepperoni (*Pappalo's* Traditional, 12"), 1/4 pie . . . 360
and pepperoni (*Totino's Pan Pizza*), 1/6 pie 330
supreme (*Pappalo's* Pan Pizza), 1/5 pie 340
supreme (*Pappalo's* Traditional, 12"), 1/4 pie 350
supreme (*Pillsbury Oven Lovin'* Microwave), 1/2 pie 310
vegetable (*Celeste*), 1/4 pie 310
vegetable (*Celeste* Pizza For One), 1 pie 490
vegetable, mixed (*Ellio's Healthy Slices*), 1/6 pie 150
Pizza, French bread, frozen:
Canadian style bacon (*Stouffer's*), 1/2 pkg. 370
cheese (*Healthy Choice*), 5.6 oz. 300
cheese (*Lean Cuisine*), 5 1/8-oz. pkg. 300
cheese (*Pillsbury Oven Lovin'*), 1 pie 350
cheese (*Stouffer's*), 1/2 pkg. 350
cheese, double (*Stouffer's*), 1/2 pkg. 420
cheese, three (*Lean Cuisine*), 5.5-oz. pkg. 330
combination (*Pillsbury Oven Lovin'*), 1 pie 420
deluxe (*Healthy Choice*), 6.25 oz. 330
deluxe (*Lean Cuisine*), 6 1/8-oz. pkg. 320
deluxe (*Stouffer's*), 1/2 pkg. 420
hamburger (*Stouffer's*), 1/2 pkg. 410
pepperoni (*Healthy Choice*), 6.25 oz. 320
pepperoni (*Lean Cuisine*), 5.25-oz. pkg. 330
pepperoni (*Pillsbury Oven Lovin'*), 1 pie 410
pepperoni (*Stouffer's*), 1/2 pkg. 400
pepperoni and mushroom (*Stouffer's*), 1/2 pkg. 410
sausage (*Lean Cuisine*), 6-oz. pkg. 330
sausage (*Pillsbury Oven Lovin'*), 1 pie 400
sausage (*Stouffer's*), 1/2 pkg. 430
sausage, Italian, turkey (*Healthy Choice*), 6.45 oz. 320
sausage and pepperoni (*Stouffer's*), 1/2 pkg. 460
vegetable deluxe (*Stouffer's*), 1/2 pkg. 420
Pizza snack chips, all varieties (*Keebler Pizzarias*), 1 oz. 140

Pizza crust (*Pillsbury* All Ready), 1/8 of crust 90
Pizza Hut, 2 slices of medium pie, except as noted:
hand-tossed, cheese, 7.8 oz. 518
hand-tossed, pepperoni, 6.9 oz. 500
hand-tossed, supreme, 8.4 oz. 540
hand-tossed, super supreme, 8.6 oz. 463
pan pizza, cheese, 7.2 oz. 492
pan pizza, pepperoni, 7.4 oz. 540
pan pizza, supreme, 9 oz. 589
pan pizza, super supreme, 9.1 oz. 563
Personal Pan Pizza, pepperoni, 1 pie, 9 oz. 675
Personal Pan Pizza, supreme, 1 pie, 9.3 oz. 647
Thin 'n Crispy, cheese, 5.2 oz. 398
Thin 'n Crispy, pepperoni, 5.1 oz. 413
Thin 'n Crispy, supreme, 7.1 oz. 459
Thin 'n Crispy, super supreme, 7.2 oz. 463
Pizza pocket sandwich, frozen:
(*Lean Pockets* Pizza Deluxe), 1 pkg. 280
deluxe (*Weight Watchers Ultimate 200*), 4 oz. 200
pepperoni (*Hot Pockets*), 5 oz. 380
pepperoni or supreme (*Jeno's*), 1 piece 370
sausage (*Hot Pockets*), 5 oz. 360
sausage or sausage and pepperoni (*Jeno's*), 1 piece 360
Pizza rolls, frozen:
cheese (*Jeno's Pizza Rolls*), 3 oz. 200
combination, hamburger, or pepperoni (*Jeno's Pizza Rolls*), 3 oz. 220
sausage (*Jeno's Pizza Rolls*), 3 oz. 210
Pizza sauce:
(*Prince*), 2 oz. 25
(*Ragú*), 3 tbsp. 25
(*Ragú Pizza Quick* Traditional), 3 tbsp. 35
garlic-basil (*Ragú Pizza Quick*), 3 tbsp. 40
pepperoni (*Master Choice*), 3 tbsp. 25
Plantain (baking banana), fresh:
raw, 1 medium, approx. 9.7 oz. 218
cooked, sliced, 1/2 cup 89
Plum:
fresh, pitted, sliced, 1/2 cup 46
fresh, Japanese or hybrid, 1 medium, 2 1/8″ diam. 36
canned, purple, in juice (*Featherweight*), 1/2 cup 80
canned, purple, in light syrup (*Stokely*), 1/2 cup 100
canned, purple, in heavy syrup (*Stokely*), 1/2 cup 130
canned, purple, in extra heavy syrup (*S&W* Fancy), 1/2 cup . . 135
Pokeberry shoots, boiled, drained, 1/2 cup 16
Polenta mix* (*Fantastic Polenta*), 1/2 cup 106

Polish sausage (see also "Kielbasa"):
(*Hillshire Farm* Links), 2 oz. 190
(*Hormel*), 2 links 170
hot (*OHSE*), 1 oz. 70
Pollock, meat only:
fresh, Atlantic, baked, broiled, or microwaved, 4 oz. 134
fresh, walleye, baked, broiled, or microwaved, 4 oz. 128
Pomegranate, fresh, 1 medium, 3³/₈″ diam. × 3³/₄″ 104
Pompano, Florida, meat only, baked, broiled, or microwaved,
  4 oz. 239
Popcorn, popped:
plain, air-popped, 1 oz. 108
plain, oil-popped, 1 oz. 142
(*Cape Cod* Light), ¹/₂ oz. 60
butter flavor (*Wise*), ¹/₂ oz. 80
caramel (*Bachman*), 1 oz. 110
cheddar (*Orville Redenbacher*), 3 cups 160
cheddar, white (*Bachman*), ¹/₂ oz. 70
cheddar, white (*Smartfood*), ¹/₂ oz. 80
honey caramel (*Keebler* Deluxe), 1 oz. 120
microwave, 3 cups popped:
  (*Newman's Own Oldstyle Picture Show*) 90
  natural or butter flavor (*Orville Redenbacher's* Light) 70
  natural or butter flavor (*Pop·Secret/Pop·Secret* Pop Qwiz) . . . 100
  butter toffee (*Orville Redenbacher's* Gourmet) 252
  caramel (*Orville Redenbacher's* Gourmet) 288
  cheddar cheese flavor (*Orville Redenbacher's* Gourmet) 130
  sour cream and onion flavor (*Orville Redenbacher's* Gourmet) 160
Popcorn seasoning (*McCormick/Schilling Parsley Patch*), 1 tsp. 10
Popover mix* (*Washington*), 1 piece 150
Poppy seeds (*McCormick/Schilling*), 1 tsp. 13
Porgy, see "Scup"
Pork, fresh (see also "Ham" and "Pork, cured"), boneless, 4 oz.,
  except as noted:
ground (*JM*), 3 oz. 190
loin:
  blade, braised, lean with separable fat 465
  blade, braised, lean only 355
  blade, roasted, lean with separable fat 413
  blade, roasted, lean only 316
  center, braised, lean with separable fat 401
  center, braised, lean only 308
  center, roasted, lean with separable fat 346
  center, roasted, lean only 272
  center rib, braised, lean with separable fat 416
  center rib, braised, lean only 314

Pork, fresh, loin (cont.)

center rib, roasted, lean with separable fat 361
center rib, roasted, lean only 278
sirloin, broiled, lean with separable fat 375
sirloin, broiled, lean only 276
sirloin, roasted, lean with separable fat 330
sirloin, roasted, lean only 268
shoulder:
  arm (picnic), braised, lean with separable fat 391
  arm (picnic), braised, lean only 281
  arm (picnic), roasted, lean with separable fat 375
  arm (picnic), roasted, lean only 259
  Boston blade, braised, lean with separable fat 421
  Boston blade, braised, lean only 333
  Boston blade, broiled, lean with separable fat 397
  Boston blade, broiled, lean only 311
  Boston blade, roasted, lean only 290
spareribs, braised, lean with fat, 6.3 oz. (1 lb. raw with bone) 703
tenderloin, roasted, lean only 188
top loin, broiled, lean with separable fat 408
top loin, broiled, lean only 293
top loin, roasted, lean with separable fat 374
top loin, roasted, lean only 278

Pork, canned:

(*Hormel*), 3 oz. 240
chopped (*Hormel*), 3 oz. 200

Pork, cured (see also "Ham"), boneless, shoulder:

arm (picnic), roasted, lean with separable fat, 4 oz. 318
arm (picnic), roasted, lean only, 4 oz. 193
blade roll, unheated, lean with separable fat, 1 oz. 76
blade roll, roasted, lean with separable fat, 4 oz. 325

Pork dinner, frozen, loin of (*Swanson*), 10.75 oz. 280
Pork entree, canned, chow mein (*La Choy* Bi-Pack), 3/4 cup . . . 80
Pork entree, frozen or refrigerated:
barbecued:
  back ribs (*John Morrell Pork Classics*), 4.75 oz. 240
  chops, center cut (*John Morrell Pork Classics*), 4.5 oz. 230
  loin (*John Morrell Pork Classics*), 5 thin slices, 3 oz. 150
  spareribs (*John Morrell Pork Classics*), 4.5 oz. 250
  tenderloin (*John Morrell Pork Classics*), 3 oz. 130
sandwich, barbecued (*Hormel New Traditional*), 4.3 oz. 350
sweet and sour (*Chun King*), 13 oz. 400

Pork gravy:

canned (*Heinz*), 2 oz. or 1/4 cup 25
mix* (*McCormick/Schilling*), 1/4 cup 20

Pork seasoning and coating mix:

plain or barbecue (*Shake'n Bake* Original Recipe), 1/8 pouch . . .	40
chop (*McCormick/Schilling* Bag'n Season), 1 pkg.	102
extra crispy (*Shake'n Bake Oven Fry*), 1/4 pouch	120

Pot roast, see "Beef dinner" and "Beef entree"

Pot roast seasoning (*McCormick/Schilling* Bag'n Season), 1 pkg.	55

Potato (see also "Potato dishes"):

baked in skin, 1 medium, 4³/₄″ × 2¹/₃″ diam.	220
baked in skin, pulp only, 1/2 cup	57
baked in skin, skin only, 2 oz.	112
boiled in skin, pulp only, 1/2 cup	68
microwaved in skin, 1 medium, 4³/₄″ × 2¹/₃″ diam.	212
canned, whole, new (*Hunt's*), 4 oz.	70
canned, whole or sliced (*Del Monte*), 1/2 cup	45

Potato, frozen, 3 oz., except as noted:

whole, white, boiled (*Seabrook*), 3.2 oz.	60
diced and hash shred (*Seabrook*), 4 oz.	80

fried and french-fried:

(*Ore-Ida*)	170
(*Ore-Ida Country Style Dinner Fries/Homestyle Potato Wedges*)	110
(*Ore-Ida Crispy Crowns*)	190
(*Ore-Ida Golden Crinkles/Golden Fries*)	120
(*Ore-Ida Golden Twirls*)	160
(*Seabrook*)	120
battered (*Ore-Ida Crispy Crunchers*)	180
battered (*Ore-Ida Zesties!*)	160
crinkle cut (*Ore-Ida*)	160
crinkle cut (*Ore-Ida* Lites)	90
crinkle cut (*Ore-Ida Pixie Crinkles*)	140
ridged (*Ore-Ida Crispers!*)	220
round (*Ore-Ida* Cottage Fries)	130
shoestring (*Ore-Ida*)	150
skinny (*MicroMagic*)	350

hash brown:

(*Ore-Ida*), 2 oz.	110
(*Ore-Ida Golden Patties*), 2.5 oz.	130
with butter and onions (*Heinz* Deep Fries)	110
with cheddar (*Ore-Ida Cheddar Browns*)	90
shredded (*Ore-Ida*)	70
toaster (*Ore-Ida*), 1.75 oz.	100
O'Brien (*Ore-Ida*)	60
puffs (*Ore-Ida Tater Tots* Microwave), 4 oz.	210
puffs, plain or bacon flavor (*Ore-Ida Tater Tots*)	140
puffs, with onion (*Ore-Ida Tater Tots*)	150

Potato, mix* (see also "Potato dishes, mix"), 1/2 cup:

(*Betty Crocker Potato Buds*)	130

Potato, mix* (cont.)

American or cheddar cheese (*Betty Crocker* Homestyle)	140
au gratin, cheddar with bacon, or smoky cheddar (*Betty Crocker*)	140
bacon and cheddar (*Betty Crocker* Twice Baked)	210
broccoli au gratin (*Betty Crocker* Homestyle)	130
butter, herbed (*Betty Crocker* Twice Baked)	220
cheddar, mild, with onion (*Betty Crocker* Twice Baked)	190
country style (*Fantastic Foods*)	85
hash brown with onions or scalloped and ham (*Betty Crocker*)	160
julienne (*Betty Crocker*)	130
mashed (*Pillsbury Idaho*)	120
mashed (*Pillsbury Idaho Spuds*)	130
scalloped or sour cream and chive (*Betty Crocker*)	140
scalloped, cheesy (*Betty Crocker* Homestyle)	140
sour cream and chive (*Betty Crocker* Twice Baked)	200
western (*Idahoan*)	120

Potato chips and crisps, 1 oz.:

plain, regular or rippled	152
all varieties (*Snacktime Krunchers!*)	150
all flavored varieties (*Bachman*)	150
barbecue or onion-garlic flavor (*Wise/Wise Ridgies*)	150
dill, onion-garlic, or sour cream and onion (*King Kold*)	150
hot (*Wise*)	160
mesquite or ranch (*Ruffles*)	160
ranch (*Eagle* Ridged)	160
skins, all varieties (*Tato Skins*)	150
sour cream and onion (*Lay's*)	160

Potato dishes, canned or packaged:

au gratin or escalloped (*Del Monte Vegetable Classics*), 3/4 cup	190
au gratin (*Green Giant Pantry Express*), 1/2 cup	120
nacho (*Del Monte Vegetable Classics*), 3/4 cup	170
scalloped, and ham (*Hormel Micro Cup*), 7.5 oz.	260

Potato dishes, frozen (see also "Potato, frozen"):

au gratin (*Stouffer's*), 1/3 of 11½-oz. pkg.	110
baked, broccoli and cheese (*Ore-Ida* Twice Baked), 5.63 oz. . . .	160
baked, broccoli and cheese sauce (*Healthy Choice*), 10 oz.	240
baked, butter flavor (*Ore-Ida* Twice Baked), 5 oz.	200
baked, cheddar cheese (*Ore-Ida* Twice Baked), 5 oz.	210
baked, chicken divan (*Weight Watchers*), 11.25 oz.	280
baked, ham Lorraine (*Weight Watchers*), 11.5 oz.	240
baked, sour cream and chive (*Ore-Ida* Twice Baked), 5 oz.	190
baked, turkey, homestyle (*Weight Watchers*), 11.25 oz.	230
baked, vegetable primavera (*Ore-Ida* Twice Baked), 6.13 oz. . . .	160
baked, vegetable primavera (*Weight Watchers*), 11.15 oz.	320
and broccoli, in cheese sauce (*Green Giant* One Serving), 5.5 oz.	130
cheddared (*The Budget Gourmet* Side Dish), 1 serving	260

cheddared, broccoli (*The Budget Gourmet* Side Dish), 1 serving 150
pancakes, see "Potato pancake"
scalloped (*Stouffer's*), 1/3 of 111/2-oz. pkg. 90
three cheese (*The Budget Gourmet* Side Dish), 1 serving 220
Potato dishes, mix* (see also "Potato, mix"), 1/2 cup:
au gratin or two cheese (*Kraft* Potatoes & Cheese) 130
au gratin, tangy or cheddar and bacon (*Pillsbury*) 140
broccoli au gratin, scalloped with ham, or sour cream and chives
    (*Kraft* Potatoes & Cheese) 150
pancakes, see "Potato pancake"
scalloped (*Kraft* Potatoes & Cheese) 140
scalloped, cheesy, white sauce, or sour cream-chive (*Pillsbury*) . . 150
Potato flour, 1 cup 628
Potato juice (*Biotta*), 6 fl. oz. 144
Potato pancake:
frozen (*Golden*), 1 piece 80
frozen, Mexican (*Golden*), 1 piece 70
mix* (*Pillsbury*), 3 pieces, 3″ each 90
Potato salad, canned:
German (*Joan of Arc/Read*), 1/2 cup 120
homestyle (*Joan of Arc/Read*), 1/2 cup 34
Potato starch (*Featherweight*), 1 cup 620
Potato sticks, canned, shoestring (*Allens*), 1 oz. 140
Poultry seasoning, 1 tsp. 5
Pout, ocean, meat only, baked, broiled, or microwaved, 4 oz. . . . 116
Preserves, see "Jam, jelly, and preserves"
Pretzel, 1 oz., except as noted:
all varieties (*Eagle*) 110
all varieties (*Mr. Phipps*) 120
all varieties, except fat-free (*Mr. Salty*) 110
cheddar flavor (*Combos*), 1.8 oz. 240
fat-free, all varieties (*Mr. Salty*) 100
frozen (*Super Pretzel*), 2.25 oz. 170
frozen, bite size (*Super Pretzel Soft Pretzel Bites*), 1.5 oz. 110
Prickly pear, 1 medium, approx. 4.8 oz. 42
Prosciutto, boneless (*Hormel*), 1 oz. 90
Prune:
canned, in heavy syrup, 1/2 cup 123
dried, with pits (*Sunsweet*), 2 oz. 120
dried, pitted (*Del Monte*), 2 oz. 140
cooked, unsweetened, with pits, 1/2 cup 113
cooked, unsweetened, pitted, 4 oz. 121
Prune juice (*Del Monte*), 6 fl. oz. 120
Pudding, ready-to-serve, 4 oz., except as noted:
all varieties (*Del Monte* Lite Pudding Cups), 4.5 oz. 100
all varieties (*Hunt's Snack Pack* Light) 100

Pudding, ready-to-serve (cont.)

all varieties (*Jell-O* Light Pudding Snacks)	100
all varieties (*Swiss Miss* Lite)	100
all varieties, except chocolate-peanut butter and tapioca (*Del Monte* Pudding Cups), 4.5 oz.	150
all varieties, except butterscotch-chocolate-vanilla and vanilla-chocolate (*Jell-O* Pudding Snacks Swirl)	170
banana (*Hunt's Snack Pack*), 4.25 oz.	145
butterscotch or chocolate (*Swiss Miss*)	180
butterscotch-chocolate-vanilla swirl (*Jell-O* Pudding Snacks)	180
butterscotch or chocolate (*Hunt's Snack Pack*), 4.25 oz.	170
butterscotch or vanilla, frozen (*Rich's*), 3 oz.	130
chocolate (*Hershey's* Chocolate Bar)	180
chocolate, all varieties (*Jell-O* Pudding Snacks)	170
chocolate, frozen (*Rich's*), 3 oz.	140
chocolate, double or milk, with yogurt (*Yoplait*)	180
chocolate, fudge or pudding sundae (*Swiss Miss*)	220
chocolate parfait (*Swiss Miss*)	170
chocolate-peanut butter (*Del Monte* Pudding Cup), 4.5 oz.	160
chocolate-vanilla (*Hershey's Kisses* Pudding Pack)	180
lemon (*Hunt's Snack Pack*), 4.25 oz.	150
rice (*Lucky Leaf/Musselman's*)	120
tapioca (*Del Monte* Pudding Cups), 4.5 oz.	140
tapioca (*Hunt's Snack Pack*), 4.25 oz.	150
tapioca (*Swiss Miss*)	160
vanilla (*Hunt's Snack Pack*), 4.25 oz.	170
vanilla (*Swiss Miss*)	190
vanilla, with yogurt (*Yoplait*)	150
vanilla parfait (*Swiss Miss*)	180
vanilla pudding sundae (*Swiss Miss*)	220
vanilla-chocolate swirl (*Jell-O* Pudding Snacks)	180

Pudding mix*, 1/2 cup:

all varieties (*Salada Danish Dessert*)	130
banana cream (*Jell-O* Microwave)	150
banana cream or butterscotch (*Jell-O* Instant)	160
banana cream or butterscotch (*Royal*)	160
banana cream or butterscotch (*Royal* Instant)	180
butter almond, toasted (*Royal* Instant)	170
butter pecan (*Jell-O* Instant)	170
butterscotch (*Jell-O/Jell-O* Microwave)	170
butterscotch (*My-T-Fine*)	160
chocolate:	
(*Jell-O* Microwave)	170
(*My-T-Fine*)	170
(*Royal/Royal* Dark'n Sweet)	180
all varieties (*Jell-O*)	160

all varieties (*Jell-O* Instant)	180
almond (*My-T-Fine*)	170
chocolate chip or mint (*Royal* Instant)	190
coconut, toasted (*Royal* Instant)	170
coconut cream (*Jell-O* Instant)	180
custard, golden egg (*Jell-O Americana*)	160
custard or flan with caramel sauce (*Royal*)	150
flan (*Jell-O*)	150
lemon (*Jell-O* Instant)	170
lemon (*My-T-Fine*)	160
lemon or key lime (*Royal*)	160
pistachio (*Jell-O* Instant)	170
pistachio nut (*Royal* Instant)	170
rennet custard, all flavors (*Junket*)	120
rice (*Jell-O Americana*)	170
tapioca, vanilla (*Jell-O Americana*)	160
tapioca, vanilla (*My-T-Fine*)	160
tapioca, vanilla (*Royal*)	160
vanilla (*Jell-O/Jell-O* Microwave)	160
vanilla (*Jell-O* Instant)	170
vanilla (*Royal*)	160
vanilla (*Royal* Instant)	180
vanilla, French (*Jell-O*)	170
vanilla, French (*Jell-O* Instant)	160
Puff pastry, see "Pastry sheets and shells"	
Pummelo, sections, 1/2 cup	36
Pumpkin:	
fresh, boiled, drained, mashed, 1/2 cup	24
canned (*Del Monte*), 1/2 cup	35
Pumpkin butter (*Smucker's* Autumn Harvest), 1 tsp.	12
Pumpkin flower, boiled, drained, 1/2 cup	10
Pumpkin pie spice, 1 tsp.	6
Pumpkin seeds:	
roasted, whole, in shell, 1/2 cup	143
dried, shelled, 1/2 cup	374
Purslane, raw, trimmed, 1/2 cup	4

Q

Food and Measure	Calories

Quail:

fresh, raw, meat with skin, 2 oz.	108
fresh, raw, meat only, 2 oz.	76
frozen, meat only (*Manchester Farms*), 4 oz.	153
Quince, 1 medium, 5.3 oz.	53
Quinoa seed (*Arrowhead Mills*), 2 oz.	200

R

Food and Measure	Calories

Rabbit, meat only:

domesticated, roasted, 4 oz.	223
domesticated, stewed, 4 oz.	234
wild, stewed, 4 oz.	196
Radicchio, raw, shredded, 1/2 cup	5
Radish:	
black, trimmed, 1 oz.	5
Oriental, raw, sliced, 1/2 cup	8
Oriental, boiled, drained, sliced, 1/2 cup	13

Oriental, dried, 1 oz.	77
red, raw, 10 medium, 3/4"–1" diam., approx. 1.8 oz.	7
red, raw, sliced, 1/2 cup	10
white icicle, raw, sliced, 1/2 cup	7
Radish sprouts, raw, 1/2 cup	8
Raisins:	
golden seedless, 1/2 cup not packed	219
seeded, 1/2 cup not packed	214
seedless, 1/2 cup not packed	217
Raspberry:	
fresh, trimmed, 1/2 cup	31
canned, red, in heavy syrup, 1/2 cup	117
frozen, in light syrup, red (*Birds Eye* Quick Thaw Pouch), 5 oz.	100
Raspberry fruit syrup (*Polaner's* Pourable Fruit), 1 fl. oz.	72
Raspberry juice:	
red (*Smucker's* 100%), 8 fl. oz.	120
blend (*Dole Pure & Light* Country Raspberry), 6 fl. oz.	90
Raspberry-cranberry juice (*Apple & Eve***),** 6 fl. oz.	90
Ravioli, canned or packaged, 7.5 oz., except as noted:	
beef (*Chef Boyardee* Microwave Meals)	190
beef (*Libby's Diner*), 7.75 oz.	240
beef, in tomato sauce (*Hormel Micro Cup*)	250
beef, mini, in tomato sauce (*Hormel Kid's Kitchen Micro Cup*)	270
cheese, in meat sauce (*Chef Boyardee* Microwave)	200
meat, in sauce (*Buitoni*)	180
Ravioli, frozen or refrigerated:	
(*Celentano*), 6.5 oz.	380
cheese (*Buitoni*), 4 oz.	360
cheese, mini (*Master Choice*), 4 oz.	380
mini (*Celentano*), 4 oz.	250
Ravioli entree, frozen:	
cheese (*The Budget Gourmet* Light & Healthy), 1 serving	290
cheese, baked (*Healthy Choice*), 9 oz.	240
cheese, baked, with tomato sauce (*Lean Cuisine*), 8.5 oz.	240
Red Lobster:	
appetizers, 1 serving:	
seafood gumbo, Bayou-style, 6 oz.	180
shrimp cocktail, with sauce	120
shrimp in shell, chilled, with sauce	160
seafood combinations, 1 serving:	
bay platter, with rice pilaf	500
Alaskan snow crab legs, 16 oz.	120
flounder, broiled, 5 oz.	150
rock lobster, broiled, 9 oz.	250
Maine lobster, 18 oz.	200
seafood lover's sampler	650

Red Lobster, seafood combinations (cont.)

shrimp scampi	310
shrimp skewers, grilled	170

Today's Fresh Catch, 5 oz. lunch portion:

catfish	220
Atlantic cod or grouper	150
haddock or mahi mahi	160
ocean perch or sea bass	180
orange roughy or rainbow trout	220
red rock fish	140
salmon, Atlantic	230
salmon, coho	240
salmon, king	290
snapper, sole, or lemon sole	160
swordfish	150
walleye pike or yellow lake perch	170

chicken and sandwiches, 1 serving:

chicken, grilled, with shrimp	490
chicken breast, grilled, 8 oz. dinner	340
chicken salad, grilled, with lite dressing	120
chicken sandwich, grilled	340
fish fillet sandwich, broiled	300
ice cream, 4.5 oz.	260
sherbet, 4.5 oz.	180

Red snapper, see "Snapper"

Redfish, see "Ocean perch"

Refried beans, see "Beans, refried"

Relish:

hamburger or piccalilli (*Heinz*), 1 oz.	30
hot dog (*Vlasic*), 1 oz.	40
jalapeño (*Old El Paso*), 2 tbsp.	16
pickle (*Claussen*), 1 tbsp.	14
sweet (*Heinz*), 1 oz.	35

Rhubarb:

raw, trimmed, diced, 1/2 cup	13
frozen, cooked, sweetened, 1/2 cup	139

Rice, plain, cooked (see also "Rice dishes, mix"), 1/2 cup:

basmati, white, long grain (*Texmati*)	82
brown, long grain	108
white, long grain	132
white, long grain, instant (*Carolina/Mahatma* Enriched)	110
white, long grain, instant (*Minute Rice* Boil-in-Bag)	90

Rice, wild, see "Wild rice"

Rice cake, 1/2 oz., except as noted:

all varieties (*Hain/Hain* Unsalted), 1 piece	40
plain (*Chico San* Salt Free Mini)	50

apple cinnamon (*Chico San* Mini) 60
barbecue, nacho, popcorn, or ranch (*Hain* Mini) 70
brown rice (*Konriko* Original Unsalted), 1 piece 30
cheddar or sour cream and onion (*Chico San* Mini) 70
cheese, honey nut, or popcorn, plain or cheddar (*Hain* Mini) . . . 60
teriyaki (*Hain* Mini) 50
Rice dishes, canned:
fried (*La Choy*), ¾ cup 180
Spanish (*Old El Paso*), ½ cup 70
Rice dishes, frozen:
and broccoli (*Green Giant Rice Originals*), ½ cup 120
and broccoli, au gratin (*Birds Eye For One*), 5.75 oz. 180
and broccoli, in cheese sauce (*Green Giant* One Serving), 5.5 oz. 160
Country Style (*Birds Eye* International), 3.3 oz. 90
Florentine (*Green Giant Rice Originals*), ½ cup 140
French or Spanish style (*Birds Eye* International), 3.3 oz. 110
fried, with chicken (*Chun King*), 8 oz. 260
fried, with pork (*Chun King*), 8 oz. 270
medley (*Green Giant Rice Originals*), ½ cup 100
Mexicana (*The Budget Gourmet* Side Dish), 1 serving 230
Oriental and vegetables (*The Budget Gourmet* Side Dish),
1 serving 230
pilaf (*Green Giant Rice Originals*), ½ cup 110
pilaf, green beans (*The Budget Gourmet* Side Dish), 1 serving 230
white and wild rice (*Green Giant Rice Originals*), ½ cup 130
Rice dishes, mix*, ½ cup, except as noted:
Alfredo, without butter (*Country Inn*) 140
almondine (*Hain* 3-Grain Side Dish) 130
au gratin, herbed, without butter (*Country Inn*) 140
beef flavor, without butter (*Lipton Golden Sauté*) 120
beef flavor or Cajun (*Lipton* Rice and Sauce) 150
broccoli stir-fry (*Suzi Wan* Dinner Recipe), 7.5 oz. 370
broccoli and cheddar (*Lipton* Rice and Sauce) 180
brown and wild, with butter (*Uncle Ben's*) 150
cheddar, zesty (*Rice-A-Roni Savory Classics*) 180
cheddar and broccoli (*Minute* Microwave Family/Single Size) . . . 160
chicken and chicken flavor:
(*Minute* Microwave Family Size) 160
without butter (*Lipton Golden Sauté*) 130
and broccoli (*Lipton Golden Sauté/Lipton* Rice and Sauce) . . . 150
creamy, and mushroom, without butter (*Country Inn*) 140
drumstick (*Minute*) 150
Florentine (*Rice-A-Roni Savory Classics*) 130
homestyle, and vegetables, without butter (*Country Inn*) 140
honey lemon (*Suzi Wan* Dinner Recipe), 7.5 oz. 370
royale, without butter (*Country Inn*) 120

Rice dishes, mix*, chicken and chicken flavor (cont.)
stock, with butter (*Uncle Ben's*) 160
  and vegetables, without butter (*Suzi Wan*) 120
Florentine, without butter (*Country Inn*) 140
fried, with almonds (*Rice-A-Roni*) 140
green bean almondine casserole, without butter (*Country Inn*) 120
herb and butter (*Lipton Golden Sauté*) 150
long grain and wild (*Near East*) 130
long grain and wild, with butter (*Uncle Ben's* Original) 120
Mexican (*Old El Paso*) 140
mushroom, creamy, and wild rice, without butter (*Country Inn*) 140
Oriental (*Hain* 3-Grain Goodness) 130
Oriental snow peas and (*Fantastic Foods*), 10 fl. oz. 160
Oriental style, without butter (*Lipton Golden Sauté*) 130
pilaf (*Lipton* Rice and Sauce) 170
pilaf, plain, beef, or chicken flavored (*Near East*) 140
pilaf, French style (*Minute* Microwave Family Size) 130
pilaf, lentil (*Near East*) 170
pilaf, vegetable, without butter (*Country Inn*) 120
risotto (*Rice-A-Roni*) 200
Spanish pilaf (*Casbah*), 1 oz. dry or ½ cup cooked 90
sweet and sour, without butter (*Suzi Wan*) 130
teriyaki, without butter (*Suzi Wan*) 120
three flavor, without butter (*Suzi Wan*) 120
vegetable medley, without butter (*Country Inn*) 140
yellow (*Mahatma/Success*) 100
Rice snack, chili cheddar, herb and garlic, or seasoned original
  (*Amsnack* Rice Snax), ½ oz. 60
Rigatoni, canned (*Chef Boyardee* Microwave), 7.5 oz. 210
Rigatoni entree, frozen:
bake, with meat sauce (*Lean Cuisine*), 9.75 oz. 250
with chicken (*Healthy Choice* Pasta Classics), 12.5 oz. 360
with chicken and tomato sauce (*The Budget Gourmet Quick Stirs*),
  1 serving 310
in meat sauce (*Healthy Choice*), 9.5 oz. 240
with meat sauce and green beans (*Stouffer's* Homestyle), 9 oz. 250
Rockfish, meat only, baked, broiled, or microwaved, 4 oz. 137
Roe, mixed species (see also "Caviar"):
raw, 1 tbsp. 22
baked, broiled, or microwaved, 4 oz. 231
Roll, 1 piece, except as noted:
(*Arnold Bakery* Light) 80
(*Arnold Bran'nola* Buns) 100
(*Arnold Francisco*, 8") 210
brown and serve:
  (*Pepperidge Farm* Hearth) 50

club (*Pepperidge Farm* European Bake Shoppe)	100
French (*Pepperidge Farm* European Bake Shoppe, 3/pkg.) . . .	240
gem style or buttermilk (*Wonder*)	80
Italian, crusty (*du Jour*)	80
sourdough (*Arnold Francisco*)	100
crescent, butter (*Pepperidge Farm* European Bake Shoppe)	110
dinner (*Arnold/August Bros.*)	90
dinner, plain or sesame (*Arnold* 24 Dinner Party)	50
dinner, country style (*Pepperidge Farm* Classic)	50
dinner, potato, hearty (*Pepperidge Farm* Deli Classic)	90
dinner, wheat (*Home Pride*)	70
egg, Dutch (*Arnold*)	150
egg, sandwich (*Arnold* Dutch)	123
finger, poppy seed (*Pepperidge Farm*)	50
finger, sesame seed (*Pepperidge Farm*)	60
frankfurter (*Arnold/Arnold Bran'nola*)	110
frankfurter (*Pepperidge Farm* Top or Side Sliced)	140
frankfurter (*Wonder*)	80
frankfurter, Dijon (*Pepperidge Farm*)	160
French (*Arnold Francisco, 6"*)	210
French, mini (*Arnold Francisco*)	130
French style (*Pepperidge Farm* European Bake Shoppe)	100
hamburger (*Arnold*)	110
hamburger (*Pepperidge Farm*)	130
hoagie, soft (*Pepperidge Farm* Deli Classic)	210
Italian (*Arnold/Savoni, 8"*)	210
kaiser (*Arnold/Arnold* Deli)	170
kaiser (*Arnold Francisco*)	180
onion (*Arnold/August Bros.*)	160
onion (*Arnold* Deli)	170
Parker House (*Pepperidge Farm*)	60
party, petite (*Arnold*), 2 pieces	70
sandwich (*Pepperidge Farm* Fat Free)	130
sandwich, onion, poppy seed (*Pepperidge Farm*)	150
sandwich, potato (*Pepperidge Farm*)	160
sandwich, salad (*Pepperidge Farm* Deli Classic)	110
sandwich, sesame seed (*Pepperidge Farm*)	140
sandwich, soft, plain or sesame (*Arnold*)	110
sesame (*Arnold/August Bros.*)	170
sourdough (*Arnold Francisco*)	100
sourdough French (*Pepperidge Farm* European Bake Shoppe)	100
twist, golden (*Pepperidge Farm* Heat 'n Serve)	110
wheat or white (*Arnold* Old Fashioned)	80
Roll, frozen or refrigerator (see also "Roll, sweet"):	
butterflake, butter flavor (*Pillsbury*), 1 piece	140
cinnamon (*Pepperidge Farm*, 2/pkg.), 1 piece	280

Roll, frozen or refrigerator (cont.)

crescent (*Pillsbury*), 1 piece 100

Roll, mix*:

hot (*Dromedary*), 2 pieces 239

hot (*Pillsbury*), 1 piece 120

Roll, sweet (see also "Bun, sweet"), 1 piece:

apple cinnamon (*Aunt Fanny's* Old Fashioned), 2 oz. 178

caramel nut, rectangular (*Aunt Fanny's*) 180

cinnamon (*Aunt Fanny's*), 2 oz. 181

cinnamon (*Aunt Fanny's* Duos), 3.75 oz. 340

cinnamon (*Hostess Breakfast Bake Shop*) 140

cinnamon or cinnamon raisin, rectangular (*Aunt Fanny's*), 2 oz. 181

pecan, rectangular (*Aunt Fanny's*), 2 oz. 184

strawberry, rectangular (*Aunt Fanny's*), 2 oz. 165

refrigerator, caramel with nuts (*Pillsbury*) 160

refrigerator, cinnamon, iced (*Pillsbury*) 110

Rosemary, dried (*McCormick/Schilling*), 1 tsp. 5

Rotini entree, frozen, seafood (*Mrs. Paul's*), 9 oz. 240

Roughy, orange, meat only, baked, broiled, or microwaved, 4 oz. 101

Roy Rogers:

chicken, fried, 1 serving:

breast, 4.4 oz. 324

breast and wing, 6 oz. 466

leg (drumstick), 1.7 oz. 117

thigh, 3.5 oz. 282

thigh and leg, 5.2 oz. 399

wing, 1.5 oz. 142

sandwiches, 1 serving:

bacon cheeseburger, 6.3 oz. 581

bar burger, 7.3 oz. 611

cheeseburger, 6.1 oz. 563

hamburger, 5 oz. 456

roast beef sandwich, regular, 5.4 oz. 317

roast beef sandwich, large, 6.4 oz. 360

roast beef sandwich, with cheese, 6.4 oz. 424

roast beef sandwich, with cheese, large, 7.4 oz. 467

Hot Topped Potato, 1 serving:

plain, 8 oz. 211

with margarine, 8.3 oz. 376

bacon'n cheese, 8.7 oz. 397

broccoli'n cheese, 11 oz. 376

sour cream'n chives, 10.5 oz. 408

taco beef'n cheese, 12.7 oz. 463

side dishes, 1 serving:

biscuit, 2.2 oz. 231

coleslaw, 3.5 oz. 110

french fries, 3 oz.	268
french fries, large, 4 oz.	357
macaroni, 3.5 oz.	186
potato salad, 3.5 oz.	107
desserts and shakes, 1 serving:	
shake, chocolate	358
shake, strawberry	315
shake, vanilla	306
sundae, caramel, 5.2 oz.	293
sundae, hot fudge, 5.4 oz.	337
sundae, strawberry, 5 oz.	216
Rum extract, imitation (*McCormick/Schilling*), 1 tsp.	19
Rutabaga:	
fresh, boiled, drained, mashed, 1/2 cup	41
canned, diced (*Allens*), 1/2 cup	20
Rye, whole grain, 1 cup	567

S

Food and Measure	**Calories**
Sablefish, meat only:	
baked, broiled, or microwaved, 4 oz.	284
smoked, 4 oz.	291
Saffron, 1 tsp.	2
Sage, ground (*McCormick/Schilling*), 1 tsp.	4
Salad dressings, 1 tbsp., except as noted:	
all varieties, except tomato vinaigrette (*Hain* Canola Oil)	50
bacon and buttermilk (*Kraft*)	80
bacon and tomato, Caesar, coleslaw, or cucumber (*Kraft*)	70
blue cheese (*Healthy Sensation*)	19
blue cheese (*Roka* Brand)	60
blue cheese, chunky (*Wish-Bone*)	73
blue cheese, chunky (*Wish-Bone* Lite)	40
buttermilk (*Seven Seas Buttermilk Recipe*)	80

Salad dressings (cont.)

buttermilk, creamy (*Kraft*)	80
buttermilk, old fashioned (*Hain*)	70
Caesar (*Lawry's* Classic), 1/2 oz.	65
Caesar, creamy (*Hain/Hain* Low Salt)	60
Caesar, olive oil (*Wish-Bone* Lite)	28
cheese vinaigrette, Italian (*Hain*)	55
citrus, tangy (*Hain* Canola Oil)	50
cucumber dill (*Hain*)	80
Dijon mustard (*Great Impressions*)	57
Dijon vinaigrette (*Hain*)	50
dill, creamy (*Nasoya Vegi-Dressing*)	40
French:	
(*Catalina/Kraft*)	60
(*Healthy Sensation*)	21
(*Wish-Bone* Deluxe)	57
creamy (*Hain*)	60
garlic (*Wish-Bone*)	55
red (*Wish-Bone*)	64
garlic, herb (*Nasoya Vegi-Dressing*)	40
garlic and sour cream (*Hain*)	70
herb, savory (*Hain* No Salt Added)	90
herb and spice (*Seven Seas Viva*)	60
homestyle (*Dorothy Lynch*)	55
honey Dijon (*Healthy Sensation*)	26
honey and sesame (*Hain*)	60
Italian:	
(*Hain* Canola Oil)	50
(*Healthy Sensation*)	7
(*Seven Seas Viva*)	50
(*Wish-Bone* Blended Italian)	36
(*Wish-Bone* Robusto)	46
with bleu cheese (*Lawry's* Classic), 1 oz.	186
with cheese (*Wish-Bone*)	85
creamy (*Wish-Bone*)	54
creamy or traditional (*Hain*)	80
olive oil (*Wish-Bone* Classic)	33
zesty (*Kraft*)	50
lemon garlic Caesar (*Cains Light Hearted*)	35
mayonnaise type, plain or coleslaw (*Miracle Whip*)	70
Mexican chili ranch (*Cains Light Hearted*)	45
mustard, spicy French (*Hain* Canola Oil)	50
oil and vinegar (*Kraft*)	70
olive oil vinaigrette (*Wish-Bone*)	30
orange Dijon (*Cains Light Hearted*)	18
orange marmalade fruit salad (*Great Impressions*)	87

oregano Greek, classic (*Cains Light Hearted*) 30
peppercorn ranch (*Cains Light Hearted*) 45
poppy seed (*Hain* Rancher's) 60
ranch (*Healthy Sensation*) 15
ranch (*Wish-Bone*) 76
raspberry vinaigrette (*Cains Light Hearted*) 20
red wine olive oil vinaigrette (*Wish-Bone*) 34
Russian, creamy or with honey (*Kraft*) 60
sesame garlic (*Nasoya Vegi-Dressing*) 40
sour (*Friendship Sour Treat*), 1 oz. 36
Swiss cheese vinaigrette (*Hain*) 60
Thousand Island (*Healthy Sensation*) 20
Thousand Island, regular or bacon (*Kraft*) 60
Thousand Island, creamy (*Seven Seas*) 50
tomato vinaigrette, garden (*Hain* Canola Oil) 60
vinegar, red wine, and oil (*Kraft*) 60
Salad dressing mix*, 1 tbsp.:
all varieties, except buttermilk and ranch (*Good Seasons*) 70
bleu cheese (*Hain* No Oil) 14
buttermilk (*Good Seasons* Farm Style) 60
buttermilk (*Hain* No Oil) 11
buttermilk, French, or Thousand Island (*Hain* No Oil) 12
Caesar or garlic and cheese (*Hain* No Oil) 6
herb or Italian (*Hain* No Oil) 2
ranch (*Good Seasons*) 60
Salad mix* (see also "Pasta dishes, mix"), 1/2 cup:
Caesar (*Suddenly Salad*) 170
macaroni, creamy (*Suddenly Salad*) 200
ranch and bacon (*Suddenly Salad*) 210
Salad seasoning (*McCormick/Shilling* Salad Supreme), 1 tsp. 11
Salami:
beef (*Hebrew National* Original Deli Style), 1 oz. 80
beef (*Kahn's*), 1 slice 70
beef (*Oscar Mayer* Machiaeh Brand), .8-oz. slice 60
beer (*Eckrich*), 1-oz. slice 70
beer (*Oscar Mayer* Salami for Beer), .8-oz. slice 50
beer, beef (*Oscar Mayer* Salami for Beer), .8-oz. slice 65
cooked (*OHSE*), 1 oz. 65
cotto (*Kahn's* Family Pack), 1 slice 45
cotto (*Oscar Mayer*), .8-oz. slice 55
cotto, beef (*Oscar Mayer*), .8-oz. slice 45
Genoa (*Hormel/Hormel* Gran Valore), 1 oz. 110
Genoa (*Oscar Mayer*), .3-oz. slice 35
hard (*Hormel/Hormel* Sliced), 1 oz. 110
hard (*Oscar Mayer*), .3-oz. slice 35
piccolo (*Hormel* Stick), 1 oz. 120

Salisbury steak, see "Beef dinner" and "Beef entree"

Salmon:

fresh, meat only, 4 oz.:

Atlantic, baked, broiled, or microwaved	206
Chinook, baked, broiled, or microwaved	262
Chinook, smoked	133
Chinook, lox	133
chum, baked, broiled, or microwaved	175
coho, boiled, poached, or steamed	210
pink, baked, broiled, or microwaved	169
sockeye, baked, broiled, or microwaved	245

canned:

coho, Alaska (*Deming's*), 1/2 cup	140
pink (*Libby's*), 73/4 oz.	310
pink, chunk, in water (*Deming's*), 3.25 oz.	120
pink, skinless, boneless, with liquid (*Bumble Bee*), 3.25 oz.	120
pink or keta, with liquid (*Bumble Bee*), 3.5 oz.	160
red, with liquid (*Bumble Bee*), 3.5 oz.	180
red, blueback (*Rubenstein's*), 1/2 cup	170
red, skinless, boneless, with liquid (*Bumble Bee*), 3.25 oz.	130
red, sockeye (*Libby's*), 73/4 oz.	380
red, sockeye, Alaska, medium (*Deming's*), 1/2 cup . . .	150

frozen, steaks, without seasoning mix (*SeaPak*), 8-oz. pkg.	270

Salmon seasoning mix (*Old Bay Salmon Classic*), 1 pkg. . . . . . | 159

Salsa, canned or in jars:

all varieties (*Chi-Chi's*), 2 oz.	15
all varieties (*Rosarita*), 3 tbsp.	25
green chili (*Old El Paso* Thick'n Chunky), 2 tbsp.	3
green chili, hot (*Ortega*), 1 oz.	10
hot (*Hain*), 1/4 cup	22
mild (*Hain*), 1/4 cup	20
mild, medium, or hot (*Old El Paso* Thick'n Chunky), 2 tbsp. . . .	6
picante, all varieties (*Ortega*), 1 oz.	10
Texas (*Hot Cha Cha*), 1 oz.	6
verde (*Old El Paso* Thick'n Chunky), 2 tbsp.	10

Salsa dip (*Eagle*), 1 oz. . . . . | 12

Salsify, fresh, boiled, drained, sliced, 1/2 cup . . . . | 46

Salt:

plain, all varieties, 1 tbsp.	0
seasoned (*McCormick/Schilling* Salt'n Spice), 1/4 tsp. . . .	1
seasoned, butter (*McCormick/Schilling* Spice Blends), 1 tsp. . . .	2

Salt pork, raw, 1 oz. . . . . | 212

Salt substitute, seasoned (*Morton*), 1 tsp. . . . . | 2

Sandwich sauce, see "Sloppy Joe sauce"

Sandwich spread:

(*Best Foods/Hellmann's*), 1 tbsp. . . . . | 50

with meat (*Oscar Mayer*), 1 oz.	65
Sapodilla, fresh, trimmed, 1/2 cup	100
Sapote, fresh, 1 medium, approx. 11.2 oz.	301
Sardine, canned:	
Norway, in oil, drained (*Empress*), 3.75-oz. can	260
in mustard sauce (*Underwood*), 3.75 oz.	220
in soya oil (*Underwood*), 3.75 oz. drained	230
with *Tabasco* (*Underwood*), 3.75 oz. drained	220
in tomato sauce (*Underwood*), 3.75 oz.	220
kippered (*Brunswick Kippered Snacks*), 3 1/2 oz.	185
Sauces, see specific listings	
Sauerkraut, canned or in jars, 1/2 cup:	
(*Claussen*)	17
(*Del Monte*)	25
(*Snow Floss*)	28
(*Stokely* Bavarian)	30
shredded and chopped (*Stokely*)	20
Sauerkraut juice (*Biotta*), 6 fl. oz.	21
Sausage (see also specific listings):	
beef (*Jones Dairy Farm* Golden Brown), 1 link	80
beef, roll (*Jones Dairy Farm* Cello Roll), 1-oz. slice	130
beef and cheddar (*Hillshire Farm* Flavorseal), 2 oz.	190
brown and serve:	
(*Hormel*), 2 cooked links	140
(*Jones Dairy Farm*), .8-oz. link	100
(*Jones Dairy Farm* Light), 1 link	60
bacon or beef (*Jones Dairy Farm*), .8-oz. link	90
with bacon, maple, or smoked (*Swift Premium*), 1 link	120
country (*Hillshire Farm* Country Recipe), 2 oz.	180
patty, hot or mild, canned (*Hormel*), 1 patty	150
pickled, all varieties (*Penrose*), .5-oz. link	40
pork:	
(*Jimmy Dean*), 2 cooked links	180
(*Jones Dairy Farm* Dinner Link), 2-oz. link	280
(*Jones Dairy Farm* Light Little Link), 1-oz. link	70
(*Jones Dairy Farm* Little Link), 1-oz. link	140
(*Jones Dairy Farm* Golden Brown Light), 1 link	60
(*Oscar Mayer*), 1 cooked link	85
mild or spicy (*Jones Dairy Farm* Golden Brown), 1 link	100
patty (*Jones Dairy Farm*), 1 patty	180
patty, extra mild, hot, regular, or sage (*Jimmy Dean*), 1 cooked patty	120
patty, mild (*Jones Dairy Farm*), 1 patty	150
patty, square (*Jimmy Dean*), 1 cooked patty	140
roll (*Jones Dairy Farm* Original Cello Roll), 1-oz. slice	100
roll, hot country (*Jones Dairy Farm* Cello Roll), 1-oz. slice	110

Sausage, pork (cont.)

and bacon (*JM* Tasty Link), 2 cooked links 100

smoked:

(*Eckrich* Lite), 1 link 150

(*Hillshire Farm* Country Recipe Flavorseal), 2 oz. 180

(*Hillshire Farm* Lite), 2 oz. 160

(*Hormel* Smokies), 2 links 160

(*Oscar Mayer* Smokie Links), 1.5-oz. link 125

all varieties, except hot (*Eckrich Smok-Y-Links*), 2 links 160

plain or beef (*Hillshire Farm* Bun Size), 2 oz. 190

plain or beef and cheddar (*Hillshire Farm* Flavorseal), 2 oz. . . 190

plain, hot, or hot beef (*Hillshire Farms* Links), 2 oz. 190

beef or cheese (*Oscar Mayer* Smokies), 1.5-oz. link 125

beef or hot (*Hillshire Farm* Flavorseal), 2 oz. 180

cheddar (*Eckrich* Lite), 1 link 190

hot (*Eckrich Smok-Y-Links*), 2 links 150

Italian seasoned (*Hillshire Farm*), 2 oz. 200

turkey, see "Turkey sausage"

"Sausage," vegetarian, patties (*Morningstar Farms* Breakfast

Patties), 2 patties, approx. 2.7 oz. 190

Sausage sandwich, frozen, 1 serving:

biscuit (*Jimmy Dean* Microwave) 170

biscuit, breakfast (*Swanson Great Starts*), 4.7 oz. 410

biscuit, breakfast (*Weight Watchers*), 3 oz. 220

Italian sausage (*Quaker Oven Stuffs*), 1 piece 350

turkey and pork sausage, biscuit (*Jimmy Dean* Light Microwave) 110

Sausage entree, frozen, gravy, with country biscuit (*Stouffer's*

Homestyle Favorites), 9 oz. 470

Savory, ground (*McCormick/Schilling*), 1 tsp. 5

Scallion, see "Onion, green"

Scallop, meat only:

fresh, mixed species, raw, 2 large or 5 small, approx. 1.1 oz. 26

frozen, fried (*Mrs. Paul's*), 3 oz. 200

Scallop squash, boiled, drained, sliced, 1/2 cup 14

Scallop and shrimp dinner, frozen, marinara (*The Budget

Gourmet* Hearty & Healthy), 1 serving 320

Scrapple (*Jones Dairy Farm*), 1.5-oz. slice 90

Scrod, see "Cod, Atlantic"

Scup, meat only, baked, broiled, or microwaved, 4 oz. 153

Sea bass, meat only, baked, broiled, or microwaved, 4 oz. 141

Sea trout, mixed species, meat only, baked, broiled, or

microwaved, 4 oz. 151

Seafood entree, frozen (see also specific listings):

Creole, with rice (*Swanson* Homestyle Recipe), 9 oz. 240

Gumbo (*Cajun Cookin'*), 17 oz. 330

Newburg (*The Budget Gourmet*), 1 serving 350

Newburg (*Healthy Choice*), 8 oz. 200
Seafood seasoning (*Old Bay*), 1 tsp. 5
Seafood and crabmeat salad (*Longacre* Saladfest), 1 oz. 45
Seaweed:
agar, dried, 1 oz. 87
Irish moss, raw, 1 oz. 14
kelp, raw, 1 oz. 12
laver, raw, 1 oz. 10
spirulina, dried, 1 oz. 82
wakame, raw, 1 oz. 13
Sesame butter:
paste, from whole sesame seeds, 1 tbsp. 95
tahini, organic (*Arrowhead Mills*), 1 oz. 170
Sesame seasoning (*McCormick/Schilling Parsley Patch*), 1 tsp. 15
Sesame seed (*McCormick/Schilling*), 1 tsp. 9
Shad, American, meat only, baked, broiled, or microwaved, 4 oz. 286
Shallot:
fresh, raw, chopped, 1 tbsp. 7
freeze-dried, 1 tbsp. 3
Shark, mixed species, meat only, raw, 4 oz. 148
Sheepshead, meat only, baked, broiled, or microwaved, 4 oz. 143
Shells, stuffed, entree, frozen:
(*Celentano*), 10 oz. 410
in tomato sauce (*Healthy Choice* Pasta Classics), 12 oz. 330
with vegetables (*Legume* Provençale), 11 oz. 240
Sherbet (see also "Sorbet" and "Ice"):
all flavors (*Sealtest*), 1/2 cup 130
orange (*Borden*), 1/2 cup 110
bar, fudge (*Borden*), 1 bar 90
bar, fudge (*Fudgsicle*), 1 bar 70
bar, fudge (*Häagen-Dazs*), 1 bar 210
bar, fudge nut dip (*Fudgsicle* Sugar Free), 1 bar 130
bar, orange, and cream (*Häagen-Dazs*), 1 bar 130
Sherry extract, pure (*McCormick/Schilling*), 1 tsp. 14
Shortening, vegetable, all varieties (*Crisco*), 1 tbsp. 110
Shrimp, mixed species, meat only:
fresh, boiled, poached, or steamed, 4 oz. 112
fresh, boiled, poached, or steamed, 4 large, approx. .8 oz. . . . 22
canned, 1 cup 154
frozen (*SeaPak* PDQ), 3.5 oz. 60
frozen, popcorn (*SeaPak* Oven Crunchy), 4 oz. 290
Shrimp dinner, frozen:
Creole (*Armour Classics Lite*), 11.25 oz. 260
Creole (*Healthy Choice*), 11.25 oz. 230
marinara (*Healthy Choice*), 10.5 oz. 260
Shrimp entree, canned, chow mein (*La Choy* Bi-Pack), 3/4 cup 70

Shrimp entree, frozen:

and batter, plain or with crabmeat stuffing (*SeaPak*), 4 oz.	260
breaded (*Gorton's* Microwave), 2 oz.	150
breaded (*Gorton's* Original), 5 pieces, 2.7 oz.	210
breaded (*Mrs. Paul's* Special Recipe), 5.5 oz.	300
breaded, butter flavor (*Mrs. Paul's*), 5.5 oz.	320
breaded, Oriental seasoning (*Gorton's*), 5 pieces, 2.7 oz.	170
breaded, popcorn style (*Gorton's*), 2.7 oz.	220
breaded, scampi seasoning (*Gorton's*), 5 pieces, 2.7 oz.	240
Cajun style (*Mrs. Paul's* Light), 9 oz.	230
and clams with linguini (*Mrs. Paul's* Light), 10 oz.	240
Creole (*Cajun Cookin'*), 12 oz.	390
etouffee (*Cajun Cookin'*), 17 oz.	360
with fettuccine (*The Budget Gourmet*), 1 serving	370
garlic and herb breaded (*Mrs. Paul's*), 5.5 oz.	250
jambalaya (*Cajun Cookin'*), 12 oz.	450
Mandarin vegetables (*The Budget Gourmet Quick Stirs*), 1 serving	300
primavera (*Mrs. Paul's* Light), 9.5 oz.	180
scampi, with vegetables and linguine (*The Budget Gourmet Quick Stirs*), 1 serving	220

Sloppy Joe sauce:

(*Hunt's Manwich*), 2.5 oz.	40
(*Hunt's Manwich* Extra Thick & Chunky), 2.5 oz.	60
Mexican (*Hunt's Manwich*), 2.5 oz.	35

Sloppy Joe seasoning:

(*Lawry's* Seasoning Blends), 1 pkg.	126
mix (*French's*), 1/8 pkg.	16
mix (*Hunt's Manwich*), .25 oz.	20
mix (*McCormick/Schilling*), 1/4 pkg.	26

Smelt, rainbow, meat only, baked, broiled, or microwaved, 4 oz.   141

Snack chips (see also specific listings):

(*Doo Dads*), 1 oz.	140
multigrain (*Keebler Quangles* Original), 1 oz.	140
multigrain (*Sun Chips* Original), 1 oz.	150
multigrain, harvest cheddar or french onion (*Sun Chips*), 1 oz.	140
regular or cheddar (*Zings*), 15 pieces	70
crisps, all flavors (*Pepperidge Farm* Flavor Crisps), 1/2 oz.	60
crisps, cheddar or Italian, swirl (*Pepperidge Farm*), 1 piece	70

Snack mix:

(*Eagle*), 1 oz.	140
classic or spicy (*Pepperidge Farm*), 1 oz.	140
herb, nutty, or lightly smoked (*Pepperidge Farm*), 1 oz.	150

Snails, sea, see "Whelk"

Snapper, mixed species, meat only, baked, broiled or microwaved, 4 oz.   145

Snow peas, see "Peas, edible-podded"

Soft drinks and mixers, 6 fl. oz., except as noted:

berry, wild (*Health Valley*)	71
birch beer (*Canada Dry*)	80
cactus cooler or wild cherry (*Canada Dry*)	80
cherry (*Sundrop*)	90
cherry, black (*Canada Dry*)	100
cherry, black (*Shasta*)	80
cherry cola (*Coca-Cola*)	76
cherry cola (*Pepsi* Wild Cherry)	82
cherry cola (*Shasta*)	74
cherry or grape (*Crush*)	100
cherry-lime (*Spree*)	79
chocolate (*Yoo-Hoo*), 9 fl. oz.	140
citrus (*Shasta* Citrus Mist)	96
club soda or seltzer, all brands, all flavors	0
cola (*Coca-Cola* Classic)	72
cola (*Pepsi* Regular/Caffeine-free)	80
cola (*Shasta/Shasta* Caffeine Free)	80
cola (*Spree*)	74
cola, Jamaica (*Canada Dry*)	80
collins mixer (*Schweppes*)	70
cream (*Hires*)	90
cream (*Shasta* Creme)	82
(*Dr. Diablo*)	78
(*Dr Pepper*)	78
ginger ale (*Canada Dry/Canada Dry* Golden)	70
ginger ale (*Shasta*)	66
ginger ale (*Schweppes*)	70
ginger ale, cherry (*Canada Dry*)	80
ginger ale, lemon (*Canada Dry*)	70
ginger ale, raspberry (*Schweppes*)	80
ginger beer (*Schweppes*)	70
grape (*Canada Dry*)	100
grape (*Fanta*)	86
grape or kiwi-strawberry (*Shasta*)	88
grapefruit or lemon sour (*Schweppes*)	80
half & half or bitter lemon (*Canada Dry*)	80
lemon-lime (*Shasta*)	74
lemon-lime (*Schweppes*)	70
lemon-lime (*Slice*)	75
lime, island (*Canada Dry*)	100
orange (*Fanta*)	88
orange (*Shasta*)	92
orange or peach (*Canada Dry*)	90
orange or pineapple (*Crush*)	100
peach (*Shasta*)	88

Soft drinks and mixers (cont.)

pineapple (*Shasta*)	106
pineapple-orange (*Shasta*)	94
raspberry creme (*Shasta*)	90
red pop (*Shasta*)	88
root beer (*Barrelhead*)	80
root beer (*Fanta*)	78
root beer (*Health Valley* Old Fashioned)	60
root beer (*Hires*)	90
root beer (*Shasta*)	80
sasaparilla root beer (*Health Valley*), 12 fl. oz.	77
(*7Up*)	72
(*Sprite*)	71
strawberry (*Shasta*)	76
strawberry, California (*Canada Dry*)	80
strawberry or vanilla cream (*Crush*)	90
strawberry-peach (*Shasta*)	86
(*Sundrop*)	100
sweet and sour (*Canada Dry*)	110
Tahitian treat (*Canada Dry*)	100
tonic (*Shasta*)	64
tonic with twist (*Canada Dry*)	70
vanilla cream (*Canada Dry*)	80
vichy water (*Schweppes*)	0
(*Wink*)	90

Sole:

fresh, see "Flatfish"	
frozen (*Van de Kamp's* Natural), 4 oz.	100
Sole dinner, frozen, au gratin (*Healthy Choice*), 11 oz.	270

Sole entree, frozen:

breaded (*Van de Kamp's* Light), 1 piece	250
with lemon butter sauce (*Healthy Choice*), 8.25 oz.	230

Sorbet (see also "Sherbet" and "Ice"):

all flavors, except strawberry (*Dole*), 4 oz.	110
strawberry (*Dole*), 4 oz.	100
and ice cream, blueberry/strawberry sorbet (*Breyers*), 1/2 cup	150
and ice cream, lemon sorbet (*Breyers*), 1/2 cup	160
and ice cream, orange sorbet (*Häagen-Dazs*), 1/2 cup	200
and ice cream, raspberry sorbet (*Häagen-Dazs*), 1/2 cup	180
Sorghum, whole grain, 1 cup	650

Soup, canned, ready-to-serve:

barley and mushroom (*Rokeach*), 7.5 oz.	100
bean (*Grandma Brown's*), 1 cup	190
bean, black (*Health Valley*), 7.5 oz.	160
bean, seven (*Rokeach*), 7.5 oz.	130
bean with bacon and ham (*Campbell's* Microwave), 7.5 oz.	230

bean with ham (*Campbell's* Home Cookin'), 10.75 oz. 210
bean and ham (*Healthy Choice* Microwave), 7.5 oz. 220
bean and ham (*Hormel Micro Cup* Hearty Soups), 7.5 oz. 190
beef:
   (*Progresso*), 9.5 oz. 160
   barley (*Progresso*), 9.5 oz. 140
   broth (*College Inn*), 7 fl. oz. 16
   broth (*Swanson*), 7.25 oz. 18
   broth, seasoned (*Progresso*), 8 oz. 20
   hearty (*Healthy Choice*), 7.5 oz. 120
   minestrone or noodle (*Progresso*), 9.5 oz. 170
   vegetable (*Hormel Micro Cup* Hearty Soups), 7.5 oz. 80
   vegetable (*Progresso*), 9.5 oz. 150
   vegetable, chunky (*Healthy Choice* Microwave), 7.5 oz. 110
   with vegetables, pasta (*Campbell's* Home Cookin'), 10.75 oz. 140
borscht (*Rokeach*), 1 cup 96
borscht, with beets (*Manischewitz*), 1 cup 80
chickarina or hearty chicken (*Progresso*), 9.5 oz. 130
chicken:
   (*Campbell's* Chunky Old Fashioned), 10.75 oz. 180
   barley (*Progresso*), 9.25 oz. 100
   broth (*Campbell's* Low Sodium), 10.5 oz. 30
   broth (*College Inn*), 7 fl. oz. 35
   broth (*College Inn* Lower Salt), 7 fl. oz. 20
   broth (*Progresso*), 8 oz. 16
   broth (*Swanson*), 7.25 oz. 30
   corn chowder (*Campbell's* Chunky), 10.75 oz. 340
   cream of (*Progresso*), 9.5 oz. 190
   gumbo with sausage (*Campbell's* Home Cookin'), 10.75 oz. 140
   hearty (*Healthy Choice* Microwave), 7.5 oz. 150
   minestrone (*Progresso*), 9.5 oz. 130
   noodle (*Campbell's* Microwave), 7.5 oz. 100
   noodle (*Hormel Micro Cup* Hearty Soups), 7.5 oz. 110
   noodle (*Progresso*), 9.5 oz. 120
   noodle, hearty (*Campbell's Healthy Request*), 8 oz. 80
   noodle, old fashioned (*Healthy Choice* Microwave), 7.5 oz. . . . 90
   noodle and vegetable (*Healthy Choice* Microwave), 7.5 oz. . . . 160
   rice (*Progresso*), 9.5 oz. 130
   with rice (*Healthy Choice* Microwave), 7.5 oz. 140
   vegetable (*Hain*), 8 oz. 110
   vegetable (*Progresso*), 10.5 oz. 150
   vegetable and rice (*Hormel Micro Cup* Hearty Soups), 7.5 oz. 110
chili beef (*Campbell's* Microwave), 7.5 oz. 190
clam chowder:
   Manhattan (*Campbell's* Chunky), 10.75 oz. 160
   Manhattan (*Progresso*), 10.5 oz. 140

Soup, canned, ready-to-serve, clam chowder (cont.)

New England (*Campbell's* Chunky), 9.5 oz.	260
New England (*Hormel Micro Cup* Hearty Soups), 7.5 oz.	120
New England (*Progresso*), 9.25 oz.	190
corn chowder (*Progresso*), 9.25 oz.	200
Creole style (*Campbell's* Chunky), 10.75 oz.	240
escarole in chicken broth (*Progresso*), 9.25 oz.	30
lentil (*Progresso*), 10.5 oz.	140
lentil, hearty (*Campbell's* Home Cookin'), 10.75 oz.	170
lentil, vegetarian (*Hain/Hain* No Salt Added), 9.5 oz.	160
lentil, vegetarian (*Hain* 99% Fat Free), 9.5 oz.	150
lentil with sausage (*Progresso*), 9.5 oz.	170
macaroni and bean (*Progresso*), 10.5 oz.	150
minestrone:	
(*Campbell's* Home Cookin' Old World), 10.75 oz.	140
(*Hain/Hain* No Salt Added), 9.5 oz.	160
(*Healthy Choice* Microwave), 7.5 oz.	160
(*Hormel Micro Cup* Hearty Soups), 7.5 oz.	110
(*Rokeach*), 7.5 oz.	140
extra zesty (*Progresso*), 9.5 oz.	150
hearty (*Campbell's Healthy Request*), 8 oz.	90
mushroom, cream of (*Progresso*), 9.25 oz.	160
mushroom barley (*Hain*), 9.5 oz.	80
mushroom barley (*Hain* 99% Fat Free), 9.5 oz.	90
pea, split:	
(*Grandma Brown's*), 1 cup	208
with egg barley (*Rokeach*), 7.5 oz.	160
green (*Health Valley*), 7.5 oz.	190
with ham (*Campbell's* Home Cookin'), 10.75 oz.	230
with ham (*Healthy Choice* Microwave), 7.5 oz.	170
with ham (*Progresso*), 9.5 oz.	150
vegetarian (*Hain/Hain* No Salt Added), 9.5 oz.	170
vegetarian (*Hain* 99% Fat Free), 9.5 oz.	160
pepper steak (*Campbell's* Chunky), 10.75 oz.	180
potato leek (*Health Valley*), 7.5 oz.	130
schav (*Gold's*), 8 oz.	25
steak and potato (*Campbell's* Chunky), 10.75 oz.	200
tomato:	
(*Progresso*), 10.5 oz.	120
garden (*Campbell's* Home Cookin'), 10.75 oz.	150
garden (*Healthy Choice* Microwave), 7.5 oz.	130
with tomato pieces (*Campbell's* Low Sodium), 10.5 oz.	190
tortellini (*Progresso*), 9.25 oz.	130
tomato beef with rotini (*Progresso*), 9.5 oz.	170
tortellini, creamy (*Progresso*), 9.25 oz.	240
turkey rice (*Hain*), 8 oz.	80

vegetable:

(*Progresso*), 10.5 oz.	80
(*Rokeach*), 7.5 oz.	100
beef (*Healthy Choice* Microwave), 7.5 oz.	130
beef, chunky (*Campbell's* Home Cookin'), 10.75 oz.	180
broth (*Hain*), 9.5 oz.	45
broth (*Hain* 99% Fat Free), 10.5 oz.	45
chicken (*Hain*), 9.5 oz.	120
country (*Healthy Choice* Microwave), 7.5 oz.	120
country (*Hormel Micro Cup* Hearty Soups), 7.5 oz.	90
hearty (*Campbell's Healthy Request*), 8 oz.	110
Mediterranean (*Campbell's* Chunky), 9.5 oz.	170
pasta, Italian (*Hain*), 9.5 oz.	160
vegetarian (*Hain/Hain* No Salt Added), 9.5 oz.	150

Soup, canned, condensed or semicondensed*, 8 oz., except as noted:

asparagus, cream of, with water (*Campbell's*)	80
bacon, lettuce and tomato, with water (*Pepperidge Farm*)	110
bacon, lettuce and tomato, with low-fat milk (*Pepperidge Farm*)	170
bean, black (*Campbell's*)	110
bean with bacon (*Campbell's Healthy Request*)	140
beef or beef noodle (*Campbell's/Campbell's* Homestyle)	80
beef broth or bouillon (*Campbell's*)	16
broccoli, cream of, with water (*Campbell's*)	80
broccoli, cream of, with milk (*Campbell's*)	140
celery, cream of (*Campbell's*)	100
cheese, cheddar or nacho, with water (*Campbell's*)	110
cheese, nacho, with milk (*Campbell's*)	180
chicken barley (*Campbell's*)	70
chicken broth (*Campbell's*)	30
chicken curry (*Pepperidge Farm*)	150
chicken mushroom, creamy (*Campbell's*)	120
chicken noodle or rice (*Campbell's Healthy Request*)	60
chicken vegetable (*Campbell's*)	70
chicken with wild rice (*Pepperidge Farm*)	80
clam chowder, Manhattan (*Snow's*), 7.5 oz.	70
clam chowder, New England, with milk (*Gorton's*), 1/4 can	140
clam chowder, New England, with milk (*Snow's*), 7.5 oz.	140
corn chowder, with water (*Pepperidge Farm*)	140
corn chowder, with low-fat milk (*Pepperidge Farm*)	180
crab (*Pepperidge Farm*)	110
fish chowder, with milk (*Snow's*), 7.5 oz.	130
gazpacho (*Pepperidge Farm*)	90
hunter's (*Pepperidge Farm*)	90
lobster bisque, with water (*Pepperidge Farm*)	150
lobster bisque, with low-fat milk (*Pepperidge Farm*)	190

Soup, canned, condensed or semicondensed* (cont.)

minestrone (*Campbell's*)	80
mushroom, cream of (*Campbell's Healthy Request*)	60
mushroom, golden (*Campbell's*)	70
mushroom, shiitake (*Pepperidge Farm*)	70
noodle, curly, with chicken (*Campbell's*)	80
noodle and ground beef (*Campbell's*)	90
onion, cream of, with water (*Campbell's*)	100
onion, French (*Pepperidge Farm*)	80
oyster stew, with water (*Pepperidge Farm*)	150
oyster stew, with milk (*Pepperidge Farm*)	180
pea, green, with water (*Pepperidge Farm*)	210
pea, green, with low-fat milk (*Pepperidge Farm*)	270
pea, split, with ham and bacon (*Campbell's*)	160
potato, cream of, with water (*Campbell's*)	80
potato, cream of, with water and milk (*Campbell's*)	120
Scotch broth (*Campbell's*)	80
seafood chowder, with milk (*Snow's*), 7.5 oz.	140
shrimp, cream of, with water (*Campbell's*)	90
tomato (*Campbell's Zesty*)	100
tomato, with water (*Campbell's Healthy Request*)	90
tomato, with skim milk (*Campbell's Healthy Request*)	130
tomato, cream of, with milk (*Campbell's Homestyle*)	180
tomato rice (*Campbell's Old Fashioned*)	110
vegetable (*Campbell's Healthy Request*)	90
vegetable beef (*Campbell's Healthy Request*)	70
watercress, with water (*Pepperidge Farm*)	60
watercress, with low-fat milk (*Pepperidge Farm*)	100
won ton (*Campbell's*)	40

Soup, frozen or refrigerated, 6 fl. oz., except as noted:

asparagus, cream of (*Kettle Ready*)	62
barley and bean (*Tabatchnick*), 7.5 oz.	130
bean, black, with ham (*Kettle Ready*)	154
bean, northern (*Tabatchnick*), 7.5 oz.	164
beef vegetable, hearty (*Kettle Ready*)	85
broccoli, cream of (*Kettle Ready*)	94
broccoli, cream of (*Tabatchnick Fresh*)	72
cabbage (*Tabatchnick*), 7.5 oz.	110
cauliflower, cream of (*Kettle Ready*)	93
cheddar, creamy (*Kettle Ready*)	158
chicken (*Tabatchnick*), 7.5 oz.	65
chicken, cream of (*Kettle Ready*)	98
chicken gumbo or chicken noodle (*Kettle Ready*)	94
chili, traditional (*Kettle Ready*)	161
clam chowder, Boston (*Kettle Ready*)	131
clam chowder, Manhattan (*Kettle Ready*)	69

clam chowder, New England (*Kettle Ready*) 116
corn and broccoli chowder (*Kettle Ready*) 102
lentil (*Tabatchnick*), 7.5 oz. 170
minestrone (*Tabatchnick* Fresh) 110
minestrone, hearty (*Kettle Ready*) 104
mushroom, cream of (*Kettle Ready*) 85
mushroom barley (*Tabatchnick*), 7.5 oz. 92
New England chowder (*Tabatchnick*), 7.5 oz. 98
onion, French (*Kettle Ready*) 42
pea, split (*Tabatchnick* Fresh) 140
potato, cream of (*Kettle Ready*) 121
spinach, cream of (*Tabatchnick*), 7.5 oz. 85
tomato Florentine (*Kettle Ready*) 106
tomato rice (*Tabatchnick*), 6 oz. 73
tortellini in tomato (*Kettle Ready*) 122
vegetable (*Tabatchnick* Fresh) 77
vegetable, garden (*Kettle Ready*) 85
zucchini (*Tabatchnick*), 6 oz. 80

Soup mix*:
all varieties (*Campbell's* Cup 2 Minute Soup), 6 fl. oz. 90
asparagus (*Knorr*), 8 fl. oz. 80
barley, country (*Knorr*), 8 fl. oz. 120
beef, hearty, and noodles (*Lipton*), 7 fl. oz. 107
broccoli (*Knorr*), 8 fl. oz. 160
broccoli, creamy (*Lipton Cup-A-Soup*), 6 fl. oz. 62
cauliflower (*Knorr*), 8 fl. oz. 100
cheddar, creamy, with noodles (*Fantastic Noodles*), 7 oz. 178
cheese and broccoli (*Hain* Soup & Recipe Mix), 6 fl. oz. 310
chicken or chicken flavor:
   creamy, with vegetables (*Lipton Cup-A-Soup*), 6 fl. oz. 93
   hearty, supreme (*Lipton Cup-A-Soup*), 6 fl. oz. 107
   noodle (*Campbell's* Cup Microwave), 1.35-oz. pkg. 140
   noodle (*Knorr*), 8 fl. oz. 100
   noodle (*Mrs. Grass* Chickeny Rich), 1/4 pkg. 70
   noodle, hearty, creamy (*Lipton Lots-A-Noodles Cup-A-Soup*),
     7 fl. oz. 179
   noodle, spicy (*Nissin Cup O'Noodles*), 2.25-oz. pkg. 290
   noodle with diced white meat (*Lipton*), 8 fl. oz. 81
   and pasta (*Knorr* Chick'n Pasta), 8 fl. oz. 90
clam chowder, Manhattan (*Golden Dipt*), 1/4 pkg. 80
clam chowder, New England (*Golden Dipt*), 1/4 pkg. 70
fine herb (*Knorr*), 8 fl. oz. 130
hot and sour, Oriental (*Knorr*), 8 fl. oz. 80
leek (*Knorr*), 8 fl. oz. 110
lentil (*Hain* Savory Soup Mix), 6 fl. oz. 130
lobster bisque (*Golden Dipt*), 1/4 pkg. 30

Soup mix* (cont.)

minestrone, hearty (*Knorr*), 10 fl. oz.	130
mushroom (*Knorr*), 8 fl. oz.	100
mushroom, beef flavor (*Lipton*), 8 fl. oz.	38
noodle:	
all varieties (*Nissin Cup O'Noodles* Twin Pack), 1.2 oz.	150
all varieties, except pork (*Campbell's* Ramen), 8 oz.	190
all varieties, except beef vegetable or old-fashioned vegetable	
(*Hearty Cup O'Noodles*), 2.25 oz.	300
beef (*Nissin Cup O'Noodles*), 2.25-oz. pkg.	290
beef onion (*Nissin Cup O'Noodles*), 2.25-oz. pkg.	280
beef vegetable or old-fashioned vegetable (*Hearty Cup*	
O'Noodles), 2.25 oz.	290
chicken (*Nissin Cup O'Noodles*), 2.25-oz. pkg.	300
with chicken broth (*Campbell's* Cup Microwave), 1.35-oz. pkg.	130
chicken mushroom (*Nissin Cup O'Noodles*), 2.25-oz. pkg.	280
crab (*Nissin Cup O'Noodles*), 2.25-oz. pkg.	270
curry vegetable or miso vegetable (*Fantastic Noodles*), 7 oz.	150
hearty, with vegetables (*Campbell's* Cup Microwave), 1.7 oz.	180
lobster or shrimp (*Nissin Cup O'Noodles*), 2.25-oz. pkg.	290
pork or garden vegetable (*Nissin Cup O'Noodles*), 2.25-oz. pkg.	280
onion (*Mrs. Grass* Soup & Dip Mix), 1/4 pkg.	35
onion, French (*Knorr*), 8 fl. oz.	50
onion, golden, with chicken broth (*Lipton*), 8 fl. oz.	62
onion mushroom (*Lipton*), 8 fl. oz.	41
oxtail, hearty beef (*Knorr*), 8 fl. oz.	70
pea, split (*Hain* Savory Soup Mix), 6 fl. oz.	310
potato leek (*Hain* Savory Soup Mix), 6 fl. oz.	260
seafood chowder (*Golden Dipt*), 1/4 pkg. dry	70
shrimp, with vegetables (*Campbell's Cup-A-Ramen*), 8 oz.	280
shrimp bisque (*Golden Dipt*), 1/4 pkg. dry	30
spinach (*Knorr*), 8 fl. oz.	70
tomato (*Hain* Savory Soup & Recipe Mix), 6 fl. oz.	220
tomato basil (*Knorr*), 8 fl. oz.	90
vegetable:	
(*Campbell's* Quality Soup and Recipe), 8 fl. oz.	40
(*Knorr*), 8 fl. oz.	35
curry, with noodles (*Fantastic Noodles*), 7 oz.	150
garden (*Lipton Lots-A-Noodles Cup-A-Soup*), 7 fl. oz.	123
harvest (*Lipton Cup-A-Soup* Country Style), 6 fl. oz.	91
spring, with herbs (*Knorr*), 8 fl. oz.	30
tomato, with noodles (*Fantastic Noodles*), 7 oz.	158
Sour cream, see "Cream"	
Sour cream and onion dip (*Bachman* Premium), 1 oz.	50
Sour cream sauce mix (*McCormick/Schilling*), 1/4 pkg.	44

Soy "milk":
fluid, 4 oz. 37
(*Soy Moo*), 1 cup 125
Soy sauce:
(*Kikkoman*), 1 tbsp. 10
(*La Choy*), 1 tsp. 4
(*La Choy* Lite), 1 tsp. 2
Soybean:
dried, boiled, 1/2 cup 149
green, boiled, drained, 1/2 cup 127
Soybean sprouts:
raw, 1/2 cup 43
steamed, 1/2 cup 38
Spaghetti dinner, and meatballs, frozen (*Swanson*), 12.5 oz. . . . 390
Spaghetti dishes, canned or packaged:
with meat sauce (*Healthy Choice* Microwave), 7.5 oz. 150
and meatballs (*Hormel Micro Cup*), 7.5 oz. 204
and meatballs (*Libby's Diner*), 7.75 oz. 190
and mini meatballs, in tomato sauce (*Hormel Kid's Kitchen Micro
    Cup*), 7.5 oz. 218
rings (*Healthy Choice* Microwave), 7.5 oz. 140
in tomato sauce, with cheese (*Franco-American*), 7 3/8 oz. 180
Spaghetti entree, frozen:
(*Dining Lite*), 9 oz. 220
with Italian style meatballs (*Swanson* Homestyle Recipe), 13 oz. 490
with meat sauce (*Banquet Entree Express*), 8.5 oz. 220
with meat sauce (*Healthy Choice*), 10 oz. 280
with meat sauce (*Lean Cuisine*), 11.5 oz. 290
with meatballs (*Stouffer's*), 12 5/8 oz. 380
with meatballs and sauce (*Lean Cuisine*), 9.5 oz. 280
Parmesan, with green beans (*Stouffer's* Homestyle), 10.25 oz. 240
Spaghetti sauce, see "Pasta sauce"
Spaghetti squash, baked or boiled, drained, 1/2 cup 23
Sparerib seasoning mix (*McCormick/Schilling* Bag'n Season),
    1 pkg. 185
Spice loaf:
(*Kahn's* Family Pack), 1 slice 70
beef (*Kahn's* Family Pack), 1 slice 60
Spinach:
fresh, raw, trimmed, 1 oz. leaf or 1/2 cup chopped 6
fresh, boiled, drained, 1/2 cup 21
canned, whole or chopped (*Del Monte*), 1/2 cup 25
frozen:
    (*Green Giant Harvest Fresh*), 1/2 cup 25
    creamed (*Birds Eye* Combinations), 3 oz. 60
    creamed (*Green Giant*), 1/2 cup 70

Spinach, frozen (cont.)
in butter sauce, cut (*Green Giant*), 1/2 cup 40
Spinach au gratin, frozen (*The Budget Gourmet* Side Dish),
1 serving 160
Spinach soufflé, frozen (*Stouffer's*), 4 oz. 140
Spiny lobster, mixed species, meat only, steamed, 4 oz. 162
Split peas, boiled, 1/2 cup 116
Spot, meat only, baked, broiled, or microwaved, 4 oz. 179
Squab, fresh, meat with skin, raw, 4 oz. 332
Squash, see specific listings
Squid, mixed species, meat only, raw, 4 oz. 104
Steak sauce:
(*A.1.*), 1 tbsp. 12
(*French's*), 1 tbsp. 25
(*Heinz* Traditional), 1 tbsp. 12
(*Lea & Perrins*), 1 oz. 40
regular or hickory smoke (*Heinz 57*), 1 tbsp. 16
Steak seasoning (*McCormick/Schilling* Grillmates), 1 tsp. 7
Stir-fry sauce (*Kikkoman*), 1 tsp. 6
Stir-fry seasoning (*Gilroy*), 1 tsp. 6
Strawberry:
fresh, trimmed, 1/2 cup 23
frozen, in light syrup, whole (*Birds Eye*), 4 oz. 80
frozen, in syrup, halved (*Birds Eye* Quick Thaw Pouch), 5 oz. . . 120
Strawberry extract, imitation (*McCormick/Schilling*), 1 tsp. 7
Strawberry flavor drink mix*:
(*Wyler's*), 8 fl. oz. 81
wild (*Wyler's* Crystals), 8 fl. oz. 85
Strawberry fruit syrup:
(*Knott's Berry Farm*), 1 fl. oz. 120
(*Polaner's* Pourable Fruit), 1 fl. oz. 72
Strawberry juice blend, country (*Del Monte*), 6 fl. oz. 100
Strawberry mousse mix* (*Oetker* Mousse Light), 1/2 cup 53
Strawberry topping (*Smucker's*), 2 tbsp. 120
Stroganoff sauce mix (*Lawry's*), 1 pkg. 123
Stuffing, 1/2 cup, except as noted:
all varieties (*Arnold*), 1/2 oz. 50
all varieties, except country style (*Pepperidge Farm*), 1 oz. 110
apple and raisin, cheese and broccoli, classic chicken, or
vegetable almond (*Pepperidge Farm* Distinctive), 1 oz. 110
corn bread, honey-pecan (*Pepperidge Farm* Distinctive), 1 oz. . . 120
country style (*Pepperidge Farm*), 1 oz. 100
herb, country garden (*Pepperidge Farm* Distinctive), 1 oz. 120
wild rice and mushroom (*Pepperidge Farm* Distinctive), 1 oz. . . . 130
mix*, all varieties (*Betty Crocker*) 180
mix*, all varieties, except chicken (*Stove Top* Microwave) 170

mix*, beef, chicken, long grain and wild rice, mushroom and
  onion, or with rice (*Stove Top*) 180
mix*, chicken (*Stove Top* Microwave) 160
mix*, corn bread, pork, savory herb, or turkey (*Stove Top*) 170
Sturgeon, mixed species, meat only:
baked, broiled, or microwaved, 4 oz. 153
smoked, 4 oz. 196
Succotash:
canned (*S&W* Country Style), 1/2 cup 80
frozen (*Frosty Acres*), 3.3 oz. 100
Sucker, white, meat only, baked, broiled, or microwaved, 4 oz. 135
Sugar, beet or cane:
brown, 1 cup, packed 821
granulated, 1 cup 770
granulated, 1 tbsp. 46
granulated, 1 pkt. 23
powdered or confectioners', 1 cup, unsifted 462
powdered or confectioners', 1 tbsp., unsifted 31
Sugar, maple, 1-oz. piece 99
Sugar apple, trimmed, 1/2 cup 118
Summer sausage (see also "Thuringer cervelat"):
(*Hormel* Perma-Fresh), 2 slices 140
beef (*Hillshire Farm*), 2 oz. 190
with cheese (*Hillshire Farm*), 2 oz. 200
Sunfish, pumpkinseed, meat only, baked, broiled, or microwaved,
  4 oz. 129
Sunflower seeds:
all varieties (*Fisher*), 1 oz. 170
dried, kernels (*Arrowhead Mills*), 1 oz. 160
dry-roasted, kernels (*Flavor House*), 1 oz. 180
Surimi (from Alaska pollock), 1 oz. 28
Sweet potato:
baked in skin, 1 medium, 5″ × 2″ diam. 118
baked in skin, mashed, 1/2 cup 103
boiled without skin, mashed, 1/2 cup 172
canned, 1/2 cup:
  in water, cut (*Allens*) 70
  in syrup, cut (*Kohl's*) 110
  in extra heavy syrup (*S&W* Southern) 139
  candied (*S&W*) 180
  mashed (*Joan of Arc/Princella/Royal Prince*) 90
frozen, candied (*Mrs. Paul's*), 4 oz. 190
frozen, candied and apples (*Mrs. Paul's* Sweets'n Apples), 4 oz. 160
Sweet and sour sauce:
(*Kikkoman*), 1 tbsp. 18
(*Sauceworks*), 1 tbsp. 25

Sweet and sour sauce (cont.)
regular or duck sauce (*La Choy*), 1 tbsp. 25
Swiss chard, boiled, drained, chopped, 1/2 cup 18
Swiss steak, see "Beef dinner"
Swiss steak seasoning mix (*McCormick/Schilling* Bag'n Season),
  1 pkg. 81
Swordfish:
fresh, meat only, baked, broiled, or microwaved, 4 oz. 176
frozen, steaks, without seasoning mix (*SeaPak*), 6-oz. pkg. 210
Syrup, see specific listings

T

Food and Measure	Calories

Tabbouleh mix* (*Fantastic Foods*), 1/2 cup 161
Taco Bell,1 serving:
burrito:
  bean 381
  beef 431
  Burrito Supreme 440
  chicken 334
  combination 407
chilito 383
cinnamon twists 171
Meximelt, beef 266
Meximelt, chicken 257
nachos 346
Nachos BellGrande 649
Nachos Supreme 367
pintos 'n cheese 190
pizza, Mexican 575
taco:
  regular 183
  chicken, soft 213

soft	225
Supreme	230
Supreme, soft	272
taco salad	905
taco salad without shell	484
tostada	243
sauces and condiments:	
green sauce, 1 oz.	4
guacamole, .7 oz.	34
jalapeño peppers, 3.5 oz.	20
nacho cheese sauce, 2 oz.	103
Pico De Gallo, .7 oz.	6
red sauce, 1 oz.	10
salsa, .35 oz.	18
sour cream, .7 oz.	46
taco sauce, 1 pkt.	2
taco sauce, hot, 1 pkt.	3
Taco casserole mix (*McCormick/Schilling*), 1 pkg.	526
Taco dip:	
(*Wise*), 2 tbsp.	12
and sauce (*Hain*), 1/4 cup	35
Taco salad seasoning (*Lawry's* Seasoning Blends), 1 pkg.	124
Taco sauce (see also "Salsa"):	
all varieties (*Heinz*), 1 tbsp.	6
all varieties, jars (*Old El Paso*), 2 tbsp.	10
hot or mild (*Ortega*), 1 oz.	12
red, mild (*El Molino*), 2 tbsp.	10
Taco seasoning mix:	
(*Hain*), 1/10 pkg.	10
(*McCormick/Schilling*), 1/4 pkg.	31
(*Old El Paso*), 1/12 pkg.	8
meat (*Ortega*), 1 oz.	90
Taco shell, 1 piece, except as noted:	
(*Gebhardt*)	50
(*Old El Paso*)	55
(*Old El Paso* Super Size)	100
(*Rosarita*)	50
corn (*Azteca*)	60
miniature (*Old El Paso*), 3 pieces	70
salad shell, flour (*Azteca*)	200
Tahini mix (see also "Sesame butter") (*Casbah*), 1 oz. dry	25
Tamale, canned:	
(*Derby*), 2 pieces	160
(*Old El Paso*), 2 pieces	190
beef (*Gebhardt*), 2 pieces	290
beef (*Gebhardt* Jumbo), 2 pieces	400

Tamale dinner, frozen (*Patio*), 13 oz. 470
Tamale pie mix (*McCormick/Schilling*), 1 pkg. 689
Tamarind, 1/2 cup 144
Tangerine:
fresh, 1 medium, 2³/8″ diam. 37
fresh, sections, 1/2 cup 43
canned (*Dole* Mandarin Orange), 1/2 cup 70
canned, in light syrup (*Del Monte*), 1/2 cup 40
canned, in heavy syrup (*S&W*), 1/2 cup 76
Tangerine juice:
fresh, 6 fl. oz. 80
bottled or chilled (*Dole Pure & Light*), 6 fl. oz. 100
Tapioca, pearl, dry, 1/2 cup 260
Taro, cooked, sliced, 1/2 cup 94
Taro chips, 1 oz. 135
Taro leaves, steamed, 1/2 cup 18
Taro shoots, cooked, sliced, 1/2 cup 10
Tarpon, Atlantic, meat only, raw, 4 oz. 104
Tarragon, ground (*McCormick/Schilling*), 1 tsp. 5
Tart shell, see "Pastry sheets and shells"
Tartar sauce:
(*Bennett's* Premium), 1 tbsp. 70
(*Bright Day* Cholesterol Free), 1 tbsp. 50
(*Heinz*), 1 tbsp. 70
lemon and herb flavor (*Sauceworks*), 1 tbsp. 70
Tea, 8 fl. oz., except as noted:
brewed 3
brewed, caffeine free (*Celestial Seasonings*) 4
iced, canned (*Shasta*), 12 fl. oz. 136
iced, instant*, lemon or raspberry flavor (*Lipton*) 3
iced, mix*, peach or raspberry flavor (*Lipton* Sugar Free) . . 5
iced, mix*, sweetened, lemon flavor (*Lipton*), 6 fl. oz. . . . 55
Tea, herbal, brewed, 8 fl. oz.:
all varieties except *Roastaroma* (*Celestial Seasonings*) . . . <6
all varieties except spice (*Lipton*) . . . . <5
(*Celestial Seasonings Roastaroma*) 11
spice (*Lipton Toasty Spice*), 8 fl. oz. 6
Tempeh, 1/2 cup 165
Tempura batter mix (*Golden Dipt*), 1 oz. 100
Teriyaki sauce:
(*Kikkoman*), 1 tbsp. 15
(*La Choy/La Choy* Lite), 1/2 tsp. 5
barbecue marinade (*Lawry's*), 1/4 cup 164
basting (*La Choy*), 1/2 tsp. 2
Thuringer cervelat (see also "Summer sausage"):
(*Hillshire Farm*), 2 oz. 180

regular or beef (*Oscar Mayer*), .8-oz. slice	70
Thyme, ground (*McCormick/Schilling*), 1 tsp.	5
Thymus:	
beef, braised, 4 oz.	362
veal, braised, 4 oz.	197
Tilefish, meat only, baked, broiled, or microwaved, 4 oz.	167
Toaster muffins and pastries, 1 piece:	
all varieties, except fudge frosted (*Toastettes*)	190
apple or cinnamon (*Pillsbury Toaster Strudel*)	200
apple cinnamon (*Pepperidge Farm* Croissant Toaster Tarts)	170
banana-nut (*Thomas' Toast-r-Cakes*)	110
blueberry (*Thomas' Toast-r-Cakes*)	100
blueberry or strawberry (*Pillsbury Toaster Strudel*)	190
cheese or strawberry (*Pepperidge Farm* Croissant Toaster Tarts)	190
corn (*Thomas' Toast-r-Cakes*)	120
fudge, frosted (*Toastettes*)	200
raisin bran (*Thomas' Toast-r-Cakes*)	100
Tofu:	
raw, firm, 1/2 cup	183
flavored, all varieties (*Nasoya*), 5 oz.	150
okara, 1/2 cup	47
Tofu spread, chili or herb (*Natural Touch Tofu Topper*), 2 tbsp.	50
Tomatillo, fresh, raw, 1 medium, 15/8" diam.	11
Tomato, red, ripe:	
fresh, raw, 1 medium, 23/5" diam., approx. 4.75 oz.	26
fresh, raw, chopped, 1/2 cup	19
fresh, boiled, 1/2 cup	32
canned, 1/2 cup, except as noted:	
whole, peeled (*Del Monte*)	25
whole, peeled, or Italian-style pear (*S&W*)	25
crushed (*Progresso*)	40
crushed, in puree (*Contadina*)	30
diced, in rich puree (*S&W*)	35
puree (*Progresso*)	45
wedges (*Del Monte*)	30
with green chilies (*Old El Paso*), 1/4 cup	14
Italian style, with liquid (*Progresso*)	18
and jalapeños (*Old El Paso*), 1/4 cup	11
stewed, all varieties (*Del Monte*)	35
dried, sun-dried, dry-packed, 1/2 cup	70
dried, sun-dried, oil-packed, drained, 1/2 cup	118
Tomato, green:	
fresh, 1 medium, 23/5" diam., approx. 4.75 oz.	30
pickled (*Claussen* Kosher), 1 oz.	5
Tomato juice, canned:	
(*Del Monte*), 6 fl. oz.	35

Tomato juice (cont.)
(*Hunt's*), 6 fl. oz. 30
(*Sacramento*), 6 fl. oz. 35
Tomato paste, canned:
(*Del Monte*), 1/4 cup 50
(*Progresso*), 2 oz. 50
with garlic or Italian style (*Hunt's*), 2 oz. 50
Tomato sauce (see also "Pasta sauce"):
(*Del Monte* Regular/No Salt Added), 1 cup 70
(*Hunt's* No Salt Added/*Hunt's* Special), 4 oz. 35
(*Progresso*), 1/2 cup 40
with garlic or herb flavored (*Hunt's*), 4 oz. 70
Italian style (*Hunt's*), 4 oz. 60
marinara or plum, refrigerated (*Contadina Fresh*), 7.5 oz. 100
for meat loaf (*Hunt's* Meatloaf Fixin's), 2 oz. 20
with mushrooms (*Hunt's*), 4 oz. 25
with onions (*Hunt's*), 4 oz. 40
with tomato bits (*Hunt's*), 4 oz. 30
Tomato and chili cocktail (*Snap-E-Tom*), 6 fl. oz. 40
Tomato-clam juice cocktail (*Clamato*), 6 fl. oz. 96
Tom Collins mix, bottled (*Holland House*), 1 fl. oz. 47
Tongue:
fresh, beef, simmered, 4 oz. 321
fresh, veal, braised, 4 oz. 229
canned, pork, cured (*Hormel,* 8 lb.), 3 oz. 190
Tortellini, frozen or refrigerated:
beef or tri-color cheese (*Master Choice*), 4 oz. 380
egg or spinach, with cheese or meat (*Contadina Fresh*), 4.5 oz. . 380
nondairy, regular or spinach (*Tofutti*), 2 oz. 210
Tortellini dishes, frozen:
cheese (*The Budget Gourmet* Side Dish), 1 serving 200
cheese, in Alfredo sauce (*Stouffer's*), 87/8 oz. 600
cheese, in tomato sauce (*Birds Eye For One*), 5.5 oz. 210
cheese, with tomato sauce (*Stouffer's*), 95/8 oz. 360
Provençale (*Green Giant Garden Gourmet Right for Lunch*),
    9.5 oz. 260
Tortilla, 1 piece:
corn (*Azteca*) 45
corn, enchilada style (*Tyson Mexican Original*) 54
flour (*Azteca*), 9″ diam. 130
flour (*Azteca*), 7″ diam. 80
flour, burrito style, hand stretched (*Tyson Mexican Original*) . . . 182
flour, burrito style, heat pressed (*Tyson Mexican Original*) 173
flour, burrito style, small (*Tyson Mexican Original*) 106
flour, fajita style (*Tyson Mexican Original*) 84
flour, soft (*Tyson Mexican Original*) 121

Tortilla chips, see "Corn chips and similar snacks"
Tostaco shell (*Old El Paso*), 1 piece 100
Tostada shell, 1 piece:
  (*Old El Paso*) 55
  (*Pancho Villa*) 55
  (*Rosarita*) 60
Tree fern, cooked, chopped, 1/2 cup 28
Tripe, beef, raw, 1 oz. 28
Trout, fresh, meat only (see also "Sea trout"):
  mixed species, baked, broiled, or microwaved, 4 oz. 215
  rainbow, baked, broiled, or microwaved, 4 oz. 171
Tuna, meat only:
  fresh, bluefin, baked, broiled, or microwaved, 4 oz. 209
  fresh, skipjack, baked, broiled, or microwaved, 4 oz. 150
  fresh, yellowfin, baked, broiled, or microwaved, 4 oz. 158
  canned in oil, drained 2 oz., except as noted:
    chunk light or chunk white, with liquid (*Bumble Bee*) 160
    chunk or solid light (*Star-Kist*) 150
    chunk or solid white, Albacore (*Star-Kist*) 140
    solid light (*Progresso*), 1/3 cup 150
    solid white, albacore, with liquid (*Bumble Bee*) 130
  canned in water, drained, 2 oz.:
    chunk light (*Star-Kist* Select 60% Less Salt) 65
    chunk light, with liquid (*Bumble Bee*) 60
    chunk or solid white, with liquid (*Bumble Bee*) 70
    solid white, albacore (*Star-Kist*) 70
  frozen, steak, without seasoning mix (*SeaPak*), 6-oz. pkg. 180
Tuna entree, frozen or packaged:
  and noodles (*Dinty Moore American Classics*), 10 oz. 240
  noodle casserole (*Stouffer's*), 10 oz. 310
Tuna entree mix*, with water-packed tuna:
  au gratin or buttery rice (*Tuna Helper*), 6 oz. 280
  fettucini Alfredo (*Tuna Helper*), 7 oz. 300
  mushroom, creamy (*Tuna Helper*), 7 oz. 220
  noodle, cheesy (*Tuna Helper*), 7.75 oz. 240
  noodle, creamy (*Tuna Helper*), 8 oz. 300
  pot pie (*Tuna Helper*), 5.1 oz. 420
  Romanoff (*Tuna Helper*), 8 oz. 290
  salad (*Tuna Helper*), 5.5 oz. 420
  tetrazzini (*Tuna Helper*), 6 oz. 240
Tuna salad (*Longacre* Saladfest), 1 oz. 52
Tuna seasoning mix (*Old Bay Tuna Classic*), 1 pkg. 117
Turbot, European, meat only, baked, broiled, or microwaved, 4 oz. 138
Turkey, fresh, 4 oz. (see also "Turkey, ground"):
  fryer-roaster, roasted:
    meat with skin 195

Turkey, fryer-roaster (cont.)

meat only	170
breast, meat with skin	174
breast, meat only	153
leg, meat with skin	193
leg, meat only	180
wing, meat with skin	235
wing, meat only	185

young hen, roasted:

meat with skin	247
meat only	198
breast, meat with skin	220
leg, meat with skin	242
wing, meat with skin	270

young tom, roasted:

meat with skin	229
meat only	191
breast, meat with skin	214
leg, meat with skin	234
wing, meat with skin	251

Turkey, canned, white (*Swanson*), 2½ oz. — 80

Turkey, frozen or refrigerated:

breast, cooked:

(*Land O'Lakes*), 3 oz.	100
(*Louis Rich*), 1 oz.	45
barbecued, hickory-smoked or honey-roasted (*Louis Rich*), 1 oz.	30
barbecue or oven prepared, quarter (*Mr. Turkey* Chub), 1 oz.	34
oven-roasted (*Louis Rich*), 1 oz.	25
roast, slices, steaks, or tenderloins (*Louis Rich*), 1 oz.	40
smoked, quarter (*Mr. Turkey* Chub), 1 oz.	35
drumettes (*Louis Rich*), 1 oz. cooked	50
drumsticks (*Land O'Lakes*), 3 oz.	120
drumsticks, wings, or wing portions (*Louis Rich*), 1 oz. cooked	55
hindquarter roast or young, butter basted (*Land O'Lakes*), 3 oz.	140
thigh (*Louis Rich*), 1 oz. cooked	65
white meat, skinless, roasted (*Swift Butterball*), 3.5 oz.	160
whole, cooked, without giblets (*Louis Rich*), 1 oz.	50
wings (*Land O'Lakes*), 3 oz.	120

Turkey, ground, cooked:

(*Louis Rich* 85% Fat Free), 1 oz.	60
(*Mr. Turkey*), 1 oz.	54
plain or natural flavoring (*Louis Rich* 90% Fat Free), 1 oz.	50

Turkey, luncheon meat (see also "Turkey bologna," etc.):

breast:

(*Butterball* Cold Cuts), 1 oz.	30

(*Butterball Fresh Deli*), 1 slice	10
(*Tyson*), 1 slice	20
all varieties (*Hillshire Farm Deli Select*), 1 oz.	31
barbecue seasoned (*Butterball Slice 'n Serve* BBQ), 1 oz.	40
honey-roasted (*Louis Rich*), 1 oz.	35
oven-roasted (*Louis Rich*), 1 oz.	30
oven-roasted (*Louis Rich Deli-Thin*), .4-oz. slice	10
oven-roasted or smoked (*Oscar Mayer*), .7-oz. slice	20
oven-roasted or smoked (*Oscar Mayer Healthy Favorites*), 1 slice	12
roast or smoked (*Oscar Mayer Deli-Thin*), .4-oz. slice	12
smoked (*Butterball* Cold Cuts), 1 oz.	35
smoked (*Longacre*), 1 oz.	35
smoked (*Louis Rich*), .7-oz. slice	20
smoked (*Louis Rich Deli-Thin*), .4-oz. slice	10
smoked, chunk (*Louis Rich*), 1 oz.	35
breast and white, browned, roasted (*Longacre Deli Chef*), 1 oz.	40
luncheon loaf (*Louis Rich*), 1-oz. slice	45
luncheon loaf, spiced (*Mr. Turkey*), 1 oz.	51
smoked (*Louis Rich*), 1-oz. slice	30
Turkey bacon, see "Bacon, substitute"	
Turkey bologna:	
(*Butterball Deli/Slice 'n Serve*), 1 oz.	70
mild or regular, sliced or chunk (*Louis Rich*), 1 oz.	60
Turkey and cheese combinations, 5-oz. pkg.:	
breast, oven-roasted, and cheddar (*Louis Rich* Lunch Breaks)	410
smoked, and Monterey Jack (*Louis Rich* Lunch Breaks)	400
ham, and Swiss (*Louis Rich* Lunch Breaks)	380
salami, and cheddar (*Louis Rich* Lunch Breaks)	430
Turkey dinner, frozen:	
(*Banquet Extra Helping*), 17 oz.	460
(*Swanson Hungry Man*), 17 oz.	550
breast, grilled, glazed (*Le Menu New American Cuisine*), 10 oz.	410
with dressing and gravy (*Armour Classics*), 11.5 oz.	320
tetrazzini (*Healthy Choice*), 12.6 oz.	340
Turkey entree, frozen or packaged:	
à la king, with rice (*The Budget Gourmet*), 1 serving	380
breast, homestyle, vegetables (*The Budget Gourmet Quick Stirs*), 1 serving	290
breast, roast, gravy, stuffing (*Stouffer's* Homestyle), 7⁷/₈ oz.	300
breast, sliced (*Kraft Eating Right*), 10 oz.	250
breast, sliced, with dressing (*Lean Cuisine*), 7⁷/₈ oz.	200
breast, sliced, mushroom sauce, rice pilaf (*Lean Cuisine*), 8 oz.	220
breast, stuffed (*The Budget Gourmet* Light & Healthy), 1 serving	250
croquettes (*On•Cor* Deluxe Entree), 8 oz.	227
Dijon (*Lean Cuisine*), 9.5 oz.	230

Turkey entree, frozen or packaged (cont.)

and dressing (*Dinty Moore American Classics*), 10 oz.	290
and dressing (*On•Cor* Deluxe Entree), 8 oz.	238
with dressing and potatoes (*Swanson* Homestyle Recipe), 9 oz.	290
glazed (*The Budget Gourmet* Light & Healthy), 1 serving	260
and gravy (*On•Cor* Deluxe Entree), 8 oz.	129
gravy and, with dressing (*Banquet Entree Express*), 7 oz.	220
and gravy, with dressing (*Banquet Healthy Balance*), 11.25 oz.	270
homestyle, with vegetables and pasta (*Lean Cuisine*), 9³/₈ oz.	230
open faced, potatoes (*The Budget Gourmet* Hot Lunch), 8.25 oz.	320
pie (*Stouffer's*), 10 oz.	530
pie (*Swanson Hungry Man*), 16 oz.	650
pie (*Tyson* Premium), 9 oz.	370
roast, and mushrooms, in gravy (*Healthy Choice*), 8.5 oz.	200
sliced, with gravy and dressing (*Healthy Choice*), 10 oz.	270
tetrazzini (*Stouffer's*), 10 oz.	380

Turkey frankfurter:

(*Health Valley* Weiners), 1 link	96
(*Louis Rich*), 1 link	100
(*Louis Rich* Bun Length), 2-oz. link	130
(*Mr. Turkey* Bunsize), 1 link	130
cheese (*Louis Rich*), 1.6-oz. link	110

Turkey giblets, simmered, chopped or diced, 1 cup — 243

Turkey gravy:

canned (*Heinz*), 2 oz. or ¹/₄ cup	25
mix* (*McCormick/Schilling*), ¹/₄ cup	22

Turkey ham, 1 oz., except as noted:

(*Butterball* Cold Cuts)	35
(*Butterball Fresh Deli*), 1 slice	10
(*Louis Rich Deli-Thin*), .4-oz. slice	15
(*Tyson*), 1 slice	23
breakfast, smoked (*Mr. Turkey*)	33
chopped (*Louis Rich*), 1-oz. slice	45
chunk (*Longacre*)	37
honey cured (*Louis Rich*), .7-oz. slice	25
round (*Louis Rich* 95% Fat Free), 1-oz. slice	30
sliced (*Butterball* Deli Thin)	35
smoked, regular or chub (*Mr. Turkey*)	32

Turkey ham salad (*Longacre* Saladfest), 1 oz. — 58
Turkey kielbasa (*Louis Rich* Polska), 1 oz. — 40
Turkey nuggets, breaded, cooked (*Louis Rich*), .7-oz. piece — 60

Turkey pastrami, 1 oz., except as noted:

(*Butterball* Cold Cuts)	30
(*Louis Rich Deli-Thin*), .4-oz. slice	10
chunk, round, or sliced (*Louis Rich*), 1 oz.	35

Turkey patty, breaded, cooked (*Louis Rich*), 1 patty — 210

Turkey pie, see "Turkey entree"
Turkey salami:
(*Butterball* Cold Cuts), 1 oz.   50
cotto, sliced, or chunk (*Louis Rich*), 1 oz.   55
cotto (*Mr. Turkey*), 1 oz.   45
Turkey sandwich, frozen:
with cheddar and bacon (*Quaker Oven Stuffs*), 1 piece   350
pocket, with ham and cheese (*Hot Pockets*), 5 oz.   320
Turkey sausage, 1 oz., except as noted:
(*Butterball*)   50
breakfast (*Mr. Turkey*)   58
breakfast, ground, cooked (*Louis Rich*)   55
breakfast, links, cooked (*Louis Rich*), .8-oz. link   45
smoked (*Louis Rich*)   40
smoked, with cheddar (*Louis Rich*)   45
Turkey and pork sausage (*Jimmy Dean* Light), 1 cooked patty   80
Turkey turnover, frozen, and Swiss (*Quaker Oven Stuffs*), 1 piece   320
Turkey seasoning mix (*McCormick/Schilling* Bag'n Season),
1 pkg.   146
Turkey spread, canned, chunky (*Underwood* Light), 2⅛ oz. .   75
Turkey sticks, breaded, cooked (*Louis Rich*), 1-oz. piece   80
Turkey summer sausage (*Louis Rich*), 1-oz. slice   55
Turmeric, ground (*McCormick/Schilling*), 1 tsp.   7
Turnip:
fresh, boiled, drained, mashed, ½ cup   21
canned, diced (*Allens*), ½ cup   16
frozen, diced (*Southern*), 3.5 oz.   17
Turnip greens:
fresh, raw, trimmed, 1 oz. or ½ cup chopped   7
fresh, boiled, drained, chopped, ½ cup   15
canned, chopped, with diced turnips (*Stokely*), ½ cup   20
frozen, chopped, with or without turnips (*Seabrook*), 3.3 oz. . . .   20
Turnover, 1 piece:
frozen, apple or blueberry (*Pepperidge Farm*)   280
frozen, cherry (*Pepperidge Farm*)   290
frozen, peach or raspberry (*Pepperidge Farm*)   310
refrigerated, apple or cherry, flaky (*Pillsbury*)   170

V

Food and Measure	Calories
Vanilla extract, pure (*McCormick/Schilling*), 1 tsp.	12
Vanilla mousse mix* (*Oetker* Mousse Light), 1/2 cup	53
Veal, boneless, 4 oz.:	
cubed (leg and shoulder), braised or stewed, lean only	213
ground, broiled	195
leg (top round), roasted, lean with separable fat	181
leg (top round), roasted, lean only	170
loin, braised, lean with separable fat	322
loin, braised, lean only	256
loin, roasted, lean with separable fat	246
loin, roasted, lean only	198
rib, roasted, lean with separable fat	259
rib, roasted, lean only	201
shoulder, arm, braised, lean with separable fat	268
shoulder, arm, braised, lean only	228
shoulder, blade, braised, lean with separable fat	255
shoulder, blade, braised, lean only	224
sirloin, roasted, lean with separable fat	229
sirloin, roasted, lean only	191
Veal dinner, frozen:	
Parmesan (*Le Menu New American Cuisine*), 10.25 oz.	360
parmigiana (*Armour Classics*), 11.25 oz.	400
parmigiana (*The Budget Gourmet* Hearty & Healthy), 1 serving	390
parmigiana (*Swanson*), 12.25 oz.	430
Veal entree, parmigiana, frozen:	
(*On•Cor* Deluxe Entree), 8 oz.	350
(*Swanson* Homestyle Recipe), 10 oz.	330
and pasta Alfredo (*Stouffer's* Homestyle), 9.25 oz.	350
patties (*Banquet Family Entrees*), 7 oz.	320
Vegetable chips (*Eden*), 1 oz.	130

Vegetable flakes (*French's*), 1 tbsp. 12
Vegetable juice:
("*V-8*" Light'n Tangy), 6 fl. oz. 40
(*Welch's* 100% Pure), 6 fl. oz. 40
all varieties, except light'n tangy ("*V-8*"), 6 fl. oz. 35
hearty or hot and spicy (*Smucker's*), 8 fl. oz. 58
cocktail (*R.W. Knudsen Very Veggie*), 8 fl. oz. 40
Vegetable pattie mix (*Fritini*), 3.5 oz., for 2 patties 358
Vegetable pie, frozen:
with beef (*Morton*), 7 oz. 430
with beef or turkey (*Banquet*), 7 oz. 510
with chicken (*Banquet*), 7 oz. 550
with chicken or turkey (*Morton*), 7 oz. 420
Vegetable sticks, breaded, frozen (*Stilwell Quickkrisp*), 3 oz. . . . 240
Vegetables, see specific listings
Vegetables, mixed (see also specific listings):
canned or packaged, 1/2 cup:
(*Del Monte*) 40
(*Green Giant Garden Medley/Pantry Express*) 35
Chinese (*La Choy* Fancy Mix) 12
chop suey (*La Choy*) 10
Dijon (*Del Monte Vegetable Classics*) 70
frozen, prepared without added ingredients:
(*Birds Eye* Portion Pack), 3 oz. 50
(*Green Giant* Polybag), 1/2 cup 40
all varieties, except New England, Santa Fe, and western style
(*Green Giant American Mixtures*), 1/2 cup 25
for beef fajitas (*Birds Eye* Easy Recipe), 7 oz. 80
for beef Burgundy (*Birds Eye* Easy Recipe), 7 oz. 120
breaded (*Ore-Ida* Medley), 3 oz. 160
in butter sauce (*Green Giant*), 1/2 cup 60
for chicken Alfredo (*Birds Eye* Easy Recipe), 7 oz. 160
for chicken primavera (*Birds Eye* Easy Recipe), 7 oz. 80
for chicken teriyaki (*Birds Eye* Easy Recipe), 7 oz. 160
Chinese (*Birds Eye* Stir-Fry), 3.3 oz. 35
chow mein, seasoned sauce (*Birds Eye* International), 3.3 oz. 90
Dutch style (*Frosty Acres*), 3.2 oz. 30
Italian, seasoned sauce (*Birds Eye* International), 3.3 oz. . . . 100
Mandarin (*The Budget Gourmet* Side Dish), 1 serving 160
with mustard sauce, Dijon, for chicken or fish (*Birds Eye*
Custom Cuisine*), 4.6 oz. 70
New England recipe (*The Budget Gourmet* Side Dish), 1 serving 230
New England style (*Green Giant American Mixtures*), 1/2 cup 70
for Oriental beef (*Birds Eye* Easy Recipe), 7 oz. 100
pasta primavera (*Birds Eye* International), 3.3 oz. 120

Vegetables, mixed, frozen (cont.)

San Francisco style, seasoned sauce (*Birds Eye* International),
3.3 oz. 100
Santa Fe style (*Green Giant American Mixtures*), 1/2 cup 70
spring, cheese sauce (*The Budget Gourmet* Side Dish),
1 serving 130
with tomato basil sauce, for chicken (*Birds Eye Custom
Cuisine*), 4.6 oz. 110
stew (*Ore-Ida*), 3 oz. 50
western style (*Green Giant American Mixtures*), 1/2 cup 60
with wild rice in white wine sauce for chicken (*Birds Eye
Custom Cuisine*), 4.6 oz. 100
Venison, meat only, roasted, 4 oz. 179
Vienna sausage, canned, beef broth (*Libby's*), 3 1/2 links 160
Vinegar:
all varieties (*Heinz*), 1 tbsp. 2
wine, all varieties (*Regina*), 1 fl. oz. 4

W

Food and Measure   **Calories**

Waffles, frozen, 1 piece:
(*Aunt Jemima* Original) 173
(*Downyflake*) 60
(*Eggo* Mini) 90
(*Eggo Special K*) 80
(*Roman Meal*) 140
apple cinnamon, blueberry, nut and honey, or strawberry (*Eggo*) 130
with apples, peaches, or strawberries (*Eggo Fruit Top*) 190
Belgian, regular or multigrain (*Weight Watchers*) 120
blueberry or hot-n-buttery (*Downyflake*) 90
buttermilk (*Downyflake* Jumbo) 95
buttermilk or homestyle (*Eggo*) 120
multigrain (*Downyflake*) 125

oat bran (*Downeyflake*) 130
oat bran, fruit and nut (*Eggo Common Sense*) 120
plain, multibran, or raisin and bran (*Eggo Nutri-Grain*) 120
whole grain wheat (*Aunt Jemima*) 154
Waffle breakfast, frozen:
with bacon (*Swanson Great Starts*), 2.2 oz. 230
Belgian, and sausage (*Swanson Great Starts*), 2.85 oz. 280
Belgian, with strawberries and sausage (*Swanson Great Starts*),
    3.5 oz. 210
Walnut:
black (*Fisher*), 1 oz. 170
English or Persian (*Diamond*), 1 oz. 192
English, raw, chopped or ground (*Fisher*), 1 oz. 180
Walnut extract, black, imitation (*McCormick/Schilling*), 1 tsp. 12
Walnut topping, in syrup (*Smucker's*), 2 tbsp. 130
Wasabi, powder, 1/4 oz. 24
Water chestnut, Chinese:
fresh, sliced, 1/2 cup 66
canned, whole (*La Choy*), 4 average 14
canned, sliced (*La Choy*), 1/4 cup 18
Watercress, fresh, trimmed, chopped, 1/2 cup 2
Watermelon:
1/16 of 10"-diam. melon, 1"-thick slice 152
diced, 1/2 cup 25
Welsh rarebit, canned (*Snow's*), 1/2 cup 170
Welsh rarebit entree, frozen (*Stouffer's*), 10 oz. 350
Wendy's, 1 serving:
bacon cheeseburger, Jr. 440
Big Classic 480
cheeseburger, Jr. 320
cheeseburger, Kids Meal 310
chicken club sandwich 520
chicken nuggets, crispy, 6 pieces 280
chicken sandwich, breaded 450
chicken sandwich, grilled 290
chili, small, 8 oz. 190
fish fillet sandwich 460
fries, small 240
hamburger, Jr. 270
hamburger, Kids Meal 270
hamburger, single with everything 440
nugget sauce, barbecue or sweet mustard, 1 pkt. 50
nugget sauce, honey or sweet and sour, 1 pkt. 45
potatoes, baked, hot stuffed:
    plain 300
    bacon and cheese 510

Wendy's, potatoes (cont.)

broccoli and cheese	450
cheese	550
chili and cheese	600
sour cream and chives	370

salads, prepared:

Caesar	160
chicken, grilled	200
deluxe garden	110
side	60
taco	640

salad dressings, 1 tbsp.:

bacon and tomato, reduced calorie	45
blue cheese	90
celery seed	65
French	60
French, sweet red	65
Hidden Valley Ranch	50
Italian, golden	45
Italian, reduced calorie	25
Italian Caesar	75
Thousand Island	65

desserts:

Frosty, medium, 16 oz.	460
chocolate chip cookie, 1 piece	280
Western-style dinner, frozen (*Banquet* Meals), 9 oz.	300

Wheat, whole grain:

durum, 1 cup	650
hard red winter, 1 cup	628
soft red winter, 1 cup	556
soft white, 1 cup	571
Wheat bran, toasted (*Kretschmer*), 1 oz., approx. 1/3 cup	57

Wheat germ:

(*Kretschmer*), 1 oz., approx. 1/4 cup	103
honey crunch (*Kretschmer*), 1 oz., approx. 1/4 cup	105
Whelk, meat only, raw, 4 oz.	156
White sauce mix* (*McCormick/Schilling McCormick Collection*), 1/4 cup	59

Whitefish, mixed species, meat only:

baked, broiled, or microwaved, 4 oz.	195
smoked, 4 oz.	122
Whiting, fresh, meat only, baked, broiled or microwaved, 4 oz.	130
Wild rice (*Fantastic Foods*), 1/2 cup cooked	83

Wine:

dessert, 31/2 fl. oz.	140
table, dry, red, 31/2 fl. oz.	75

table, dry, white or champagne, 3 1/2 fl. oz. 80
Wine, cooking:
marsala (*Holland House*), 1 fl. oz. 9
red (*Holland House*), 1 fl. oz. 6
sherry (*Holland House*), 1 fl. oz. 5
vermouth or white (*Holland House*), 1 fl. oz. 2
Wolf fish, Atlantic, meat only, baked, broiled, or microwaved,
 4 oz. 139
Wonton skin (*Nasoya*), 1 piece 23
Worcestershire sauce:
(*Heinz*), 1 tbsp. 6
(*Lea & Perrins*), 1 tsp. 5
white wine (*Lea & Perrins*), 1 tsp. 3

Y

Food and Measure	Calories

Yam:
fresh, baked or boiled, drained, 1/2 cup 79
canned or frozen, see "Sweet potato"
Yam bean tuber:
raw, sliced, 1/2 cup 25
boiled, drained, 4 oz. 52
Yeast, baker's (*Fleischmann's* Active Dry/RapidRise), 1/4 oz. . . . 20
Yellow squash, see "Crookneck or straightneck squash"
Yellowtail, mixed species, meat only, baked, broiled, or
 microwaved, 4 oz. 212
Yogurt:
plain (*Breyers* Lowfat), 8 oz. 140
plain (*Colombo* Classic), 8 oz. 130
plain (*Colombo* Nonfat Lite), 8 oz. 110
plain (*Yoplait* Nonfat), 8 oz. 120
all flavors (*Axelrod Easy Dieter*), 8 oz. 100
all flavors (*Borden* Light/*Viva* Nonfat), 6 oz. 90

Yogurt (cont.)

all flavors (*Colombo* Classic Fruit on the Bottom), 8 oz.	230
all flavors (*Colombo* Nonfat Fruit on the Bottom), 8 oz.	190
all flavors (*Colombo* Nonfat Lite Minipack), 4.4 oz.	100
all flavors (*Crowley* Swiss Style), 1 cup	240
all flavors (*La Yogurt*), 6 oz.	190
all flavors (*La Yogurt* Light), 6 oz.	80
all flavors (*Yoplait* Fat Free Fruit on the Bottom), 6 oz.	160
all flavors, except black cherry and vanilla (*Breyers* Lowfat) 8 oz.	250
all flavors, except cherry, mixed berry, and vanilla (*Yoplait Custard Style*), 6 oz.	190
all fruit flavors (*Borden* Lowfat Fruity), 6 oz.	168
all fruit flavors (*Yoplait*), 6 oz.	190
all fruit flavors (*Yoplait* Light), 6 oz.	80
apricot-mango or wild blueberry (*Stonyfield Farm* Nonfat), 8 oz.	160
banana berry (*Light n'Lively*), 4.4 oz.	130
berry, wild (*Light n'Lively*), 4.4 oz.	140
cherry, black (*Breyers* Lowfat), 8 oz.	260
cherry or mixed berry (*Yoplait Custard Style*), 6 oz.	180
strawberry (*Colombo* Classic), 8 oz.	180
strawberry (*Stonyfield Farm* Nonfat), 8 oz.	160
vanilla (*Yoplait/Yoplait Custard Style*), 6 oz.	180
vanilla (*Yoplait* Nonfat), 8 oz.	180
vanilla, French (*Colombo* Classic), 8 oz.	190
vanilla, French (*Stonyfield Farm* Nonfat), 8 oz.	155
vanilla bean (*Breyers* Lowfat), 8 oz.	230

Yogurt, frozen, 1/2 cup, except as noted:

banana-strawberry or chocolate (*Häagen-Dazs*)	170
cherry, black (*Breyers*)	140
cherry or chocolate (*Borden* Premium)	100
chocolate (*Breyers*)	150
chocolate, double chunk (*Frusen Glädjé*)	160
coffee (*Häagen-Dazs*)	180
peach, raspberry, strawberry, or vanilla (*Breyers*)	140
peach, strawberry, or vanilla (*Häagen-Dazs*)	170
praline almond (*Frusen Glädjé*)	170
raspberry, strawberry, or vanilla (*Borden* Premium)	100
raspberry-vanilla swirl (*Dolly Madison*), 3 fl. oz.	70
strawberry (*Frusen Glädjé*)	120
strawberry or vanilla (*Dolly Madison*), 3 fl. oz.	70
strawberry banana (*Breyers*)	130
strawberry cheesecake twist (*Colombo Shoppe Style*), 3 fl. oz.	90
vanilla (*Frusen Glädjé*)	130
vanilla-almond crunch (*Häagen-Dazs*)	200
vanilla-peach twist (*Colombo Shoppe Style*), 3 fl. oz.	90

Yogurt bar, frozen, 1 bar:
chocolate or strawberry (*Yoplait* Lowfat) 45
chocolate, strawberry, or vanilla, chocolate dipped (*Yoplait Triple Dipped*) 100
chocolate chip (*Yoplait* Lowfat) 55
coffee-chocolate or vanilla-chocolate (*Häagen-Dazs*) 210
peach or raspberry (*Häagen-Dazs*) 100
vanilla, milk chocolate-almond coated (*Elan*) 260

Z

Food and Measure	Calories

Ziti dishes, frozen:
marinara (*The Budget Gourmet* Side Dish), 1 serving 200
with zesty tomato sauce (*Healthy Choice* Pasta Classics), 12 oz. 350
Zucchini:
fresh, raw, trimmed, sliced, 1/2 cup 9
fresh, raw, baby, 1 medium, 5/8″ diam. × 25/8″ 2
fresh, boiled, drained, sliced, 1/2 cup 14
canned, Italian style (*Progresso*), 1/2 cup 50
canned, in tomato sauce (*Del Monte*), 1/2 cup 30
frozen (*Southern*), 3.5 oz. 18
frozen, breaded (*Ore-Ida*), 3 oz. 150
frozen, with carrots, pearl onions, and mushrooms (*Birds Eye* Farm Fresh), 4 oz. 30